# BEAUTIFUL SACRIFICE

# BEAUTIFUL SACRIFICE

### ELIZABETH LOWELL

**Doubleday Large Print
Home Library Edition**

*wm*

WILLIAM MORROW
*An Imprint of* HARPERCOLLINS*Publishers*

BEAUTIFUL SACRIFICE. Copyright © 2012 by Two of a Kind, Inc. All rights reserved. Printed in the United States of America. No part of this book may be used or reproduced in any manner whatsoever without written permission except in the case of brief quotations embodied in critical articles and reviews. For information address HarperCollins Publishers, 10 East 53rd Street, New York, NY 10022.

ISBN 978-1-61793-956-3

Printed in the USA

**This Large Print Book carries the
Seal of Approval of N.A.V.H.**

**For Matt and Heather,**
**who never cease to amaze and please me**

ANCIENT MAYA PROPHECY

**If the covenant be kept on the night of December 21, 2012, then the Great Wheel shall grind the old world to dust, Kukulcán shall blow it beyond the Bacabs, and the followers of Kawa'il will rule in the Age of Kings.**

—MODERN TRANSLATION FROM THE LOST CODEX OF KAWA'IL

# Chapter One

Dr. Lina Taylor drove into the staff parking area of Houston's Museum of the Maya.

*Good,* she thought in relief. *Nearly empty. I can park close to the back entrance. Thank God for winter break.*

In a gesture that had become automatic over the past few months, Lina checked around the area before she turned off her little Civic. Nobody was paying any attention to her. There was no reason for the back of her neck to tingle in primal warning.

Yet it did.

Just before she opened the locked doors, her cell phone rang. The tone told her that it was her mother, Cecilia Reyes Balam—Celia to her friends, business associates, and family.

*Is she calling for family or business?* Lina wondered, hesitating. *Some of both, probably. No doubt my great-grandmother is talking about a bad heart and a great-granddaughter who doesn't visit often enough and should be long married, hip-deep in children.*

It would be Celia, her mother, who carried the complaint. Celia orbited between family and business like a planet with two suns. Lina wished she could handle the balancing act with half of her mother's grace. Lina was more like her father, an academic with a deep love of working in the field, discovering ancient cities and temples a single brushstroke at a time. Yet it was being one of the public faces of the Museum of the Maya that paid Lina's salary, not working on the isolated Yucatan digs she loved.

For the third time, Lina's cell phone burbled out its merry little jingle, a hot salsa beat. She thought about letting the call go to voice mail, but decided against it. If Celia wanted to talk to her daughter, she'd track her down in person. With a glance at her watch—plenty of time before she had to teach class—she opened the cell phone.

"Morning, Celia. Are you in town?" Lina asked.

"Not unless I have to be."

"Is everything all right with the family?"

"Abuelita complains of her heart," Celia said. "She calls me daily, asking when you will visit. So does *mi primo*."

"Your cousin Carlos has always done whatever Abuelita wants."

"Do not disrespect him," Celia said. "Without Carlos, you would not be surrounded by the artifacts you love more than anything else."

*Oh, I don't know,* Lina thought. *Hunter Johnston might give the artifacts some real competition . . . if he ever stayed put.*

Guiltily she yanked her attention back to her mother. "No disrespect intended. I don't know Carlos as well as you do."

"You do not see him enough."

Lina couldn't argue that. Growing up, she had never felt close to her mother's cousin Carlos. She felt no need to pretend closeness now, despite his recent, repeated invitations to confer with him about

Reyes Balam artifacts, and how they might be used to celebrate the coming baktun in a worthy way. The Turning of the Wheel of time was a great celebration among the Maya in general and her great-grandmother in particular.

**If Carlos wants help decorating for the baktun, let him go to Philip. Neither one of them has asked me for so much as a nod in the past.**

No matter how hard she had tried to please her father, she'd never managed that feat.

"What's up?" Lina asked, ignoring the past and its disappointments.

"Was there anything good in the Belize shipment Philip sent? The market is humming with rumors."

"Define 'good.'"

"Worth a great deal of money at auction, what else?"

Lina winced. "Please, Celia. Someone could overhear and misunderstand you. After the scandal—"

"You and Philip," Celia interrupted, "always harping on what turned out to be nothing."

*After many thousands spent to grease bureaucratic wheels,* Lina thought, *and academic reputations ruined. Philip's and mine. It didn't do the family export-import business any favors either.*

"Sorry," Lina said, trying to get the conversation back on track.

"Yes, yes," Celia cut in. "You have a reputation to maintain. I understand. So long as Philip keeps discovering artifacts on our land and the Reyes Balam family keeps 'donating' some of the artifacts to the Museum of the Maya—and a lot more to Mexican museums—you have nothing to worry about."

"Philip also supplies you with artifacts for your export-import business." Lina's voice was mild, though she knew trying to bridge the gap between her parents was useless.

Her parents might still be married, but they lived separately because they fought constantly.

"Each artifact I receive is thoroughly documented, with proper export papers, and all fees and taxes duly paid," Celia said as though reciting from memory. "What other shipments have you received in the last few weeks?"

"It would be faster if you tell me what you're looking for. Then I can tell you if I have it."

"There are rumors. Many rumors."

Lina waited.

"The rumors whisper of an obsidian mask carved from a single piece of stone, a god bundle never opened, a sacred scepter with obsidian teeth, a foot-long jade Chacmool, an exquisitely made obsidian knife created solely to let the blood of kings. Even an unknown codex. All and more, of the very highest quality, appearing and then disappearing again, like ghost smoke."

Mind ablaze with possibilities, Lina could hardly speak.

"Separate artifacts?" she managed finally.

"Yes."

"That's . . . impossible."

Celia laughed. "Not impossible. But very, very expensive. You've heard nothing?"

"No. Even one of those artifacts would create a sensation in the archaeological world. All of them together? A dream. Just a dream."

"If you hear of anything, you will call, yes?"

"Call? I'd scream it from the rooftops."

"No! You would keep it very, very quiet and call me."

For a moment Lina didn't say anything. She was remembering the feeling of being watched. Followed. Perhaps her mother wasn't the only one who thought Lina had an entrée to some incredible black-market Maya finds.

"I'll show you everything in the museum," Lina said. "You'll see that there's nothing like what you've described. Please tell everyone you know."

"Nothing at all?"

"Not one thing," Lina said distinctly.

"Then I won't waste any more time. I have other sources to check, but you were my best hope. Promise you won't miss Abuelita's birthday. Only a few days."

"Four."

"Promise."

"Yes, I'll be there," Lina said. "I can't stay long because I have a lot of work to—"

"So do I," Celia interrupted. "Good-bye, see you soon."

The line went dead.

Lina laughed in the empty car. Celia in pursuit of exceptional artifacts was a force of nature.

After a glance around the parking lot—still alone—Lina popped the locks and got out of the car. Beginning a class at seven in the morning wasn't Lina's first choice, but many of her students worked for a living. The museum scheduled its classes accordingly.

Lina locked the car and headed quickly for the staff entrance. As she walked, she looked over her shoulder.

Twice.

There was nothing to see in the shadows and early sunlight, no visible reason for the haunted, hunted feeling that made the skin on the back of her neck prickle. There was no one behind her, no one on either side, nothing but a hot, lazy wind stirred on the grounds.

**Maybe I'm getting paranoid, like my father.**

But Lina didn't feel crazy. She felt watched.

Hurriedly she entered the code on the electronic pad beside the staff door. It clicked open, a loud sound in the hushed acreage surrounding the museum's ziggu-rat building. Such land was very expen-sive in metropolitan Houston, but the Reyes Balam family was nothing if not smart about where to put its money for maximum business impact.

She walked quickly through the open door and closed it firmly behind her. The second security door ahead of her was heavy glass, reflecting a young woman of medium height, dark hair, large dark eyes, full lips, and a black silk business suit that struggled to hide her curves.

Lina barely noticed her reflection. She had accepted long ago that she would never be tall, skinny, and blond. She punched in a different sequence on the number pad beside the glass door. It opened softly, closed with a solid sound behind her.

Slowly she let out a long breath. She didn't feel as watched now. Or maybe it was just the two security doors between her and the city outside.

The inside air was cool, dry, comfort-able for humans, and excellent for the arti-facts that were the heart and soul of the museum. She glanced at her watch. She would be barely on time. She hurried toward the small wing that held meeting rooms and a cramped lecture hall.

She told herself that her bubbling impatience had nothing to do with the chance of seeing Hunter Johnston again, then admitted that it had everything to do with hurrying. The man was both fascinating and exasperating. In the past few months they had talked after her classes—when he managed to show up—occasionally shared coffee, and circled each other with equal parts desire and wariness.

Then two weeks ago Hunter had disappeared. He'd missed classes before, but not for so long a stretch. Maybe he'd tired of the subject matter. Or her.

She shook her head and told herself that Hunter didn't matter. She had a class to teach. She was down to the homestretch, racing toward the coffee and time off waiting at the finish line.

# CHAPTER TWO

"YOU THERE, MAN? I NEED YOU."

Frowning, ignoring the fatigue that kept dragging at the edges of his vision, Hunter Johnston listened to the message. He had known Jase for a lifetime, yet he'd never heard quite that sound from his friend. He prayed it didn't have anything to do with Jase's wife or kids. Especially his children. Kids were so innocent, so fragile.

The thought made Hunter open the apartment window with a vicious snap. It was the eighteenth of December, and Houston had to be seventy-five degrees already in the simmering morning. Summer simply hadn't given up.

*Better than the Yucatan,* he told himself. *No one shooting at me.*

Hot air bathed him, bringing with it the smell of the city—gas, diesel, asphalt, concrete, dust, a whiff of stuffed Dumpster, and dueling Mexican and Chinese take-out joints. Hunter preferred the mixture of odors to his stale apartment and food that had been forgotten in his rush to get to Mexico in time to keep a young woman from being bought and sold like tamales on a dirty street corner.

A world away from Dr. Lina Taylor's safe, well-lighted classroom.

*Dream on, fool,* Hunter told himself. *I had to run out on our last sort-of coffee date. I'll be lucky if she speaks to me.*

Business and apartment lights glimmered against the hazy sky. Across the city avenue, Jase's apartment already had the windows open and the blinds lifted to catch every breeze. A woman's silhouette paced past one window, holding an arm-waving toddler. Ali, Jason's high-school sweetheart and his wife, mother of his children.

Hunter both envied and feared what Jason had. The pain of losing what had once been part of his soul would always haunt him.

In the faint breeze, the gauzy privacy curtains by Hunter's face did a shy and languid dance, like the last girl watching the last boy from across the gymnasium, that tantalizing moment of *will I or won't I?*

He'd met Suzanne's mother on a day like this. Seven years after that day, both mother and daughter were dead.

**Get past it. The world sure has.**

It had ended almost eight years ago, and it still cut like broken glass.

The breeze danced over Hunter like laughter, like memories, burning. He slammed the window down. The curtains hung, lifeless. No more dance, no more shyness.

No more.

He picked up his cell phone and punched in a text message to Jase. Border Patrol types stuck together, even when it was officially called Immigration and Customs Enforcement, even though Hunter had quit years ago. He hadn't liked having his hands tied by orders from on high while the bad guys ran free. ICE's ropes were covered in velvet benefits, but they still cut his wrists after a while.

**Are your wrists bleeding, Jase?**

Somebody knocked on the apartment door. Hard. Jase's voice came in, low and urgent.

"Hunter, you in there? I saw lights."

Three long strides took Hunter to the door. When he opened it, Jase stood there, a thick manila envelope under his left arm. He was dressed in jeans and a T-shirt, his feet in worn leather sandals, his thick, short hair standing on end. His broad face looked tired. From the amount of dark stubble on his jaw, it had been at least a week since his last shave.

"Hey, bro," Hunter said, grabbing him. "I was just texting you. I've been in the Yucatan for two weeks."

Grinning, Jase stepped into the one-armed hug and mutual back whacking. "Figured that. Haven't seen the blinds open until a few minutes ago."

"Ali and the kids okay?"

"Colds, spit-ups, Christmas gotta-haves—the usual."

Hunter let out a silent sigh of relief. The kids were okay. Anything else that was wrong could be dealt with. He motioned Jase in and shut the door behind him.

"You home for a while?" Jase asked.

"Until the phone rings. The family business is exploding like popcorn. All the narco violence has people on both sides of the border checking under the beds."

"I don't blame them." Jase threw his manila envelope on the kitchen counter. "The crap going down now has to be seen to be believed."

"That why you need me?"

Jase's smile faded and his face looked years older than thirty-four. "They're going to fire me on the twenty-second. Merry Christmas, mope."

Hunter went still. "What the hell?"

"Some stuff went missing from ICE's warehouse. You know what that place is like—lockers crammed to the ceiling with guns and goodies, drugs and money."

"Brubaker thinks you're selling drugs out of evidence lockers?" Hunter asked, not hiding his shock.

"No." Jase sighed, poured himself some coffee, and took it to the small café table. He slumped into one of the two mismatched chairs. "I've never flipped an investigation or taken a drop of all that black money pouring through our hands and he knows it. But if I don't find this missing stuff before the twenty-first, I'll be cleaning bathrooms at Mamacita's. With my tongue."

"Three days?" Hunter demanded, unbelieving.

Jase nodded. He was counting down the minutes. Hell, the seconds.

"What went missing?" Hunter asked. "Guns?"

"Maya stuff. Or Aztec. Or what's that early one?"

"Moche? Olmec? Mixtec?"

"Whatever. I don't know diddly or squat about that stuff. That's why I need you." Suddenly Jase put his face in his hands. "Ali told me she's pregnant. I was grinning at the moon. Then this. I don't know what to tell her. It's not like the missing stuff is gold or coke or anything, but Brubaker's dick is in a knot and it all has to do with politics. How do you explain politics to a pregnant mother with children to feed and a husband who's about to get sacked?"

*And I'm your Hail Mary option,* Hunter thought unhappily. *Damn, Jase, no wonder you're halfway to panic.*

Hunter took the remaining chair at the tiny kitchen table. Their knees knocked. The men automatically shifted to make room. They had been raised around small tables in small kitchens.

"Walk me through it," Hunter said. "How did ICE come across the artifacts?"

"About two, three weeks ago," Jase said, rubbing his eyes like a man who hadn't had enough sleep. "Around the first of December. I'm out there supervising a training session at the Matamoros crossing. Everything is dry like burned toast. Everyone out there is swearing and edgy. Beagles start howling just because they're so miserable."

"Beagles? What, you're gonna lick the bad guys to death?"

"Those beagles are unstoppable. Noses that won't quit. Stubborn and cute as puppies. They're a lot more tourist-friendly for airports and cruise-ship terminals than your average German shepherd." Jase glanced up from his coffee. "Politics, you know. Nobody's afraid of beagles. Ali swears she's gonna steal one and take it home to the kids."

Hunter almost smiled. "Okay. You're

out on a beagle training session. Then what?"

"It's a joint training session. ICE and DEA, getting along just like stepbrothers. But when the president tells you to play nice, then you damn well don't get caught playing dirty."

"What happened?"

"We get a stake-bed truck with plates out of Quintana Roo. The dogs freak. Howling and pawing the air and stretching leashes all over the place. All we see are commercial bags of concrete and some boxes of tools."

"Coke?" Hunter asked.

"Yeah, the dogs hit on coke stashed with the concrete bags. But not a lot of it. A few kilos, nothing like a full shipment."

Hunter's mouth quirked at one corner. "And the dumb driver swears he didn't know coke from concrete mix, right?"

"How'd you guess?" Jase asked dryly. "The coke was packed amateur, and it looked like at least one of the packages had gotten messed up before it was wrapped. Dogs locked onto the smell of the coke even though it had been doctored with kerosene or jet fuel."

"Bad night for the driver," Hunter said.

"I suppose, but he seemed almost relieved to get caught. Was real eager to talk. Acted like we would protect him from the witch doctors. He gave us the address he was supposed to be taking this load to."

"He talked before he had a lawyer?"

Jase shrugged. "He didn't care about lawyers. All he wanted was to get away from the shipment quick as he could. We processed him the snitch route, even ran a transfer to Cameron County custody on an empty charge just so he wouldn't be kept with us or labeled as a DEA collar. He got shanked anyway within a few days."

Hunter whistled softly. "Someone is connected like muscle to bone."

"Welcome to the border, where money is black, coke is white, and you never know who's got a rocket in his pocket." Jase's voice was weary rather than bitter. The border was what it was—a war zone.

"Who did the hit?"

"Some gangbanger from the Latin Kings out of Harlingen."

"Did he give a reason for the killing?"

"Said the dude looked at him funny. He's already in for life on killing four people, including two kids asleep in their beds, but he's not giving up whoever told him to do the driver from Quintana Roo."

"Not even to get some time shaved off a life sentence?"

Jase looked like he wanted to spit. "Cameron County's D.A. is ambitious. He wants to run for governor and makes no secret of it. You don't score a lot of points by making deals with kiddy whackers."

"You can get a lot of points for nailing whoever ordered the whack."

"Bird in the hand, man. Can't guarantee what's in the bush." Jase drank some cooling coffee. "The ADA went ahead and tried to make a deal. The gangbanger acted like he was alone in the room."

"Which tells me that whoever gave the order for the hit on the Q Roo driver pulls some serious weight. Is it a Latin King?"

Jase shook his head. "Ain't none of the LKs ever had a lick of interest in the artifact trade. The amount of coke we found might get someone killed, but . . ." He shrugged, the liquid movement of a man whose ancestors came from both sides of the border.

"So would a handful of dirt," Hunter said.

"Yeah. The driver didn't have a drug background. Pretty much a Q Roo dirt farmer, not someone the Kings would be dealing with directly."

"What about the artifacts? Do you think they were the real cargo?"

"DEA must have. They sneered at the five kilos of coke. That's a lot of personal use, but not really a blip on DEA's radar. But they were real eager to hand the artifacts over to Mexico for a big gold star in their good-neighbor file. So was our very own AIC Brubaker."

Hunter shook his head and spit out a single word. "Politics."

"Oh yeah. There was the usual pushing and shouldering. Then we cut a deal. DEA got the drugs and ICE got the artifacts. Since they weren't evidence of anything prosecutable—the driver was dead—Brubaker fast-tracked the artifacts for the repatriation photo op." Jase breathed out from the soles of his feet, deflating. "Man, I wish I'd given them to the feds. They're politically radioactive."

Hunter sorted through what he'd been told. "So the coke was the driver's payday for taking everything over the border?"

"That and the lives of his family. You know how it works."

Hunter grimaced. He knew. He just didn't like it.

"The artifacts," Jase continued, "weren't carelessly wrapped like the coke. They were all tight and in sacks of concrete mix just like the kerosene-laced dope was. At first we thought the packages were opium tar or something else thrown in for the trip up. The shapes were really odd."

"What about the address the driver gave you before he was shanked?"

"We checked it out." Jase swallowed hard, remembering what he really wanted to forget. "I saw things in that place I'm not ever going to un-see."

For a few moments Jase stared at his coffee cup, trying not to remember the unspeakable. He did anyway. "It wasn't a single psycho rocking out. No bodies. Just blood everywhere, places you can't believe blood would get. Blood from more than one person, more than ten. Fresh. Old. Blood and candle wax and rotting flowers." He shook his head, hard, trying to throw off memories. "That place was . . . evil."

"What's the theory? Gang bloodbath? Death cult? Killing ground for rent?"

"ICE will take bets on any of those. We're assuming the bad guys got word that the shipment had been popped, figured that the house was next on the list, so they ran like the cockroaches they are."

"And resumed business in another place," Hunter said grimly.

"Don't they always? Hell, for all I know, they have lots of places like that house. The drug business lives on blood as much as money."

For the space of several long breaths, Hunter tried to plug Jase's new information into the framework of his own lifetime knowledge of the Texas borderlands. It didn't fit. "Anything connect to cold cases?"

Jase drank some coffee, rinsed it around, and swallowed. "I don't know. We handed the death house off to the sheriff's department with the understanding that ICE wanted info on anything covered in our mission statement. All they told us was that something was taken off the wall, and there were signs that a table had been moved."

"Or an altar?"

"I don't like to think about that, but yeah, I wondered."

"Okay. You busted artifacts and small-time coke. Followed an address to a bloody dead end. Cataloged the artifacts into the ICE warehouse."

"With that Maya apocalypse 2012 all over the media, Brubaker was practically lap-dancing about the chance to add the artifacts to the pool of stuff that's being repatriated to Mexico on the twenty-first. It's a big-ass deal. Vice president, governor, senators, everybody under the Homeland Security umbrella will be there, shaking hands across the border and giving Mexico back pieces of its history as we walk shoulder to shoulder into the future, blah blah blah."

"But the artifacts go poof from ICE storage," Hunter said. "Then what?"

"I don't have to tell you the theft has 'inside job' written all over it."

"I remember the warehouse. Cameras, locks, finger pads, guards, everything but the ever-popular alien butt probes."

Jase smiled faintly. "Brubaker was thirty-two flavors of pissed off. He looked around for an ass to pin the tail on. Must have been my lucky day, huh? He put me on paid leave, told me I had until the twenty-first to find those artifacts, then said if I even breathed the word 'ICE' in my investigation, much less showed my badge, I was road-kill. No word of the theft was to get out."

Hunter stared at him. "That's a joke, right?"

Jase looked back with hard, dark eyes.

"When did this happen?" Hunter asked.

"About two weeks ago. I tried to call you, but . . ."

"Cell phones don't work where and when you want them to," Hunter finished. "I was up to my pits in jungle and limestone scrub."

"I hear those beaches on Riviera Maya are primo."

"Didn't get that far. You have pictures, file numbers, descriptions?"

"Of the artifacts?"

"What else?"

Jase reached for the manila folder on the counter. "You never saw these."

"Saw what?"

Hunter opened the envelope and started looking at photos he never should have seen.

# Chapter Three

"THERE ARE STILL MANY AREAS OF MAYA MY-thology that are wide open to interpretation," Lina Taylor said clearly to her more-or-less attentive students. "This is to be expected, given that people are still fighting over the meaning of texts that have been widely available, translated from culture to culture, and practiced for more than two thousand years."

Nobody coughed or stirred. The truly uninterested students were still asleep in various beds. Part of Lina envied them, especially if they were with lovers, but nothing of her simmering emotions showed in her face or voice.

"The fact that so much of Maya myth and lore was lost in one night, at the hands of Bishop Landa, means that we may never know the actual names of deities such as 'God K'—suggested as Kawa'il by some—much less the subtle distinctions in their hierarchy and powers, religious and civil lives."

An unlikely blonde who was dressing like her teenage daughter dutifully took notes from the front-center seat.

*Does she ever look in the mirror?* Lina thought. *Does she need glasses?*

"The nuances of the ancient Maya may be lost to us," Lina continued, "but the broad strokes are reasonably clear. And in many ways, unchanged since the first glyph was chiseled into limestone."

She clicked a remote and the room lights dimmed. Another button on the remote brought the overhead projector to life, displaying an image of jungle broken only by the reclaimed ruins of a Maya ziggurat in the distance. The ancient building was pale and jagged under a cloudy sky.

In the foreground, several people were gathered at a bonfire, dressed in bright shawls worn over a variety of very colorful garments. Each person carried an offering of flowers, handmade crosses, or small glass bottles of liquor. When the people withdrew, the offerings remained behind at the feet of traditional Maya deities overlaid by a veneer of Christian names.

"Notice the syncretic nature of the celebration," Lina said, using her laser pointer, "the mixing of elements of Christianity and indigenous deities. This picture was taken last year during the Días Perdidos celebration, not far from Chichén Itzá. The celebration roughly translates as their version of Mardi Gras—a syncretic festival which also mixes Christian and other religious elements—for a holiday directly before the season of Lent."

The jungle image was replaced by that of a wooden cross, taller than the man standing next to it. The heavy beams were covered in cornstalks and leaves, as if the cross were living, growing.

"The question that this image begs is, Which is more important to the villagers living here? The cross or the maize? You could separate the corn from the cross, but without the corn to sustain them, there would be no worshippers for the cross. The two can't be separated, but neither side is truly ascendant here."

Immediately the reporter who had been allowed into the final class for a feature about "December 21, the End of the World" spoke up.

"The images of the cross and the corn you showed—aren't you concerned about backwash from people who take their religion seriously?" the reporter asked.

"The Maya were, and are, very serious about their religion. They just don't approach it in the typical Western Christian way. Understanding that is fundamental to understanding the Maya of any time or place."

"Still, it's not reassuring to mainstream religion," he said. "Altars have been found everywhere along the border. It's rumored that bloody sacrifices are made, just like in the old days."

"Doubtful," Lina said cheerfully. "Among the most important sacrifices a Maya king could make was his own blood, produced by piercing his foreskin with a stingray spine and slowly drawing knotted twine through the slits. Do you think men today have the belief to carry through with such a painful sacrifice?"

The reporter winced and shifted as though to protect himself. "I was thinking more of human sacrifice."

"What could be more human than genital self-mutilation in the name of a god you hope to please?" Lina asked, just to see the reporter squirm.

"What about tearing out a victim's heart?" the man asked hurriedly.

"Sometimes noble war prisoners were sacrificed—literally *made holy*—by having their heart removed while it was still beating. But those weren't the most valued sacrifices."

"What was?"

"When the life of ruling royalty itself was given. To the Maya, blood continuity was fundamental to their reality. The people's safety, sanity, and soul depended on being led by a priest-king who could claim unbroken descent from his guiding deity, who was also his blood ancestor. To sacrifice someone of royal blood was a tremendous gift, a desperate gift, done only in times of extreme need."

"What kind of need could drive people to tear out living hearts?" the reporter asked.

Lina told herself to be patient. The man was only doing what he thought was his job. Chasing headlines. Sensation.

"There are glyphs describing such sacrifices," she said, "usually after the people of a kingdom lost a war or suffered intense famine or drought. Such a calamity was proof that your priest-king had lost his connection to his guiding deity. The priest-king himself was sacrificed, often with his blood kin, and the people moved on to follow another, more powerful leader. One who had the blessing of the gods."

"Rather barbaric, don't you think?"

"To paraphrase Shakespeare," Lina said dryly, "uneasy lies the head that wears the crown. Any crown. The Maya are human, no more or less barbaric than Europeans or Chinese of the same time."

From the corner of her eye, Lina saw a tall, muscular figure slide into the classroom. His skin was like his body, sun-weathered and tight. Hair that was neither brown nor black, simply dark, gleamed under the fluorescent lights. The shirt he wore was a guayabera. It would have been at home in any Maya marketplace—faded, boxy, designed to be worn outside the pants to allow the body to breathe in the hot, humid jungle. His jeans were equally faded, equally clean. The boots he wore were so old they were the color of asphalt. Even with clean-shaven cheeks, the man had a roughness about him that wasn't a fashion statement. It was simply real.

Hunter Johnston was back.

## CHAPTER FOUR

LINA'S HEARTBEAT PICKED UP EVEN AS SHE TOLD herself that she was a fool. A few months of on-again, off-again shared coffee and conversation didn't equal anything that should lift her pulse.

The reporter was talking again, his tone impatient.

"I'm sorry," she said to the reporter, "what was the question?"

"The Santa Muerte shrines and the offerings of food and bullets and—some say—blood? How do they tie into the Maya and the end of time in three days?"

"You're assuming that they do."

"Are you saying they don't?" the reporter shot back.

"You'll have to ask the people who visit the shrines."

Hunter quietly took a seat at one side of the room, close to the front. He put a heavy manila envelope on the seat next to him.

"But the shrines began appearing along with talk of the Maya millennium," the reporter said.

"There have been shrines as long as there have been indigenous people," Lina said. "It's simply their way of communicating with their gods. As for the Maya in particular, when they move away from their homelands, their need for shrines goes with them."

"What of three days from now—December twenty-first, 2012?" he insisted.

"It will be followed by December twenty-second, 2012."

The reporter gave up trying to get a headline from her. "Ah, yeah. But a lot of people don't believe that."

"A surprising number of people believe that the earth is flat," Lina said neutrally. "To my knowledge, that belief hasn't affected the shape of the planet."

Hunter snickered.

"So you think this Maya millennial belief is garbage?" the reporter persisted.

"Hale-Bopp was a real comet," Lina said. "It came and went. People who believed it was the Mother Ship come to take them home were disappointed. Another group of people believed in the Y2K frenzy. Our European millennium calendar turned to January first, year 2000. Computers kept on working and the world kept on turning." She smiled. "Think about that on the twenty-second of December."

Lina turned to the rest of class. "I'll see everyone in a few weeks for the exam. I won't be in my office until after New Year's Day. If you have any questions, the line forms after Mr. Sotomayor of the *Houston News*."

The reporter laughed and shook his head. "I'm done."

As the students rustled and murmured on their way out of the room, Lina turned to the two people who hadn't left. One was the woman whose clothes didn't match her age.

Hunter was the other.

"If you have any questions, please come

forward and we'll talk informally," Lina said.

Hunter unfolded his long frame and started walking toward the lectern. As he approached, he was again struck by the difference between Lina's starkly simple clothes and the lush mystery of her golden-brown skin. Up close her eyes were very dark. When the light caught them a certain way, there were surprising shards of gold radiating out from the pupils.

"I'm sorry about running out on coffee a few weeks ago," Hunter began.

The hurried clacking of high heels on the tile floor accompanied by an equally sharp voice drowned out anything else he might have said.

"Dr. Taylor, I'm simply breaking out with questions."

Lina's lips tightened as she turned to the student rushing toward her. She wore carefully distressed black jeans, very tight, and a black sequined shirt, equally tight. The designs on the shirt were meant to be edgy, like jailhouse tattoos. She was as thin as a famine victim, her face all sharp angles and points, with the telltale deer-in-headlights look of too much plastic surgery.

*And they call the Maya barbaric,* Lina thought.

"But first," the woman said, "I just wanted to thank you for your really interesting take on the whole subject."

Perfume hit in a wave.

Hunter tried not to breathe.

"You're more than welcome," Lina said.

"Call me Melodee."

Lina vaguely remembered having been told that before. "Of course, Melodee. How can I—"

"So I wanted to ask about the whole 2012 thing, you know, the Turning of the Great Wheel for the last time," her new best friend cut in without pause. "I mean, if the world is going to end, I really want to know about it and go out having a good time."

She aimed the last words squarely at Hunter, who'd been doing his best to be invisible. He'd run across some of the millennial types while on various trips to the Yucatan and had been forced to make polite conversation by way of keeping his cover intact. But that wasn't required right now, so he didn't bother.

He ignored the woman.

Melodee turned back to Lina. "So Kali

Yuga meets the Age of Aquarius or just a cosmic burp?"

Lina managed not to roll her eyes like her mother. "The ancient Maya were, as some people are today, obsessed with numerology. It was deeply integrated into the Maya culture. It's a very human thing to create significance where realistically there is none."

Deliberately Lina began packing up her lecture materials, signaling an end to the woman's questions.

Melodee plowed right ahead. "But the end of the age? And then there's the whole passing-through-the-galactic-center thingy. We can't just ignore alignments that are so rare."

*I can,* Hunter mouthed from behind Melodee.

Lina managed not to smile. "You are, of course, entitled to your beliefs."

"But—"

"It's very exciting to believe that you're living at a pivot point in human history," Lina continued, talking over the relentless Melodee. "People make a lot of money polishing that lure and it gets buckets of page views on the Internet, even though the movie didn't sell as many tickets as its backers hoped. That, I believe, will be the only millennial Maya cataclysm."

"The Maya will begin the Fourteenth Baktun," Hunter added, "and the rest of us will continue counting down the shopping days until Christmas."

"That's so . . . so ordinary," Melodee said.

"The beginning of a new baktun," Lina said smoothly, "especially this one, which will end the Long Count and begin another, is a cause for celebration all across the Maya world."

"But the sunspots," Melodee said. "And the reversal of the magnetic poles and Nostradamus and—"

"None of those things concerned the Maya," Lina said, "and they were incredible astronomers and mathematicians. They tracked the seasons, followed the path of Venus—their sacred star—and invented a very abstruse language to describe how their universe worked."

"But the sun will cross the galactic equator and the plane of the ecliptic or something like that and the galactic alignment and everything in the *Chilam Balam* and . . ." Melodee ran out of breath and buzzwords at the same time.

"The Maya don't need a fourth catastrophe to be complete," Hunter said, not bothering to conceal his impatience. "The Spanish took care of it for them."

"Very good, Mr. Johnston," Lina answered, biting her lower lip to hide a smile. "In Maya mythology, they have already gone through three separate cataclysms, leading to the age that the fifteenth-century Maya knew, which was their present day. But much of how we perceive the Maya today is filtered through the lens of the Spanish, who weren't interested in the Maya as a culture, but as a resource."

"The Maya died three times before the Spanish came?" Melodee asked faintly.

"It's a metaphor," Hunter said, readjusting the envelope under his left arm. "A story. It took the gods four tries to get the world right. First with people made of mud, then made of wood, then monkeys. Then us."

"Precisely," Lina said. "And between each of the worlds, the gods erased their works and started over, finally culminating with the world the Maya lived in, with the covenant between the gods and humans. Things were as they needed to be and life was good and bad in cycles. But there was never going to be one total apocalypse at the end of the Long Count."

"But the *Chilam Balam* says there will be."

"The Maya writings you refer to were composed after the Spanish conquest. They're a mixture of Maya and Christian beliefs, with a good dose of wishful mysticism."

"Then why aren't the Maya still here?" Melodee asked. "Living in their palaces and all?"

Melodee's bizarre take on reality left Lina speechless.

*Hasn't this idiot learned anything from my classes?* she asked herself silently.

"I am part Maya," Lina finally said. "Through my mother, my lineage can be traced back at least to Tah Itzá in modern Quintana Roo. The Maya are a people, not ancient architecture and a religion based on sacrifice to appease the gods."

Melodee looked to Hunter. No support

there. Then to Lina. "So there's no grand revelation coming?"

"The only revelation is that there won't be one," Hunter said. "That help?"

"No," Melodee said, turning on her high heels like a pole dancer. "It's as boring as you are."

With that, she strode up the aisle. The curious group of students who had overheard the exchange began to drift away to their mundane lives.

"My God, when will this craziness end?" Lina muttered. "I can't wait for December twenty-second. I'm tired of breaking the news to wide-eyed adrenaline freaks that the earth will turn and life will go on as always."

"People like Melodee make my head ache," Hunter agreed. "Shall we try that coffee again?"

Lina hesitated, then smiled up into his eyes, eyes that were almost as light as her father's but silvery blue rather than gray. Beautiful in a way her father's would never be, because Hunter was vividly *there,* his attention focused only on her.

"Is your cell phone with you?" she asked wryly.

"I set it to vibrate." A slow smile. "Cheap thrill is better than no thrill at all."

She told herself not to laugh. It didn't work. The idea that a man like Hunter had to get his adrenaline rush from a phone shaking against his butt was ridiculous.

"Coffee," she agreed.

"Thank you."

"For what?"

"Giving me another chance."

She gave him a sidelong look. "I'm addicted to coffee."

As they walked to a local coffee shop, Hunter waited for her to ask where he had been, why he'd run out on her with a rushed apology. He was still waiting when they took their coffee to a back booth. Lina had been too busy glancing over her shoulder and looking at people who passed by to pay much attention to him.

Maybe she hadn't noticed that he had been gone for the last two weeks.

Lina slid into the booth, then bent over and inhaled the rich scent of coffee, cinnamon, and chocolate rising from her reinforced paper cup. She closed her eyes and sighed with pleasure.

Hunter's jeans started not to fit.

*Damn,* he thought. *It's been way too long if a bit of simple, sensual female appreciation makes me hard.*

But there was something about her thick, dark eyelashes and full lips, the slick pink of her tongue as she caught a drop of coffee on the rim of the cup. It was sexier than watching most women undress.

"You're very quiet," he said.

"I told you," she said, taking another sip, "I love coffee."

"Can you look and lick—er, sip—at the same time?"

"Depends."

"On what?"

"What I'm looking at." She glanced up and saw him watching her mouth. Suddenly the booth felt very small, intimate. When she spoke, her voice was husky. "I can multitask."

Hunter didn't know Lina well enough to be thinking what he was thinking, much less to say it. He let out a silent breath and shifted on the seat.

"I have some photos," he said.

"Please, no etchings."

He laughed. "Nothing that clichéd."

"Bring it," Lina said. "For this coffee I'll look at almost anything."

Silently Hunter took a handful of photos from the manila envelope and fanned them across the table, facing her.

Lina looked down.

The world shifted.

She squeezed her coffee cup so hard the heavy paper gave and coffee slopped over, scalding her.

Hunter whipped the photos out of the way, grabbed napkins, and began cleaning up. "You okay? Burn yourself?"

Silently she shook her head, refusing to meet his eyes.

**No wonder he looks dangerous. He's a damned grave robber.**

She told herself that the disappointment breaking coldly over her was way out of line. Hunter was nothing to her. Less than nothing.

**Thief of the dead.**

"I've had enough coffee," Lina said abruptly.

Before she could stand, his hand snaked across the table and grabbed her wrist, pinning her in place. The grip was gentle.

And unbreakable unless she wanted to make a scene.

"Let's see that hand," Hunter said.

"It's fine."

"Okay. Then tell me about the photos."

"I didn't really look at them." She hadn't had to. An instant was all she needed to know she shouldn't be here, with him.

"What's wrong?" Hunter asked.

His voice was gentle, but his eyes were as implacable as the hand around her wrist.

"I don't talk about artifacts without provenance," she said flatly. "Or are certificates of export and import in that envelope, too?"

Hunter glanced around the coffee shop with eyes gone as flat as her voice. Too many people. Too close.

"How about we talk in your office?" he asked.

"Until I see papers for those artifacts in the photos, I have nothing to talk about with you."

"The artifacts were taken in a drug bust at the Texas-Mexico border."

"Who are you?" Lina asked.

"A man who bought you coffee. That's all. No badges, no official inquiries, no headlines in academic magazines and reputations muddied. At least, there don't have to be."

*He knows,* she thought, hoping her face didn't show her fear. *Somehow he knows about the scandal that nearly brought the Reyes Balam family down. And he's threatening another.*

**Isn't he?**

"Your office?" he asked again.

"I don't bring grave robbers into the museum."

"Good. I'm not one."

"Or slimy middlemen or collectors who troll the black markets."

"Still good," he said.

She stared back at him with eyes gone dark.

"Look," he said. "We need privacy or you'll be facing another scandal. My apartment isn't far way. Neither is yours."

"How do you know?" she asked, torn between anger and a fear that made her even more angry.

"Same way I know a lot of things. I checked you out. It's what I do. Find things, especially if they're lost in Mexico. I'm private. Very private. But if a public badge would make you feel better, I can call my friend. He's with Immigration and Customs Enforcement. I'm working with him on these." Hunter tapped the photos on the edge of the table.

"My office," Lina said tightly. "I know men there with badges."

*Rent-a-cops,* Hunter thought sardonically. *But if they make fear go away from those beautiful eyes, rent-a-cops are my new best friends forever.*

"Your office," he agreed.

A few minutes later, Lina locked her office door behind her and watched Hunter fan the damning photos over her mostly clear desk. The locked door was a signal to students and professionals alike that she didn't want to be disturbed.

But she was more than disturbed. She was scared.

If Hunter was lying to her about keeping his silence, her career was over. And if he wasn't lying to her, her career probably still was over. From the little she had seen in the photos, they could easily have been the pieces her mother had been sniffing after this morning.

**Celia, what have you done now?**

With an expertise that came from years of experience caught between her warring parents, Lina smoothed all expression from her face.

"These pieces were seized at the border by ICE," Hunter said again, figuring she didn't need to know about DEA and the beagle brigade.

"You can prove that?"

"If it will reassure you, I can bring in an ICE badge. Depending on where Jase is, it will take about half an hour."

"Jase?"

"Jason Beaumont," Hunter said. "My closest friend."

Lina walked over to her desk, trying not to stare at the photos.

Failing.

The fear that had rooted in her kept growing. Fumbling slightly, she slid into her office chair without looking away from the photos.

Hunter studied Lina's face as she studied the photos. Unlike the flash of panic or disgust he'd seen in the coffee shop, she appeared entirely composed now. Since she came from a high-test family, he wasn't surprised at her calm. The Reyes Balam bloodlines were as blue as they came, New World and Old combined.

"What do you want from me?" Lina asked.

He wanted more than information, but that was his personal problem. It wouldn't get in the way of his professional needs. Or Jase's.

"First and foremost," Hunter said, "a promise that this goes no further than the two of us."

"Why?"

"A man's job hangs on finding those artifacts. Fast. He has two kids and another on the way. To help him, I need the kind of knowledge you have."

It wasn't what Lina had expected to hear. She blew out her breath. "Just the two of us. And that goes both ways, Hunter."

"Three. Jase already knows I was going to contact you."

"Is it his butt on the line?" Lina asked bluntly.

"Yes."

"All right. The three of us. If this gets out, I'm ruined."

"Just for talking to me?" Hunter asked.

"There is no shade of gray in the academic view of unprovenanced items. You're pure white or you're garbage waiting for the disposal to be turned on."

"The Caesar's wife syndrome?"

"Exactly. My family's reputation wouldn't survive another scandal. Neither would mine. As you well know," she added coolly.

"The sooner you help me find these artifacts, the quicker you'll be left with the purists."

She looked at him for a long moment, her eyes dark and measuring. Then she looked at the photos. "Do you know where the artifacts came from?"

"All I know is that the plates on the truck caught at the border were from Quintana Roo."

"The driver?"

"The same."

"Has he mentioned any specific area or ruins?" Lina asked without looking up. Holding her breath. "Q Roo is a big state."

"He's dead," Hunter said. "He didn't talk about anything but getting shuck of the artifacts. He was afraid of them, or of whoever would take delivery."

"You're not making this any easier," she said under her breath.

"Easy or hard, it'll get done. Somebody knows where those artifacts came from. Somebody looted them, sold them, maybe they were resold a few times before they were packed in bags of cement mix and taken north. When I find the looters or the middlemen, I'll find the name of the end buyer. Somewhere along that line, someone will talk. Someone will know about these artifacts."

Lina was still caught on the bags of cement. "Was it a commercial load in a commercially licensed truck?"

"No. I had a source check it out. The truck was stolen from a building site on the Riviera Maya."

*Thank God,* Lina thought. "You know that part of my family's business in Mexico and the U.S. is cement?"

Hunter nodded. "The bags weren't from Chel Balam International."

Not that the wrapping proved anything. Buying bags of cement mix was about as complex as buying tortillas.

"Yet you still came to me," she said.

Silently he watched her, waiting for her to realize there was no way out.

"This is extortion," she said.

"You want me to walk away, I'll walk," he said, reaching for the photos.

"And talk, no doubt," she said bitterly, smacking his hand away from the photos.

"Does that mean you want me to stay?"

"It means that I have no choice. And we both know it."

"I'll pay for your time and expertise," Hunter said, letting out a hidden breath of relief.

"I'm not a whore with a Ph.D. Now shut up and let me concentrate on these photos."

Hunter shut up.

# CHAPTER FIVE

SOMEWHERE BEHIND HUNTER, A MAN WHISTLED down the hallway outside Lina's office. Someone else called out a greeting. The air conditioner made mechanical sounds.

Hunter counted the books in one of Lina's bookcases. Twice.

After a very long silence, Lina asked, "May I take notes?"

"As long as you don't show them to anybody but Jase or me," Hunter said.

Without another word, she pulled over an electronic notebook, turned it on, tapped the screen to create a new document and a keyboard, and began typing.

"You said you could multitask," Hunter said, "so talk while you type."

"The knife is most likely obsidian, which is volcanic glass. Unusually refined, delicate flaking pattern. The goal was beauty, not durability. Ceremonial. Probably to be used only once, or at most in a brief series of highly important ceremonies. There is a sigil etched into the blade."

"What does it mean?"

"Unknown. The photographer used too much flash for me to read beneath the glare."

Hunter came and stood behind the desk, close to her. Too close. He knew it and he didn't care. He really liked the scent and feel of her near him.

"Show me," he said.

"Here," she said, pointing to the photo.

The flash had made an explosion of light against the highly reflective obsidian. The result obscured part of the knife while throwing the rest into relief.

"Go on," he said.

Her full lips tightened, but all she said was "These are first, very quick reactions to the artifacts. A gut response. If you want academic detail, I need more time."

"Give me what you can right now. I'll wait for the rest."

*There was no double meaning in that,* Lina told herself. *And he's not breathing in the scent of my skin.*

She forced herself to think, to multitask despite the looming presence of Hunter Johnston, but every breath she took was flavored with warmth and something clean, healthy, male.

"Give me room," she said tightly.

He shifted an inch away. When she met his eyes, she knew that he was as aware of her as she was of him. She set her teeth and forced herself to concentrate on the second photo.

"A mask," she said. "Those are feathers or wings flaring away from the sides of the face." *Inhuman lips parted, a god's words pouring out.* "Gaping mouth, eyes large and not filled in with shell or obsidian. This was designed to be worn, to give some visual freedom to the wearer. Again, likely for ceremonial use."

Her fingers paused.

"What?" Hunter said instantly.

She shook her head as though throwing

off cobwebs. "It . . . echoes something, but I've never seen a piece like it before."

"What's the echo of?"

"I don't know. It was just a feeling. Nothing academic."

"I do feelings."

Lina felt a wild laugh bubbling in her throat. She swallowed it. Twice. The idea of someone as hard-looking as Hunter "doing feelings" was far too intriguing. She forced herself to look at the third photo.

Her breath caught.

"Talk to me," Hunter said, his voice flat.

"The bundle is vaguely heart-shaped, wrapped in clear plastic." Her fingers moved silently over the electronic keyboard. "Color beneath could be white or beige. Again, the flash interferes."

"What are the stains?"

"Mud, blood, coffee, cinnamon, chocolate. Impossible to say without chemical analysis."

Hunter grunted. He wasn't getting much that was useful. He watched her fingers—clean, short nails, no rings—touch the edge of the first photo.

"The glyph in this," she said, tapping the

photo of the ritual knife, "looks like it has some jagged lines. Or it could be glare."

She shifted the photo of the knife, changing the light, trying to peer through the glare.

It was impossible.

"Is it a common glyph?" he asked.

"As I can't really see it, I can't make a judgment."

"This isn't academia. Give me your best guess."

"If the artifacts came from the same area as the stolen truck—a big 'if'—then the glyph might possibly be related to Kawa'il, a Maya deity worshipped after the destruction of the Maya rule by the Spanish."

Lina's father probably knew more about Kawa'il than she did, but she had no intention of mixing Hunter with her obsessive, erratic father.

"Do you have an electronic image of the knife?" she asked. "You might be able to run a digital photo through a computer program and clean up the glare from the flash."

"I'll check into it, but I doubt it. Looks like it was taken right after the raid. ICE uses a lot of digital cameras. The photos on the card were probably printed out with the report and then wiped from the card's memory to make digital room for the next bust. How much does it matter?"

"Kawa'il wasn't a common deity. His worship was confined to small areas of the Quintana Roo and, perhaps, Belize. Many Maya scholars don't even believe Kawa'il existed."

"But you do."

"Yes. Some glyphs related to Kawa'il have been found on . . ." Her voice died.

"Reyes Balam land."

It wasn't a question.

"If you already know so much, why mousetrap me into helping you?" she asked sharply.

"The presence or absence of Kawa'il was central to the scandal that got your father thrown out of academia."

"He is still a Harvard professor."

"Technically," Hunter agreed. "He's on indefinite leave to 'pursue scholarly interests.' You have to look real hard to find Dr. Philip Taylor's name attached to a university of any repute, including in Mexico."

Lina didn't say anything. It was the harsh

truth, one that had driven Philip to ever greater lengths of obsession and secrecy. He was determined to regain his reputation no matter what it took.

"If my father knows of these artifacts," she said quietly, "I'm useless to you. Philip doesn't confide in anyone, including me."

Hunter nodded. "It was a long chance, but one I had to eliminate."

"You believe me?"

"Until I find a reason to do otherwise." He smiled thinly. "That's more slack than the academic community will cut you."

Again, a harsh truth.

"Well, at least you don't fancy things up," she said.

"I'm a simple man."

"I don't believe it. The bunch of fabric," she said, tapping her finger on the photo of the cloth, "could be rubbish or it could be a god bundle. Again, without tests, I can't be more precise."

"If it's a god bundle?"

"It would be highly, *highly* rare. Pretty much unique, as far as I know. Such bundles are represented in glyphs and verbal legends, but none have survived to modern times."

"So it's worth a lot of money on the market," he said.

"Without proper provenance, no reputable dealer or establishment would touch it."

As Hunter had arrived at the same conclusion himself, he wasn't surprised. Disappointed, but not surprised.

"That covers some of the market," he said. "What about the rest of it?"

Lina frowned. "Frankly, I doubt anyone would pay or trade anything significant for it. So unique an object is automatically suspect. Fraud is a fact of life when you're dealing without provenance. And a god bundle . . ."

He watched her face, the change in her eyes, like she was looking at something far more distant than the photos.

"A god bundle was the most sacred of artifacts," Lina said. "It was believed to contain talismans created by the god himself. The talismans were said to literally hold the strength of that god given in promise to the village or city-state that worshipped and was guarded by the god. The bundle was carried in a carved box at the forefront of soldiers going into battle. Capturing a god bundle meant the end of a deity and the people who followed it. We have no analogue to it in modern times."

"National flags?"

Her short nails drummed on the desk. "Not really. It's like comparing a tennis game to World War Two. You must realize the depth of the Maya belief system. That god bundle was the god itself. It was *real,* like birth or death. A fact."

She looked at him, saw that he understood what she was saying, and shifted her focus back to the photo.

"Losers in a war lost their real god," Lina said after a moment. "The belief that the clash of armies was in fact a clash of deities is one of the things that made the Maya relatively easy to conquer. If an enemy's god was more potent, you abandoned your losing god. You accepted the victorious god, worshipped it, and shared in its power. Because the Spanish were more powerful than the Maya, it followed that their god was more powerful. Christ rather than Kukulcán, as it were. Of course, not everyone gave up their god. Some only gave lip service."

"Good," Hunter said. "That's the kind of thing I need to know. I looked at those photos and I saw a bunch of probably Late Terminal Classic artifacts. The mask was totally unfamiliar, and the fabric was a mystery blob."

"We don't know it's a god bundle."

"But we do know that unloading it for significant cash on the black market isn't likely."

"Yes. Too many wealthy collectors have been stung in the past. If an artifact is too good to believe, they don't believe it without the kind of provenance that would boggle even an ancient Chinese bureaucracy."

"What kind of provenance?"

"If the artifact came into the U.S. before the passage of various international antiquities laws, you would have to be able to prove at least three legitimate previous owners. If the artifact was in the hands of the original owner's family, you would need proof that the object had been collected and cataloged before the antiquities laws were in place, and hadn't passed out of the first owner's hands without proper paperwork. That's the minimum."

"What if the object entered the marketplace more recently?" Hunter asked.

"Proof of proper export and import papers, signed by any involved governments and stamped with various and explicit official approvals. Again, that's the minimum. Legitimate collectors and institutions are often more demanding."

Hunter braced a hand on the desk, half enclosing Lina.

"Tell me about the less demanding ones," he said.

She tried and failed not to breathe him in, realized at a primal level why many cultures felt breath was the essence of the soul. Breathing in.

Breathing him.

"Buyers and sellers alike get stung in the gray or black market," she said in a low voice. "It's the price of doing business on the wrong side of antiquities laws."

Hunter rubbed the back of his neck. The motion reminded him that his hair was too long. Downright shaggy. "But some people risk it."

"I'm not one of them. My reputation can't take another hit, no matter that I never did anything wrong," Lina said flatly. "I can't even be seen with the loose type of dealer or collector, much less be associated with any. If a branch of my family didn't own this museum, I probably wouldn't have been let in the door, much less hired."

"What about your mother?" Hunter asked.

Lina stiffened. "What are you implying?"

"Nothing. Just asking."

Grimly Lina got a grip on herself. "As far as I know, Celia learned her lesson years ago. The charges of dealing with looted Maya antiquities nearly destroyed the Reyes Balam family. But you already know all of this, don't you? It's why you're here."

Hunter barely managed not to wince. Her voice had gone from the husky warmth that made him think of foot rubs and creamy desserts to the kind of ice that could cut skin. Whatever her family might or might not be into, Lina had embraced the purity of Caesar's wife.

Professionally it was a disappointment to Hunter. Personally, it made her all the more appealing.

*You're trusting her,* he warned himself.

*Only until I find a reason not to,* he defended himself.

Problem was, he wasn't certain he wanted to see that kind of reason.

"I'm here because you're an expert in Maya artifacts," Hunter said evenly.

Lina measured his stark, angular features, his brilliant, patient eyes, and knew she was outmatched. All he had to do was whisper a few words and she wouldn't be trusted in academic circles with a handful of twentieth-century potsherds. And her family . . .

She stuffed down her anger at being trapped and went back to studying photos. Yet her hands wanted to tremble. Everything she was seeing pointed to Kawa'il, to the family estates in Quintana Roo, to the illicit artifact trade.

*These must have been looted,* she told herself. *It's the only rational explanation. My parents might be foolish, sometimes even childish, but they aren't stupid.*

Feeling more sure of herself, Lina pointed toward the fourth picture. "This is a stone scepter. The cup on the end could have been for corn pollen or blood or some other ritual material. There's no way of knowing without examining the object itself."

"Blood again."

"Blood was central to Maya sacred rituals. Everything depended upon and sprang from blood." She shifted the photo. "Again, this is ceremonial, finely made. Note that the protruding, carefully worked obsidian flakes run the entire length of the scepter. Whoever gripped this would be cut deeply enough to bleed freely. It's a sign of a priest's or king's willingness to sacrifice his own blood for the god or gods."

"Beats the foreskin-piercing routine," he said.

"I'll have to take your word on that." A hint of huskiness was back in Lina's voice, ice melting, white teeth sinking into her full lower lip as she bit back a smile.

Hunter's body came alert. He leaned over, getting closer to the photo. And Lina. There was a hint of cinnamon in her scent, either from the spilled coffee or just a natural part of her.

He wanted to taste.

"So this scepter goes with the ceremonial theme of the other artifacts," he said.

The extra depth in his voice was like a stroke over her senses. "Yes."

The word was breathless. She yanked her mind back from Hunter's male body so close to her.

**He blackmailed me into helping him.**

*For a friend,* she reminded herself. Hunter wasn't after personal gain.

Part of her wondered if he would really ruin her reputation. Then she remembered the look on his face when he said that Jase had two kids and his wife was expecting a third. To protect the children, Hunter would do what he had to.

She couldn't really blame him, but she didn't have to like it.

**Just once, I'd like to be the most important thing in someone's life.**

Lina squashed the thought as soon as it came to her. Her childhood was what it was. Her adulthood was her own responsibility.

She cleared her throat and said crisply, "Yes, ceremonial."

"Late Terminal Classic?"

"From all appearances."

"What about the Chacmool?" he asked.

He was so close to Lina now that he could see his breath stirring the tendrils of hair that had escaped the severe bun at the nape of her neck. Goose bumps rippled over her skin, telling him just how sensitive she was, how aware of him.

"Ceremonial." It was more a husky whisper than a word. Then, "Stop it."

"What?" he asked, his breath against her ear.

She opened her mouth to tell him precisely what he was doing, then realized how easily he could deny everything, making her feel a fool for noticing him so intensely, allowing him to affect her so much.

*It could be an accident,* she told herself. *I've often leaned over someone's shoulder to look at something.*

But it hadn't made her skin feel too tight, her breath too short.

"I have an American's sense of personal space," she said. "You must have spent a lot of time in Mexico."

"Busted." He moved away just enough that she could no longer feel his breath. "Better?"

She let out a long, almost silent rush of air. "Chacmool figure, including a bowl to catch blood. Ceremonial. New World jade. Jaguar glyphs engraved around the edge of the figure. The glyphs around the lip of the bowl appear to be Late Terminal Classic."

Hunter barely kept himself from leaning closer. He'd liked the scent of Lina's skin, the creamy texture, the pulse beating rapidly at the base of her neck.

"So, this represents the god's mouth?" he asked, pointing to the shallow bowl that was the reason for the Chacmool's existence.

"Are you sure you need me?"

"Very sure."

Lina told herself there was no double meaning in his words. She couldn't quite believe it. But then, she'd never been flirted with in such a bold yet indirect way.

"If you already know the purpose of the Chacmool . . ." she began.

"Your course work covered it—a reclining man-god figure with knees bent and head raised, providing a rest for a shallow bowl."

"You missed half the classes."

"The syllabus was excellent."

Lina gave up and concentrated on the photo. "The glyphs I can see are what I would expect on a ceremonial object. The date. The royal hierarchy. Man's reverence. The gods' awful power."

"Is Kawa'il a part of the Chacmool and its ritual?"

"Without seeing the entire rim, I can't answer that."

"Is it possible?"

"I'm told anything is possible, including the Maya millennium," she said dryly. "Ask Melodee."

"Pass. I prefer women who haven't been cut-and-pasted."

Lina shook her head, smiling. Hunter Johnston was very much to her taste. Too bad he was little better than a blackmailer.

"You still mad that I twisted your arm to help me?" he asked.

"Are you a mind reader?"

"No. You were smiling, then you looked like someone had asked you to eat a bug. Since I'm the only insect-eating SOB here, it was a logical connection."

Hunter was entirely too quick, or she was too easy to read. Or both.

"The fifth photo fits with the time frame and ceremonial theme," Lina said, sticking to what she knew rather than what she feared or desired. "The censer appears to be clay, beautifully crafted so that the incense smoke would seem to be pouring from the mouths of gods."

"Looks like snakes to me."

"The feathered serpent was a common Maya theme. If the censer was originally found with the other objects—"

"Unknown."

"—the assumption would be that you have the trove of a high priest or a king."

"You keep saying priest *or* king," Hunter said.

"The English language makes the distinction. There is no proof that the Mayan language did. From all we have learned, it appears that nobility supplied the priest-kings. The duties, if they were separate at all, overlapped so heavily as to make a distinction meaningless."

"I love it when you go all academic on me. Such a contrast to your—" Abruptly Hunter closed his runaway mouth.

Lina raised one dark, wing-shaped eyebrow.

"Off the subject," he said. "I'm a man. My thoughts sometimes wander."

She didn't ask where they went. She knew. And she liked it, which confused her.

He had strong-armed her into helping him, but she wasn't as mad as she should be. He was flirting with her, and she liked it way too much. She'd slapped down less aggressive males without a thought.

Hunter took thought.

"The Maya believed that a god's words could be seen in smoke, in dreams," she said.

"Drug-induced?"

"Perhaps. Peyote enemas are a documented archaeological reality, as are mushroom and other psychotropic substances. But there are other ways to induce visions."

"Such as?"

"Pain. Enough pain, enough self-bloodletting, can cause what Western people label hallucinations and Maya called communication with the gods."

The part of herself that was instinctive, bone-deep, knew that the censer in the photo had been used in just such rituals.

"I wonder what the gods told him," she said softly.

"Him? What about women?"

"Maya weren't, and aren't, much for equal opportunity between sexes. A Maya queen could never ascend the throne unless she was pregnant and her husband was recently dead."

"So women weren't part of ritual ceremonies?" Hunter asked.

"The queen was, and perhaps the wives of the highest nobles. A female let blood through her tongue. Knotted twine was pulled through a vertical cut."

"Ouch."

"They were a visceral people. And are today. Only the ceremonies change. Not that the Maya lacked intellectual accomplishments," Lina added quickly. "Their mathematical system understood the necessity of a zero. The fact that their numerical system was based on twenty rather than ten makes it difficult for us to fully understand and appreciate. Our problem, not theirs. Their astronomy was superb, the equal of any world culture."

"You admire them."

"Don't you?"

"The more I know, the more there is to admire."

*Not touching that one,* Lina thought. *He will not suck me into a world of double meanings.*

"The last photo," she said, forcing her thoughts away from Hunter's temptations, "is as incredible as the cloth bundle. Perhaps more so."

"I'm ready."

Lina barely resisted the temptation to check out the fit of his jeans.

*Focus,* she told herself.

It was hard.

Like him.

"This." She cleared her throat and tried to remember all the reasons she should be angry with him. But breathing in his male scent, sensing the muscular warmth of this body, made anger as impossible as her attraction to Hunter Johnston. "This is as unique as the cloth bundle." She let the photo of a mask draw her in and down, back into a past that was as fascinating as it was lost. "Maybe more unique. If it's real."

"Looks real to me."

"Frauds are real, too," Lina murmured.

"Are you saying that the mask is a fraud?"

"I'm saying that I can't be sure until I've examined it under a microscope for machine marks."

"Somebody killed to keep its secrets," Hunter said. "Assume it's real."

"Killed?"

"The driver. Maybe others. Life is cheap."

"Not to me."

"Or me." An echo of Suzanne's death twisted through him, scraping his soul. "We're creatures of our culture. Other cultures, other creatures."

"Assuming this is real," Lina said, "it's the single most extraordinary artifact I've ever seen. Obsidian is rare in the Yucatan, though not in what became Mexico."

"So the object isn't from the Yucatan?"

"Trade was commonplace. The Maya had huge canoes that ferried merchandise along the Gulf and around the Yucatan peninsula. I've seen a fragment of a mask so intricately inlaid with obsidian that the artifact was a complex mosaic of black with silver-gold light turning beneath. But I don't see any sign of inlay in this photograph of the mask, just a solid, unbroken surface."

"Could it have been made of a single chunk of obsidian?" he asked.

"If you're asking if obsidian comes in pieces this large, yes. I've seen obsidian boulders as big as a car. But . . ."

Hunter waited. He was good at it.

"The time and effort that would go into flaking and polishing a piece of obsidian into a mask is extreme," she said finally. "Obsidian is friable, it shatters. It's very difficult to make it smooth."

*Like your skin,* Hunter thought, leaning close again. *Smooth.*

"Making this would be the same as taking a ragged hunk of glass the size of a washing machine and slowly working it into a mask the size of a human face," Lina said, breathing him in, wanting him to understand just how astonishing the mask was. "Chipping, flaking, grinding, polishing. Starting all over with a new chunk when something came apart. Big pieces of obsidian have natural flaws that make the material fracture in surprising ways."

He watched her with eyes the silver blue of a glacier beneath the sun, framed in the darkness of a winter past.

*A woman could get lost in those eyes.* Lina felt a shiver go over her at the thought. She tried to believe that it was fear, not desire, cold rather than heat. But she had been curious about Hunter for too long, and he was so close to her now.

"The Chinese worked jade," Hunter

said. "Some pieces took generations to finish. It's not impossible that the Maya did the same."

"No," she said huskily, "it's not impossible." *But you are, Hunter Johnston. You're the most impossible thing about this whole situation.*

Lina forced herself to look away, to concentrate on the obsidian mask, volcanic glass lovingly worked and polished until it shone like a gold-tinted mirror beneath the harsh flash used to take the photo. *Hunter's like that. The surface isn't what is important.*

"Lina?" he asked.

Belatedly she realized that she was looking at him again, falling into darkness and light.

"The central part of the mask is human," she said, her voice low. "The eyes are heavy-lidded, half open. The nose is a blunt blade of nobility, the cheekbones high and broad, the mouth a grim slit of judgment. This is a god on the brink of a catastrophic temper tantrum."

"Not a gentle god."

"The Maya revered the jaguar, a climax predator. If tenderness was valued, we've seen little indication of it in their religious-civic art."

"Sounds like the Yucatan I know and love," Hunter said dryly, thinking of his last assignment. Being a courier in a kidnap-ransom scheme wasn't his favorite job, but it brought a lot of money into the family business. And saved lives. Sometimes. If he was very lucky, very careful.

"Do you know the Yucatan?" Lina asked, surprised.

"Better than most, not as well as you do. What are these things along the edges?" he asked, pointing to the mask. As he touched the photo, it shifted, making it seem alive, breathing, waiting.

"Symbolic feathers or flames or even lightning. It's difficult to tell against the flash." As Lina spoke, she typed into her notebook. "These are very vigorous symbols, incised and brought into relief. Delicate and vivid, polished to the same hard gleam as the face itself. See the drill holes that would hold cord or leather, allowing it to be fastened to a man's head? Amazing, incredible artisans created this."

Hunter watched her profile, a more feminine, much more elegant echo of the mask.

"Imagine this in torchlight," Lina said. "It would be inhuman, terrifying, awesome in the original sense of the word. It's clearly a ceremonial piece, but who wore it? For what purpose? It must have been traded for, but why and when?"

She made an exasperated sound and smacked her palm on the desk.

Hunter waited.

"This is maddening," she said. "Without context, my questions can't be answered. I might get a chemical analysis and be able to match the obsidian to the original quarry site, but that's such a tiny part of this mask's history. To date it, I would need to know where it was found, in what layer of dirt, with what other objects or signs of habitation. All I have is this photograph."

Hunter noted the flush of temper darken her high cheekbones. The lady had passion. It was part of what attracted him to her. Then he watched anger fade into something close to puzzlement.

Silence stretched.

"What?" he asked.

She flinched as though she'd forgot he was there. "I'm not sure. I feel like I've seen something similar to this, but I can't remember where or when. The shining . . ." She smacked the desk again with her palm. "Damn the grave robber who cared more about money than knowledge!"

"Grave robbers are poor. Only the end-game is rich."

She blew out a hard breath. "I know. I spent most of my childhood running bare-foot through villages that depended on my family's generosity for food, clothing, every-thing but water. And sometimes even that. I didn't understand then. I just laughed and played with the village children while Philip and their fathers dug through the jungle, seeking Maya heritage."

"You can't eat heritage."

The air-conditioning kicked on, a cool breath settling over the office.

Suddenly Lina looked defeated. She shook her head. "I know. If my child was hungry, I'd be in the front line of grave dig-gers, shoveling hard."

His hand squeezed her shoulder, lin-gered.

"So would I," he said. "Tell me more about Maya and masks."

She looked into his silver-blue eyes and saw shadows. She knew he understood loss at a level as deep, even deeper than hers. She tried to remember why she should be angry with him.

She couldn't.

"Masks," she said, gathering herself. "Masks were an integral part of Maya rituals. The nobles/priests wearing them would take on the aspects of the god whose mask they wore, or the god would speak through the mask wearers. Either or both."

"I don't think the news coming from that obsidian mask would be good."

"All masks are fearsome to some degree, because the gods are fearsome. But this one gives me chills."

**Yet I know this mask.**

**Or will.**

A movement at the ground-level window caught her attention. Whatever it was vanished before she could focus. Just like all the other times she'd looked over her shoulder, feeling watched.

"You okay?" Hunter asked.

"Yes," she said automatically, even as her instincts shouted *no.*

Hunter's phone vibrated against his butt. A text had just come in. He fished out the device, hit the button, and read Jase's message: NEED U. NEW INFO.

"I have to go," Hunter said, gathering up the photos and stuffing them into their envelope.

"But—" she began.

"For now, you'll have to work from your notes," he cut in. "I'll call as soon as I'm free. Have something good for me."

The office door closed behind Hunter before she could say anything. The man moved like a cat.

Then she remembered why she was mad at him.

With a muttered word, Lina booted up her big computer and went to work. It wasn't like she had a lot of choice, after all.

And if she kept telling herself that, she might not have a case of rapid pulse every time he came near her.

# CHAPTER SIX

WHEN HUNTER LEFT THE MUSEUM BUILDING, HE didn't notice the rising, oddly dry heat of the day. His long legs moved with deceptively lazy speed as he covered ground to the parking lot where he had left his beat-up Jeep. As he walked, he speed-dialed Jase's number.

"What's up?" Hunter asked as soon as Jase answered.

"While you were sniffing around the sexy professor, I reviewed those warehouse tapes until my eyes started to bleed."

"I was working, not sniffing," Hunter said. A half-truth.

"Nice work if you can get it. I found something interesting."

*So did I,* Hunter thought as he slid into the Jeep with its open windows and canvas cover. *Her skin smells like cinnamon.*

"One of the nights covered on those security tapes," Jase said, referring to the digital record that got wiped every three weeks, "the custodian made an extra trip through the warehouse. Other than that, he was as regular in his rounds as a robot."

"Huh." Hunter turned the key. The engine started instantly. Only the exterior looked careless. Every working part was better than new. "You at my apartment?"

"Yeah, I don't want Ali to suspect that anything's wrong, that I didn't take the bus as usual to work. Can you pick me up? It's Ali's shopping day."

"Buses are a pain," Hunter agreed, "especially with kids and groceries."

"And pregnant." There was a smile in Jase's voice, the sound of a man who was pleased with his woman.

"On my way," Hunter said.

A few minutes later he pulled to a stop in front of his apartment building. Jase was waiting, dressed in jeans, sandals, and a clean blue shirt whose sleeves were already rolled up against the heat. A light wind jacket made an unnecessary layer, which told Hunter that Jase was carrying.

"How close did the janitor get to the stuff?" Hunter asked as Jase slid into the passenger side of the Jeep.

"That's tough to tell. The recording devices are only triggered by movement. Some of the guys had complained about that and the lack of enough cameras to cover every angle, but the brass blew it off."

"Cameras cost money. Where we going?"

As Jase told Hunter the address, the Jeep poked out into city traffic. People and faces flowed by on all sides, shades of pale sliding into rich mahogany. Cowboy hats were common, whether they were made of leather or felt or straw.

"The janitor could've spent a few minutes in the area where the artifacts were," Jase said. "I could see him come and go on the record, but not exactly what he did. That whole aisle wasn't covered well."

"Budget is a bitch. Is this a regular janitorial guy?"

"He's on the crew, more or less checks out. But get this, he's taken a few days of unannounced vacation, starting about three days ago."

Hunter's eyebrows lifted. "Interesting."

"Yeah. So let's go knock on his door, ask a few questions."

"How'd you get the address?"

"Usual way."

"A warrant?" Hunter asked.

"Ha-ha. I told the head of PR of DeWatt Industrial Solutions that he could talk to me or I'd come back with a warrant for his personnel files, checking so-called Social Security numbers against government databases."

"Oh. That usual way. Thought you weren't supposed to show your badge."

"Brubaker can sit on it and spin."

Hunter smiled. "You do know where the address is?"

"Dirtbag central," Jase said.

"Just so you know."

"Why do you think I wanted company? Going in there solo would be stupid. My mama didn't raise no stupid kids."

When Hunter finally beat his way through

traffic to the address, he was glad he and Jase were bilingual. In this area, English wasn't even a second language.

"I get to be the bad guy," Hunter said as he parked the Jeep.

"You always get to be bad."

"People look at your big brown eyes and trust you with their firstborn."

Jase grinned. "I always knew you were jealous. Serves you right for those icy Anglo eyes."

Hunter parked along the cracked, dirty curb a block away and half a block down a side street. Bits of paper trash lifted on the occasional breeze. With an automatic motion, he pulled the Jeep's key, shoved it deep in his front pocket, and got out. He didn't need to worry about locking up. Most of the time there was nothing inside the Jeep but dirt from both sides of the border. No radio, no antenna, no tire iron, no tools, no baggage. Nothing worth stealing.

A few minutes later Jase studied the two-story apartment building. "Hard to imagine it new."

"Instant slums, built to sag and lean and rust overnight."

"Bet the rooms smell like mildew on a good day, cat piss the rest of the time."

In the heat, the smell reached right out to the curb.

"Tell me this is the wrong address," Hunter invited.

"I never lie to you."

"What about the blonde, the redhead, and the Siamese twins?"

"What about them?" Jase asked.

Hunter shook his head and walked around the broken glass security door that hung drunkenly, allowing wind, dirt, and anyone who was interested into the hallway beyond. Inside, an aggregate concrete stairway held up by rusty iron gave access to the second floor. Every step was broken, cracked, or both. A ragged pyramid of Tecate cans stood unevenly off to one side of the bottom step, waiting to fall.

"If this guy's a thief," Jase muttered, following Hunter, "he's lousy at it. Like a pickpocket with no hands."

"Poor impulse control has been the downfall of more than one master criminal," Hunter said dryly. "Is this call hard or soft?"

"Soft. Just wondering how he is, we haven't heard from him, blah blah."

The steps up from street level grated underfoot. The crumbling stoop was crusted with dirt and greasy debris.

Behind an apartment door, a dog barked madly. The dog's bark changed to hysteria when he caught their scent. Someone yelled in Spanglish for the dog to *cállete* the hell up. The dog yipped and went silent.

Hunter scanned the upper balcony for unpleasant surprises. Nothing moved.

"Looks like everyone's tucked in with TV and cerveza," Jase said.

Hunter grunted.

"You armed?" Jase asked.

"The usual." For Hunter, that was a knife in his boot. "What's the dude's name?"

"LeRoy Ramirez Landry. First door on the right."

"Let's hope Mr. Landry doesn't do anything stupid."

"Paying rent here is stupid," Jase said.

"You take the door," Hunter said. "I'll cover you."

Jase stepped past Hunter, whose narrowed eyes were scanning the other closed doors. Landry's apartment was closest to the stairs. That would make a fast retreat easier.

Feeling watched from behind, Hunter looked over his shoulder and out at the street. His neck had felt like he was in someone's crosshairs since he'd left the lecture room with the professor on his arm. It wasn't a good feeling.

Nothing moved below but a feral cat scrounging for fast-food scraps and slow rats.

Jase knocked on Landry's apartment door. The door sounded dry and hollow, empty as a cracked bone.

"It's been kicked out of the jamb," Jase said in a low voice.

"Saw it from the stairs."

"Cat eyes. You've been out in the jungle too long."

"I like being in one piece," Hunter said.

"Not arguing, just saying."

Jase knocked again. He didn't want to shout out "ICE" if he didn't have to. No reason to get trampled in the stampede out of the building.

A gust of wind licked through the broken street door, toppling the empty beer cans at the bottom of the stairs. Across the hallway, a dog whined once.

Silence spread like dirt in the hallway.

Hunter and Jase knew that all the televisions had just been turned down.

"Dude isn't home or he's hiding," Hunter said in a low voice. "Everyone else knows we're here."

"What a surprise."

"Yeah. If you happen to lean on that door and it gives way, technically it isn't breaking and entering," Hunter offered.

He pointed to the finger-wide gap between the barely open door and the frame.

"Man, and I was hoping to get in another misdemeanor today," Jase said.

"Stay tight. A felony might be just around the corner."

Jase scratched at the spot where his reversed baseball hat met the back of his head. "Well, I'm concerned about the well-being of this citizen who may or may not have become involved in a crime. We really should check out the place. I mean, it's for his own safety."

"You're such a good citizen," Hunter said. "How do you do it?"

"Clean living."

"You forgot constant prayer."

"That's Ali's job." Jase put the back of his hand on the door, pushed. It scraped open. "Oops. Look at that. Busted. We better check that Mr. Landry is okay."

Jase pushed the door wide open and stepped to the other side of the frame. Hunter was already at Jase's blind side. They had both been trained the same way, by the same life.

Nothing was behind the door. No one was within sight. Curtains shifted. They were dirty enough to have been used as napkins.

Not one sound came from inside the apartment.

The cramped room seemed to cringe at the afternoon sunlight flooding through the open door. A coffee table was littered with envelopes torn open carelessly. Empty bottles of malt liquor stood sentinel by crushed cigarette packs and overflowing ashtrays. Cigarette butts stuck out of the ashes like finger bones.

"Guess he lives on nicotine and alcohol," Jase said. "No fast-food trash."

"Lotto tickets," Hunter said.

The colorful stubs were ripped up, tossed everywhere in a kind of loser's confetti.

Jase walked a bit farther into the room. Hunter's movements mirrored his partner's.

The television was off, and Hunter could see where the screen had been dusted with an open palm. The ring of grime at the edges clung. He moved the back of his hand close to the screen. Cold. Like the room, despite the cracked door. Air-conditioning hummed and rattled as it came on.

"Looks like he hasn't been here for a while," Jase said. "But I'm not going to open that fridge to check expiration dates."

"How long?" Hunter asked.

Jase understood the rest of the question. "Feels like days. Maybe more."

"It smells bad, but not dead-body bad. Back room?"

Nodding, Jase headed farther into the apartment.

"Unmade bed," Jase said, looking into the tiny bedroom.

"I'd be surprised if it was made."

Jase pushed the door wide open, flat against the wall. Nothing

"No obvious signs of struggle."

"Just the everyday fight to keep in beer, cigarettes, and lotto tickets," Hunter said. "No sign of any artifacts either."

"Man, I really don't want to wreck this

place to find them," Jase muttered. "Just standing here makes me want to wash my hands."

He pulled a wad of exam gloves from his jacket pocket and handed a pair to Hunter. Both men snapped them on. Jase opened what he could of the closet's sliding door before it jammed on the gritty rails.

"A few shirts, pants, some of the clothes have DeWatt janitorial service logos," Jase said quietly. "Ratty tennis shoes. Flip-flops. Dirty socks."

Hunter was glancing around the coffin-size bathroom. No cupboards. Drawers half open, empty of everything but used razors and crusty soap. The bathtub held the rest of the dirty laundry, but there wasn't enough of it to hide anything interesting underneath.

"Do we toss the place?" Hunter asked neutrally.

"Son of a bitch," Jase snarled, ripping off his hat and slamming it onto the dirty linoleum floor near the bed. A faint ring of dust rose and spread from the impact.

"Take it easy," Hunter said, approaching Jase. "We'll find the artifacts. If not here, somewhere else."

He crouched down, reaching for Jase's hat. As he grabbed it, he spotted something.

"We need a warrant to take anything from under the bed?" Hunter asked.

"You thought you saw a scorpion run across your shoe, stomped, and crouched down to make sure you nailed it," Jase said instantly.

"Oh, right. Huh, the bug got away. But lookee here."

Hunter hauled out a dark blue duffel bag.

"He can't have had it long," Jase said. "It's clean."

Manufactured by some company called Élite, the duffel was crisply cut from a thick, woven nylon that looked like it could stop a bullet. A cardboard sales tag still hung on one of the handles, fastened by thin nylon line. Academy Sports.

"About a mile from here," Jase said. "Big place. Sells cheap. Open the damn thing."

"The artifacts won't be inside. Not heavy enough," Hunter said, turning the top flap over.

Jase kneeled down and rooted around in the bag. He pulled out wadded-up paper

towels. All of it came in three-sheet segments.

"Spread it out," Hunter said. He took a
double handful of the stuff and smoothed
it over the dirty floor. "We're not going to
have the time or money to CSI this stuff,
are we?"

"That's only for big murder cases, not
my-ass-is-in-traction moments."

Hunter looked over the towels. There
wasn't much to see. "Even if the artifacts
were wrapped up in these, there wouldn't
be much evidence of it. The obsidian
wouldn't shed and . . ."

"What?" Jase demanded when Hunter's
voice died.

"Most worked obsidian is sharp. It would
tear the paper towels. See? This bunch of
towels has little slits, like maybe they were
wrapped around something sharp and it
cut through."

"Hey, there's some dirt or something on
this one!" Jase said, pouncing.

"Dial it down," Hunter said. "The walls
are listening. What do you have?"

"Looks like a piece of . . . pottery?"

"Wrap it up. I know an expert who can
tell us."

While Jase took care of the find, Hunter undid all seven zipper compartments in the duffel and ran his hands around the slick interior of the nylon. He found nothing but an inspection card and tissue paper put in by the original manufacturer to make the duffel look solid.

"This bag is really new," Hunter said.

Jase scooped up everything but the tissue paper, pulled clean plastic bags from his wind jacket, and folded all the paper towels away. Everything disappeared into his pockets.

"I'd really like to talk to LeRoy Landry," Jase said.

"I'd like to help."

Hunter stuffed the tissue paper back in the seven compartments, zipped everything, and shoved the bag back under the bed. Together he and Jase did a fast, discreet search of the apartment. No cell phone, no regular phone. Nothing in plain sight, and no place to hide anything in the empty cupboards. The refrigerator held two beers and a few moldy lumps of something organic. There was a piece of paper halfway under the trash can. The top of the paper had an ICE logo. The rest was blank.

"Short of pulling up the floor, tearing apart the mattress, and axing the walls, we're done," Jase said. "Let's haul—"

Squeaky brakes came to an ear-ringing stop in front of the apartment.

Hunter eased over to the side of the window in the main room, looked out carefully at the street, and held up two fingers.

"We're outta here," Jase said. "I don't like jail food."

Hunter followed Jase out the apartment door, pulling it almost closed, just the way they had found it. They shucked the exam gloves and crossed the concrete balcony to the top of the stairs just before company appeared.

Two well-dressed men, relaxed and hard-eyed, stepped through the useless security door and headed up to the second floor. In the sun, their long black hair was shiny, straight, their features more Maya than Mexican, and their cowboy boots blindingly expensive. Though neither man was above medium height, they carried themselves like they were ten feet tall.

One of the men showed a flash of recognition when he saw Hunter. Then the man's face became expressionless again.

Silently the two men climbed the stairs and stepped past Jase and Hunter, going single file.

Jase started down the stairs in a hurry.

Hunter swore loudly in Tex-Mex Spanish and grabbed the rail. "Damn cramp is back," he said in the same dialect. He clung to the railing and flexed his left leg violently. His face was a grimace of pain.

Jase started to say something, then thought better of it.

The two strangers hesitated outside Landry's door. They spoke in a language that sounded like one of the many native dialects that pocked Mexico, words from a time before Spanish sails had ever been seen in the New World.

Hunter couldn't figure out a damn word.

"You okay, man?" Jase asked clearly in the same kind of border Spanish Hunter had used.

"Yeah, I'll live," Hunter answered in the same language, kneading his left calf and knee. "I'm too old to get beaten up in soccer scrums."

Jase understood Hunter's game immediately. "Sorry. I didn't mean to dump you on your ass."

"Yeah, yeah. Help me down. If we're late to pick up your sister, she'll kick my other leg."

Both he and Jase were careful to keep their back to Landry's door, but Hunter had unusually good peripheral vision.

One of the men knocked hard on Landry's broken door.

"You want to lean on me?" Jase asked.

"I'll walk. You get ready to catch me." Hunter took a tentative first step and then hobbled very slowly down the steps, toward the busted street door.

Behind them Landry's apartment door scraped open.

As soon as Hunter and Jase got out of sight of the building, they walked quickly to his Jeep.

"Let's keep an eye on this place," Hunter said softly in English. "The liquor-store parking lot down and across the way should work."

"You like those dudes for something? They sure were too expensive for around here."

"No crime to be a dude. But if their business is with Landry, then hell yeah, I like them."

Hunter waited in the parking lot while Jase went inside. He came back out with a box of incredibly greasy burritos and something in two brown paper bags. Jase climbed in, handed over half the grease and one paper bag. They sat swigging water from the anonymous brown bags, wolfing down lousy food, and waiting.

Half an hour.

No one reappeared.

An hour.

Nothing but locals.

Another twenty minutes.

"I'm going in," Jase said.

"What's your excuse?"

Jase touched his shoulder holster under his wind jacket. "It's called a nine-millimeter warrant."

Hunter started to argue, but got out instead. It was Jase's butt on the line, so it was Jase's call.

They walked back slow and quiet. The afternoon was settling into heat with a slanting promise of evening. Eventually. The river birches that had been planted along with the buildings were the only break in the concrete and dirt.

The car with the squeaky brakes was

still parked in front of the apartment building. The steps leading from the street to the apartment were still dirty, the security door was still broken, and the staircase to the second floor still complained. The only thing that had changed was the opening in Landry's door. Now a small pony could walk through without sucking in its breath.

Beyond the door was chaos. Overturned table, chairs, TV knocked down, bedroom door wide open, ripped sheets, and trashed mattress.

"This was a message, not a search," Jase said.

He drew his pistol, holding it parallel to his leg in case any civilians opened an apartment door. He and Hunter stepped into the destroyed apartment. Hunter went straight to the bedroom.

The blue duffel was gone.

Jase began swearing in the kind of gutter Spanglish his mother wouldn't have allowed. Hunter joined him.

"Can't believe they walked out right past us," Jase said.

"Bet there's a fire escape at the back. Or they just walked into a ground-floor apartment, threatened the occupants, and went through the window," Hunter said. "Either way, they're gone and we're standing here with refried beans on our face."

"What now?" Jase asked.

Hunter didn't point out that it was the other man's case. "Give me the paper towels and piece of pottery. I'll drop you at your apartment. Or use mine if it's too soon for you to be home. Can you run the plates on their vehicle from there?"

"Ten to one it's stolen."

"No bet. It's a piece of junk. The two men were expensive."

"I'll do it anyway," Jase said. "And I'll see what I can shake out about LeRoy Landry. What are you going to do?"

"Find out what Dr. Taylor can tell me about the pottery."

"A hot Latina and all you can think about is a broken pot. My man, I taught you better."

Shaking his head, Hunter stalked out, leaving the apartment as he had found it.

# CHAPTER SEVEN

LINA SAT IN HER OFFICE, STARING AT THE LINES she had so hastily entered into her electronic notepad. She printed them out and stared some more, hoping to see something other than Hunter's slow grin and long body.

Nothing new or old spoke to her.

*The artifacts have to be fake,* she thought.

Unfortunately, Hunter didn't really care. Fake or straight from the ground on a sponsored dig, he wanted them.

*If they're fake, it doesn't matter where or how they were "found,"* she reminded herself.

The relief was intense.

But she couldn't afford to assume the artifacts were fake. If they were real, and her family was involved . . .

"Damn it, Philip. Return my call."

But her cell phone remained quiet. So did her desk phone. Not that she was surprised. Out on a salvage dig in Belize, Philip couldn't care less about the rest of the world. Even her use of the word "scandal" hadn't piqued his interest.

**It will take dynamite to get through that limestone block he calls his head.**

Lina breathed out a few choice words and nerved herself to do what she didn't really want to do—call Mercurio ak Chan de la Poole. During the looted artifacts scandal that had shaken her family, Mercurio had logically decided that being mentored by Philip was no longer a fast road to academic recognition. It hadn't been a difficult decision. Not only was Philip an exacting master on dig sites, he wasn't going to make room for anyone other than himself at the top of the pyramid. The scandal made a hat trick on the side of Mercurio working alone.

Lina had been there on the hot, steamy

night when Mercurio and Philip had un-
loaded years of mutual tension. Mercurio
had left at dawn and had never come back.
He had kept in touch with Lina, though.

Sometimes too much touch. Especially
after the scandal had died down. Lina never
had been sexually drawn to the handsome
young Mexican, no matter how delicate or
deliberate his pursuit. Yet they had retained
an odd kind of remember-when friendship
rooted in past digs and present interest in
Yucatec Maya artifacts.

Reluctantly she punched in the number
Mercurio always made sure she had. The
phone rang several times before a male
voice answered in Spanish. Around his
words she heard the sound of a sea breeze
through open windows and the cry of birds.
A cross between homesickness and nos-
talgia swept over her. There was no place
on the earth like the Yucatan.

"*Hola,* Mercurio. It's Lina Taylor," she
said, mouth dry.

"Lina! It's so good to hear your voice
again," he said. "It has been much too long."

"I know. I'm sorry. I just don't get down
to Tulum as often as I used to. And when I
do it's to see family or digs."

"Ah, but you never find time to see *my* digs," he said, his voice teasing. "You know that you're more than welcome anytime."

"Of course. You're very gracious, Mercurio. You always have been."

Somehow Lina managed the long minutes of polite small talk—family and digs and weather, new friends and old—while she waited for the right moment to introduce the reason for her call.

"Though truth to tell, I won't be on the digs as much as I used to," Mercurio said. "I'm in line for director of the department. Funny, no?"

"A desk instead of a dig? You never seemed the type. Always happier out in the dirt, like me."

"Ah well, things change. Except for your father. His only change is to get more . . ."

"Difficult?" Lina suggested dryly.

She could almost hear Mercurio's stifled laughter.

"I should thank King Philip for teaching me the importance of being politic," Mercurio said after a moment.

"Are you kidding?" Lina asked. "Philip hates anything that doesn't have him measuring a dig level, marking and mapping artifacts in situ, or gently brushing dirt away. He's the least political academic I know."

"Exactly," Mercurio said. "Which is why he'll be out in the rough instead of on the fairway."

"When did you take up golf?"

Mercurio laughed. She found herself smiling. Laughter was one of the reasons they had remained friends despite the professional and personal tensions.

"But really, if not for Philip's example of how *not* to do things," Mercurio said, "I probably would have made a mess of my career."

**Like Philip did.**

But neither of them said it aloud.

"Philip is the best technical archaeologist I've ever known," Mercurio continued. "Sites he's named are referred to constantly. Yet he, himself, is almost never cited directly. It is excellent that he enjoys his digs. He will be working them until he dies, and then all he will have to show for his life is dirty fingernails."

Part of Lina wanted to disagree. The adult part told her to shut up and listen.

Mercurio was her best sounding board for what was happening in the Maya artifact community outside the Reyes Balam family.

"But I'm sure that you didn't call to hear what I think of your father," Mercurio said smoothly. "We're adults, and that is behind us. So tell me the reason for this delightful break in my boring day."

Lina reminded herself that Mercurio was only being polite in the Mexican way, not actually flirting with her.

Too bad she knew better.

"I have a favor to ask, I'm afraid," she said.

"For you? Everything. Tell me."

"Could you check your incoming acquisitions for some pieces? I believe that they came out of Tulum, but Belize is a possibility."

"Why are you calling me? You should be talking to your mother."

"Because you know about every single legitimate dig that's going on in Q Roo. And you'd be lying if you said that you didn't know about some of the shady ones, too."

"Ah, another sticking point with your dear father. Yes, I can tell you what has been dug on an unsanctioned basis. But that's also common knowledge for anyone who has an ear to the ground."

"Not for my mother. Not this time. I've seen pictures of these artifacts, but she hasn't."

Sounds of the sea wind, an undertone of traffic, the sharp call of birds. Then Mercurio's toneless whistle.

He was thinking.

"You interest me, as always," he said after a minute. "How would Cecilia let something truly splendid escape her delicate claws? What were the artifacts?"

Lina paused, rethinking her jump off the brink. There were only two known site groups of origin for Kawa'il cult artifacts. One of them was near Tulum, on Reyes Balam family land, and was investigated solely by Philip Taylor. The other was a smaller and much less significant site in Belize, which had been explored by de la Poole himself. Of course, ask Philip and he'd say that the Belize site was at best a misinterpretation of other worship practices, and at worst a fabrication that was meant to ride on Philip's own coattails of discovery.

Lina had never known whether Philip's opinion was based on Mercurio having discovered the Belize site or something less emotional, more scholarly.

"Where is the cat with your pink little tongue?" he asked.

She edged closer to the brink of trusting through necessity rather than true choice. "There was at least one sacrificial knife, a scepter with sharp inserts, a Chac-mool, an incense burner and . . ." Her mouth dried.

"You need to be more specific," Mercurio said. "We have hundreds of artifacts in the museum here that might fit such description."

Lina went over the edge and hoped that something would break her fall. Hunter would be her first choice.

"They were all finely made. Obsidian, jade, intricate pottery. They might have been pieces from the Kawa'il cult," she said. "The photo quality was too poor for me to be certain."

Only the sea breeze whispered across the open line.

"Now where is that cat with the missing tongue?" Lina asked.

"Send me the photos," Mercurio said, his tone businesslike.

"I don't have them. The source is far from reputable and very wary." It was only half a lie.

"Are you sure about this?"

"The photos or the lack of provenance?" she shot back.

"A moment."

The sounds of a door shutting and windows being closed came over the phone. Mercurio was sealing up his office against possible eavesdroppers.

"I've heard rumors," he said, coming back to the phone. "No photos, though. I'm swamped with departmental needs and directives that will keep me busy for the next month, but I will do what I can for my oldest friend."

Lina winced. She really didn't want to be in the position of owing Mercurio a handsome favor.

"Nothing elaborate, please," she said. "I just hoped you could check your incoming storage or computer records. Despite the sharing agreement between our two museums, I can't access what I need from here by computer."

"Perhaps you should come down here. It is your winter break, no? I could go through the storage area with you."

"Don't you have a student or two you could throw at this? Just a quick search?"

"You know what it is like in the Yucatan leading up to Christmas," Mercurio said. "Everybody is home or partying or both. I don't have the resources to handle my own needs, much less outside requests. Perhaps you could find a way for Celia or Carlos to fund a position for—"

"Don't be ridiculous," Lina cut in. "Your funding comes from the state. I know that your eyes are bigger than your funding when it comes to acquisition—whose aren't?—but I was hoping for a little help with this."

"If you should make your way down here for the festivities, you're welcome to look at whatever you like. Otherwise, I can't help you. No matter how much I would like to. And *cara,* I would."

Lina wondered what Mercurio wasn't saying. "I'll see what I can do about wedging in a visit during my family's Christmas celebrations. And Abuelita's birthday."

"Sooner rather than later, yes?"

She made one last try. "If these artifacts are what I think they are, they should be in a museum. Your museum. This is the sort of thing that you and Philip both worked on."

"Not anymore. I have my own sites to work and my own problems to deal with. If these artifacts are Kawa'il cult objects, then they're not mine. I doubt they're Philip's either. His salvage dig in Belize is just that. Salvage. The permits run out very soon, after which the Brits are turning the area into a bombing range."

*No wonder Philip didn't take the time to call,* she thought.

Lina knew how desperately Philip would be working to save what he could before the destruction began. It infuriated her that history could be so casually thrown away, but it was something that happened with "unusable" land more often than she wanted to think about. Yucatan and Belize—much of Mexico, in truth—was a mound of history waiting to be dug and understood. But the modern world needed space and modern people needed crops to eat, and various militaries needed training ranges.

Damn it.

"Have you talked to Philip about this?" Mercurio asked. "It would be like him to hide a significant find of Kawa'il artifacts."

"You're being a bit of a bastard," Lina pointed out graciously.

"I learned from the very best. King Philip. My offer and my storeroom are still open to you, should you find yourself in Tulum Pueblo at any time."

"Thanks," she said through her teeth. "I'm sorry to cut this short, but my other line is blinking." A lie.

"But of course." Mercurio's rich laughter came over the line. "I look forward to seeing you, *mi amiga muy hermosa.*"

Lina disconnected and stared at the paperwork on her desk. Silently she cursed her father's inability to yield even the smallest inch of possible prestige or scholarly credits when it came to his work. It was his and his alone. No sharing.

Mercurio had recognized that and moved on to a place where the work could be just as much his. To Philip that was unforgivable.

*Mercurio can be a bastard, but he's right this time,* Lina admitted silently.

She had learned about her father's limitations and his brilliance the hard way. Now she simply kept as much distance as she could, though she intensely missed being on his digs.

It was the same for her mother. Celia was brilliant in her chosen field of marketing artifacts. She had human manipulation down to a fine art—except for Philip. Lina hated the poison that flowed between the two fonts of knowledge in her chosen field. She could go thirsty or poison herself.

*Pull it out of the past,* Lina told herself harshly. *No matter how much I wish otherwise, those two won't change. All I can control is my own reaction to their reality.*

She went back to her work, immersing herself in researching what she could about the artifacts in the photos.

A knock came on her office door. The loud, impatient sound told her it wasn't the first time the person had knocked.

"Lina?" called Hunter's voice. "You still in there?"

"Yes." The sound was hoarse. She swallowed. "I'm here."

"You eaten lunch?"

She realized that she had forgotten the

time, not unusual when she was working. "Ah, no."

"Neither have I," Hunter said, opening the door. "Missed breakfast, too. Grab what you need and let's go. There's a place called Omar's. You been there?"

"I've heard it's great," she said, shutting down her computer.

"Never tried it?"

"Not the kind of place or area that I wanted to go in alone," she said.

"Smart lady."

Lina looked up. Hunter seemed to fill the doorway. Whatever he'd been doing in the past hours hadn't left him in a good mood. There was an edge to his mouth and his eyes that made her glad she hadn't made him mad.

At least she hoped she hadn't.

"Long day already?" she asked.

"It'll do."

"Know the feeling."

"Wait," he said as she stood up. "Better to do this here than over sloppy enchiladas."

She watched as he carefully removed something from the pocket of his shirt. It looked like a small wad of white paper towels.

"I should probably be flogged in front of a lectern for carrying it like this," he said, gently unwrapping the paper towel. "Didn't have much choice at the time. There you are, you little devil."

Lina walked over and stood close to him. She saw a potsherd nestled in the white paper. The sherd had a fragment of what looked like a blue glyph painted on it.

"Well?" he asked.

"Nice sherd," she said neutrally. "A lot of them don't have any paint at all."

"Jase and I found it in the apartment of a man who has gone missing, probably after stealing the artifacts from the ICE warehouse. There were wads more towels inside a duffel, but nothing else."

Her breath came in sharply. "I see."

"Some of the paper towels had been cut. I think they were wrapped around something sharp. Like worked obsidian blades."

"May I?" she asked, reaching for his palm.

"Anytime."

Lina gave him a sideways look, but

otherwise ignored him. Carefully she lifted the towel and sherd to her nose. "Smell is . . . odd."

"It was packed with cocaine inside a bag of cement mix. Could be some turpentine or jet fuel filtered through. That stuff stinks."

"I can't be certain of anything about this sherd unless I do specialized tests."

"Expensive and time-consuming?"

"Oh yeah. Even with money in hand, our lab connection has a waiting list and it's the happy holiday season."

He breathed out a curse. "Figured. Anyway, it doesn't really matter whether this is from a genuine artifact or a recent manufacture. What I need is your best guess if this piece could be related to the stuff that was stolen."

"Assuming that the missing man is the one who lifted the missing artifacts," she said, then shook her head.

"Go on."

"In order for that potsherd to have any significance, it would have to have come from the censer in your photographs. To assume that, you have to assume that this missing man didn't have a regular sideline in stealing artifacts, that this robbery was a one-off."

"I love a logical mind," Hunter said.

"My logical mind isn't loving this," she said. "You've got about five big 'ifs' between you and even a circumstantially useful connection to the potsherd."

"There are some plus marks in the column."

"Really?"

"Two dudes came to LeRoy's apartment. They spoke a Mexican Indian dialect and looked the part. Maya faces and bodies. Shorter than you. Darker. Expensively turned out. They wrecked the place and took the blue duffel where we found the paper towels. Then the dudes went invisible. The car they were driving was stolen."

"Charming," she muttered. "They could be disappointed middlemen who have nothing to do with your case."

"I hate a logical mind."

"Then don't look in the mirror when you shave," she said.

A slow smile changed Hunter's face. "Let's get some food. You can tell me what you've learned about the artifacts while we eat."

"It won't take that long."

"Was afraid you'd say that. Let's go anyway. We still have to eat. Or at least I do."

Hunter followed Lina out of the building. The instant he was outdoors, the feeling of being watched made his neck and shoulder blades tingle. Without making a fuss about it, he checked out the surroundings. No one seemed to be staring at him.

Lina was looking around, too. She wasn't as subtle about it as he was, but she got the job done.

**Wonder if she'll talk about who is following her. If anyone is. I sure can't make the bastard.**

Hunter led her to the parking lot where his well-used Jeep waited. She swung into the vehicle like a pro. And she was smiling like it was a tricked-out Italian sports car.

"Most women don't think much of this rig," Hunter said, starting it.

"Most women have never driven on unpaved tracks in the Yucatan. This is great transport. The tires have deep tread, the oil pan won't bleed out on a sharp rock, and the engine sounds like a jaguar."

"Don't say another word. I'm halfway in love."

Lina gave Hunter a startled look, smiled rather uncertainly, and shut her mouth. The feeling of being watched prickled over her, but no matter how long or how often she looked behind her, she couldn't see anyone who seemed to be paying special attention to them.

*Philip would be proud of me,* Lina thought unhappily. *He senses spies everywhere, trying to steal his precious knowledge. He's just never caught anyone doing it.*

As Hunter gained speed on the metro roads, the hot, unusually dry wind coming through the open windows began to take apart Lina's sleek bun. By the time they arrived on the wrong side of town and parked, her hair was flying around like a witch on Halloween. She tried to smooth the black mess back into a bun.

"Let it go," Hunter said, catching her hand in one of his. "It's beautiful loose."

Her pulse kicked at his touch, the look in his eyes.

"It looks unprofessional," she said.

"I don't see anyone here with an academic scorecard."

Lina hesitated, then shook her hair fully free. His smile didn't help her pulse rate one bit.

Hunter got out of the Jeep and came around to her side before she had picked up her purse. He reached in and lifted her out. His hands were hard, his strength startling. Before she could object, she was standing on the sidewalk. She stared at Hunter and revised her first estimate of his strength. The man must have serious muscles beneath his loose shirt.

"This way," he said, slowly releasing her.

He tucked his hand into hers and led her down the street. Everywhere she looked, the signs were in Spanish, with the occasional English word used like an exclamation mark. It was the same for the language of the people standing in groups, getting into cars, or smoking and watching the world go by. Hats, boots, jeans, work shirts. Occasional flashes of colorful clothes and hot black eyes from women in high heels. Otherwise, the visible population was overwhelmingly male and Latin.

She felt like she was in semirural Mexico.

Omar's was a rustic brick building that smelled of chili and onions and meat, with the scent of fresh tortillas curling through it all like a golden ribbon. The café was close enough to downtown that tourists might wander through, but authentic enough that only locals would stay. The tempera paints on the outside of the window were faded from sun and heat, not yet melted by rain. Yard-high red letters spelled out *BIENVENIDOS Á OMAR'S.*

Lina smiled. The smells of food and the language being spoken on all sides surrounded her like a lover.

"You look like you've been handed a piece of heaven rather than an invitation to a Mexican dive," Hunter said. He knew his voice was too husky and he didn't care. The more he discovered about Lina, the more he liked her.

Wanted her.

*Good thing I'm wearing a loose shirt,* Hunter thought wryly. *I'm throwing wood like a teenager.*

"I've missed this kind of Mexican food," Lina said.

"Greasy?"

"Real. Country food meant to feed people who have little money and hard physical jobs."

As they walked into the tiny restaurant, the sun flooding through the red letters on the window made the interior glow carmine. The three Latina women making tortillas behind the grill waved at Hunter and then giggled.

*"Buenos días, señoritas,"* Hunter called to them. His lilting accent was all Mexican, as easy as his English. "Omar, how's business?"

Behind the counter, Omar grinned. He was six foot two—six foot six if his turban was counted. His dark complexion might have helped him to blend in, if not for his height and aquiline features, which would've been more at home in the Punjab. He wore his long beard carefully kept and his eyes glittered behind thin lenses. He insisted often and loudly that he was the only Sikh running a Mexican restaurant in all of Texas. No one argued. The food was too good.

"Excellent," Omar said. "What may I serve you?"

"I'll have the usual."

"Machaca, half a stack of corn tortillas, eggs soft, extra salsa nuclear," Omar called over his shoulder. "And for the beautiful young lady?"

Lina looked behind her, laughed, and said, "Machaca, frijoles refritos, corn tortillas, salsa, and orange soda."

"The salsa," Omar said, looking at her, "gringo, medium, hot, or nuclear?"

Darkness shot through with gold flashed as she rolled her eyes. "Just hot."

Omar grinned, revealing black gaps and white teeth. "Coffee and water are in the customary place," he said to Hunter as he totaled their order on an adding machine. "Soda is in the cooler."

Hunter paid before Lina could open her purse. She would have argued, but it wasn't worth it. At the moment she was very much in a man's world.

Lina glanced over at the wall to the left. The cooler beckoned in cheerful, chipped colors next to a worn linoleum-surfaced table holding coffee, water, sugar, cream, and plastic utensils wrapped in napkins. By the time she and Hunter found an empty table—about two feet square—and two metal chairs, their order arrived.

For a few minutes the only sounds the two of them made were "Mmm," "Wow," and scraping utensils. Hunter ate with the same efficiency he did everything else. He never moved fast, but everything disappeared at an astonishing pace.

After destroying two skimpy napkins—his and hers—Lina gave up and simply licked her fingers.

Hunter watched and wished he could offer to help. Insist, actually. Her agile tongue was hotter than his salsa, which was hot enough to melt plastic.

"I missed breakfast as well as lunch," Lina said as she mopped her plate with a last bit of corn tortilla. "These tortillas . . . fantastic. Like the corn was ground by hand with a limestone metate."

"Could have been. Omar's wife is Mexican, from Tamaulipas. So is Omar. The narco violence drove them across the border to Texas about five years ago. He has some pull with the feds, so he and his family have refugee status here."

"I hear it's bad," Lina said. "Even the Yucatan." She shook her head. "Zetas, Gulf Cartel, and others are making life hell for the common people."

Hunter almost told her about the blue-painted, headless, heartless bodies being found by ICE, but didn't. No use spoiling her meal. He liked watching a woman who didn't push lettuce around on her plate and call it eating.

"I've been thinking about the . . . items," she said in English, glancing around.

The tables around them had filled up. People came and went through the tiny eatery like waves on a beach. Tex-Mex was the predominant dialect, but she heard accents that went farther south than Mexico City.

It would be stupid to assume that they were the only English speakers present.

Hunter moved his chair right next to hers, so close the metal legs scraped. "Go on. I'll keep an eye out for eavesdroppers."

"If they are fakes," she said in a low voice, "why would anyone go to the trouble of painstakingly counterfeiting objects that less than a handful of people would recognize as relating to an obscure, forgotten god?"

He thought about her words as he checked out the occupants of the café with his unusually wide peripheral vision. "You're saying that fake or real, the market is limited?"

"Very."

"Outside your family, who would care?"

She flinched. "There are several museums in the Yucatan that specialize in local ar—ah, items." Her voice dropped. "My father has made enemies. These could be a trap for him. Or them."

"What's the profit in that for anyone?"

"Revenge."

Hunter hesitated, considered, nodded. "Anything else?"

He watched Lina's pulse work furiously beneath her skin as she looked around yet again.

"Whatever cat you're trying to keep bagged up is already out," she said in a low voice.

He leaned closer, so close she felt his words as much as heard them. "How do you know?"

"Rumors of unusual ar—items are making the museum and collector rounds." She looked at her fingers, clenched in a stained napkin. "You must understand. What you're looking for, if real, could make a collection, and a museum, famous."

"Even without provenance?" he breathed into her ear.

"That can be manufactured if you have the right connections," she said reluctantly. It was one of the realities of the artifact world that really made her angry, so she tried not to think about it. "It would cost a great deal, but it could be worth it to some people."

"And the provenance would be accepted, if the right people were on board?"

She nodded slowly, unhappily. "There would be academic carping, but it would be written off as professional jealousy."

Three men walked in. They were of the same ethnic type as the men Hunter had seen at LeRoy's apartment. Long hair, black, straight, clean. They weren't as richly dressed as the apartment wreckers had been, but silence followed them through the small restaurant like a spreading shadow. Several patrons crossed themselves as the men passed.

"Interesting world you live in," Hunter said.

He threw some money on the table for the cleanup crew, pulled Lina to her feet, and headed out.

The Jeep was waiting for them, as hot and dirty as the streets. Houston's usual humidity was making a comeback from the earlier dry air. The sky had turned to steel, but it didn't feel like rain was coming. Traffic was its usual relentless self. Lina was relieved to get inside the museum building again.

Inside her office, she stared at the photographs until they seemed to shimmer, breathe smoke, drip blood. Sitting next to her, close enough to rub thighs beneath her office worktable, Hunter was using her computer to search databases she really hoped didn't leave any cookies on the hard drive. Auction houses weren't on the academically approved list, much less some of the sleazy "archaeological specialties" sites he'd visited.

Apparently, some people really got into Maya bloodletting rituals. Or what they thought of as Maya rituals.

While Hunter worked he exchanged texts with his friend Jase. From the set of Hunter's mouth, none of the news was good.

Lina knew how he felt. Even in the Reyes Balam private databases, none of the artifacts she'd seen were like those in the photos. Artifacts similar in form and function? Yes. Identical in substance and detail? No.

Hunter stretched and yawned. Not boredom. Fatigue. The darkness beneath his eyes told of missed sleep and too much adrenaline.

"Why don't you go home and nap?" Lina asked. "Yawning is catching."

"You saying I'm boring you?"

"I'm saying you're tired. How much sleep did you get last night?"

"A few hours." It was the time of year he acutely remembered Suzanne's death. Sleep was hard.

"Git," Lina said in her best way-east Texas drawl.

Hunter hesitated.

She knew he was thinking about Omar's and the men who had spread silence like darkness behind them.

"I'm in a museum that is guarded all day, every day," she pointed out. "Go home and sleep. I've got a lot more work to do on these photos before I'm ready to talk about them. When I leave, I'll have the guard walk me out to my car. My apartment is very secure." *Because my family is paranoid.* "I assume I'll see you tomorrow."

"I can't leave the photos here."

"I have an excellent memory and lots of notes." She didn't mention the quick sketches she'd made. She just scooped up Hunter's photos, stacked them neatly, and handed them over. "Go."

Reluctantly, Hunter went. Lina was right. He couldn't do all-nighters the way he once had.

"Call me if anything breaks loose," he said.

She waved her hand in a shooing motion. She was already at work, making cryptic notes. A thick book of glyphs stood open at her elbow.

Silently Hunter let himself out of the office.

## CHAPTER EIGHT

HUNTER GROANED, TWISTING IN THE COILS OF A nightmare.

Suzanne, trapped in a beat-up truck, hammering against the window with her little palms flat and red, her eyes so wide that they're more white than brown. The truck is parked on a frozen lake, so cold that Hunter feels his skin split and bleed.

Icy blue fog claws its way around the truck tires while something laughs like breaking bones.

No, not bones. The ice is breaking, the blue fog rising in fingers shaped like a shaman's smoke dreams. Ancient glyphs smiling death.

He runs and gets nowhere, heart slamming, open mouth screaming "NOOOOOO," and his cries are more glyphs, more death.

More bones breaking, ice smoking into blue nothing.

The back end of the rusty Ford slips away first, shards of blue teeth chewing up the truck bed. Suzanne with her father's eyes staring at Hunter, beating on the window with small fists, smears of blood. She is sideways now and the icy teeth and glyph, blue fire and red death, chewing, chewing.

Sweat glazes Hunter's body, his heart beating like his daughter's fists, his body frozen in blue ice and fire.

The car slips deeper into the hungry blue while Hunter, frozen in a glyph, watches helplessly, screaming, Suzanne dying—

The phone trilled at Hunter, dragging him from the nightmare. For long moments he didn't know where he was, who he was, how he was alive. A last ripple of thunder came through the apartment walls. A storm, not ice breaking, not him screaming, his body slicked with sweat.

**Goddamn. Goddamn.**

He hadn't had a dream that bad since Suzanne had died in a single-car rollover accident with her mother and drunken father. No ice, no water, except in his nightmares.

The phone stopped ringing, then started up again. Hunter grabbed it.

"Yeah?" he asked hoarsely, looking at his alarm clock.

He'd slept well into the next day. No wonder he felt like roadkill.

"Hunter?" Jase asked. "You sound like something the cat dragged in and rammed down the garbage disposal."

"What's up?" Hunter asked. The last thing he wanted to talk about was why he sounded the way he sounded.

"I got a tip from someone who owes me. A bust is going down that sounds like it might be interesting. I'm out front."

"My car or yours?"

"Mine. Some of the agents are used to seeing it."

Hunter swigged the dregs of yesterday morning's coffee straight out of the carafe, jammed his feet into his jungle boots, and went out to meet Jase. It was hot, stinking hot. The thunder that echoed in the distance hadn't brought any rain.

Hunter got into Jase's white minivan, slammed the door, and fastened his belt.

"I'm not going to say anything," Jase said. "Don't want to prejudice you."

Hunter grunted. Silence was just fine with him

Jase drove through Houston to Willerton Lane. Going through this part of Houston was like peeling back time, skinning away years and watching things get meaner and meaner until the low stucco buildings went feral. Sunbaked and blasted, mangy lawns reverted to swatches of prairie yellow, dead for lack of water. Weeds grew waist-high and finally starved out, leaving behind a prickly thicket that you could lose bodies in.

ICE and Houston PD had cordoned off the area. Patrol cars were sitting with rollers blinking urgent colors, moving aside only for official vehicles. Neighborhood people watched from porches, nursing the second or third cerveza of the day while the children played with faded plastic toys

in a heat that was more summer than winter. The sky reflected the neighborhood.
Sullen.

Jase flashed his badge and got waved
through with a nod and a glare of sun from
the cop's mirrored aviator sunglasses. Nobody seemed to care that Hunter was in
the passenger seat, probably because he
looked rough enough to be an undercover
agent. Jase pulled over to the decaying
curb behind a newly minted Houston blue-
and-white. Under other circumstances,
the high-gloss finish would have been ir-
resistible to neighborhood taggers.

Jase didn't move to get out.

"Now what?" Hunter asked. He needed
something to keep his mind off his nightmare or his second taboo line of thought—
Lina's scent, her warmth, her lush lips
made for the sweetest kind of sin.

**She must think I've disappeared
again.**

"We don't get to move in until after the
door is cracked," Jase said.

The house on Willerton had been left to
abscess for a long time. It was rotten to its
foundation. But that wasn't what kept
neighbors at a distance.

"The bad guys live here," Hunter said. "No graffiti."

Every other house on the block had been tagged, broken into, and then patched up. But this old house would be standing long after the neighborhood was abandoned and stripped. Nobody would be messing with the sun-faded stucco, because real predators lived here. The only things new about the house were the security doors and bars on the windows. They were black steel, powder coated, and looked like they could turn a bullet shot from the street.

"Nice bars," Jase said.

"Stupid," Hunter said. "Limits your field of fire from the inside."

"Dude, sometimes I worry about you."

Nearby a tactical van was parked close enough to do some good, but not close enough to get in the way. Two snipers lay on the van's roof, covering the front of the house and yard. Hunter knew there would be another van just like it on the opposite side of the house, with ICE troops ready to come over the back fence if anyone tried to rabbit.

An electronically amplified voice boomed

from the van in front of the house, advising the occupants of the house that they were officially required to quit the premises with hands on head.

The house stayed quiet.

"That's the third warning," someone shouted. "Take it down."

A group of men cut the chain on the fence's gate and moved in fast, marching up the cracked walkway in black fatigues and vests that clearly spelled out ICE in what seemed to be mile-high yellow silk-screen. All of them carried handguns at a precise forty-five-degree angle from the ground.

The agents swept up the short stoop. They didn't bother knocking. One of them stepped to the side and yelled, "Clear!"

"Det cord?" Hunter asked. Explosive cord made short work of locks.

"No, on houses like this—"

Gunshots rang out. The door shuddered and swayed, held on only by the dead bolt.

"—they shoot out the hinges and kick in the rest," Jase finished.

Someone wrapped his climbing cord around the doorknob and took a good five steps back, bracing to pull. A big agent went to work around the dead bolt with a pry bar. The door clattered to the ground and skidded out into the front yard.

"THIS IS YOUR LAST WARNING. COME OUT BEFORE WE COME IN."

No response.

An agent armed two flash-bangs and tossed them inside the open doorway. He counted down with his fingers, starting at three, two, one.

For an instant the gloom of the darkened interior went thermite bright. Sounds like a fireworks display gone psycho rolled through the neighborhood. Glass shattered behind one of the barred windows. Agents streamed into the house two by two, sweeping the rooms.

Hunter was relieved no more shooting came. Despite his training, he really didn't want to have to go med-tech on anyone right now.

Soon six men were sitting cross-legged in the prickly yellow weeds that made up the front yard. Their hands were cuffed behind their backs. Eight cops stood around them, weapons low but attentive.

"Bet those bad boys have jailhouse tats and iron-pile abs," Jase said.

"Sucker bet." Hunter rolled the window down, flinched, and swore under his breath. "Something's been dead for a while."

"And not buried," Jase agreed. "Stay here until I make sure it's cool for a visitor."

Hunter settled back. It would take time to Mirandize the gangbangers in the weeds and secure the house. He checked the glove compartment and found the little pair of binoculars Jase always kept there, just in case.

Quietly Hunter focused on the seated men. Only one of them tripped his radar. The man was darker than the others, calmer, and had tats like multicolored serpent scales winding up his brawny arms. No reptilian head in sight.

While agents hauled out the rock cocaine and precursors from the kitchen, others pulled enough weapons from the house to start—and finish—a war. The guns came out in green nylon rucksacks that looked like they had been dragged up and down the Dirty Coast a few hundred times. And then there were the knives. From what Hunter could see, Gerbers and Ontarios were the local favorites. One Bowie-style knife as long as his forearm had *DULCE BESO* engraved on the blade.

"'Sweet Kiss,'" Hunter muttered to himself. "Those are some whacked-out dudes."

All of the agents who came out of the house looked a little paler than when they had gone in—even Jase, who had emerged to chat up the agent who was questioning the gangbangers in the weeds.

Finally Jase came back to the van. "With me," he said to Hunter. "Be seen but not heard."

"Got it. The dude with the snake tats looks like a cousin to LeRoy's visitors."

"The agent questioning him thinks he has a Yucatec accent," Jase said. "Can't be sure. The agent's mother was born in Guatemala, near the border, but they still visit family."

Hunter followed Jase across the weeds that were being trampled by all the traffic. Once they were inside, the house was dark with more than a lack of light. Beneath the smell of flash-bangs was something grim. Not simply dirty, but foul.

The living room was jammed with leather furniture that had once been expensive.

Then had come years of being used for everything from ashtrays to whetstones. The coffee table was supported by cinder blocks stamped with a colorful flower pattern. The table itself was made of mismatched boards that probably had been stolen from a construction site. Spanish-language *telenovela* magazines were scattered about, as well handled as the centerfolds tacked to the grimy walls. The tits-and-ass needed no translation.

*Wonder if they hoped Juan Carlos would choose Tilde or Mariana for eternal bliss,* Hunter thought.

"Guess these gangbangers and my mom have something in common," Jase said. "The magazines, not the skin pics."

"Scary idea," Hunter muttered.

The kitchen was dominated by a gigantic, soot-caked gas range. Butcher-block tables had been pushed together to make a large work surface. On it was a cardboard box filled with tiny Ziploc bags.

"Your mom's kitchen smells better," Hunter said.

"Drugs stink like the crap they are."

The counter was covered by red plastic

cylinders filled with white powder and chunks, or pale salmon-colored flakes.

"Could be the candles that stink," Hunter said.

The stalks of wax were black, as thick around as a strong man's arm. Near them was an eerie snake-man statue. Maya in style, it looked like smoke made solid as it escaped a snake's mouth. Glyphs marched down the length of the piece.

"Not antique," Hunter said before Jase could ask. "Mass-produced, on sale in any tourist trap in the Yucatan, Belize, or Guatemala."

"Huh. The dudes out in the weeds aren't Latin Kings or any of the other gangbangers around here. I didn't recognize their tats. Neither did the agents I talked to. Which just makes the strange even stranger. The tip on this house came from the cellmate of the gangbanger that shanked the artifact driver."

"Nice to know somebody still wants reduced time," Hunter said.

"I just overheard an agent say the dude that ordered the hit on the driver of the load was at this address."

"Señor Snake has my money."

"Yeah. He's the lion in this bunch of jackals."

An agent stormed up the basement steps and shoved by Jase, hand over mouth, throat working, face pale and sweating. He made it out the back door before he threw up everything but his toenails.

"Oh, this will be fun," Jase said, turning toward the basement.

Hunter followed.

On the way down the stairs, they passed a female agent headed up. She was pale but otherwise fine.

"How is Chuy?" she asked.

"He made it outside," Jase said.

"If you can give the basement a pass, you'll sleep better," she said through pale lips.

"Wish we could," Jase said, "but thanks."

She nodded and went to check on her partner.

Halfway down the stairs, Hunter knew why someone was out in the back puking. The smell of death was thick enough to cut and serve at a demon brunch. Hunter started to breathe through his mouth. So did Jase. It didn't help much, but it was all they had to fight the smell.

While Jase went to talk to the lone agent protecting the scene, Hunter made himself invisible in the shadows near the stairs.

A fluorescent lantern held by the agent revealed the basement in slightly swaying arcs that matched the man's careful breaths. There were racks of unlit candles and stands for larger torches. The floor was concrete, worn smooth in places, cracked in others, gleaming dully. There were patches of what looked like oil, so dark that they sucked up and swallowed any light. The splotches were mute testimony to something so revolting that the only thing left to do was bolt for fresh air and throw up.

Hunter's hackles rose. He'd seen death sites before, but not like this. This basement told him why people believed in evil.

The radio feeding information into the agent's ear crackled and the lantern jerked. Then it steadied at a different angle, revealing something in the far corner of the room. A pale stone table glistened in the light. The legs were carved to look like a large cat's paws, ending in sharp claws that dug into the concrete floor itself. Given the context, Hunter assumed that the paws were meant to represent a jaguar, the sacred animal of Maya royalty. Blood had dripped down, wrapping around the legs like snakes. It had happened so often that the legs looked black. But for all the evidence of past bloodletting, only a small amount had ended up on the basement floor near the altar.

*Jase mentioned another bloody crime scene, but the table was missing,* Hunter though grimly, remembering the killing house his friend had described. *Don't really want to know how many people died on that stone altar, here or there.*

The smeared darkness on the floor made sense, now. Bleeding bodies had been dragged off the table, across the cement, and ignored until it was time to dispose of them.

Jase swore, his ugly words fitting the basement like the smell. Then his voice dropped again as he and the agent holding the lantern continued their conversation in the low tones of people who don't want the devil to overhear.

As the lantern swayed, Hunter memorized every bit of the room that he could see. The stone face mounted on the wall over the altar was as carefully made as the jaguar table itself. Savage and grim, the face was that of a god who would never be appeased, no matter the quantity or quality of blood sacrifices that came to its hungry table. The face proudly displayed the features of Maya nobility, topped off by a crown of lightning or claws or knives that scored deep into forehead and temples. The gently swaying light made the wounds appear to bleed.

Whatever that artifact's age, the stone face was genuine in a way that had nothing to do with provenance and everything to do with the darkest side of human nature.

Ignoring the slow crawl of his flesh, Hunter stared at the face. *I've seen something like this before. Was it in Tulum? Cancun? A roadside shrine?*

The god's features were broad and strong. Like the table, the craftsmanship was surprisingly fine. The eyes were empty yet stared through him, through the basement, through the world to a different reality Hunter really didn't want to share.

The lantern swung as the agent turned toward the stairs. A pool of darkness became a tarp someone had pulled aside to reveal what was beneath. A single look told Hunter more than he wanted to know.

No head. No hands. No feet. A black gash where the heart should be. Blue glyphs, the paint blurred by sweat before death. A wad of clothes the body didn't need anymore.

The gold DeWatt logo gleamed as light passed over it.

After a few more minutes of low conversation, Jase left the agent and walked quickly through the gloom to where Hunter waited.

"Need to see anything more?" Jase asked very softly.

"No."

"The chicken will hit the fan real soon. Let's get out of range."

With the attitude of men on a mission, they climbed the stairs and strode to the van.

The eyes of the prisoner they had dubbed Snake followed them across the weedy yard.

"Hope somebody shanks that reptilian son of a bitch," Jase said as they got into the minivan.

"I'd like to talk to him first."

"In your dreams." Jase cranked the engine hard. "He's already lawyered up."

"Anybody we know?" Hunter asked.

"The biggest narco defense lawyer in Texas."

"Adios, information."

"That's the way the game is played. Mopes die, lawyers get paid, nobody cries."

Jase drove away from the rotting house, handling the controls with an edgy speed that didn't suit the minivan.

"The stone face and the table," Hunter said. "Could they have been taken from that other killing house you told me about while I looked at your photos yesterday morning?"

"Good catch. I'll tip the sheriff. Always good to play nice with local law. You see anything else?"

"A DeWatt logo on the clothes in the corner."

"Damn, I knew there was a reason I brought you," Jase said, smiling.

"Did your schmoozing pay off?"

Hunter had never known anyone who could suck out information like Jase. He could walk through a half-empty parking lot and come up with three new friends and enough street information to fill a telephone book.

"There's an ICE Special Detachment agent back there," Jase said. "He's out of Brownsville. They've been on both houses for a while. They think the mopes we bagged are LDX."

"Los de Equis?"

"He called them Los de Xibalba."

"*Xibalba*. That's the Mayan word for the underworld. For hell."

"Figures."

"Are these guys involved in the artifact trade?" Hunter asked.

"No such luck. They've taken a lot of ancient Maya imagery for their tats and jewelry, but all ICE knows for sure is that they're narco terrorists of the worst kind. LDX is used as an elite enforcement arm by the Q Roo cartel. Killers every one."

"So they're like the Zetas? Only they haven't branched out into their own business yet?" Hunter asked.

"Yes and no." Jase found an opening in city traffic and shouldered into the flow. "The Zetas started out as a Mexican military unit that was meant to take apart the cartels. Then some Zetas cut loose and went to work for the narcos."

"So they started as hired guns and finished as head of their own cartel," Hunter said. "Can't trust an assassin long enough to blink."

"But LDX doesn't seem to have profits as their driving force," Jase said. "ICE is going nuts trying to get inside their organization. No go."

"Is Snake LDX?" Hunter asked.

"The special agent didn't think so. It seems that genuine LDX don't mark themselves up for the world to see."

"Gang culture's all about bragging, flashing the signs, wearing the colors."

"LDX isn't a gang like we know it," Jase said. "The special agent didn't want to come right out and say it, but LDX is more a cult than anything else."

Hunter was silent while Jase pushed the minivan like it was a sports car, darting in and out of traffic lanes.

"It fits," Hunter finally said.

"What?"

"One of my best sources in the Yucatan told me that LDX works with the Q Roo drug cartel, but it's only to get paid for what

LDX would do for free. The Q Roo boasts of having the baddest badasses of them all. LDX makes good on the boast."

"Beautiful," Jase said sarcastically. "ICE special investigations first got wind of these guys through some makeshift shrines and the like showing up in prisons. Weird stuff. Crucifixes with snakes wrapped around them and stone faces with rosaries. Monsters made out of scrap stolen from the shops or trash or whatever. Doesn't matter that Corrections took them down as fast as they found them. It spread. Maybe it started in jail, maybe it got imported."

"Better and better. A death cult. Serial killers serving a ravenous god."

"That's what the special agent thinks," Jase said unhappily.

A horn blared at someone who had double-parked in front of a coffeehouse. Jase swerved around the vehicle without lifting his foot from the accelerator.

"I've seen those cult trappings in the Yucatan," Hunter said, ignoring the near miss. "Places where real blood is believed to have real power, not just the Santa Muerte drug shrine garbage. This is old, old belief coming back in a new form. The Spanish couldn't kill it, and they had the Church and the guns on their side. Hard to shut down an idea. Especially if it's an idea that makes you feel stronger, better."

"Stronger or crazier?" Jase asked.

"Whichever gets the job done." Hunter's hand fisted on the dash. "Damn, I don't want Lina anywhere near this, yet those artifacts . . . Damn!"

"I don't blame you. The body count at the place we just left was four, and they haven't even begun to dig."

"But the altar hadn't been there long enough for the blood running down those table legs to reach the floor."

"Maybe they wore the old one out." Jase shrugged. "Kill in the name of cartel profits. Kill in the name of an unknown god. Same result. Dead."

Hunter clenched his teeth and wished that Lina's job was curating *Teddy Bears Through the Ages.* But it wasn't. No matter how much he hated it, Lina was on the trail of death.

"I don't like any of this," Hunter said. "You want to just bag it and come to work for my uncle?"

"What?"

"Just what I said. There's always a job waiting for you. You know that."

"Not until ICE throws me out," Jase said stubbornly.

Silently Hunter hoped that wouldn't be too late.

## CHAPTER NINE

LINA SAT IN HER OFFICE, LOOKING OUT AT THE hazy afternoon. She felt like she was sixteen again, waiting for the phone, willing it to ring.

Unlike when she had been sixteen, it actually rang. She grabbed it.

"Hello," she said.

"It's Philip," her father's voice said. "What do you want?"

"Are you still in Belize?" she asked, ignoring his curt greeting. Nothing personal, just the way he was.

"No. I'm at the estate, getting ready to

work a new site. What's this nonsense about another scandal?"

Briskly Lina put herself in the proper frame of mind to deal with her father. He was a man of extremely limited interests and less ability to deal with people, especially his family. He simply didn't know how to express affection.

"There are rumors of a group of artifacts reaching the marketplace," Lina said carefully. It was hard to keep Hunter's secret and still get information. "Has Celia mentioned them to you?"

"Don't be ridiculous. She hides artifacts from me."

"The descriptions I received point to artifacts that could relate to the cult of Kawa'il. Have you heard anything?"

"Damn de la Poole!"

Lina added the missing parts of the conversation and winced. "The artifacts weren't connected with Mercurio."

"Then they don't concern me."

"What about looters on Reyes Balam lands?" she asked, as blunt as her father.

"They wouldn't dare. Carlos and I feed

all the villages on our land and they protect my sites."

"Then you haven't heard any rumors of sensational artifacts appearing on the market?"

"No. Is that all?"

"Yes."

The connection ended.

Lina wasn't surprised. Philip was infamous for his curt conversations. Once she had dreamed of being important to her father, if only through her own ability to interpret texts he simply lacked the gut-sensitivity to understand. Then she'd grown up and accepted her parents for what they were—brilliant in their work, indifferent as parents.

A knock on her locked office door and Hunter's voice saying "You in there, Lina?" made her heart kick. The man who had blackmailed her had shown her more respect than her parents ever had.

More approval, too.

"Yes," she said. "Let me get the lock."

"Jase Beaumont is with me."

"Nice to meet you, Mr. Beaumont," Lina said as she unlocked the door.

"Same goes, Dr. Taylor." Jase shook her hand and gave her an easy smile.

Hunter locked the door behind him. His glance went over Lina like a man who had been cold and finally was standing close to a fire.

She felt stroked.

Feeling a blush darken her cheeks, she looked away from Hunter to Jase. He was shorter than Hunter, with dark chocolate eyes and bittersweet-chocolate hair. His skin was the kind of brown than went deeper than a tan. A gold wedding band gleamed on his left hand. Both men were freshly showered, their clothes clean, and their eyes weary. She took a folding chair from behind the door and placed it next to the visitor's chair across from her desk.

"Sit down," she said. "I've got half a pot of coffee if you're interested."

"Thanks," Jase said.

"Black," Hunter said. "I'll get it."

Lina waved him off and started pouring coffee into mugs that held the museum logo. "If you want something to eat, the cafeteria is still open."

Jase and Hunter exchanged a look. After

what they had seen, they didn't feel particularly hungry. Or clean, despite showers hot enough to burn.

"We're good," Hunter said to Lina. All he really wanted from her was a kiss to drive out the basement's deadly cold. He wished he had the right to simply go to her, hold her, feel her living warmth. "Do you have a sketch pad and a pencil?"

She smiled. "That's like asking if I've worked on digs."

She opened a desk drawer and pulled out a sketchbook, plus three grades of pencils, and handed them to Hunter.

He caught her hand and the pencils, holding her, breathing her in, eyes half closed. Her swiftly inhaled breath told him she liked it. Slowly he took the pad and pencils, drinking her warmth through his fingertips.

Jase gave Hunter a sideways look that told him he could feel the heat.

"Thanks," Hunter said to her, his voice deep. Forcing himself to focus on something other than his blunt hunger for Lina, he opened the pad and flipped past sketches of glyphs and artifacts—some of which he recognized—until he found an empty page. As he began to sketch, he asked, "Have you made any progress on your end of the artifact chase?"

"No." She leaned against her desk for the simple reason that her knees wanted to shake. The hunger she'd felt radiating from him was more complex than plain old sex. "When I mention new artifacts, everyone wants to buy them but nobody has them. My father, who has been on a dig in Belize, hasn't heard anything. Mercurio de la Poole, who is the only other recognized expert on the cult of Kawa'il, was coy. He wouldn't say anything unless I was there in person."

"Do you think he has them?" Jase asked instantly.

"I don't know," Lina said. "Mercurio has no particular motivation. His museum is run by the state of Quintana Roo with money from the Mexican federal government and artifacts from Reyes Balam land channeled through state and federal governments. He has his own digs in Belize, where he has found some indications of the cult of Kawa'il. Since the government funds him, if he had your missing artifacts he would study them, publish, and take his bows."

"How well do you know him?" Jase asked.

"Quite well. He and my father worked together for years. I spent summers, vacations, and every moment I could beg from Celia on the digs where Philip and Mercurio were."

"How did de la Poole and your father get along?" Jase asked.

"Nobody 'gets along' with Philip," Lina said. "You just go along and understand that he won't ever change. All you can do is control your own response to him."

Hunter heard what she didn't say, the child hoping and trying and always failing to find approval. *My uncles would love her to death,* he thought. So would his mother, if she hadn't been killed by a hit-and-run driver in a crosswalk ten years ago. His father had been with her. He had lived a day in ICU. Then he died of his injuries.

"So you don't think de la Poole stole the artifacts from your father," Jase said, "for revenge, professional jealousy, plain old spite?"

"If Mercurio had done that, Philip would have tracked him down, cornered him, and taken the artifacts back."

"But you don't think that's likely," Jase said.

"Nope."

"Describe Philip in three words," Hunter said without looking up from the sketch pad. He didn't trust himself to. He wanted to hold Lina so much he ached.

"Curt, obsessive, brilliant," Lina said.

"Mercurio?" Hunter asked, needing to know, yet his voice was neutral.

"Charming, ambitious, very smart."

Hunter relaxed. There was nothing particularly affectionate in her voice.

"That's why I don't think he has the artifacts," Lina added. "He can't publish them, can't display them, can't sell them. They're of no use to his ambitions and he's smart enough to know it."

"Your mother?" Hunter asked, still not looking up.

"Gorgeous, shrewd, formidable businesswoman."

Hunter sketched, listening to what was said and what wasn't. Her words told him that her childhood hadn't exactly overflowed with love and approval. He heard respect, understanding, and little else. He wanted to ask whether she enjoyed or avoided her mother and father, but Lina's emotions had no bearing on finding the artifacts, so he kept quiet and let Jase work.

"How about your mother's competition in the artifact sales game?" Jase asked.

"They're all variations on Celia's theme. Few have her connections when it comes to accessing legitimate Yucatec artifacts from the end of the Maya rule and the continuation of Maya life under the Spanish rule, so Celia's pretty much at the top of her heap."

"Where does she get her artifacts?"

"Reyes Balam lands. Family lands."

"So your father's digs are on private land."

"With the full blessing of the Mexican state and federal governments," Lina said.

"Did your family buy the land because of the ancient ruins?" Jase asked.

"No. The family lands are from the time before the Spanish came."

"How'd you keep them?" Jase asked curiously. "Damn few natives did."

"The Balam family was among the first Maya nobility to accept the Spanish rule and sign formal treaties with the Spanish king," Lina said. "In return, the Balams were granted a good chunk of the Yucatan and a Spanish noble title. Thus the Reyes Balam line began."

"Your ancestors were Maya royalty," Jase said. "Wow. Should I bow?"

"Only if my mother was here. And she would tell you about the minor Spanish royalty who married into the Balam family to exploit New World wealth." Lina's voice was wry. "As for me, I really don't care. I'm American."

"Huh. I'm a mix of Spanish, *indio,* Irish, and Japanese," Jase said. "But I sure ain't no royal."

"Neither am I," Lina said.

"Japanese?" Hunter said. "I never knew that."

"My grandfather was half Japanese. By the time it got to me, it didn't show."

"It does in your sister," Hunter said, remembering. "Beautiful almond-shaped eyes."

"But they're blue," said Jase.

"It's the shape that matters," Hunter retorted.

Lina felt some of the tightness flow out of her, and only then realized that both men had been humming like high-tension wires when they walked in. She wondered what had happened. Maybe Hunter would tell her later . . . if she could get him alone.

Or maybe they'd do more interesting things.

*He's almost a blackmailer,* she told herself.

*So what?* herself snapped back.

"Do you think your mother's competition has the artifacts?" Jase asked.

"If they did," Lina said, "Celia wouldn't have come to me asking about them."

"Not even to throw you off the scent?"

Lina paused, considering. "Celia can be manipulative as the devil, but she doesn't treat her family that way. Whatever she's feeling about family, she's in-your-face about it. Certainly with Philip and me. Carlos, too."

"Who's Carlos?" Jase asked.

*"Mi primo,"* Lina said. "Americans would say second cousin."

"Also royalty, huh?" Jase asked with a smile.

"Carlos Porfirio Chel Balam," she said. "And proud of it. He's an international businessman of Mexican citizenship, but he never forgets his royal Maya heritage."

"Powerful family you come from," Jase said, meaning it.

Lina shrugged. "On paper. These days, 'nobility' puts tortillas and beans on the table by working just like real people."

Jase grinned, liking her. "I've met some who don't look at it that way."

"So have I. That's why I'm in America and they aren't."

"Can you tell us about this Kawa'il cult?" Jase asked, thinking of the basement he and Hunter had seen that morning. But it seemed a little more distant now. Bearable.

"As you would expect of a transitional religion—" Lina began.

"Transitional?" Jase interrupted.

"End of Maya rule, beginning of Spanish," Hunter said without looking up from whatever he was sketching.

"Gotcha," Jase said. He smiled at Lina. "Sorry for the interruption. I'm a cop, not a scholar."

Lina smiled back. "Ask whatever and whenever you want. It's how we both learn."

"That's why you're a good teacher," Hunter said. "You know that learning flows both ways."

She enjoyed the warmth going through her at Hunter's offhand compliment entirely too much. She shifted against the desk, trying to fit into skin that felt a little too tight.

"The end of any culture through war is a violent time," Lina said, her voice husky, her eyes on Hunter, not Jase. "The cult of Kawa'il reflected that. He was a god of blood sacrifice and death. If my interpretations of the glyphs associated with him are correct, Kawa'il communicated exclusively through blood and sacred smoke."

"Didn't all the Maya?" Jase asked.

"It's a matter of degree," Lina said, looking at him. "Some gods are appeased with corn pollen, flowers, liquor, jade objects, food, that sort of thing. Kawa'il demanded more blood and sacrifice than other gods. Apparently a great deal more. I suspect that nobles who survived the ongoing war with the Spanish and the anger of their own people were in high demand as, er, conduits to Kawa'il."

Hunter's pencil paused.

Lina saw his bleak expression, and Jase's, and hurried to explain. "Keep in mind that it was a horrible time for the Maya. War, subjugation, disease, their already declining civilization in pieces around them. They must have been desperate to know the minds of their gods, to understand why such calamities had come."

Jase nodded. "So this Kawa'il ruled?"

"Only after the Spanish conquest, that we know of, and only in a very small part of Maya territory. On Reyes Balam land in Quintana Roo and government land in Belize. The presence of a god Kawa'il isn't accepted by most of the academic community. My father has spent his life trying to prove it."

"What do you think of the artifacts you saw in the photos?" Jase said.

"My gut says Kawa'il. My mind needs proof."

"How about this?" Hunter asked, handing her the sketch pad.

Lina looked at the surprisingly good rendition of a jaguar altar, but it was the second sketch that drew a quick breath from her.

Hunter waited, savoring the scent of her

and the warmth of her breasts swaying so close to him that if he moved his hand just a few inches . . .

"How big was the first artifact you sketched?" Lina asked.

Hunter forced himself to focus on the drawing rather than her tempting breasts. "The table was big enough to hold a man. From where and in what condition we found it, the table was associated with . . . rituals."

"An altar, then. Was there a channel to allow blood to run off into a Chacmool?"

"The light wasn't good enough to tell," Hunter said.

"Where did you see this?" Lina asked.

"The other side of town," Jase said. "One of the barrios."

His voice caressed the Spanish word in a way that told her he was fluent in the language, perhaps had been raised speaking it. Not unusual along the Mexican-American border.

"Is it Kawa'il?" Jase asked, touching the edge of the drawing.

"It could be. It certainly is patterned after sacrificial altars of the time just before the

Spanish came." She frowned. "You said a basement. Is the altar in private hands?"

"Not any more," Jase said. "We arrested the gangbangers on murder and drug charges. The table will be entered as evidence and stored in someone's evidence warehouse."

"Could I see it?"

"If necessary," Jase said.

"You don't want to," Hunter said at the same time.

"Why?" Lina asked, looking at Hunter.

"Let's just say it seemed to be a bloody active altar."

Lina's eyes narrowed. "Sacrifice?"

"Oh yeah," Jase said.

"Lots," Hunter said.

"Human," Lina said. It wasn't a question.

"We'll know for sure when the tests come back," Jase said. "But judging from the shape of the body I saw and what I've heard since . . . yeah, human. Past tense."

"You believe the altar was used at least once," she said to Jase.

"Every time I get a text message, the count goes up."

Hunter said something bleak under his breath and changed the subject, wanting to spare Lina the nightmare of that basement.

"One of the men arrested had tats like a brightly scaled snake winding up his arms. No head in sight," Hunter added.

"Is that usual?" Lina asked.

"Never seen it before," Hunter said.

"Me neither," Jase said. "Snake seemed to be the chief badass in charge. The rest of them had the usual jailhouse-gangbanger tats."

"The Maya had a scaled serpent associated with the gods, but not specifically with Kawa'il," Lina said slowly. "Except, once again, in a very small territory."

"Reyes Balam lands?" Hunter asked.

She nodded, hugging herself as though chilled. With an effort she forced her mind toward academic knowledge rather than the kind that shadowed Jase's and Hunter's eyes. It was one thing to study texts on ancient blood sacrifice. It was horrifying to hear about it happening in her own time and place.

Hunter gave Jase the sketchbook and pencils. Gently Hunter's big hands closed over Lina's arms, rubbing up and down, sharing warmth as though he understood the chill of violence sliding over her skin.

"Sorry." She gave him an unsettled smile. "I don't think of myself as being in an ivory tower, but to sacrifice people without the context of societal and religious approval is just . . . sick. Seriously sick. No meaning except depravity."

"Don't apologize for your reaction," Jase said. "Cops exist to keep the criminally sick from the average healthy citizen. So ignore the whack jobs and tell me about Maya and snakes."

Lina drew a deep breath. "Normally my sensitivity to cultural nuance is very useful in my studies. This time, not so much." She took another deep breath. "So, snakes and Maya. Usually the serpent was a generalized sacred symbol connecting the underworld with the overworld. The snake was often drawn as smoke or having wings, perhaps both. Why a modern gang-banger would choose the sacred snake over a more recognized Western symbol— such as skull and bones—is a question for a psychiatrist to answer. I can't."

Carefully Hunter eased his hands away

from Lina. The temptation to pull her onto his lap for some serious cuddling was simply too great.

"I can tell you that the jaguar was the exclusive province of Maya royalty," she added. "Your altar was modeled after ancient Maya royal practices."

Jase's thick eyebrows rose. "Huh. Snake dude didn't seem real royal to me."

"You're assuming he was the one using the table," Hunter said. "I'd bet he was more palace guard than king."

"If we get lucky, his snaky fingerprints are all over that altar," Jase said.

"Oh, I think Snakeman is more than capable of murdering people just because he can," Hunter said. "But he didn't strike me as the religious type, old or new." He took back the sketchbook and pointed to the second drawing. "What about this?"

Lina hadn't been looking forward to that question. The jaguar altar could have come from a relatively large number of sites. But the mask . . .

"It depends on your interpretation of the symbols around the mask," she said.

"It's stone," Hunter said. "Couldn't tell what kind. Too dark. It could even have been cement. Bigger than life by about twice."

"If the artifact is only a tenth as well done as the sketch, I doubt that it's made of cement," Lina said.

"Was that a compliment?" Jase asked, looking at Hunter with a sly smile.

"Truth," Lina said to Hunter. "You should be an artist."

He looked bemused. "Pay sucks."

"If you could take the Yucatan jungle, you'd be real useful on a dig," she said,

Jase laughed. "Ma'am, Hunter spends half his time in Mexico, on back roads or worse."

She looked at Hunter as though seeing him for the first time. "Really."

He tapped the second drawing. "Let's stay on topic."

Visibly, Lina thought over whether to accept the change of subject. When she did, Hunter suspected he'd be hearing more about art later. That was okay. He'd be glad to get naked and talk about whatever she wanted.

At length.

Depth, too.

"This looks like an elaborate stone mask,"

she said. "The crown or whatever is unusual, more like stylized sun rays or something shining from or through the mask. It reminds me of . . ."

"What?" Hunter asked.

"Come with me. I have a piece of wood I want you to look at."

Jase made a choking sound and looked sideways at Hunter's lap.

Hunter flipped him off.

But he was grateful for the walk through the museum's maze, because his pants fit better at the end of the stroll than at the beginning.

*Gotta get my mind off sex,* Hunter told himself, watching Lina's prim and proper body striding ahead of him. *Yeah, like that's going to happen. The lady has an outstanding ass. Perfect for my hands, perfect for my—*

**Stop thinking about it.**

Quickly Lina walked toward a room that held special, temporary cases—locked, controlled for temperature and humidity. Every step of the way she told herself that she was imagining the waves of sexual heat coming off Hunter. Her outfit was a simple dark pantsuit, nothing clingy, nothing feminine, no peekaboo tease, nothing to make her feel like Hunter's glance was caressing her hips.

**What is it about that man? He makes me feel . . . odd. Fizzy.**

**Sexy.**

*Try stupid,* she advised herself. *He's the one who's sexy, not me. And he's the next thing to a blackmailer, remember?*

She remembered, she just didn't care. Maybe her previously unsuspected bad-girl self was coming out to play.

Automatically Lina punched in her code, held the door for the men to enter the room, and made sure the door locked again.

The door opened into a room flooded with cool, blue-white light. The illumination was indirect, bounced from hidden lights, with no obvious source. Inside a transparent, humidity-controlled case, a sheet of very dark red wood rested on a stark white sheet. The wood was perhaps twenty inches long, two-thirds as wide, and appeared to be the top of a sacred box that had once held a god bundle.

Each time Lina saw the artifact, it took her breath and set her mind on fire. There was something richly organic and alive about the wood, as if it might flow right out of the case into a Maya priest's smoke dreams. A crack ran across the lower third of the artifact, a new break that told of a missing wedge of wood.

Hunter looked from the dark wood to Lina's face. The distance between this room and the bloody evil of the basement was so great he had a hard time holding it in his mind. Belatedly he realized Lina was talking.

"Then we'll verify the age by several kinds of analysis," Lina said. She looked at him. "Hunter?"

"Sorry. The contrast between this museum room and that barrio basement . . ." He shook his head

She put her hand on his arm. "The job you and Jase do must be nearly impossible."

"One of the reasons I'm no longer with ICE," Hunter agreed, putting his hand over hers.

Jase looked from one to the other and felt invisible. He had always accepted Hunter's differences—especially his intense awareness of things most other people didn't notice—but every so often Jase was reminded all over again. Like now. He had a sense of what Lina and Hunter were talking about, yet he didn't quite understand it.

But they certainly did. Even Jase could feel the sexual energy between them. It made him think about going home and nibbling on his wife. All over.

Lina cleared her throat and turned to the artifact case and the oddly radiant wood, taking refuge in professionalism. It was either that or start undressing Hunter with more than her mind.

"After I saw your photos," she said, "I reviewed every bit of private and published research on the Kawa'il cult. When I found nothing to explain most of your artifacts, I looked for reasons why someone might create counterfeits. Only a few people in the world care enough to go to those lengths. My father does, but he couldn't. It's not a matter of professional standards so much as creating those artifacts would take an act of imagination that he simply isn't capable of."

She looked at Hunter, trying to see if he understood.

He nodded. "What about Mercurio?"

"Possible, of course. But impossible to

keep secret. Take the mask in your photo," she said. "Even today, creating that from a piece of obsidian would take artisans of enormous sophistication a very long time to complete. No matter where you find those people, they will have friends, associates, competitors, whatever. Over time, that number of people can't keep a secret. If the piece is machined, rather than handmade, the 'secret' is out as soon as someone who knows what they're doing examines it under a microscope."

"In other words, why bother?" Hunter said.

"Exactly. To me, that mask looks even more sophisticated than Aztec mask work, which is considered by many to be the zenith of the art."

"Anything else?" Hunter asked.

"Your mask glowed and reflected like a smoking mirror, which is one interpretation of glyphs associated with priests of Kawa'il."

Hunter whistled tunelessly. "And Kawa'il is a god of death. Then and now."

"It makes a whacked sort of sense," Jase said. "Cartels are always looking for an edge in the fear department. Living human sacrifices made to a god of death are scarier than the narco's Santa Muerte cult with its ghosts and groans."

"That's a travesty of the original intention of sacrifice, literally to be made holy," she said. "In the past, the ritual was an act of awe and reverence, a way to communicate with the gods, with the very structure of the Maya universe. Look at this piece of wood. Look with your mind and emotions as well as your eyes and experience."

Jase and Hunter leaned closer, but it was Hunter's warmth she felt.

"This"—Lina traced the glyphs in the wood, not quite touching the case itself—"is the radiance of the gods and their wisdom shared, brought to the Maya by a priest-king-god who climbed up from the earth wearing a mask like a smoking mirror, his very breath the exhalation of gods."

Hunter's eyes narrowed. He followed her words, her finger, her voice describing a sacrament rather than the barbarism of the basement in a crumbling stucco house.

"The carving is of dream serpents," Lina said. "See the delicate tracery of individual feathers on the mouths of the beasts? The carver didn't see these creatures as monsters in the modern sense of the word. They were guardians, keepers of knowledge that was sometimes bestowed upon the wise, the brave, the worthy."

Jase grunted. "I'll take your word for it."

Hunter didn't look up from the case. Lina's voice curled around him, sank into him like smoke, like dreams.

"The central image," Lina said softly, almost reverently, "shows a human figure emerging from the fanged mouth of a huge serpent. The man is astride its jaws, forcing it open from within. Instead of being consumed by the knowledge, he is escaping with it, returning to his people to share the teachings of the gods."

Hunter unfocused his eyes just slightly, imagined light from fire rather than electricity . . . and felt his skin ripple in primal response.

"Now look below the escaping man," she said, her voice low. "Look where his face is watching. His mouth is open and he's speaking."

With a frown, Jase tried to see Lina's words in the artifact. He looked sideways at

Hunter. His friend was rapt, intent, a predator scenting game.

"See the masked figure?" she asked, tapping lightly on the case over the glyph. "He is himself emerging from the ground like a flower, legs as roots in the soil below. He seems to be looking up. His face is covered in an elaborate and—to modern eyes—terrifying mask, with something like wings flaring out from the sides, displaying fantastic feathers. There is even a marking that seems to indicate light coming from this mask, subtle rays, almost like a reflection."

"Is it the mask shining?" Hunter asked. "Or is something shining on him?"

"Professionally, I can't be certain."

"What about your instincts?"

She hesitated, then said, "I think the mask is made of something reflective."

"Gold?" Jase asked instantly.

"Not even silver," she said. "Wrong time, wrong place, wrong material. In fact, the more I look at it, the more I believe it represents something translucent enough to be shining from within." She laughed. "Never mind. That's my fancy, not my training. The point is, I think the wood might have originally been carved in Tulum, near our estates. There's something about the style of the glyphs."

"Where did you get it?" Jase asked.

"On loan from Mexico's Museum of Anthropology. We're dating it."

Silently Hunter studied the piece, then tapped lightly on the case. "What is this? The man the snake is swallowing?"

"I think that figure emerging from the snake is handing his bestowed wisdom to the figure below," she said. "My guess is it's a priest of Kawa'il passing something to man."

"The man with the mask and his feet in the underworld?" he asked, shifting his position, watching the wood.

"Yes. Look between the figures, where the wood is cracked." She indicated a place where there was a wedge of wood missing, but pointed at a spot on the high side of it. "If you study this area, you can see the hint of something. Like a section of zigzag line."

"So?" Jase asked.

"It's not a glyph I recognize—too many straight lines. But it seems to represent something being passed from one side to another. Those kinds of transactions only go one way," she said. "Gods to man."

"The break looks very recent," Hunter said. "The wood along the edges hasn't had time to age. Did you use it for dating?"

"You have a good eye," she said. "No, we didn't—wouldn't—break the wood. It came to us in that condition."

Slowly Hunter nodded. "Wonder what's on the missing piece."

"Whatever was passing from the priest-king to his people," she said. "Probably instructions on how to perform certain rituals."

"Verbal?" he asked.

"Not according to the narrative I see. No smoke coming from his mouth or any common sign of speech."

"Moses and the stone tablets," Hunter murmured. "Could he be passing on written commands? Like a codex?"

"It would have to be one that postdates Bishop Landa, after the Spanish conquest."

"Surviving that would be worth commemorating," Hunter said.

Silently he and Lina stared at the wooden piece, awed by something Jase didn't see.

"Okay. Shining mask and all the rest,"

Jase said. "How does this get us closer to finding the artifacts?"

Lina frowned. "I guess it doesn't. Not directly. I'm just trying to give you an idea of how profoundly rare something like the mask is. If the other artifacts you're looking for were associated with the mask, then it's the equivalent of someone sacking a great church and stealing the most sacred of religious objects."

"Makes sense, if you're trying to get a new religion off the ground," Hunter said.

"Are you talking about another Maya revolt, like in the twentieth century?" she asked. "That didn't end well for the natives."

"Wouldn't be the first time blood, politics, and religion mixed it up." He turned to Jase. "I haven't heard about anything beyond the usual millennial garbage. Have you?"

"I have a friend or two in Special Investigations. If this is real, it'd be special. I'll make some calls."

Lina looked at her watch. "I think Mr. Beaumont—"

"Jase," he cut in.

"—Jase, needs to understand what's

available on the high end of the Maya artifact market in Houston today," she said. "Without that understanding, it's easy to miss something important."

Jase grunted. "That's why we're here."

"Sometimes knowledge is emotional," Lina said. "I'm not always with you. And frankly, you have no particular feel for the artifacts you're chasing. They transcend the word *special.*"

"She's got you there," Hunter said.

Jase sighed but didn't argue. He looked at Lina. "I don't have time to get a Ph.D. You got a quick fix in mind?"

"Sort of. Pre-Columbian Dreams is open. It's a gallery just across from Shandy's."

"Legitimate?" Jase asked. "The gallery, not the restaurant."

Lina shrugged. "The owner says she can provide papers for anything in the front or back of the gallery."

"Is the ink dry?" Hunter asked.

"So far, so good."

Jase smiled. "Sounds like an interesting place."

"Don't get your hopes up," Lina said quickly. "I have an academic prejudice against places that sell artifacts, but there has never been a verified incident of anything illegal in Pre-Columbian Dreams."

"Gotcha," Jase said. "I'll leave the cuffs in the car."

"Drop Lina and me off at the apartment so I can pick up my Jeep," Hunter said. "I'll take her out to Shandy's after we see the gallery."

"The lack of an invitation to dinner with you is making me bleed," Jase said.

"You have a hot meal waiting for you at home."

Jase's smile widened. "And I'm a man with a real big hunger. Let's do this gallery so I can get on home and . . . eat."

## CHAPTER TEN

PURPLE DUSK WAS SLIDING OVER THE LAST OR-ange light of day, but the parking structure still felt like a three-story oven as Hunter parked his Jeep. Jase's white minivan idled by, looking for an empty space in the gloom.

Hunter and Lina got out and stood near the Jeep, waiting for Jase. Even after he went by, she kept looking around, checking out the cars coming in. Hunter was doing the same thing, but it was a survival habit he had picked up on the job. Like most animals, he had a sixth sense that told him when he was being watched.

Every time he was around Lina, the prickly warnings would go off, a constant stretch of nerves that had nothing to do with sexual attraction.

"Do you have an ex who is a stalker?" Hunter asked Lina.

She blinked. "What?"

"You act like someone who's afraid she's being followed."

"No ex-anything, including stalker." She went back to staring at the entrance.

Hunter waited, watching her.

"Okay, I know this sounds crazy," she said after a minute, "but sometimes I feel like I'm being followed."

"How long has it been going on?"

She kept watching the garage entrance. "A month, maybe more. It didn't happen all of a sudden. Just a sort of gradual awareness until I couldn't ignore it anymore."

"You ever see anyone?"

"No. Unless a shadow here and there counts. Nothing I can put a face to. Just a . . . feeling. An almost-itch on the back of my neck. Maybe Philip's paranoia is catching."

"Or his caution," Hunter said easily.

"Sounds like your father made a few enemies along the way. What about you?"

"Oh, I'm sure I'm not everyone's best friend forever, but enemies? Not that I know of."

"Think about it."

"I have," she said, narrowing her eyes as another car came in.

Like a lot of the vehicles in the lot, it was a dark SUV with tinted windows. It turned down a different aisle and vanished.

Jase found a parking spot a few rows over. He got out, locked up, and threaded himself between parked cars until he reached Hunter and Lina.

"Let's go get a dose of education," Jase said, walking toward the garage exit.

Lina shook her head at his tone of voice. "Such enthusiasm."

"You've only been on this case for two days," Jase said. "I've spent enough time that I'm getting really cheesed about tiny steps forward, big steps backward, and most of the steps running round in circles until I feel hungover."

Hunter looked at his friend. He knew that underneath the easy tone of voice,

Jase was tight, exhausted, feeling time dripping away like blood.

"Anything new turn up from the basement?" Hunter asked.

"We're up to ten bodies now. Is that new?"

"I meant from processing the gangbangers that were arrested."

Jase smiled grimly. "Oh, we learned boatloads, but nothing that applies to this case. Snakeman has never been in our system, or in any of the law enforcement databases we've accessed. He's clean except for a lack of immigration papers. Given that his lawyer is slick as snot, he'll get off with deportation."

"That's fu—ah, crazy," Hunter said, looking sideways at Lina.

Jase made a sound that could have been a laugh. "It's scary, is what it is."

"That, too," Hunter agreed.

"All but the last body—LeRoy—died without mutilation," Jase continued in a casual voice. "Well, they were beheaded, but still intact otherwise. From the tracks the gangbangers left in the legal system, we should be giving them medals for skimming scum off the cesspool. Except for LeRoy—

who had only minor stuff in his record—I'd have done them myself for free."

"I so don't want to meet your 'clients,'" Lina said.

Jase's smile was all teeth. "Every day is a new lesson in dickheads."

After the gloomy heat and conversation in the garage, the street looked like heaven. The gallery was located on Houston's answer to Rodeo Drive, where money, fashion, money, jewelry, money, cars, and money were on display inside and outside of the shops. The gallery itself went for an ambience of exceptionally classy artifacts for exceptionally discriminating multimillionaires. Pools of white-gold light haloed objects that would be sullied by the very thought of a price being attached to them.

*But there's always a price,* Hunter thought cynically.

In that, the gallery wasn't so different from the gory basement. Just better lighting.

A woman approached, a thin blonde who had pushed ordinary good looks as far as she could with skillful makeup and clothing. She was seductive, but kept well back from the edge of the cliff called trashy. Green eyes, unlikely boobs for such a thin frame, artfully cut hair, expensive-looking clothes, and gold jewelry with pre-Columbian designs.

"I'm Ms. Arkan. If you have any questions, I'm at your disposal."

"Thank you," Hunter said. "Right now we just want to look around."

Ms. Arkan nodded and went back to a small, elegant desk tucked against the far wall. In the corner nearest the door, a man stood quietly, watching nothing and everything.

"Classy rent-a-cop," Jase murmured. "I'll bet he's Houston PD working a second shift to put tortillas and beans on the table."

"Hope so. That would mean that he knows how to use the gun that's under his coat."

Lina tried to be invisible. Unlike her mother, she didn't make a habit of trolling pre-Columbian sales galleries. Guilt by association was an established truth in academia.

Wandering off, Jase stared at a breastplate made of what appeared to be solid gold. The pectoral and abdominal muscles were suggested by squared-off shapes that managed to be graceful. The pedestal holding the breastplate spun slowly, like a runway model strutting haute couture.

"This thing is giving me a boner," Jase whispered after Hunter wandered over. "Is that normal?"

"If it lasts more than four hours, call a doctor."

Jase snickered.

Under his breath, Hunter muttered something about triumph, subjugation, and plunder. He would rather have seen the artifacts for sale in a back alley in Cozumel. But that was his prejudice. Smart people with money didn't go into a dark alley. They came to places like this and paid for the lighting and protection.

More gold and silver objects—figurines and jewelry—were carefully displayed against black velvet with pinpoint spotlights shining down, making each piece appear special, breathtakingly unique in its perfection.

"Nothing familiar here," Jase said very quietly.

"There's some pottery where Lina is standing. Masks, too."

Slowly both men worked their way

through the gallery aisles to where Lina was. Along the way they saw ancient jewelry, cloth, pottery in striking shapes, and figurines in everything from gold to clay. New World jade gleamed with ancient reverence. In another aisle there were chunks of limestone with broken pre-Columbian designs etched into them.

Jase might not have had a Ph.D., but he was a long way from stupid. Nowhere did he see anything that made his professional instincts quiver. Knives, yes. Obsidian, occasionally. But no knife was made from a single piece of obsidian. Masks, yes, many of them. One had a few obsidian inlays, as well as jade and what could have been shell. But no mask had enough obsidian to come close to the one in the photos. Pieces of cloth, yes, but no stained bundles. The only artifacts that gave him pause were in a long case. Clay censers of various degrees of intricacy were illuminated from within.

"Nope," Hunter said softly.

"Not even close?"

"Right function. Wrong time and design."

"Damn. I haven't seen anything useful. Have you?" Jase asked.

"Not yet."

As the men drew close to Lina, she lifted an eyebrow questioningly.

"Damn few Late Terminal Classic Yucatec Maya artifacts," Hunter said.

"I'm glad you said it," Jase muttered. "I couldn't have."

Lina almost smiled. "Exactly. Artifacts from that place and time period aren't thick on any ground, especially high-end galleries. My mother's galleries have the most and the best of that type of artifacts, yet she was asking *me* if I'd heard anything about some spectacular new artifacts."

Silence, then Jase nodded glumly. "Point made. I'm outta here. I've got better ways to waste my time."

"Philistine," Hunter said.

"Want to see my T-shirt?" Jase asked.

"What about the Happy Meal, boy wonder?" Hunter retorted.

"I'm getting that real soon. Later, old man. Or sooner if you come up with anything useful."

Jase headed out.

Shaking her head, Lina looked at Hunter. "Are you two always like that?"

"Like what?"

"Pushing and shoving and loving it."

"Ever since we met. He was four and I was a month older. I never let him forget it either. I called him 'boy wonder.' Now he calls me 'old man.'"

Smiling, Lina wondered what it would be like to have a friend like that. Close. Lifetime close.

"Anything else you want to do here?" Hunter asked. "I'm hungry."

"I'd rather cook something for us at home than eat at Shandy's."

Hunter paused an instant before he opened the gallery door for her, a courtesy she appreciated rather than resented.

"Shandy's doesn't take reservations," Lina explained. "It's loud, you wait for a table at the bar, and the service is slow because they want you to buy overpriced drinks. I'd rather be able to talk in a normal tone of voice and not starve to death waiting for food. Okay?"

When she looked up at him, Hunter's smile was the kind that melted ice.

"Need to shop before we cook?" he asked.

"We?"

"My parents both worked and they both shared the home jobs. I'm not a chef, but I can clean a kitchen good enough for a health inspection."

"I've got food," she said. Then, carefully, "As long as food is all you're expecting . . ."

"Food is always good. Dessert is your call, Lina."

She studied his face and knew he meant it. "I like a man who doesn't think with his package."

Hunter laughed. "Don't kid yourself, sweetheart. My package is real interested."

"But you can still think and talk like a civilized being."

"My mother did her best."

Lina's laughter made Hunter grin. He took her hand as they walked into the parking garage. Across the garage he saw Jase's van backing out of a parking slot. An SUV idled down toward the exit, passing them as they reached the Jeep. Hunter had just handed Lina into the Jeep when he heard vehicle doors open hard. Footsteps smacked and scuffed on the textured concrete, people walking fast, nearly running.

Lina's eyes widened as she looked over Hunter's shoulder. One hand dove into her purse, fingers searching frantically.

Hunter spun around in time to take the first man down with a kick to his gut. The momentum of Hunter's spin carried though as a punch to a second man's throat. The man tucked his chin in time to save his trachea, but took a solid hit to his nose. Blood sprayed as the man staggered back. Voices shouted in a language Hunter didn't understand. He went down beneath the third man and heard Lina scream. The second man piled on.

Lina kept on screaming, telling anyone with ears that something was wrong in the garage. At the side of her vision she saw strangers scrambling away from the area, running for the exits. One of the women was shouting into a cell phone.

A broad, powerful hand wrapped around Lina's arm, yanking her out of the seat and onto her knees on the concrete. She looked up into the sweating face of the man Hunter had kicked. The attacker was cursing nonstop in a mixture of Mayan and Spanish as he yanked her up to her feet.

Adrenaline sleeted through her as she aimed the pepper spray, turned her head aside, and pressed hard. The man went down, clawing at his eyes with one hand and yanking her back onto her knees with his other. Her teeth sank into his wrist and her elbow into his diaphragm.

With a desperate lunge she wrenched free of the groaning man in time to see Hunter buck off one attacker and grapple for the gun the other had drawn from beneath his jacket. She still had some pepper spray left. She rushed forward.

"No, Lina!" Hunter shouted, wrenching at the gun with all his strength. "Run to the gallery! Now, NOW!"

The driver of the SUV kept yelling the same Spanish words over and over again while two more men leaped out. The dull flash of gun barrels told Lina that her pepper spray was about as much use as spit. But Hunter was down and it was all she had.

One of the men from the van barked something. The man with the gun leaped away as his friend took aim at Hunter.

A shot exploded, echoing in the parking

garage. The man who had been drawing down on Hunter staggered back and dropped bonelessly to the ground.

Jase drove the white minivan with one hand and shot through the open windows with the other. He braked hard between Hunter and the attackers, who were scrambling to use their dark SUV as a shield from the unexpected gunfire pouring from the white van.

"Get her out of here!" Jase yelled as he slapped in a new magazine.

He aimed at the SUV, firing to keep the shooters from hitting Hunter or Lina. Bullets punched through the driver's-side window of the SUV, making a snapping, crackling sound. The driver flinched and the SUV bucked.

Bullets started ripping into Jase's white van, an endless roll of deadly thunder. Bullets whined and caromed off the concrete floor and pillars. Car alarms shrieked. Human screams echoed.

*Submachine pistols,* Hunter thought. *Bastards must have learned to use them watching TV, because they're blasting everything from the oil stains to the ceiling lights.*

The bitter smell of powdered concrete rose from the spray of bullets.

Jase yelled, "I'm hit!"

"That one is a cop, you stupid goats!" yelled the driver in Spanish. "We have to get out of here!"

More shouts in the language Hunter didn't understand but that sounded like the Yucatec Mayan he'd heard. The attackers turned and scrambled back into their dark SUV. Someone pushed the SUV's bleeding driver over the console into the passenger seat. The rest piled in the back, dragging anyone who couldn't walk. The SUV roared down the aisle as its doors started slamming shut. The stink of burning tires mingled with gun smoke. The SUV pulled into traffic amid a blare of horns and squealing tires as people braked frantically to avoid an accident.

Slowly Jase slumped over the wheel of the van. Red bloomed along his upper body.

"Stay down and call 911," Hunter shouted at Lina as he ran to Jase's van.

The smell of blood rolled over Hunter. Bracing Jase with one hand, he opened the door with the other. No sign of an exit wound on his back. He eased Jase against the seat to check his front. He was breathing, but not easily. Same for consciousness, barely there.

"She . . . okay?" Jase managed.

"Yes, thanks to you, boy wonder. Now shut up and let me see how bad it is."

Jase smile slightly at the old nickname. Then his eyes rolled white and he passed out.

Hunter ripped open his friend's ruined shirt. Blood flowed heavily from the wound on Jase's left side, but didn't pulse.

**Not an artery.**

The lack of bloody froth on Jase's lips or around the bullet hole told Hunter that if the lungs were involved, it wasn't critical.

Yet.

But the blood. God, the blood.

Quickly Hunter balled up the ripped shirt and applied pressure to Jase's chest wound, trying to slow the bleeding.

**Too much blood. Way too much.**

"Don't you die on me, Jase," Hunter growled. "Don't you damn die!"

As the car alarms slowly gave up, Hunter heard the yelp and wail of approaching sirens. Slowly he became aware that Lina was standing next to him, had been talking to him.

". . . on the way," Lina said. "What can I do?"

"Hold this while I check for other injuries."

She didn't hesitate. She simply pressed her hand over the bloody rag and watched sweat run down Hunter's face. And tears. She doubted he even knew it, any more than he knew he was cursing and praying nonstop under his breath as his hands went gently, quickly over his friend.

"He took another one, more a burn than anything else," Hunter said. "A third wound is clean, just muscle. Is he still breathing?"

"Slow, but there."

Something dripped off Lina's chin. Vaguely she realized she was crying, too. It was better than the screams that wanted to rip through her throat.

Hunter's hand covered her bloody one. Together they kept pressure on the wound and listened to electronic wails that suddenly stopped on the street outside. Emergency lights flashed in the gloom. The sound of vehicle doors and powerful engines idling, running feet. Spotlights glared, casting stark, conflicting shadows.

Lina flinched.

"It's okay," Hunter said. "These are the good guys."

"Yes." But that didn't stop her from shuddering at the sound of shoes slapping concrete, rushing toward them.

"When they question you, you don't know anything except that Jase wanted a tour of a high-end pre-Columbian artifact gallery, so I brought him to you." Hunter's voice was low, cold. "I'll talk to ICE myself. Got that?"

She glanced at his drawn, grim face. "Yes. Gallery. That's all I know."

He turned to the men rushing up. Some had weapons drawn, but they were pointed at the floor.

"Man down," Hunter said. "Bleeding bad. Let those med-techs through now!"

Being talked to in their own language reassured the cops. The guns disappeared.

"Any unsecured weapons?" asked one of the cops.

"One on the floor of the van," Hunter said. "The wounded man is with ICE."

"Any other wounded?"

"No."

"You're both bloody."

"Jase's blood," Lina said, her voice strained.

Someone passed a signal and the med-techs pushed through to the van. Very quickly Jase was hooked to an IV, field-dressed, and loaded into an ambulance for a screaming ride to the hospital.

"His wife is pregnant and he has two small kids," Hunter said. "She should be with him."

"We'll take care of it."

"Now," Hunter said. "After you're done questioning us might be too late."

The cop started to object, then looked at Hunter's face and the blood that covered him.

The officer's partner said to Hunter, "Give me her number. You ICE, too?"

"Not anymore."

As soon as he had Jase's home number, the second officer withdrew. Other officers scattered out to secure the crime scene and question everyone who had been crazy enough to hang around after the shooting started.

"What happened?" asked the first cop. "You first, ma'am. Begin with your full name."

Lina answered that question and the

following ones while leaning against Jase's van. Hunter and another cop with an agenda walked fifty feet away and began the Q-and-A process. When crime-scene techs asked Lina to move, she and her questioner went to a pillar beyond the yellow tape that was being strung around the parking garage like some kind of perverse Christmas wrap.

"How long have you known Agent Jason Beaumont?" the officer asked without a pause.

"I don't really know him. He's Hunter's friend. We came to the gallery so that Mr. Beaumont could get a feel for what's available in the high-end artifact market."

"How long have you known Hunter Johnston?"

Lina was on the hard downward spiral of an adrenaline jag, and she had answered all the questions at least three times. A fourth time was twice too many.

"As I've told you many times," she said, her tone as impatient as she felt, "Mr. Johnston has audited several of my classes over the last year. We've had coffee and conversation. Now, if you don't have any new questions for me, I'm exhausted and would like to at least wash my hands."

Hunter must have reached the same point in the questioning process because he was striding through the various remaining cops toward her. He was close enough that he heard her last sentence.

"Unless you're going to arrest us," Hunter said, "we're leaving. She's a civilian and she's kept it together better than anyone has a right to expect. She needs to chill, not to be grilled."

"You know that we're required—" began the cop.

"To ask questions," Hunter cut in. "Once, twice, fine. Three times because you're pissed. Now you're just wasting our time."

"With what you've given us, there's not much chance of catching the shooter," the cop snarled.

"No shit. Now let us leave or read us our rights."

Someone with higher rank moved in. "Thank you for your cooperation," she said to Hunter and Lina. "If we make any arrests, we'll need you to identify the suspect or suspects."

"You can reach me on my cell phone," Hunter said.

"You have my cell number," Lina said wearily.

"Your cooperation is appreciated," the woman said, smiling professionally.

Hunter and the cops all knew that devils would be ice-skating in hell before there was any arrest. If the SUV was found on this side of the border, it would be stripped, likely reported stolen. Every description of the occupants boiled down to short, swarthy, and similar. More *indio* than Mexican. Like thousands of other Houston residents.

The description was useless for catching anything but overtime.

Hunter nodded to the cops, took Lina's arm, and led her to his Jeep. It had escaped the bullets. The Mercedes parked in the next slot over hadn't been as lucky. The rear window was blown into thousands of grainy, sparkling pieces.

Before Lina had fastened her seat belt, Hunter called the hospital Jase had been taken to, only to be told that Jason Beaumont was none of his business. Swearing, he called Ali's cell number.

"It's Hunter," he said as soon as she picked up. "How is Jase?"

"In surgery," Ali said, her voice raw. "He won't be out for—hours. It's—very serious."

"I'll be there as soon as I can." *As soon as I wash Jase's blood off me.*

A hot darkness wrapped around the Jeep as it nosed out of the garage into traffic. Christmas lights sparkled everywhere in storefronts. Lina felt like she was dreaming.

*Must be shock,* she told herself.

"Your apartment is closer," Hunter said.

Lina shivered. "Yes."

"Cold?"

"No."

"Hang on, sweetheart. I'll get you home."

"No," she said tightly. "I can't go there. Those men were after me."

"What?" Hunter said, giving her a fast look.

"They were speaking in a Mayan dialect. They wanted me."

Hunter's eyes searched surrounding traffic and the driving mirrors with quick glances. "You sure?"

"I grew up with Spanish and English as my primary languages. The Mayan dialect those men spoke was my third language.

My great-grandmother prefers it, though she speaks Spanish very well. In case you didn't catch it, the driver only spoke Spanish. He knew Jase was a cop."

"I got that." Hunter wove through traffic, checking mirrors, watching for any vehicle matching his maneuvers. "What did the others say?"

"They screamed at the shooter not to hurt me or El Maya would eat their balls and tear out the heart of every living relative they had."

Hunter's eyebrows lifted. "Is that a usual curse?"

"No. They yelled variations of the threat and made it clear that they wanted to . . . take me. El Maya wants me intact and unharmed." Tears welled from her eyes and silently streaked her face, shining trails in the streetlight. "It's my fault. All that blood, Jase's blood, my fault."

"You weren't holding the guns. The blood is all on the shooters' ticket. Did you tell the PD?"

Silently she shook her head while the city's petroleum-scented wind turned tears cold on her face. "No. Was that wrong? Should I have told them?"

For an instant Hunter's fingertips slid down her cheek, bringing warmth to the cool flesh. "You did good. Right now I don't trust anyone. Narcos have ears in every police department that is important to them. Houston is real important." He put his hand on the wheel again. "You need to disappear."

"Narcos? Is this about drugs, not the artifacts?"

"I don't know. All I know is that anything we give the police will end up in places that it wasn't meant to be."

"Corruption?" she asked unhappily.

"Even if ninety-nine-point-nine percent of the Houston PD is on heaven's short list, that still leaves plenty of people to pass information on down to hell."

"God, we're turning into Mexico."

Hunter's attention never left the traffic around them. "We're as human as Mexicans are. Corruption happens. In some cultures it's accepted, even admired, and certainly exploited just like any other business opportunity. Mexico . . ." He shook his head.

Lina watched Hunter's stark profile while he told her what she didn't want to hear.

"Mexico is circling the toilet," he said bluntly. "Everybody knows it and nobody talks about it. The narcos are in open warfare with the *federales*. Silver or lead, take your pick. Bribery or blood. I don't judge the civilians who only want to survive. The cops and politicians, well, I wouldn't mind flushing those corrupt bastards before the rot goes any farther."

"I know. It's just . . ." Her voice trailed off.

"Yeah. When that greasy corruption takes a slice out of your honest life, it's a shock."

More silence, night and time flowing by.

"Anyone following?" Lina asked, her voice catching.

"Not that I've caught," Hunter said. "Ease down, sweetheart. It's going to be a long night as it is. No need to waste energy worrying about things you can't control. Deep breaths. Slow. Long."

Silently Lina practiced breathing while Hunter wove through traffic, making unexpected turns, sometimes going around whole blocks and ending up in the same place. She let herself drift, sliding down and down, back to where her heart wasn't beating double time and screams weren't clawing at her throat.

"Is your passport at your apartment?" he asked.

She looked at his face, dark planes and angles slashed by city lights. He looked as forbidding as any stone statue carved in reverence to forgotten gods.

"No," she said, her voice hoarse. "I always carry it with me. Same for Mexican travel documents."

Hunter almost smiled. "Same here. Need anything from work?"

"My computer."

"Can you access it through an outside portal?" he asked.

She closed her eyes. "Yes. I have all the passwords."

"You know how to use a handgun?"

Her eyes snapped open. "Handgun, shotgun, and rifle. Sometimes I worked alone at remote sites."

"Ever shoot anything but a target?"

"No. I don't particularly like guns."

"Neither do I," Hunter said. "But at least you understand which end bites and how to keep it from biting you. That's more than most know."

More time slid by with the night, fragmented into darkness and light, seething with unknowns.

"Why would someone called El Maya want me enough to kill for me?" she asked finally.

"I don't know. When I find out, I'll know who gave the orders that ended up with blood all over Jase."

Hunter didn't say any more. He didn't have to. Lina understood that someone now had the kind of enemy that made nightmares look cozy.

# CHAPTER ELEVEN

LINA WOKE UP WITH A START WHEN THE JEEP slowed and took an off-ramp leading to a street. Houston's flash and glitter was nowhere in sight. Nothing but an overcast night and car lights whizzing by on I-10. Her neck hurt from sleeping against the window and her skin was chapped from scrubbing blood off in a gas-station restroom on the outskirts of Houston.

"Where are we?" she asked.

"South Padre Island."

She rubbed her eyes. "The beach. That explains the salt smell." She must have slept for hours. "Any word on Jase?"

"He's out of surgery."

The tightness around Hunter's mouth made her stomach sink.

"And?" she asked unhappily.

"Still critical. Ali's parents are with her, taking care of the kids."

"I'm sorry," she whispered.

"Not your fault, any of it." He stopped for a light. "You warm enough?"

She shifted the jacket he had put over her. "Yes. What about you?"

His eyes checked the mirrors as regularly as breathing. "I run hot."

The sound of air rushing and rippling over the canvas top was white noise, something she had stopped hearing after the first half hour on the road.

"Are we being followed?" she asked.

"I lost them after the gas station."

Scattered lights told of houses and strip malls hacked out of scrubland and stilted above storm tides.

"If no one is following, why are we here?" she asked.

"Because we have to assume that whoever wants you has my Houston address by now. Ditto for Brownsville and my uncles' homes. My cousins have kids. I don't want them in the line of fire."

She opened her mouth, closed it. There was really nothing to say. He was right. She should have thought of it herself.

"My uncles are working their contacts," Hunter continued. "They hear something good, we'll hear it."

"You're obviously more used to this kind of thing than I am," she said. "What do you do when you disappear for days or weeks at a time?"

"I work for the family security company."

"Doing what?"

"Securing whatever needs it," he said.

She didn't give up. "What does that mean?"

"Exactly what I said. My uncles' company specializes in cross-border security issues for corporations and individuals." Hunter's glance flicked to the mirrors again. Still nothing that ruffled his instincts. It was late enough that traffic was light, which made checking for tails much easier.

"Where were you the past two weeks?" she asked bluntly.

"I missed you, too," he said, smiling.

"Hunter—" she began impatiently.

"My most recent job was outside of Co-zumel," he said before she could rip a strip off him with her sharp tongue, "ransoming a rich debutante who thought that bad things only happened on TV, and that get-ting knee-walking drunk was safe in a Mexican dive."

"Was it dangerous for you?"

"It had its moments. They decided to up the ransom and threw a bullet tantrum when I refused. I grabbed the young mis-tress of the universe and beat the bad guys to the airport."

"No wonder you weren't shocked by what happened in the garage," she said.

"Don't bet on it. A friend's blood is al-ways shocking. I've just had more experi-ence on the adrenaline ride than most. It doesn't hit me as hard on the up or the down."

She let out a long rush of air. "Remem-bering to breathe is the hardest part for me."

"Harder than holding a bloody rag against a wound?"

"Philip wouldn't let me go on a dig with him until I could handle weapons and had a basic understanding of field medicine," she said neutrally.

"How old were you?"

"Nine. I had to prove myself every summer I spent with him. The tests got harder every year."

"Sounds harsh," Hunter said.

She shrugged. "It was useful. I stitched and bandaged more than one deep machete cut. It was years before I understood that Philip upped the difficulty every summer because he wanted me to fail. When I figured it out, I confronted him."

"What did he say?"

"He didn't answer. He usually doesn't."

Hunter's mouth tightened but he kept it shut. She wasn't the first child to have a dickhead for a father and she wouldn't be the last.

Even at this time of night, Gulf Boulevard's party houses were flashing like beacons. With the ocean just across the boulevard, it was always vacation time for high-school and college kids, and the older men who preyed on them. The fact that it was the holiday season just put a more colorful gloss on the hunting grounds.

Hunter took it all in without really seeing

it. He was looking for the unusual, not the routine.

He turned the Jeep off the boulevard and entered a long, sandy, cracked asphalt driveway leading away from the ocean. The beach house he headed toward was small, one-story, on stilts, and old enough to have lived through too many of the Dirty Coast's hair-raising hurricanes. A latticework fence shielded the space between the floor of the house and the ground.

When Hunter turned off the Jeep, Lina heard the muted breathing of the surf beyond the boulevard, flat waves lapping against the sand. The salt air was sticky on her skin, cooler than Houston had been, but still warm enough to make the thought of walking on the beach alluring.

"You need help getting out?" Hunter asked as he came around the Jeep.

"I'm not a baby."

"No argument there," he said, standing next to her, close, breathing in her presence. "But I'm betting you're stiff from playing on concrete and then taking a long drive."

Lina took off her seat belt, grabbed the purse she had hung on to through all the chaos, and started to slide out. It was a good thing she used the roll bar to steady herself, because Hunter was right. Her knees were crying. He braced her until she worked some of the stiffness out.

"Bad?" he asked.

"Not enough to matter."

But she didn't pull away from the arm encircling her waist. She liked it there. She liked having Hunter close. He smelled of cheap restroom soap with an underlay of darkness, salt, and man.

*Breathe,* she reminded herself.

She did, and felt his scent race into her lungs, her blood. The sudden uptick in her heartbeat owed nothing to fear and everything to being a woman close to a man she wanted.

*This is crazy,* she told herself.

**No. Crazy is what I'll be if he doesn't step away.**

Nothing that had happened during the day had made Hunter less appealing to her. Everything he'd done had simply increased what had already been a compelling sensual lure. She tried not to lean on his strength, but he was there and her legs were stiff, he was warm and she was cold.

She hoped he didn't know how much she needed him close, then closer. This afternoon she had learned the difference between almost-blackmailers and murderers. In her new world, Hunter was an angel. A dark one, yes, but they were the most intriguing kind.

"Doesn't look like much, but it has what we need," Hunter said.

Still holding her, he leaned back into the Jeep. One-handed, he snagged his computer from under the passenger seat. When he straightened, his breath was against her ear, his arm around her waist comforting . . . and more, much more.

She forced herself to look away from him, to tear through the sensual web weaving around them, binding them closer.

The coastal scrub was kept away from the house by the concrete walkway that was covered with a fine coat of sand and a fringe of dirt that was blue in the moonlight. Toad calls and insect noises ebbed and flowed with the sound of the waves. The front steps were weathered gray wood.

"Looks real good to me," she said.

"I haven't been out here to clean up for a while," Hunter admitted. "I've been too busy with work to come to Uncle Danny's summer place."

"You're sure he won't mind us using it?"

"I talked to him on the phone while you were asleep. He told me the usual."

"Which is?"

"To leave it better than I found it. He probably wants me to fix the gutters or something." Hunter sounded more amused than irritated.

Motion sensors kicked on. Spotlights pointed the way to the weather-beaten porch. There was a scurry of critters racing for the shadows.

"Just like being on a dig," Lina said, laughing.

"So long as they stay outside and don't bite, my uncle don't pay them no never mind," Hunter said.

His drawl sounded just right, like he'd grown up with it. One accent for the city, one for the country.

Another light went on inside the house. At the end of the driveway Lina saw a tiny garage. Its door was closed.

"Is your uncle here now?" she asked.

"No. He only likes Padre in the summer. Then he complains about all the damn people. Think that's why he likes it," Hunter said. "Under all the gruff, he's a people person."

"What about you?"

"What do you think?" Hunter asked with a sideways look.

She smiled slightly. "I don't think you're a people person."

"Gold star on your forehead, sweetheart. I'm real choosy about who shares my time. An hour wasted on social chitchat is an hour of my life I'll never get back."

"And here I am, invading more than an hour," she said unhappily.

His arm tightened, pulling her even closer, until she could feel the flex and play of his thigh along her hip. The easy power of him pleased her in ways that kept surprising her. She'd never been much for the macho type, having seen way too many of them in Mexico. But Hunter . . . Hunter simply was what he was, no fuss, no bother, no strutting.

"You can invade my life anytime you like," he said, "for however long you want. Besides, I'm a blackmailer, remember?"

"Better than kidnappers and murderers."

"I'm relieved." And he was. He didn't

want Lina angry to be in his company. He simply wanted her.

Hunter stepped up onto the narrow porch that ran along the front of the house. Computer in one hand, he pulled a key from his jeans pocket with the other. Despite the weathered appearance of the door, the lock was bright and well oiled. The door opened without a creak or grind.

"Come on in," he said.

He put his computer on a dusty table and headed straight to a surprisingly complex security system across the room. Quickly he punched in a long code. Lights on the panel flickered from red or orange to green.

"I bet your uncle installs security systems along with rescuing debutantes," Lina said, setting her purse next to his computer.

"It was the original business. Then things started going to hell south of the border and he expanded the menu options for customers. Personal security training, threat evaluation, kidnap negotiations, bodyguards, whatever the customer wants—as long as it's legal."

"So you're a bodyguard, too?" she asked.

His mouth flattened. "Only when I don't say no fast enough, and only for very short periods—corporate meetings across the border and such. I don't have the social skills to be a high-level bodyguard. And I don't want them."

*You could guard my body anytime,* Lina thought immediately.

She had just enough self-control left not to say it aloud. For the first time in her life, she wanted to have the kind of affair that women wrote memoirs about. With Hunter.

"So your uncle comes to a crowded place and complains a lot," she said, struggling for a neutral topic. "Does he complain about other things?"

"Only on the days that end in *y.*"

She laughed softly. "Sounds like Abuelita. 'Why don't you dress better, Lina?' 'Why don't you have a man, Lina?' 'I can't wait forever for my great-great-grandchildren.'"

"Children are a gift," he said without thinking as he locked the door behind them and reset the security system.

"You sound like you have personal knowledge," Lina said.

And then she held her breath, waiting for his answer.

"I do. Did. She and her mother died."

Lina's hand went to Hunter's arm. She wanted to say she was sorry, but the words were so useless. She put her arms around him and held him, just held him, wishing she could take away the kind of pain that no one should have to know.

"It was years ago," he said, holding her in turn.

"Not for you," she said huskily. "It's there every day you wake up, fresh as dawn."

His arms tightened. For long minutes they just stood, sharing warmth and life. Slowly Hunter released her. It was that or take her to the nearest flat surface and eat her alive. But she was too vulnerable right now and he had just enough self-control left not to take advantage of her.

"Maybe I should sic my uncle on your *abuelita*," he said.

Lina took a shaky breath. "Abuelita would shred him. In Mexico, any woman who has even the smallest measure of power has to be tough and smart enough to know where and when to use it. Manipulate, manage, and never get caught with your hand on the power switch."

Hunter laughed softly. "Every culture has its version of a dragon lady."

"There's a reason. Patriarchy creates them every time." Lina took another long breath. "What's that smell?"

"Dust."

"No, not that. The flowery one."

"Plumeria. My uncle won't pay to have the house dusted, but there's a gardener to pamper the greenery."

Lina thought about the army of workers who attended the Reyes Balam estate. It was something she had taken for granted as a child. As an adult on her own, she appreciated the luxury of the estate and understood that it went two ways. The men and women of the nearby villages had steady, lifelong work on the estate, money to feed their children and to celebrate their religion. Celia sponsored the brightest kids through high school. The ones who had ambition she sent to college or technical school, whichever the child chose. Reyes Balam depended on the villagers and they depended on Reyes Balam.

"Uncle Danny claims he hates all the

flowers that my aunt planted and loved," Hunter said. "But after she died a few years back, he hired someone to keep the flowers alive."

"He loved her," Lina murmured, wondering what it would be like.

"Still does." Hunter pulled the sheet off the low, Danish Modern couch. The smell of dust rose, then settled beneath the perfume from outside. "But you'd have to shove glass splinters under his fingernails to get him to admit it. I used to think that was funny. Now I understand."

"You loved your wife," she said.

There was a taut silence, a near-silent rush of breath, and then Hunter spoke in a neutral voice. "I got Pauline pregnant when I was eighteen and she was seventeen." He smiled thinly. "Sometimes the party lasts longer than the party hat."

Lina waited. Hunter didn't show anything on his exterior, but she sensed the cost of every word he said.

"Little Suzanne was the light in my life," he said after a moment. "Four years later Pauline told me I wasn't Suzanne's sperm donor. Her boyfriend was out of jail and she wanted a divorce so she could live with the man she loved. I didn't want to let go of Suzanne, but I believed a child had a right to live with her father and mother. The three of them lived on alimony and child support until the drugged-out son of a bitch met a long-haul rig head-on at over one hundred miles an hour. The trucker got a few broken bones. Pauline and Suzanne died instantly. Her lover took a week to die. I hope he hurt like hell on fire every second of it."

Lina didn't know what to say, so she simply watched Hunter methodically tear off more slipcovers from the furniture.

"I didn't particularly love my wife, but I loved my little girl," he said finally. "How about you? Any great loves in your life?"

She had to swallow several times before she answered. His neutral voice and seething emotions made her want to weep.

"No," she said. "No loves great or small. Living north of the border for seven months a year and south of the border the rest of time . . ." She shrugged. "When I was old enough to live on my own, I was too hooked on the thrill of the digs to worry about spending quality time on anything else."

Silently Hunter folded slipcovers and put

them in a tiny hall closet. He wasn't about to say the truth out loud: he was glad she hadn't found a man, married, and settled down before he had ever known her.

Lina studied the furniture. Unlike life, it was all clean lines and smooth surfaces. The colors were solid earth tones and blacks, as if the clock had stopped at a very fashionable 1954 and never started again.

"The bedrooms are back here," Hunter said. "We'll need to get into town early and buy clothes and supplies."

"And then what?"

"See what my ICE contacts and my uncles come up with."

"I should be at the family estate soon," Lina said. "I promised Mother and Abuelita."

"I'm looking forward to seeing your family home."

Silently she absorbed the fact that Hunter assumed he was going with her. She started to object, but didn't. Everyone was always harping on how she should bring a man home to meet the family.

Hunter was all man.

"No argument?" he asked.

"We have to assume the objects came from the Yucatan," she said.

"Looks like it. More important, the tools who tried to grab you came from there. Right now I'm as worried about you as I am about Jase."

Lina gave Hunter a startled look. "Jase is in more danger."

"He's under guard in the hospital. His family is under guard. He's safer than you are."

"Under guard?"

"I talked to Stu Brubaker, Jase's boss. I told him straight up that he had sent Jase blindfolded into a firefight, and if anything else happened to him, Brubaker's political ass was on my firing line."

She looked at Hunter's eyes and saw the predator she had always sensed beneath his easy movements. It didn't worry her. Life had taught her that it was better to have a predator with her than against her.

Predators were strong enough to be gentle.

"I bet the boss didn't like that," Lina said.

"From me, no, but he got to the bottom line even before I called. He put the guards on Jase and his family. Right now Brubaker is backdating files to make it clear that Jase was officially working undercover for him on a very politically sensitive project."

"Wasn't he?"

"In a back-door kind of way. The files make it up front, which means that Jase was shot in the line of duty. Uncle Sam will take care of the bills. Every last penny of them. If Jase comes out of this injury less than one hundred percent, he'll get full disability whether he stays in the field or not. Jase's choice."

She cleared her throat. "Sounds like you and Brubaker had quite a chat."

"In our family, we call it a come-to-Jesus talk. Brubaker's a good man underneath the bureaucracy. It shook him hard to see Ali and the kids. Reminded him that more than an attaboy from the vice president was at stake in this sorry game. And Brubaker's plenty savvy enough to know that his career is gone if he doesn't take real good care of Jase."

"So he won't fire Jase over the artifacts even if they aren't found?"

"Not while I'm on watch. Brubaker and I have a Mexican standoff on that subject. If my guess is right, he's quietly twisting arms to get his hands on some objects that are close enough to pass at the repatriation ceremony. Since we're talking truckloads of goods already slated to be handed over, and there was no hoo-ha over Jase's artifacts in the first place, it should work."

"Then you don't need me anymore. Jase's job is safe." Lina's voice dried up as she looked into Hunter's eyes. They were intense, focused solely on her.

Hunter shook his head. "Sweetheart, you couldn't be more wrong. You're not going anywhere alone until I know who and what this El Maya dude is. He pulled the trigger on your kidnapping. And Jase."

"My family has bodyguards," she pointed out. "Everyone with money in Mexico does."

He nodded. "Ever think that some of the money your family has might not be clean, and that's a reason for you to worry and for men to be after you?"

She bit back her first response, which was a snarling denial. Finally she said, "I've never believed that my family was involved in anything truly illegal."

Breathing in Lina's scent, Hunter waited.

The silence drove her to speak. "Celia

sometimes lives on the thinnest edge of legal, but she knows how not to fall off. My father could make a fortune skimming artifacts, but he's too obsessive about them to let them out of his hands. As long as the family supports his digs, he has no reason to risk the black market for money. Being in charge of a dig is all Philip really cares about."

"Okay. Abuelita sounds a little old to be actively involved in the illegal artifact or drug trade."

Lina smiled. "Especially when I call her *chichi,* which is Mayan for 'grandmother.' She's my mother's grandmother."

"Anyone else?"

"If you researched the family, I'm sure you know Carlos was a small-time drug dealer/user back when he was called Carlitos. Abuelita put a stop to that little rebellion. Carlos cleaned up and began doing manual labor for Philip on the digs. When Carlos was old enough to be respected and respectable, he took over running the family cement business. Ultimately, he became a successful cross-border businessman and a respected amateur Mayanist." Lina faced Hunter directly. "Am I missing anyone on your mental suspect list? Just give me their names and I'll tell you what I know."

"Simon Crutchfeldt," Hunter said.

She blinked with surprise but didn't miss a beat. "One of Celia's best clients. He both collects and resells."

"Reputation?"

"Depends on who you talk to," Lina said.

"I'm talking to you."

"I don't like him professionally or personally."

"Has Crutchfeldt ever been arrested?" Hunter asked.

"Not that I know of."

"Would he be a likely receiver of Jase's missing artifacts?"

"He's too smart to keep them," Lina said. "He's not obsessive like Philip or true collectors."

"How about being a go-between?"

She let out a long breath. She really didn't like some of Celia's clientele. People like Crutchfeldt were why. "It's possible that Crutchfeldt is a middleman for illegal transactions."

"Anything is possible," Hunter said. "How about probable?"

Lina felt like she was being harried into a corner. "All right. Yes. My mother deals with some despicable people. Crutchfeldt is one of them."

Callused male fingertips brushed over Lina's lips. "Easy, sweetheart. I'm not attacking you or your family."

"It sure feels like it."

"Nobody's one hundred percent pure," he said. "Nobody. Once you accept that, life gets a lot easier."

"Tell that to Caesar's wife," she shot back.

Hunter's smile was a flash of warmth stroking her.

"Such beautiful eyes," he said, "hot as sin and sweeter than an angel. I'm sure glad you aren't married. Real glad."

Lina felt the ground shift under her feet. His words, the touch of his fingers on her lips, his smile, everything about him kept her unsettled.

"Hunter, what are you doing to me?"

"Not near as much as either of us would like." Reluctantly he withdrew his touch from her soft, warm lips. "Damn. We're both too tired for what I hope you want."

Deliberately she looked at the fit of his jeans. "You don't look too tired."

"I should be. The last two weeks have been hell. Except for you."

"Go to bed. I'd hate to have you fall asleep before the, er, main event."

Hunter's laughter was even warmer than his smile. She couldn't help laughing, too.

Then his mouth was over hers, his arms pulling her against every hard inch of his body. She hadn't known she was still cold until she felt his heat. She gave herself to his kiss, the hot strokes of his tongue, to him. He tasted of night and coffee, salt and man, a storm in the tropics. Her fingers clenched in his hair, holding him closer, afraid he was a dream that would vanish between one breath and the next.

"This is stupid," he said finally against her lips.

"I know." She burrowed closer, nipping his chin.

With a groan, he stepped away from her. "Help me, here. I'm trying to do the right thing."

She licked her lips. "You felt right to me." Then she shook her head like a dog coming out of water.

"Feeling bushwhacked?" he asked wryly.

"Yes. What is it about you? I'm not like this. I don't just jump into a man's arms because I like the way he looks."

"I'd love to take credit for it, sweetheart, but it wouldn't be true. Adrenaline is the most underrated drug on the market. Worse than booze for tempting people to break their own rules. So I'll make you a deal. You look at me like that in the morning and I'll jump you right back."

She closed her eyes, carefully not looking at him. Then she sighed, knowing he was right. "Tomorrow." It felt like forever to her.

His glance went over her like ghostly hands.

"To hell with it," he said, pulling her back to him. "It's already tomorrow."

# CHAPTER TWELVE

LINA CAME TO HUNTER EVEN AS HE PULLED HER closer. She breathed out his name when her mouth found his, seeking. The perfume of plumeria and their own scents and the smell of the ocean mixed into something primal, hot, like their kiss. She wasn't used to wanting a man like this, mind and body savagely insisting, explosive heat and chills and a moan that she couldn't believe was hers.

"Be sure, sweetheart," he said hoarsely after he broke the kiss. His mouth nibbled and nipped over her beautiful cheekbones, her lips. "You're so vulnerable right now."

"And you aren't?" she challenged.

Her hips moved over his erection, setting fire to everything.

"I've been hard since the first time I saw you." His voice was more a growl than words. "You get to me like no one since . . ."

"Pauline?"

Deliberately his teeth closed over Lina's full bottom lip. "We were teenagers. More hormones than brains. The way you reach into me as an adult scares me almost as much as it turns me on."

She pulled back a little, just enough to see his eyes clearly. Black rims around the iris, shards of silver and blue of every shade radiating out from the pupil, an intensity that staggered her.

"It's the same for me," she said. "I need you in too many ways. I don't know how to handle the other needs, but this one . . ." She arched into him again. "This one can be satisfied."

Hunter's smile was slow and hot. "We sure can try."

He looked at her for a long moment while the air crackled between them, lamplight poured over them, and bright dust motes pulsed around them with each breath. The electric dance of the pulse in her neck and the smell of her skin filled him as surely as Suzanne's death had emptied him. Suddenly everything inside Hunter was too strong, too much to be held by his skin. He needed something else surrounding him, holding him deep.

He needed Lina.

His mouth pressed hard against hers, as demanding as his arms pulling her so close they breathed each other. His fingers ran though the black tide of her hair and he groaned with the perfection of her—hot, woman, his.

Lina's fingertips dug into Hunter's back as they fought a sensual battle for control of the embrace. Neither won. Both won. His skin beneath his shirt was tight, hard, yet supple over muscles in a way that shouted he was male. She gloried in it, demanded it, let her hips move against him, and shuddered at the wonder of it. When one of his legs shifted to press between her thighs, breath hissed in. Hers. His. Both.

He turned and braced her against the wall even as her arms locked around him in demand. Their mouths ate at each other, sucked, savored, devoured, needing more and always more. She tried to say something, anything, but all she managed were throaty sounds of hunger and pleasure.

"You—I—we—" Her mind scattered when he bit her neck with exquisite care.

"Oh yeah." His voice was deep, hoarse. "Us. Damn, sweetheart. It's going to be so good. You want us straight up now or in the bed as fast as we can get there?"

She gave him a dazed look, eyes huge and dark with gold flashing unexpectedly when the light caught her just right.

"God, you're beautiful," he said roughly.

"I—it's you." She shook her head and fought to breathe. "Bed. I can barely stand up."

"Your knees hurt?" Hunter asked, concern shadowing the fire in his body.

"What knees?" she asked with an odd laugh. "It's not the bruises making me shaky. It's you."

He bent to kiss her hard and deep, but stopped. If he started here, they wouldn't get to bed the first time. Hell, maybe even the second.

He breathed out a rough word. "You're killing me here."

She glanced down his body and smiled, feeling less shaky, less blindsided by the heat burning through her.

"Those jeans look tight enough to bruise." Lina's hands reached for the steel buttons on his fly. "Let me see if you're hurt."

With a strangled laugh, he grabbed her hands and led her down a short hallway. The bedroom was like the house, small. Or maybe it was the bed that took up more than its share of the room.

Before Lina could draw a breath, Hunter dropped her in the middle of the mattress and followed her down, landing over her in a sprawl of muscle and heat.

"Gotcha," he said.

She smiled and slid one hand between their bodies to find him, rub against him, digging her fingernails into denim, flesh hot and hard beneath, and his breath shuddered. "Gotcha right back."

"I'm trying to slow down."

"I'll tell you if you go too fast."

"Promise?" he asked.

"Yes."

She barely got the word out before his long fingers had the business jacket off her shoulders and down to her elbows. He tugged her blouse out of the matching slacks. She tried to help him, but kept getting distracted by her own need to get his clothes off so that she could enjoy him. The fact that her jacket was around her elbows didn't help. She felt her bra suddenly loosen and then his mouth was on her, licking and nibbling at her breasts. When he sucked one nipple into his mouth, her back arched and she twisted beneath him.

Reluctantly Hunter released her nipple, his tongue teasing every bit of the way. "Too hard?"

"Get me out of this damn jacket," she said, trying to work the sleeves down her arms.

"You sure?" Hunter looked at her full breasts framed by her pushed-up blouse and her crumpled jacket. Her dark, hard nipples swayed with each breath, each movement. "You look damn good just the way you are."

He leaned down and nipped gently, then sucked her deep.

"Jacket," she gasped.

He lifted his mouth. "Can't."

"Why?"

"Your hands are in my jeans."

She made a startled sound and realized he was right. Both of her hands were inside the waistband of his pants, rubbing over the thick crest that was even now damp with his hunger for her.

"Help me, Hunter." Her voice was breathless, needy.

He reached down with one hand and tugged at metal buttons. Suddenly her fingers had freedom to move over his full, aching length.

"That wasn't what I meant," she said breathlessly. "But it's good."

Hunter groaned at her hungry caresses. Then he moved fast, stripping off her jacket and blouse, sending them flying with her bra onto the floor. He lowered his head again to the curves that had aroused him from the first time he had sensed them beneath the prim professor clothes.

"Your boots are still on," she said.

And her hands circled his erection, squeezed, and approved from base to tip.

"Keep that up," he said, "and they'll still be on when I'm inside you."

"Too fast?" she asked. Her voice was like her hands, hot and teasing.

"Just warning you."

"Just enjoying you," she said.

Then, slowly, she released him. He shuddered and forced himself to be reasonable.

"Boots," he growled. "Will you strip while I undress, or are you shy?"

"I was. Before you."

Her eyes became even more heavy-lidded. She toed off her low shoes and opened her tailored pants. Before she could lower the zipper, Hunter had kicked off his boots and was shoving his jeans over his feet. His underwear and shirt followed. By the time the narrow waist of her pants reached her curvy hips, he was naked, watching her.

And she burned, watching him in return. Slower now, she shimmied out of the bottom of her pantsuit, feeling a little embarrassed and a lot aroused by the stark male hunger in his eyes. His eyes never left her as he ripped open a foil packet from his jeans and put on a condom. Her simple underwear caught in the pants fabric. She lifted her hips and tugged harder.

"Darn my big butt," she said between her teeth.

"Big? Hell, no." His hands swept off her tangled clothes and kneaded the curves in question. "Sweetheart, you have the most amazingly perfect ass I've ever seen. Makes me want to . . . bite."

He leaned down and did just that, sucking hard, his mouth leaving a brand against her rich skin. She cried out in surprise and pleasure, then in shock as his mouth moved lower.

"I—can't," she said, writhing beneath his hungry tongue. "I've never—"

Turning away from the shy feast he'd barely tasted, he kissed the inside of her thighs and murmured, "Next time. Or the time after. I want you like I've never wanted a woman. All of you, sweetheart. Everywhere. Everything."

Lina moaned at the same time a rush of liquid heat left her core. Before she could draw another breath, he came back up her body like a storm tide, covering her, tumbling her around and around, entering her, engulfing her. She hung on to him with her arms, her legs, her mouth, everything she was, moving as he did, giving and taking and demanding. Then she cried out as her body bowed in an arc of passion that turned her inside out, breaking her and remaking her with each wave of release.

Hunter locked deep inside her and rode her orgasm until he could no longer hold back his own. Release pulsed and racked him until he was empty, fulfilled, and knew only her. Breathing hard, he licked the slow tears from her cheeks.

"Did I hurt you?" he asked.

"No. You . . ." Another wave rippled through her. Deep inside, she clamped down on him, milking him. "So good."

"Amen." He shuddered as he felt her caressing him, holding him sweet prisoner.

When she was finally still, he rolled aside. He knew he should separate their bodies and get rid of the condom, but he felt too damn good to move.

"This could be addictive," he said against her skin.

Her breath sighed out and her hands stroked the slick heat of his back. "I'll risk it."

Reluctantly he pulled out of her. She made a disappointed sound.

"Condom," he said.

She mumbled something and snuggled under the covers while he disposed of the protection.

"Shower?" he asked, turning over and reaching for her.

"Sleep." She burrowed close to him, skin to skin.

He pulled the bedspread over them and was asleep before his head hit the pillow. So was she.

HUNTER AWOKE AS HE HAD SLEPT, A SENSUAL tangle of heat and flesh, female and male. He watched the sun spill across Lina's face. Dark hair, eyelashes black half circles against her creamy brown skin, her lips full and red. Her beauty made his heart ache. They had reached for each other again and again during the night and he still wanted her. Knowing that she wanted him in the same way was a miracle he was still trying to absorb.

He looked at the digital clock on the small bedside table. It was early, but tourist towns worked long hours. Crutchfeldt and his staff should be awake. From what Hunter had found out about the man, he was up at dawn and lying in the sun like a lizard until the sun went down. All work was conducted at poolside.

The clock told Hunter it was time to get

going, to find out who El Maya was and make sure he would never threaten Lina again.

But all Hunter wanted to do right now was sink into Lina so deep they would never be separate.

Caught between what he should do and what he wanted to do, he forced himself to slide slowly from the bed. The room was warm, not only with the day but with a whole summer's worth of heat still captured in the cinder-block walls. He retrieved his cell phone from his jeans and went to the living room with long, silent strides.

The first call he made was to the nurses' station on Jase's hospital floor. Ali had told them that he was Jase's brother, so getting information wasn't a problem. A nurse reassured Hunter that Jase was doing well, a lot better than expected. His condition had been upgraded to good.

Relief went like wine through Hunter's system. He savored it for a moment before he went to the living room, where his computer had been plugged in for a charge. The workstation in the corner of the living room was mildly messy and quite dusty. He booted up his computer and read quickly—e-mails from contacts answering his queries, and from his uncles concerning background checks.

Snakeman had been deported in record time.

The body count at the second death house was up to eleven, but only a few of them had had their hearts removed.

**Why them? Why not the others, too?**

No one had any answers, or even hints of answers. None of the gangbangers who had been arrested had talked. They didn't know nothing from nothing. Each one of them had claimed he was just couch-surfing at a friend's place and he'd been arrested for no reason but racism.

**And rats have wings covered in booty dust.**

The dead janitor had a mother and two teenage sons living across the border. When questioned, they admitted that the sun rose in the east and set in the west. Other than that, they only knew that the dead man had sent money south and now he didn't. The grandmother was terrified. The grandsons were sullen.

The crime-scene photos an ICE contact

had sent were as ugly as Hunter's memories.

Nothing new.

Certainly nothing useful.

The quick, but not careless, background checks his uncles had done yielded little more than Hunter had already guessed or known. Lina's parents lived separately. Other than a single scandal about artifacts that were sold from Reyes Balam land without government approval and a public drunkenness charge when Philip was a freshman, there were no flags in any official files that had been searched.

Carlos had indeed been a bad boy in his early teens, but had grown into a citizen in good standing with two governments. There were bare hints that he might be unofficially working for and/or being investigated by DEA. Not surprising for the Mexican-born CEO of a cross-border enterprise in these days of open narco warfare. Two ex-wives, serial mistresses, no children.

De la Poole was single, upper class, educated, connected, and clean.

Crutchfeldt not so much, but he didn't

have any official black marks on his record on either side of the border. Reading between the lines, there was a good probability that he snitched on illegal artifact middlemen from time to time, which kept the cops off his own back.

*Probably taking down competitors, just like the narco "informants" do,* Hunter thought.

He kept reading swiftly. Everything he saw made him believe that if he was going to find the shooters and whoever they worked for, it wasn't going to happen north of the border. The people in the United States who might have answers were dead or lawyered up. As much as he'd like to beat the truth out of the gangbangers, he had a gut feeling that any real knowledge had been lost when Snakeman went south.

Hunter punched up a travel Web site and checked availability. From the look of it, they'd just added more flights to Cozumel to accommodate the holiday-season demand. He booked several different flights on the family business account, paying extra for fully refundable tickets.

**Wonder how good the Reyes Balam bodyguards are?**

Good or bad, Hunter would find out. He wasn't letting Lina out of his sight until he was sure she was protected. Then he'd go hunting in Mexico, where rules were different and life was lived a lot closer to the bone.

But first, Crutchfeldt.

"Hunter? Where are you?"

Lina's voice floated through the silence like music. The huskiness told him that she had just awakened.

"I'm just checking on Jase."

"How is he?" Her voice was as anxious as Hunter had been before he talked to the hospital.

"Good," Hunter said. He left the computer and headed toward the bedroom. "Out of danger, stable, recovering faster than anyone expected."

"That's wonderful!"

When he got to the bedroom, she was propped on one arm, the sheet loose around her breasts. She was more beautiful to him than ever, goddess and woman, as deep inside him as his heartbeat. Deeper.

She watched him with equal intensity.

"Don't look like that, sweetheart," he said huskily.

"Like what?"

"Like I have another party hat in my jeans."

"You're not wearing any jeans," she said, her glance traveling over him with open approval. "Not wearing anything, in fact."

"Neither are you." He bent over and kissed her slowly, thoroughly. "We'll take care of that when we get some new clothes, Padre style. Do you think Crutchfeldt would like to show us through his collection?"

Lina slowly surfaced from sleep and the desire that curled lazily through her. "Crutchfeldt? Why would he?"

"You're Celia's daughter. You've heard so much about his collection from your mother, and you happened to be in the area, yada yada."

More awake with each second, Lina thought about it. "He just might. He's arrogant, proud, and likes to be admired for his scholarly and discriminating taste."

"Perfect. Bat those fantastic eyelashes

at him, make suitable cooing sounds, and generally take his mind off of business."

She grimaced. "Ugh. That's what Celia does. The batting and cooing."

"Works, right? Men can be very simple creatures."

"Simon Crutchfeldt is odious," Lina said. "He'd wade through blood to get to an artifact he wants."

Hunter's eyes narrowed. "Literally?"

"There are rumors . . ." Lina's long fingers moved restlessly over the bedspread. "But rumors aren't truth. I don't want to spread lies, even about him."

"Are those rumors about a network of grave robbers and bloody middlemen who funnel artifacts through Mexican government contacts to Crutchfeldt?"

She gave him a startled look. "Yes. How did you know?"

"Part of any security operation is gathering information. My uncles are good, and two of my cousins are even better. Born hackers."

"Crutchfeldt." She said it like a curse. "I can't decide whether to shower before or after we see him."

Hunter laughed. "I'll shower down the hall while you decide. Because if I shower near you, we'll be in severe danger of making a baby."

Lina got up. She'd much rather have lured Hunter into bed or into the shower, and knew he felt the same way. But she didn't object aloud. They had used up all available condoms. Not that she didn't want to have a baby. She did. Just not nine months from today.

Sometimes being an adult sucked.

Hunter watched Lina's beautiful butt disappear into the bathroom. He grabbed his clothes, showered, and dressed quickly. A circuit of the house told him that nothing had changed since the last time he'd made the rounds shortly before sunrise. Nobody parked nearby, nobody sitting on a porch, no new tracks in the yard or near the Jeep.

He went back to the house and straight to his uncle's safe. The combination hadn't changed. He opened the safe, counted out a wad of cash, took one of the penlights, removed his boot knife, and left a note with his signature. He ignored the handguns and the cache of emergency documents in case he needed a new identity. He shut the safe, smiling.

Lina thought he was paranoid. His uncles *were* paranoid. They had learned the hard way.

By the time Lina had showered, taken what stains and wrinkles she could out of her clothes, and dressed, Hunter was through fixing breakfast in the kitchen. Toast, peanut butter, orange juice, coffee. Not a feast, but it would keep them going until they found better. They both ate quickly, knowing the meal was meant to be fuel rather than a dining experience.

"No complaints?" he asked as he ditched their paper plates.

"About what?"

"The food."

"We don't have freezers and green-grocers and chefs at dig sites," she said, rinsing out their coffee cups. "We eat what we pack in and are glad to have it."

He laughed, slid his arms around her waist, and nuzzled her freshly washed hair. "I really like you, Dr. Taylor. You don't need perfumes and spas and boutiques to make you sexy."

"A night with you would make any woman

feel sexy." Then Lina heard her own words and blushed.

"Same goes. I'm lucky I can walk this morning." His teeth closed gently on her ear, his tongue savored delicate skin. "Now march that beautiful ass out to the Jeep before I get us into trouble."

She took the warning and grabbed her purse on the way through the living room. She noticed the open computer, but left it for Hunter to deal with.

By the time Lina was strapped in the Jeep, Hunter was striding out, computer under his arm. All male, lithe as a big cat, he took her breath away. With a mental curse she reined in her thoughts.

"Do you want me to call Crutchfeldt now?" she asked as Hunter got into the driver's seat. "Or do you just want to show up at his door?"

"You have his number?"

"He called me a few weeks ago, looking for Celia." Lina pulled her cell phone out of her purse. "He should still be in the memory."

"Good. We're on a short clock. Get us in as soon as possible."

Hunter drove into the commercial section of town while Lina made nice on the phone with a man she would rather have sliced into fishing bait. He admired her professionalism and hated that he'd asked her to do something so distasteful to her.

But then, holding a bloody rag over a bullet wound was nobody's idea of nice either. She'd done it without a flinch or a complaint.

*I like her way too much,* Hunter realized.

Then he smiled. She was the best thing that had ever happened to him, and he knew it. At some level it scared him. He knew what loving and losing was like.

Hell on earth with no time off for good behavior.

"In an hour," Lina said, closing her phone. Like her mouth, her voice was flat. "He just oozed anticipation over meeting Celia's oh-so-respected Ph.D. daughter."

"Good work, Lina. Thank you."

"If it will help Jase and his family, I'll deal with the devil."

"And you," Hunter said quietly. "Don't forget your own safety in this. I sure don't."

Her mouth tilted in an upside-down smile, but she didn't say anything.

South Padre Island unrolled on either

side of the Jeep—malls and tourist traps sprouted like crazed mushrooms alongside new two-story houses and smaller homes that had been in place for some fifty years or more. The damage from the last hurricane was a memory gathering dust in storerooms along with the plywood used to cover windows during a blow.

It was cooler than Houston, but not by much. The morning sun caused heat ripples to rise out of the asphalt. The breeze from the sea was more hope than actual relief. The swampy smell of the slow-cooking wetlands to the west of them pervaded the humid air like invisible smoke.

Hunter parked near a strip mall with a gas station on one side and a discount chain clothing store in the middle, and tourist traps full of trinkets on the other end. In between was everything including a liquor store, a fake fingernails "spa," a check-cashing company, a small grocery store, and a Thai restaurant.

He reached into his wallet and pulled out cash. "Get what you need."

"I have credit and debit cards," she said.

"Cash only. No paper or electronic trail

until we have to show our passports to get on the plane to Cozumel."

Lina stared at him with wide, dark eyes. "Were we followed to Padre?"

"Not yet, but there's no point in leaving a trail of bread crumbs."

"You're paranoid."

"I'm alive."

She let out a breath. "I'll pay you back."

"Whatever. Just make sure you have two changes of clothes and shoes you can run in. The sort of stuff you could wear on a dig or at the beach. Are you on birth control?"

She blinked. "Ah, no."

"Good. Then we don't have to worry about getting you meds."

"I can live without vitamins, but a toothbrush would be very nice."

"No problem. We'll pick them up along with a new stock of party hats."

Lina bit back a smile. "Colors and flavors?"

He gave her a hot sidelong look. "Want to pick them out?"

She blushed, laughed, and shook her head.

With a last check around the parking lot, Hunter followed Lina into the store. His eyes were never still, but he didn't find anything that set off his internal radar. They hadn't been followed past the edge of Houston and nobody seemed interested in them now.

Once in the store, Lina quickly found what she needed. Even if she'd been the shopping kind of woman, this wasn't a place she would have lingered. But shopping was something she did when she had to, with a list in hand. Like jaguars were climax predators, she was a climax shopper; she knew what she needed, she took it when she saw it, and that was that. The only thing she tried on was a pair of all-purpose athletic shoes. She threw in socks and a pair of flip-flops and took her armload back to where Hunter waited, watching other shoppers.

"Your turn," she said.

He went through the men's department with an efficiency that spoke of long experience with unexpected trips and living off the land. His last selection was a cheap sports duffel that could hold everything the two of them had selected. He paid for the lot at one of the checkout stands. As soon as they were in the parking lot, he put everything into the duffel and headed for the market.

"Get what you need. I'll get snacks, water, and trail food. And party hats." He smiled at her. "We'll change in the gas-station restrooms after I get fuel."

She looked startled. "We aren't going back to your uncle's house?"

"Depends on Crutchfeldt."

Lina tilted her head and watched him with unblinking, bittersweet-chocolate eyes. "I don't understand."

"If he gives us a good lead, we'll work it wherever it goes," Hunter said. "If somebody picks up our trail, we're on the next plane to Cozumel. Keeping you safe is my first priority. Finding who's after you is second."

# CHAPTER THIRTEEN

GROUND FOR BUILDING ON SOUTH PADRE Island was scarce—protected wetlands thrived on one side and the ocean on the other. Simon Crutchfeldt's house was built on enough land for a small subdivision. The two-story faux Georgian clashed with the wild tangles of scrubland that surrounded all but the ocean side of the estate. The manicured lawn looked as improbable as big boobs on a skinny woman. The tall, showy rows of sabal palms lining the approach and clumped artfully around the house looked plastic.

In north Houston, the estate would have

been right at home. On Padre, it was slightly ridiculous.

"Sometimes money doesn't talk," Lina said. "It screams."

Hunter drove up the long drive and parked his Jeep in an area set aside for guests. Beyond a waist-high hedge of gardenias there was a pool set in several acres of landscaping and tilework. Although it was just after nine, their host had told them to look for him there.

"I'm along for the ride," Hunter said, turning off the Jeep and pocketing the key. "You just pursue your area of interest and don't pay attention to Mr. Harold Kerrigan. That's me."

"Is Mr. Kerrigan the strong, silent type?" she asked, smiling.

"Yeah. But if I start coming on like a middleman for a collector with an agenda, you be your usual shocked, upright academic self. I'm just a guy you've dated once or twice and you're really pissed off. That way, if the ivory tower ever gets wind of this charade, you'll be covered."

"You make me sound like a prig."

"Caesar's wife, sweetheart. 'Prig' is the first word in the job description."

Lina didn't like it, but said nothing. Hunter was hardly the first person to notice her determined respectability in all things archaeological.

They climbed out of the Jeep and headed toward the pool area. Like everything else about the estate, the pool was oversize, made of hand-set tiles, and surrounded by greenery more suitable to Hawaii than Padre. Tropical flowers made the air dense with perfume.

"Mr. Crutchfeldt has never heard of too much of a good thing," Hunter said in a low voice. "Including the man himself."

A huge human lump of white and tan lay on a mahogany chaise along the turquoise pool. He wore white cotton shorts and a short-sleeved shirt, also cotton. The buttons had been undone over his stomach, revealing a swath of tanned and hirsute flesh.

"Carpet doesn't match the drapes," Hunter muttered.

Lina looked from the body bristling with gray hair to the very dark hair on Crutchfeldt's head. His Panama hat was perched rakishly in a style more suited to Indiana Jones than Indy's father. Crutchfeldt was a thoroughly senior citizen chasing a youth he was never going to catch.

"Good morning," Crutchfeldt said, rising and buttoning his shirt. He had the voice of a man who liked to talk, supple and able to go for hours without needing a break. "Lina, it's so good to finally meet you in the flesh. Your mother talks often about your expertise." His big hands engulfed hers. "And who is your . . . friend?"

Lina introduced "Harold Kerrigan" while trying to get her hands back without being insulting about it. Despite the heat of the day, Crutchfeldt's hands were cool, almost clammy. She wondered if he had some kind of circulatory problem. It could explain why he spent so much time in the sun.

"It's good of you to interrupt your day to show us your collection," Lina said, tucking her hands in the pockets of her cargo shorts.

"Oh, my pleasure, dear. It's always nice to share conversation with someone who can appreciate the, ah, peculiarities of my little hobby." Crutchfeldt's smile was as oversize as he was.

Hunter smiled back amiably. He'd met

Crutchfeldt's type before, big and over-bearing, teeth like an all-white concert piano's keyboard. Some of those men had been vain and stupid. Crutchfeldt might be vain, but he wasn't stupid. His blue eyes watched the world with sharp, predatory intelligence.

*Maybe this won't be a complete waste of time after all,* Hunter thought.

"I'm guessing that you both would prefer to chat inside, yes? One man's paradise is another's overheated hell. Follow me, if you please."

Crutchfeldt didn't wait for their agreement. He led them at a brisk pace up a wide, paved walkway toward large double doors hanging open to the sun and heat.

The entryway was dry and cool, illuminated only by indirect sunlight and a row of small windows just beneath the line of the ceiling. Pottery was arrayed on pedestals along either side of the gallery-size hallway.

Lina didn't need the discreet brass plates to know that the artifacts were pre-Columbian, Maya, mostly of highland origin, and worthy of a wing in anyone's museum. The intricacy and balance of the blackware vases were riveting. Each one told a story of a king's rise and fall, glyphs highlighted in red pigment leading from one to another to yet another, whispering of a past beyond her reach. But not beyond her yearning.

Lina kept falling farther and farther behind as Crutchfeldt led the way down the hall. The quality of the artifacts fascinated her. The thought of sunlight from the open doors and high windows accidentally touching them made her wince inside.

**Why is Crutchfeldt displaying these pieces so recklessly? Not even a velvet rope or a UV-glass case to shield them.**

And yet, the very lack of pomp and boundaries made the artifacts all the more remarkable. They existed as they had been created to be, nothing between the eye and the object.

Reluctantly Lina admitted that such a method of display was brilliant, even if it made her academic soul flinch.

"Something to eat or drink?" Crutchfeldt asked, watching Lina.

The expression on his clean-shaved face

was that of a cat being stroked. Though Lina hadn't said a word, she obviously was entranced by the hallway artifacts.

"No, thank you," she said without looking away from the glyphs detailing the triumph of Sky Macaw over Jaguar Lily Pad. The vase was staggering, with just enough imperfection and wear to make it genuine. "We've imposed on you enough simply by being here."

Crutchfeldt smiled as Lina's gaze was drawn back to the vases. This smile was less flashy, more real.

"These are extraordinary," she said, gesturing around the hall. "Highland Maya. Late Classic. A few Terminal Classic. Just . . . incredible. I've never seen such quantity and quality."

"Lifetimes of passion," Crutchfeldt said. "My family has been exploring and collecting Maya goods for almost two hundred years."

*Convenient,* Hunter thought sarcastically. *Predates any antiquities laws in the world. Provenance? No problemo, your honor. My great-greats brought it home for Christmas.*

Lina wanted to say that these pieces

belonged in a museum, open for scholarly study, as well as the awe of people who barely understood the meaning of the word "Maya." But she bit her tongue. Her thoughts, however, were uncensored by the rules of civility.

**I can't believe these pieces are all legitimate exports. Mexico would want some of them for its own museums.**

"I'm surprised you got export permits for goods of this quality," she said before she could stop herself.

Crutchfeldt's laugh was loud enough to rattle pottery. "My dear, even leaving aside the long collecting history of my family, everything has a price, and every person. Surely your mother taught you that?"

Lina managed a noncommittal sound and hoped Crutchfeldt didn't notice how still she was. "I spent more time at the digs with my father. My, uh, passions were closer to his."

"They are very much appreciated," Crutchfeldt assured her. "Without people like you and your father, I'd find very little worthy of being added to my collection. And your mother, of course. A shrewd businesswoman after my own heart."

*Does he mean to be insulting?* Lina asked herself. *Or, like Philip, does he see the world only through the prism of his own desires?*

"Lots of stuff," Hunter said casually. "Is this it?"

Lina looked at him in disbelief. *Stuff?*

Then she realized that he was deflecting attention, giving her time to rein in her temper.

"Sorry about staring at the blackware," Lina said. "I don't mean to be rude."

"My dear, your fascination is a compliment of the most truthful kind. Whenever you're ready . . ." He gestured toward the room opening off the hall.

"I'll never be ready," she said honestly, then bit her lip.

Crutchfeldt gave her a smile, the genuine kind. "Such open interest is as fascinating to me as the artifacts are to you."

Hunter watched. *Yeah, lap it up, you bastard. Innocence and honesty are rarer in this house than sunshine in hell.*

But Hunter was a better poker player than Lina. He hid his response to the fact that the artifacts compelled him almost as much as they did her. He also hid his antagonism toward Crutchfeldt. Instead, Hunter let himself soak in the artifacts. There was something heady about being in the presence of so much beauty from a time and a place that would never come again. He didn't have Lina's detailed knowledge of the artifacts, but he shared her visceral appreciation of them.

"Of course, openness and acquisition don't always walk in each other's footsteps," Crutchfeldt said.

Hunter watched the man watching Lina. Crutchfeldt's voice was casual, but his glance was probing her as intently as a dental pick looking for decay.

*Don't let him rattle you, sweetheart,* Hunter thought urgently.

She kept staring at the artifacts.

"I'm sure," Crutchfeldt added, "that you understand how easily reputations can get tarnished when dealing with artifacts today."

Lina waved her hand without looking away from a magnificent blackware vase.

Hunter allowed himself to breathe. Lina knew the game Crutchfeldt was playing. She didn't like it one damn bit, but liking wasn't part of the game. Staying in it was.

"Acquisition is such a delicate process," Crutchfeldt said. "Naturally, everything I have purchased since the onslaught of antiquities laws has been well documented and watermarked by all necessary authorities."

"Of course," Lina said absently.

Hunter knew her well enough to understand that she was speaking through clenched teeth. But her shoulders were relaxed, her stance outwardly casual as she turned toward her host.

"I only wish other collectors were as thorough as you are," she said. "Celia has nothing but praise for your discrimination and finesse."

Smiling, Crutchfeldt drew Lina into the larger room at the end of the hall. "Your mother is a woman of rare archaeological understanding and political expertise."

Lina made a sound that said she was there.

Hunter watched from beneath hooded eyes. He wanted to hug her, to tell her she was doing a great job, but that wasn't in the rules of the game they were playing.

Carefully Lina didn't look at Hunter. Being civil to the odious Simon Crutchfeldt was like jamming splinters into her flesh. All that kept her from screaming at her smug host was the memory of bullets powdering concrete near her feet and the cruel intimacy of a man's blood welling up between her fingers.

"You've barely looked at the headdress, my dear," Crutchfeldt said. "It's one of my most recent acquisitions from your mother."

"I'm still . . . overwhelmed by the blackware," Lina managed.

Dutifully she looked where her host was pointing. Her breath came in hard and stayed there, aching, until she thought she would explode.

The artifact was extraordinary. The wood, clay, and what were probably woven fastenings looked far too new to be as old as her gut said they were. The colorful feathers were frayed and brittle, possibly as old as what they decorated. The band of glyphs that would have wrapped around a priest's skull were in the style of other finds from Reyes Balam lands.

What Lina could see of the glyphs told of power and prestige, nobility and the jaguar, god-smoke and knowledge. All that was missing was the distinct glyph signifying Kawa'il.

"Celia sold this to you?" Lina asked neutrally.

"She knew it would require a particularly discriminating buyer," Crutchfeldt said.

His tone said that "discriminating" was another word for "unquestioning."

Silently Hunter wondered why Crutchfeldt was baiting Lina. Perhaps it was simply because he could. Perhaps he had a more sinister purpose.

Servants moved behind them at the far end of the hallway, cleaning house and calling in soft Spanish to one another about church and children, faithless men and the need for more money.

Hunter hoped no one was armed, but assumed some of the faithless men under discussion worked as guards for their host. As much money as was on display here required guarding. And weapons.

"You haven't seen this before?" Crutchfeldt asked Lina blandly, referring to the headdress. "Celia assured me it was from Reyes Balam land."

"I don't spend much time on the digs there anymore," Lina replied. "The glyphs are correct for artifacts we've found in the past."

"You're certain."

"As I'm sure you know," Lina said, her smile all teeth, "glyphs are as much individual art as shared cultural meaning. Rather like Chinese calligraphy, in fact. Uniformity wasn't prized. Elegance and originality were."

Crutchfeldt tried to say something.

Lina didn't let him.

"Each artist," she said, "took commonly understood symbols and raised them to new levels of communication and beauty. Meaning becomes transformed according to the position of a glyph or the choosing of one glyph instead of others that had similar denotations but different connotations. A noble could be subtly mocked by his glyph artisan, yet the skill in execution was itself a compliment to the noble's ego."

Hunter wanted to high-five Lina. Crutchfeldt looked like a cat being stroked just right. Praise the artifact, praise the discriminating owner.

Crutchfeldt had an unusual appetite for appreciation.

"I admit I don't really understand glyphs except at an aesthetic level," he said, but his confidence belied his words. "The style on that mask is particularly pleasing to me. Celia assures me it is the hallmark of Reyes Balam goods."

Hunter tried not to think about how prime it would feel to introduce Crutchfeldt's smug face to the marble floor.

"The surviving priest-kings were blessed with the cream of the surviving artisans," Lina said. It was her classroom voice, confidently neutral in the face of a student with an agenda.

"And the Reyes Balam family has been blessed with an industrious archaeologist and a politically astute businesswoman," Crutchfeldt said.

*Still digging for something,* Hunter thought, disgusted. But he wasn't worried about Lina. If she hadn't lost her temper yet, he doubted she would.

Lina managed a nod that might be misunderstood as gracious. "Celia is an inspiration."

"Yes, indeed," Crutchfeldt said. "She

understands that there are some collectors who value ownership more than legal hairsplitting in the name of artifacts that belong to a culture and time that predated today's nations and absurd notions of 'owning' antiquity."

With a sound that could have meant anything, Lina moved farther into the room. Crutchfeldt followed her like a yapping shadow. Hunter was two steps behind both of them, alert to any change in Lina's demeanor in the face of the abundant, priceless artifacts. But she went through the room with the polite ruthlessness of someone who knew exactly what was in front of her and was looking for something else.

When Hunter finally became certain that none of the missing artifacts were in view, he decided to throw some reality into all the scholarly conversation and self-congratulation.

"If there were certain pieces that you'd heard rumors about," Hunter asked, "where would you go looking for them?"

Crutchfeldt gave him a measuring look. "What kind of artifacts?"

"Late Terminal Classic. Yucatec," Hunter said with a trace of impatience, and an accent that could only be described as worldly. "The real deal. Unique and bloody valuable."

Crutchfeldt blinked and looked at Lina.

She looked back at him.

"Hmmm," Crutchfeldt said. "Sometimes a collector simply wants a piece that will bind all the other pieces together. Take this mask." He pointed to a clay mask beautifully inlaid with stone and shell. "This is a contemporary piece, bought and sold as such. Celia found it for me because she knew that I required just such a piece."

Lina didn't bother to hide her surprise. "She didn't mention that she was handling modern art."

"If she knows one of her very good customers is looking for a specific artifact and hasn't yet found it on the market, she will sometimes find a modern version made to very exacting standards," Crutchfeldt said. "The process requires proper tools, proper materials, and very skilled artisans."

A sense of relief crept through Lina. She had noticed several artifacts in Crutchfeldt's gallery whose condition was simply too good to be believed. Part of her had feared that her mother had been involved in fraud.

"You're not alone in filling holes in your collection," Lina said. "Even in the later days of the Maya empire—and I use the term loosely, for it was less an empire than a culture that changed through time—there were artisans who were specifically commissioned to replicate items hearkening back to the kings of old. Perhaps it was a way to invoke the gods of a more powerful time, before the culture began to unravel."

"Fake is fake," Hunter said.

"Even fakes tell us about the culture they came from," Lina said. "Yet I understand your point. Authentic artifacts are always preferable."

"So who would you go to for something authentic to add to your collection?" Hunter asked the older man. "Something you've heard rumors of but have never seen."

"Well," Crutchfeldt said, "Celia Reyes Balam, of course."

"What if she didn't have it?" Hunter said. "Where would you go next?"

"If she doesn't have it," Crutchfeldt said, "no one does."

"What if it came up the chain from grave robbers?" Hunter asked casually.

Lina made a startled sound. "Then it would be illegal."

"Yeah," he said, without looking away from Crutchfeldt. "So who would be likely to have it and how would you get in touch with them?"

"That's—" Lina began.

"I'm curious," Hunter said, not looking at her. "If you aren't, go sit by the pool or something."

She didn't hide her irritation. "Mr. Crutchfeldt might not like the implications of your questions."

"You insulted?" Hunter asked Crutchfeldt.

"I'm a collector," the other man said easily. "In order to pursue the avenues you are implying, I'd have to want the item very, very badly. I don't have many such items, but . . ."

Hunter and Lina followed Crutchfeldt's glance to a nearby alcove where a teardrop light illuminated half of what appeared to be a stone knife. It was chipped, dull and unremarkable, broken into three pieces. Yet on closer inspection, the sheer craftsmanship glowed through the haze of time and damage. On one of the blade segments there was a small marking. Hunter looked at it curiously, sensing that he'd seen the sign or something much like it on one of the pieces that Jase had lost.

With a soft sound, Lina edged closer. The broken knife had a sigil on it, a marking that made her pulse spike. The mark was a cluster of four triangles all turned point out, with jagged lines joining them on their longest side.

Four corners joined by lightning.

**Kawa'il.**

"Where did you find this?" Lina asked tightly.

"If memory serves, it probably wasn't from a sponsored dig," Crutchfeldt said, his smile more a hint than a real curve. "It's from a lowland site in the Yucatan. Post-Classic period. It actually postdates the official end of the Maya civilization, though there were many artisans who kept working with motifs and styles—"

"Yes, I know," Lina interrupted curtly. "Which site."

It was a demand, not a question.

"South of Padre," Crutchfeldt said blandly.

She took a careful breath before she looked at Hunter. "You never wanted to date me. You just wanted to use me."

He stared back, unreadable.

"I'll be in the Jeep," Lina said.

Without another word, she left.

"Sensitive young lady," Crutchfeldt observed. "It's that Latin temperament."

Hunter wanted to roll his eyes. "I haven't noticed that Latins have the only tempers on earth. If you're talking temper, I come from Vikings via Genghis Khan."

For the first time, Crutchfeldt looked at Hunter with real interest. "What do you want?"

"I have a client who wants to acquire artifacts from that period." Hunter nodded toward the alcove before he added a deliberate echo of Crutchfeldt's words. "Very, very badly."

"You should have dated the mother, not the daughter."

"Celia doesn't have access to the artifacts," Hunter said.

"And you think I do."

"That's why I'm here."

Hunter reached into one of the pockets

of his cargo shorts and pulled out the pictures of the missing artifacts. The photos showed the rubs and creases of careless handling, but the artifacts were quite identifiable.

Curious, Crutchfeldt leaned closer. Hunter yanked back the photos and held them like a poker hand, close to his chest. With an impatient sound, Crutchfeldt plucked one of the photos free.

A mask, shining like a smoking mirror, ringed with glyphs of power and death.

"Kawa'il," Crutchfeldt breathed. For an instant the avarice of a collector gleamed in his eyes. Then the businessman took over. "What is the provenance?"

"My client wants the artifact," Hunter said, "not the pedigree."

"I don't have either one."

Hunter had known that the moment Crutchfeldt looked at the photo with the eyes of a man who wanted, not one who already owned.

"Who would?" Hunter asked.

There was a long silence. Then Crutchfeldt sighed. "I rarely give advice, yet . . . Dr. Taylor's exquisite appreciation of my collection was very satisfying."

Hunter waited.

"There are grave robbers on Reyes Balam lands," Crutchfeldt said. "They take, but they don't sell to me or anyone I know. Their leader is more ruthless than your Genghis Khan."

"Who is he?"

"To speak his name is death." Crutchfeldt smiled thinly and handed over the photo. "I prefer life."

"Is he Mexican?"

Crutchfeldt nodded.

"Is he called El Maya?"

Crutchfeldt's eyelids flinched. "Good day, Mr. Kerrigan. You know the way out."

Hunter wanted to argue, but he knew a losing hand when he held it. With a smooth motion, he pocketed the photos and walked out, leaving Crutchfeldt and his collection behind. The sun seemed unusually hot and vital after the mansion.

Lina was waiting in the Jeep, frowning and biting her lush lower lip.

Hunter got in and started up the engine without a word.

"Well?" she asked after they were beyond the long drive.

"I'm thinking."

"Think out loud."

Hunter almost smiled despite the anger and adrenaline racing through him.

**To speak his name is death.**

He didn't want Lina anywhere near that kind of danger.

And he didn't have any choice. Houston hadn't provided safety for her. They had been followed to the city limits and would have been followed farther if Hunter hadn't lost the tail. The fact that it was a lone follower had told Hunter that it wasn't a law enforcement agency breathing down their neck. Even the dumbest cop knew that if the subject was alert, a single tail didn't get the job done.

"Hunter?"

He flexed his hands on the steering wheel. "If I thought it would do any good, I'd turn around and hold Crutchfeldt's face in the toilet until he talked."

Lina's eyes widened in shock. "Did he recognize the photos?"

"As in knowing where they were now? No. But he knew they came from Reyes Balam land."

"How?" she demanded.

"Same way you did, even when you didn't want to. A good eye."

"What did he say?"

"That there are grave robbers on Reyes Balam land."

She made a low sound. "I was afraid of that."

"Apparently their leader is a real piece of work. Crutchfeldt was afraid to even say his real name. When I asked if it was El Maya, he invited me to leave."

Lina's long lashes lowered and she went back to nibbling on her lip. "Celia would have to know about him, wouldn't she?"

"You own a lot of land. Rough land. Remote. Tough to get around in. I doubt if anyone could keep track of every acre."

"But if she's buying from grave robbers, she'd know."

Hunter's hands flexed on the wheel again. He didn't like any of this, and everything he found out made it worse.

"Crutchfeldt said the grave robbers weren't selling to anyone he knew." Hunter's voice was like his eyes, edgy.

Relief and frustration went through Lina.

She was glad to hear that her mother wasn't trading in black-market artifacts, yet the information didn't get them any closer to the person who was.

The sounds of the tires and the road and the occasional cry of a seabird filled the Jeep.

"You're thinking again," Lina said finally.

Hunter didn't answer.

"I can't help if you close me out," she said.

"I'm trying to decide between taking you to my uncles for protection—"

"No," Lina cut in. "I don't want to drag anyone else into this."

Hunter glanced at her and knew that she was hearing bullets chewing through concrete, seeing Jase's blood.

"They know how to protect themselves," Hunter said.

"So did Jase."

Hunter let out a low curse. "I don't want you hurt."

"Neither do I." She looked out the window. "I'll go to Quintana Roo. My *abuelita* will be happy and I'll be safe. My family members might live in the jungle outside

Tulum, but they're fashionable enough to have motion sensors, guards, and a panic room. All the latest in rich, paranoid chic."

"What about the grave robbers? And El Maya?"

Lina shrugged. "They've obviously been in place for some time and nobody in the family has been harmed. Houston was where I was attacked, not the Yucatan. As for El Maya, it could be an American nickname, not Mexican. Besides . . ." Her voice died.

"What?"

"I've never felt watched in Quintana Roo."

Hunter looked at his watch. "We have just enough time to make the next flight out of Brownsville."

# CHAPTER FOURTEEN

THE SEA TURNED TURQUOISE IN THE AFTERNOON light, slapping lazily against the shore. Tourists were thick on Cozumel's ground. Expensive hotels gleamed like high-rise wedding cakes, absorbing light and spreading a shimmering kind of brilliance. Backpackers and students swarmed over the other end of the tourist rainbow, sprawling on peripheral beaches or gearing up for jungle hikes. High or low, liquor flowed, oiling the machinery of commerce and culture.

Lina breathed in deep and bloomed like an orchid. Part of her was very much at home with the heat and humidity. A whole childhood of memories poured through her—prowling the jungle, diving and swimming in the cool cenotes that pocked the land, and eating exquisitely spiced food.

"Do we have time to eat?" she asked Hunter as they walked to a cheap rental-car place. "I'd kill for a good *pibil*." She laughed. "Even a bad one."

"I'm supposed to meet Rodrigo at a place called La Ali Azúl on Avenue Escobar. I'm sure they serve a mean *pibil*. But you'll be eating alone."

"Why?"

"My contact isn't a nice man," Hunter said. "That's why he's useful."

"Is meet-and-greet with unsavory people another aspect of your job, like being an occasional bodyguard?"

"Information is our most important resource," Hunter said. "Nothing quite like knowing the weather on the ground to help an operation go smoothly."

"In other words, yes," she said.

"Savory people aren't much help when your business comes down to stopping crooks."

Hunter rented a Bronco with Quintana

Roo plates. Back-road dust had been ground into the floor mats. They drove off the rental lot and followed the Cancun-Chetumal highway south to the meeting place. The countryside was wild with greenery spilling across the limestone plateau and punctuated with even more shrines than Hunter recalled. But then, he hadn't spent a lot of time in the nicer areas of the Yucatan.

"You remember this many shrines?" he asked.

"Not really," Lina said, frowning. "Even at this time of year, it seems like an excess of religious fever, more than I've ever seen. A lot of Maya crosses."

"Maya?"

"The cross was a significant symbol to the Maya before the Spanish ever came. Some texts are interpreted as meaning that the native cross represents the plane of the ecliptic, the time when the Long Count calendar ends."

"Twenty-twelve again."

She shrugged. "The division of time was a Maya preoccupation. Rather like modern civilization, with our obsession for minutes and hours and nanoseconds. The

Maya measured bigger chunks of time, but the intent was the same. What can be measured can be controlled."

"Culture rules," Hunter said. "Like us."

"What do you mean?"

"We've been speaking Spanish since we landed."

She looked startled, then amused. "You're right. I didn't even notice the transition. Maybe Abuelita will forgive you for being a gringo after all. You're very fluent."

"Your great-grandmother sounds like a pistol."

"Oh, she is. I swear she'll outlive us all."

Hunter smiled at the affection in Lina's voice.

The vegetation thinned and low buildings sprawled to either side of the divided road. Most of them were made of stucco over cinder blocks and other masonry, fenced off with wrought iron, and walled in by a succession of low billboards and electrical lines like blood vessels nourishing every building.

The mirrors were clear. Nobody had followed them from the airport. Nobody on the highway seemed interested in them.

"You feel watched?" Hunter asked Lina.

"No."

"Let me know if that changes."

"I'm impressed," she said.

He checked the mirrors automatically. "By what?"

"You not only don't laugh at feelings, you actually listen to them."

He smiled thinly. "Anyone who doesn't won't last long in the jungle—or on the wrong side of city streets."

Hunter parked as close as he could to the address Rodrigo had given him. Not that Rodrigo had been willing, especially when Hunter had awakened him in the middle of the night. But it was smart not to give Rodrigo too much warning.

The population around them was almost one hundred percent native, which meant that Hunter stood out. Too tall. Eyes too light. Skin not dark enough. Lina's coloring mixed better with the locals, but she was taller than the men.

*Rodrigo would have to choose a native backdrop,* Hunter thought unhappily. *Probably to punish me for insisting on the meet.*

The smell of the ocean and cooking grills filled the tropical air. A little early for lunch, but not too early for a cerveza. Outdoor seating was casual—scattered plastic chairs, a bench, or just squatting on your heels. The morning open-air market had already closed. Other places were doing a slow, steady business. Bikinis and backpacks had been replaced by straw hats and loose guayaberas—shirts—in pale shades of tan and cream and blue. If Hunter had had one, he would be wearing it.

Nobody paid particular attention to him—gringos weren't that rare—but Lina drew some quiet regard. It wasn't her sweet figure people noticed, but her face. Men who swaggered elsewhere stepped out of her way. Children stared, only to be softly scolded by their mothers.

"They're treating you like royalty," Hunter said very quietly in English.

"I have Reyes Balam bone structure," Lina said, shrugging. "They see it in the ruins every day."

"Huh. Thought it was your height and beauty."

"Height, yes. The rest is in the eye of the beholder and all that."

"So your family is well known," he said.

"Think of the American Kennedy family, but with five hundred years or more of royalty."

"You don't act royal."

"When I look in the mirror, I see Dr. Lina Taylor, American. That's who I am. The rest is, quite literally, history. Something for Abuelita and Celia to care about."

"But not you," Hunter murmured.

"Like I said, I'm American by choice."

Hunter kept watching, but other than the subtle deference Lina took for granted, he saw nothing out of place. Nothing to make his neck tingle.

*Maybe we left that behind in the U.S.,* he thought.

But he wasn't going to bet Lina's life on it.

"See the café two buildings down and across the street?" Hunter asked.

"Yes. They have good *pibil*. At least they did the last time I was here."

"I wouldn't have guessed it was your kind of place."

Lina tucked a stray bit of hair behind her ear. She had twisted the heavy mass on top of her head and held it with a worn silver clip from her purse. "I was feeling adventurous, but not enough to actually eat inside. I got my *pibil* to go."

"Get a table toward the center. That way I'll be able to keep an eye on you."

"Where will you be?"

"Wherever Rodrigo is, usually near the back exit."

Lina chewed on that while she crossed the street and went into the café. Small, sturdy tables and people to match. She took a scrap of a table toward the center.

Ten steps after her, Hunter walked in. He saw Lina and Rodrigo in the same sweeping glance. As expected, Rodrigo was in a dark corner. Not that darkness was difficult to find—after the tropical sunlight outside, the café looked like a cave.

A shrine overflowing with offerings of liquor and flowers filled one corner of the bar. The shrine looked a lot fresher than anything else in the café.

The interior lights hadn't been turned on, probably to help the patrons ignore the dirt and flies. A weak glimmer of light marked the video jukebox screen. The music was a mix of urban Mexican pop and songs glorifying narco traffickers.

Rodrigo was slumped over a row of empty shot glasses and a small pile of lime rinds, squeezed and scavenged for every drop of juice. A stubby unlit candle waited on his table amid salt scattered from tequila glasses. An empty bottle of Herradura lay on its side next to the candle.

Without a word, Hunter dragged a vacant chair over and sat next to Rodrigo at the scarred table, where the view of both exits was clear.

"I told you not to come," Rodrigo said in a soft, slurred voice.

"And I told you I was coming anyway."

Hunter palmed two hundred-dollar bills and gave them to Rodrigo under the table.

"If your info is useful, there's more," Hunter said.

"That's why I'm here, for now. I'm flying out tonight. Adios, Yucatan. I'll come back when the crazies go away."

"What's with the shrine in the back corner?" Hunter asked.

Rodrigo stared at the dark blue tequila bottle lying on its side. "Ask the crazies."

"You're the one I'm talking to." *And you're the one I just laid two bills on.*

Rodrigo looked up from the bottle. Even

in the gloom, his eyes were red. "All the old demons are coming out of the jungle. All those old stories people don't believe until they see the blood and then they believe or die."

"Narcos?" Hunter asked.

The other man slowly shook his head. Gloomy light slid like oil over his ragged beard, which looked more accidental than a deliberate statement of manhood.

"You really going to Tulum like you said yesterday?" Rodrigo asked.

"Why?"

"Bad shit going down there. Worse than here."

"Who's behind it?" Hunter asked.

"Dead men don't talk. I'm playing dead."

"For two bills, get a little life."

Hunter watched Lina from the corner of his eye. She was chatting with the waitress. Both women were animated, smiling. Lina lit up the room like a fire, but the people who had watched her when she walked in were back to shoving food in their mouths.

Rodrigo stirred uneasily and stared back at the tequila bottle, a kind of pretense. If he didn't meet Hunter's eyes, he wasn't really talking to him.

"There are fires at night," the Mexican said. "Big fires in the jungles. People going missing. Parts of people showing up later."

"Q Roo cartel? Narcos?"

Sighing, Rodrigo shook his head like he was mourning the empty tequila bottle. "Those temple sites outside of Tulum that I told you about? The ones that were gonna make me and my compadres rich?"

Hunter shrugged. Rodrigo and his buddies always had a get-rich plan. And he always ended up looking at the bottom of a tequila bottle in some dive.

"Yeah. So?" Hunter asked.

"They are all dead. Hearts cut out, blue palm prints on their bodies. They were cut up, man. Cut. Up."

For the first time, Hunter realized that Rodrigo's numb stare came from more than tequila. He had the shell-shocked look of a man fresh from a bloody battle.

"You sure they didn't just cross the wrong narcos?" Hunter asked very softly.

He didn't need to glance around to discover if anyone was listening. He'd been checking since the instant he sat down. So far, all the patrons were more interested in chow than nearby chat.

"When the cartels kill," Rodrigo said, head down, in a voice too low to for anyone but Hunter to hear, "they either hang the body from a bridge or shove it into a mine shaft or a mass grave."

Hunter nodded.

"But not these bodies," Rodrigo said, a sheen of terror coating his eyes and throat. "My compadres were prepared with great care, in the old way."

"Sacrificed?" Hunter asked very softly, remembering a filthy Houston basement.

Rodrigo looked up. "If you go to Tulum, you keep away from the temples. You stay in the town. You don't stand near nobody you don't know like your own cock. Then you watch the skies and the jungle and your back. Death is out there. A hard death."

Hunter palmed another Ben, put his hand on the table so that only Rodrigo could see the money. "You hear of anyone called El Maya?"

Rodrigo wanted the money enough to sweat, but he shook his head. "I don't hear nothing."

For a moment Hunter thought of pushing hard. But he'd known Rodrigo long enough to know when he would talk and when he wouldn't. Apparently the subject of El Maya was taboo here as well as in Padre.

Yet it wasn't a name in his uncles' files. Since most narco types thrived on notoriety, the usual sources of information were coming up dry.

"What else can you tell me about Tulum?" Hunter asked finally.

Rodrigo took the bill and sagged back in his chair, looking haunted. "You ought to talk to that pretty lady so lonesome a few tables over. The one you came in just behind. She has that Tulum look about her. The eyes. See the regal shape? And the cheekbones. She's a queen among peasants."

"You're drunk."

Abruptly Rodrigo's eyes sharpened, making Hunter wonder if he'd really worked his way through a bottle of tequila after all.

"You believe what you want to," Rodrigo said clearly yet very softly. "Maybe I see you again sometime. Maybe you die on the twenty-first. Bet you wish you believed me then."

"Did your buddies get anything out of the temple sites?"

"A hard way to die."

"No artifacts?"

"Not a peso," Rodrigo said bitterly. "That's why I waited for you. Need money to fly. Another three, and you can have my pistol. Clip is full."

"Two. If I like what I see, and you throw in your boot knife, I'll give you another hundred."

Rodrigo started to protest, then decided he wanted money more than an argument. He reached beneath his loose shirt and pulled out a flat black pistol, square and chunky. He passed it under the table to Hunter.

A casual look, plus the feel of the gun itself, was all it took for Hunter to know what was for sale.

**H and K Mark 23, SOCOM variant. Nice piece.**

"Is it hot?" he asked quietly.

Rodrigo gave a liquid shrug. "Isn't it always? But I never fired it. I never had a chance to. They were dead when I got there."

Under the table, the pistol and another hundred changed hands. Hunter concealed the weapon the same way Rodrigo had, under his shirt at the small of his back. The gun felt hard, heavy with potential death. Slowly Hunter's body adjusted to the presence of the weapon. It wasn't the first time he'd worn gunmetal under his shirt, but he'd never learned to like it.

"Knife," Hunter said softly.

Rodrigo bent, pulled the knife out of its boot sheath, and gave it to Hunter. A flick of his thumb tested the edge. Clean, hard, sharp. Hunter passed over another hundred.

"Two hundred more if you talk about El Maya," Hunter said very softly.

"If you get out now," Rodrigo said, "I'll see you again."

"Three hundred."

**"Vaya con Dios."**

With that, Rodrigo stood and walked out the back door, staggering just enough to make any watchers believe he'd been drinking hard.

No one looked up as he passed. No one seemed to care.

After a few more minutes of watching, Hunter went to Lina's table.

"Your 'friend' is a drunk," Lina said.

"That's what he wants you to think," Hunter said softly as he sat near her. "You try to roll him, you get a nasty surprise. Being tricky is how he survives."

The waitress came over and put down a huge bowl of *pibil*. Steam that smelled of lime and orange and pork rose up. Bowls of corn tortillas and various condiments followed. She put plates and silverware along one edge of the table, smiled, and left.

Lina took a big bite of *pibil* and looked around as she chewed.

"See anyone you know?" he asked. "Tulum isn't that far away."

"No. I just can tell by the faces that I'm in the Yucatan. Undoubtedly, our workers have relatives here, but I don't know them by name."

"But they could know you."

"Recognize me, yes," Lina said. "Knowing me is a lot different."

"How does your neck feel?"

"Calm," she said, licking up a stray bit of spicy sauce.

"Let me know when that changes." He looked at the piles of food. "You mind sharing?"

"I was thinking of you when I ordered. The sauce in the green bowl will eat through steel. You should love it."

Hunter smiled and went to work. He ate with excellent manners, and quickly enough so that if something interrupted the meal, he wouldn't leave the table hungry. After a few minutes, he looked up. Lina was watching him, smiling in a way that said she liked seeing him enjoy the Yucatec food she loved.

"You really do feel at home in Mexico," she murmured.

"As long as I don't have to eat the worms at the bottom of the mescal bottle."

She laughed and relaxed.

Hunter ate and kept an eye on the patrons.

He didn't want any nasty surprises. But so far, so good. The café was filled mostly with chattering people, laughter, and the occasional off-color toast from a table of five young men. Their clothes labeled them as workers, not narcos.

"Rodrigo called you a queen among peasants," Hunter said.

"Now I know he was drunk."

Hunter looked at Lina's strong, high cheekbones and large, almost almond eyes. She had an extraordinary face. Haunting. Timeless.

"Rodrigo has seen more than his share of Maya ruins," Hunter said. "He lives well over the line between angels and devils. If I hadn't saved his life a few years back, he wouldn't even talk to me now. He's a hard man to frighten. Yet he's running scared, heading for the airport and the hell away from Tulum."

Lina paused just before she took a bite. "Why?"

"Some tomb robbers he knows got themselves killed." He took a big bite and watched her.

She chewed, swallowed, prepared another bite. "If I don't think of their families, I can say they had it coming."

But her dark eyes said she was thinking of wives and children, parents and siblings and cousins who would have holes torn out of their lives.

"They died the old-fashioned way," Hunter said, swallowing the *pibil,* which was as savory as it was nuclear. "As a sacrifice. Body paint, no hearts, sacred glyphs on the skin. You know of anyone local who might take ancient history a little too seriously?"

"There are many full-blooded Maya here," Lina said. She really wanted to eat more, but wasn't sure her stomach had room. "And out in the small villages . . . well, you saw the cross of corn and the like. Catholic sure, but only on Sundays. The rest of the time, they live with the gods of their ancestors."

"All the Maya are pagans underneath?"

"No. They're like every other people. When it comes to any religion, they have fanatics and unbelievers and everything in between. But as a rule, the closer the jungle, the closer the old gods."

Hunter nodded. He'd noticed the same thing himself.

"What's next?" Lina asked, giving up on the savory food.

"De la Poole. You sure you don't want to call him?"

"I'd rather surprise him."

"What if he isn't there?" Hunter asked.

"Someone at the museum will know where he is."

Without appearing to, Hunter took another look around the café. Nothing had changed. The locals might admire Lina's royal looks, but they weren't groupies.

"You finished?" he asked.

"Stuffed."

He threw some money on the table. "Let's go."

They left the café and went to their rented Bronco. Hunter didn't see anyone who cared. Lina's neck didn't itch.

"I'll drive," she said. "You check on Jase."

Hunter didn't argue. She knew the way better than he did.

The Cancun-Chetumal highway was two lanes of divided road in either direction. There was jungle crowding on both sides, giving only rare glimpses of the ocean that was close enough to taste as an underlying tang in the air pouring through the open windows.

Hunter changed chips in his phone and

called Jase at the hospital. As he waited for the call to connect, he noticed a flash of color on the right. Another shrine over-flowing with flowers and offerings of food and liquor. By the time he was put through to Jase's room, a second shrine flashed by on the left.

To Hunter's shock, Jase answered his own call.

"'Lo?"

"Jase, it's me, Hunter. What are you do-ing answering the phone?"

"Enjoying being alive." Jase's words were a bit slow and slightly breathless, but otherwise strong. "'Sup?"

"I took Lina and ran south."

"Good. Bullets hurt like a bitch."

"Brubaker off your ass?" Hunter asked. *He damn well better be.*

"Off it? Hell, he's kissing it. Dude's roll-ing in artifacts."

"What?"

"Got 'em all back and then some," Jase said.

"Wait, are you telling me that the miss-ing artifacts have been returned, obsidian mask and all?"

Lina shot Hunter a startled look, then went back to driving. But she kept listening real hard.

"Close enough for government work," Jase said.

"Amigo, you're not making sense. I'll call later."

Jase kept talking. "Snake's lawyer delivered the box, from what I heard. Said he had a client with a dirty conscience. Now it's clean."

"Snakeman's lawyer coughed up the artifacts?" Hunter asked in disbelief. "Did the lawyer say where the artifacts came from?"

"Janitor stole them to pay Snakeman a gambling bet."

"Bullshit."

"Yeah," Jase said, "but it grows mighty fine roses. Even if they aren't what you planted."

Ali's voice came in the background, talking to the nurse. It was time for Jase's pain shot.

"Give it to me while I'm on the phone," Jase said.

Hunter knew he'd have to talk fast. Pain meds tended to hit Jase like a landslide.

"So you have artifacts," Hunter said,

"even if they aren't exactly what went missing?"

"Yeah. They're in real good shape, too. Like new."

"And Brubaker's buying it?"

"Ouch! You using a twelve-gauge needle?" Then, "Brubaker ain't looking in no gift pony's mouth. ICE will be front and center at the re-pa-tri-a-tion ceremony. Gold star in my file. Maybe a raise, new title."

"Are you high?"

"Getting there. Damn, the drugs in here are prime. Hey, darling, c'mon over and give your big stud a kiss."

Ali's giggle came through the connection, then the sound of a kiss. Over Jase's muttered protests, she took the phone.

"Hunter?"

"Hi, Ali. Sounds like our boy is feeling good."

"The stuff they give him hits him hard and fast. Otherwise he wants to get up and go home."

"He said something about Brubaker."

"Whatever the boss was so upset about is over," Ali said. "I don't know the details, but Brubaker got his hands on a box of old stuff and he's doing the happy dance around Jase's bed. I don't understand any of it, but Brubaker can't say enough nice things about Jase."

"Huh." Hunter saw a riot of color whip by on the left side of the road. Another shrine. Rodrigo's words echoed in his mind.

**Death is out there. A hard death.**

And the locals were praying like hell that death didn't find them.

". . . out of danger," Ali said. "He's recovering so fast the doctors are amazed. He's in a regular hospital room now."

Hunter snapped back into focus. He smiled as a weight he hadn't realized was there shifted off his chest. "He always did heal fast. Give your big stud a kiss for me."

Ali snickered. "I'll be sure to tell him it's from you."

The instant Hunter turned off the phone, Lina said, "What's going on?"

"Someone returned the stolen artifacts, or something close enough that Brubaker doesn't care."

"That's . . ." Her voice died.

Hunter laughed without humor. "Yeah. But Jase is off the hook and recovering so fast the docs are smiling."

"So if we assume that the artifacts

and the kidnap attempt on me are connected . . ." she began.

Hunter waited.

"Because the coincidences are pretty
overwhelming otherwise," she added. "So
I should be safe now."

He didn't answer.

"Well, hell," she said.

"Pretty much. None of this makes sense.
Until it does, I'm all over you like fur on a
bunny."

A spark of color up on the right resolved
into another roadside shrine.

"Pull over," Hunter said. "I want a closer
look at that."

"And you want to make sure we're not
being followed."

"Two birds, one stone."

Lina slowed and carefully pulled off the
paved highway. They bumped to a stop ten
feet from the shrine. Unlike other parts of
the highway, no trash was scattered near
the shrine. The only bottles there were full,
offerings left by believers. The only paper
or plastic was in the flowers, though many
were fresh. The arms of the cross were
longer than was usual for a Christian
symbol.

The flowers were brilliant yellow and scarlet and purple against the white limestone crumbles of the roadside. The cascade of petals was interrupted by candles of various sizes and shapes. The cross was covered in snakeskin that the reptile hadn't shed willingly. Bright feathers were glued to the cross. They moved in the lightest breeze, like they were somehow alive, breathing.

"That's the fifth one of these that we've seen out in the open since Playa del Carmen," Hunter said.

"Normally you see a roadside shrine and they're for someone who died in a crash along the highway or something," Lina said. "They aren't really legal, but it's an old custom. They just appear overnight and gradually fade into the jungle."

"Whoever put this shrine out was pretty brazen. Or else drivers on the highway don't really care what happens on the side of the road. Must have a lot of accidents here."

"I don't remember this many shrines. And there aren't any pictures or names of loved ones." Lina rubbed her fingers together, as though trying to clean them. "Flowers don't smell like this. Like death."

"I was thinking that."

"This is creepy, Hunter. Can't you feel . . . something out here?"

The wind picked up, making the wall of vegetation rustle and shake as if something large slithered through the undergrowth. Wind whistled over the snakeskin, a sound like thin reptilian wings. The head of the snake appeared to be swallowing the cross from the top down.

For a moment everything felt dry, a forest fire or a desert riding on the restless wind.

"This is wrong," she said.

Hunter agreed. "Not a quaint little roadside shrine. Someone around here is really into ancient gods."

The snakeskin twitched in the wind, pulling like an animal wanting to be free.

Lina made a low sound.

"What?" Hunter asked instantly.

"This is an altar to Kukulcán. The cross isn't here to pay lip service to Catholicism." She shivered, though the temperature was warm. "This represents an ancient Maya belief system."

There was no photo or name to honor a relative killed along the highway. The only writing was crudely drawn glyphs painted on snakeskin or inked onto paper and tacked into place.

It was silent except for the random swish of traffic.

No one pulled off farther down the road. No one even paused. The intermittent parade of ancient cars and trucks was splashed with the shine of rich people's vehicles and the duller gleam of rentals.

Insects crawled among the shrine's offerings. Wind stirred restlessly, carrying the scent of old blood, old flesh.

"Roadkill?" Lina asked, wrinkling her nose.

"Smells like it, but I don't see any. Would the locals get upset if I looked more closely at the shrine?"

"As long as you don't deface anything, it should be okay."

Hunter went to the shrine and sat on his heels. Very carefully he lifted a mound of flowery offerings. Dull eyes stared back at him. The smell of carrion became overpowering.

"What is it?" Lina asked.

"Monkey head. Maybe a cat. Hard to tell at this point."

Her breath came in hard, coated with the odor of death. "Blood offering."

"Looks like it." Gently Hunter replaced the flowers and tried to ignore the memories of a basement where human blood had flowed red and dried black. The gun he had stuffed into the back of his jeans felt better than it had since Rodrigo had sold it to him. "You recognize any of the glyphs?"

Carefully she leaned down, breathing through her mouth in an effort to minimize the smell. "They're very rough."

He grunted.

"Blood. Power." She stood suddenly. The smell was making her stomach twist. "This shrine calls the powerful old gods, but most of all, the gods of knowledge and death. Kukulcán and Kawa'il.

"I was afraid of that. You think the others along the road are the same?"

"Not all of them. At least one had a picture nailed at the center of the cross, and the arms were shorter. That usually means a Christian commemoration of a dead friend or a family member."

"But most shrines were like this?" he asked grimly.

"Yes. Kawa'il. Death."

Hunter straightened swiftly. "Want me to drive?"

"No. I'm okay. Just . . ." She shrugged.

"Yeah, me, too. Wonder what Mercurio de la Poole thinks of this?"

"I'll be sure to ask."

Lina and Hunter got back in the Bronco and drove through a green tunnel of jungle punctuated by flaring shrines.

# CHAPTER FIFTEEN

"ARE YOU SURE YOU WANT TO DO THIS?" LINA asked Hunter after a silence lasting many miles.

"What?"

"Be here right now," she said bluntly. "You're used to dealing with people who are driven by money—kidnap, extortion, outright theft, that sort of thing. Jase is used to drug cartels and poor, ambitious civilians who want to find work by crossing illegally into the U.S."

Hunter saw a flash of color against jungle. Another shrine or altar or whatever the hell was going on.

"Whoever left that blood sacrifice," Lina said, "is different. He or she is owned by gods and a way of life you don't understand. What you think of as good or evil doesn't matter right here, right now."

"And you do understand?"

"I not only know the sources of Maya religion, I *feel* it. I was a child in isolated villages. I understand that spirits own the night, jaguars walk with kings, and humans live on the thinnest thread of approval from capricious gods."

"You're a believer?" Hunter asked.

She laughed, but it wasn't a sound of humor. "No. But I've *felt* believers. They're different. What repels us elevates them, brings them closer to the beating heart of divinity, the very breath of the gods infusing everything. We hear wind in the jungle or the cry of birds; believers hear gods, and they act on what they hear."

Hunter was silent, watching her, seeing both past and future in her striking profile. "So the blood and shrines aren't new to you?"

"No. But the intensity and amount of both is new." She tucked a piece of her unraveling hairdo behind her ear. Before she lifted her hand, the wind pouring through the open windows undid her work. "In Houston, I believed the messianic fervor around 2012 was a fad, a diversion for people who had too much money and too little life. But here . . ."

Hunter watched Lina's teeth sink into her lower lip and wished they were back in bed, where needs were clear and the celebration of life was direct.

"The altar we stopped at wasn't the product of some easy New Age belief," Lina said after a moment. "The altar was real blood, real flesh, real death. The giving of blood and the pain that came with it, the first and oldest sacrifice."

"So you're saying that the blood and flowers are a recognition of the turning of the Great Wheel, baktun, the end of the Long Count, of Maya time."

"To us, perhaps. To a believer it would be the beginning of a new world," she said. She slowed for an old pickup truck hauling a rickety crate of frazzled chickens in back. She went around the truck with a smooth surge of speed. "If there really is a resurgence of native Maya belief around here, then any calculations you make based on

New World power and drugs and money won't be valid. Someone you expect to do one thing will do something entirely different. The past won't be a predictor of the present."

"Gods change. Human nature doesn't." Hunter's hand stroked her tensed right arm in a slow, lingering caress. "I'm staying with you, Lina. Tomorrow night we'll celebrate the Maya baktun together with champagne or blood, whatever gets it done. Then we'll see who walks and who rides in the brave new Maya world."

She flicked a glance at Hunter. His face was as hard as anything she'd ever seen carved in stone.

And as compelling.

A THIN, HIGH HAZE HAD COVERED THE SKY WHILE the sun came closer to dropping into the jungle. The air was unusually dry for what was technically the end of the rainy season. Not desert dry, but not ocean-and-jungle humid either.

The Museo de Antropología de Tulum was located on the northern edge of Pueblo Tulum. It was as much a compound as a pure museum. Several modest residences were situated across a courtyard garden from the museum itself. The area was walled, with ancient stelae rising among the flowers. The museum's reception area had been designed like the anteroom to an ancient temple. Framed photos of local Maya ruins competed with colorful rubbings taken from a temple wall describing Jaguar Claw's victory over an ancient priest-king.

A black-haired woman dressed in a long skirt and a colorful native blouse stopped tapping on an old computer when the front door opened. With the ingrained training of a woman in Mexico, she passed over Lina and asked Hunter in soft Spanish how she could help him.

"Tell Mercurio that Lina Reyes Balam is here to see him," Lina said, stepping into a shaft of light from a high, vertical window.

The woman's eyes widened and she stood up with what could have been a subtle bow.

"But of course. Immediately." She hurried out through a side door.

Hunter waited until she was out of earshot. "Not royalty, huh? She didn't bow to me."

Lina rolled her dark eyes, but before she

could think of a comeback, a handsome man rushed out of a shadowed hallway and engulfed her in a hug.

"Lina, *querida,* you should have told me you were coming," Mercurio said.

His voice was as deep as his hair was black. Eyes almost as dark as his hair watched Lina with something that could only be called possessiveness. Like Lina, he was a mixture of Maya and European, an inch taller than she was and a lot stronger.

Hunter didn't enjoy watching Mercurio hug her breathless one damn bit, but he knew better than to show any emotion. Mercurio was making a statement. Now it was up to Lina to make one of her own. Impassive, Hunter watched her struggle politely to get some distance from Mercurio without being insulting about it.

"Sorry about the lack of notice," she said, finally managing to step back from the embrace.

"No, no." Mercurio held on to her hand and kissed it too long for politeness. "Such a sweet surprise you are."

Color appeared high on Lina's cheekbones, anger or embarrassment. She wasn't nearly as comfortable with Mercurio's affectionate display as he was. Nor did she like the way he was ignoring Hunter. Mercurio was usually polite to a fault.

She felt like a bone being mauled by a dog.

"Dr. Mercurio ak Chan de la Poole," Lina said crisply, "I would like to introduce Mr. Hunter Johnston. We're both very interested in the artifacts I mentioned when I called you."

Reluctantly Mercurio turned to Hunter with a meaningless smile. "Good to meet you."

Hunter murmured something polite and shook hands in the gentle Mexican way.

Mercurio had been north of the border. He ground down on Hunter's hand with enough force to establish machismo.

Hunter's smile didn't change. He waited patiently to be released. When he was, he slid his hand over Lina's and laced their fingers deeply together.

"You've come a long way from Texas," Mercurio said to Hunter.

"Lina knows I'll go anywhere with her."

She shot Hunter a look from under long, dark eyelashes, but kept her mouth shut.

She didn't want to insult Mercurio before she saw his new acquisitions.

"I would do the same," Mercurio replied coolly, "go anywhere for her." His dark eyes shifted to Lina, caressing her and ignoring Hunter like a buzzing fly. "What may I do for you, beautiful one? What has brought you all the way to my humble place of work?"

"Humble?" Lina's hand gestured to the timbered vault of the ceiling, and the Maya-inspired designs carved into the hardwood that must have taken hundreds of hours of exacting work.

"One tries," Mercurio said.

She smiled brightly. "You succeed. I know how valuable your time is, so I'll try not to take much of it."

"For you—"

She kept talking. Ruthlessly. "We'd really love permission to see your recent acquisitions. Perhaps you have some items that would be suitable for trade with my museum."

"But of course, *querida*." He took her arm and led her to the acquisitions room.

Lina kept hold of Hunter's hand like a lifeline. He decided that if Mercurio called

Lina *querida*—darling—one more time in that deep, possessive tone, there might just be an unhappy moment or three while Hunter shoved Mercurio's grasping fingers where the sun doesn't shine.

But only after Hunter got what he came for. He was liking better and better the idea that Mercurio was good for illegal artifact trading, attempted murder, and attempted kidnapping. At least Hunter's emotions liked the idea. His mind wasn't cheering quite as happily.

"Did you come down for Abuelita's birthday?" Mercurio asked, plainly not caring if Hunter could hear.

"I'm surprised you remembered," Lina said.

"This year, it would be difficult to forget. To have a Reyes Balam birthday on the day the wheel will turn is a magnificent thing, a source of much celebration. Some of the village people have prepared shrines."

Lina almost missed a step. Hunter steadied her with a hand at the small of her back. Then he nearly sent her to her knees with a slow, loving caress over her backside.

"Shrines?" she asked. Then she cleared

her throat and tried again. "Shrines with Abuelita's picture?"

Mercurio shrugged with a male grace that was unconscious.

Hunter considered tripping him.

"I look only at the flowers," Mercurio said. "From a distance, they are beautiful, yes?"

"You never got close to one of the shrines?" Hunter asked.

"The peasant beliefs are not mine," Mercurio said without looking away from Lina. "I am a civilized man educated in the civilized world."

"Have you heard that the people are getting fanatic about their gods?" Hunter asked. "You know, baktun and all."

"There are rumors." The distaste in Mercurio's voice was clear. "The villagers are very unsophisticated."

"What kind of rumors?" Lina asked before Hunter could. "Anything that might threaten my family?"

Mercurio's laugh was as richly masculine as his voice. "Their jungles might be short a few monkeys, but the villagers hold the Reyes Balam line in reverence.

Not quite gods, but close. Priest-kings, as it were."

"Priest-kings often came to a bloody end," Hunter pointed out.

"That was long ago," Mercurio said. "Like the artifacts in this museum. Beautiful reminders of a past that is no more."

Hunter thought of the blood-drenched basement, the stone altar with the face of a god brooding over it, shots echoing in a parking garage, and Jase's shirt with a terrifying stain of blood.

"Some people still take it seriously," Hunter said. "Like death."

"There are crazies in every society," Mercurio said.

"Have you ever heard of El Maya?" Hunter asked casually.

"Superstitions, but I've heard something. The peasants think he is a god."

"Yeah? Is he local?"

"He's a god," Mercurio said. "He's everywhere. And nowhere."

"I haven't heard of him," Lina said.

Mercurio made a dismissing motion with his hand. "El Maya is a combination of Robin Hood and the Grim Reaper. He's a hope and a fear. Hot air, I believe you Americans say."

"So you don't think he's real," Hunter said, remembering Rodrigo's silence.

"No," Mercurio said, focusing on Lina as he opened the door to the acquisitions room. "You have strange friends, *querida*."

Hunter wanted to show Mercurio just how strange he was—but not until Hunter was sure that he'd wrung all possible information out of the man.

Lina's breath came in swiftly as she saw the room beyond Mercurio. Shelves and tables filled every space. Most surfaces were covered by artifacts waiting to be cataloged.

"As I said, I need more help." Mercurio's tone was wry, but not apologetic.

Lina didn't take the bait.

"Good help is hard to find," Hunter said blandly.

Mercurio kept on acting as if he were alone with Lina.

She headed for the artifacts. There was a tug at her arm before Mercurio slowly, reluctantly let go. If she hadn't needed to look at his artifacts, she would have given him the kind of cold female shoulder that left ice burns.

Silently Hunter's glance raked over artifact after artifact, looking for something that matched the photos in his cargo pants.

Lina was looking just as intently. "Nice incense burner."

"Nice?" Mercurio laughed. "The censer is beautiful and you know it."

"Of course," she said, studying it.

The pottery's central motif was an intricate cutout of an idealized Maya skull, mouth open. Snakes wrapped around the cranial dome, heads pointed up to the heavens. The figure was repeated three more times around the pottery. The inside was black with smoke, probably from sacred copal, the hardened but not fossilized remains of tree sap. The outside showed traces of blue that could have been painted glyphs, faded now.

There was no piece missing in the censer that would match what Hunter and Jase had found in the murdered janitor's room. None of the glyphs had the squared, jagged lines, a sigil sacred exclusively to Kawa'il.

The blackware vases were perfect—suspiciously so to Lina, but it wasn't her collection, so she said nothing. Their glyphs were outlined in red. Kawa'il's sigil was absent.

Hunter absorbed each artifact in turn. The ornamental carved stones were new to him.

"What's their purpose?" he asked aloud.

"Perhaps good luck, perhaps simple offerings flung into a sacred cenote," Mercurio answered. "I haven't had time to translate the glyphs, which appear to be Terminal Classic on first look."

Hunter switched his attention to tiny pottery faces, misshapen and broken, as though cast aside. "These?" he asked.

"Supernatural faces," Lina said when Mercurio didn't answer. "Some of the many, many gods of the Maya. They look like imports from the highlands. Anywhere from Classic to Late Terminal Classic. Probably cenote offerings."

"Very good," Mercurio said in surprise. "But then, you always had an enviable eye. Are you certain I can't lure you to the Yucatan full-time?"

"Quite certain," Lina said absently.

Her attention was on pots with knobby animal feet at the bottom. Again, probably made as offerings to one god or another. But it was a string of pale, carved jade beads that made her breath stop. The beads looked like a snake swallowing its own tail. Some of the beads were chipped or cracked, but it didn't detract from the impact of the whole.

Lina had seen only one thing like the beads—a big jade medallion of a jaguar head wreathed in a feathered snake devouring its own tail. The piece probably had been part of a priest's regalia. She had found it at one of her father's digs.

The piece had vanished into her father's scholarly collection. She wondered if he had ever written the article he had talked about doing on the jade. If he had, it hadn't been published in any source she knew. And she knew all of the scholarly ones as well as some that were more shadowy.

"This is extraordinary, Mercurio. Where did you get it?" she asked

"I traded for it," he said.

Hunter managed not to laugh out loud. He'd bet that the beads were—at best—a gray-market trophy.

Lina frowned. "Was the previous owner Mexican?"

"He had the requisite papers," Mercurio said. "The beads came from the first dredging of Chichén Itzá. One of the worker's descendants sold them for cash before anyone had dreamed up antiquities laws. Someone strung the beads. The result came down through the years in a Maya family. They sold it to pay for doctors for their son."

"You're very fortunate they came to you," Lina said carefully.

"Yes."

She waited, but Mercurio said no more.

Listening with a small part of his attention, Hunter had ruthlessly moved from artifact to artifact while Lina and Mercurio danced around the subject of questionable provenance. Obviously Mercurio wasn't into the Caesar's wife strategy of business.

"What's that?" Hunter asked finally. "Paper?"

Instantly Lina was at his side. "Looks like it. Birch bark."

There were fragmentary symbols on

one side of the piece. She couldn't read them. There simply wasn't enough left.

"What is it?" Hunter asked.

"It looks like a bit torn from a Maya codex, but . . ." She shook her head. "All of the five surviving codices are accounted for. This could be a fragment from one of them." Her tone said it was unlikely. "Bishop Landa and his soldiers were very thorough. If there were any books they didn't find and burn, the climate eventually destroyed them. Five hundred years in a jungle . . ." She looked at Mercurio and raised one dark eyebrow. "Any comments?"

"The paper came in the same lot as the beads," he said. "The owner said it was a fragment of an unknown codex."

"You believed him?" Hunter asked.

"No," Mercurio said bluntly. "That would be too much. Simply fantastic."

"Understatement," Lina said. "Proof of an ancient, unknown codex would rock the Maya world like a nuclear bomb. Finding a sixth surviving book is the holy grail of every Maya archaeologist."

"Collectors, too?" Hunter asked.

"Of course," Mercurio said.

"It could never be displayed," Lina said at the same time. "You could have a stack of provenance going back to Bishop Landa himself, and Mexico would still scream patrimony."

"Not all collectors would care," Hunter said.

"But gossip goes through solid stone walls," Lina pointed out. "A sixth Maya book is a secret that I can't imagine being kept."

"Okay. You see anything here that looks like the photographs?"

"No."

"What photographs?" Mercurio asked.

Watching the other man, Hunter reached into one of the cargo pockets on his new pants. He spread the photos across an empty worktable and turned to watch Mercurio. The man came to a point, all but quivering like a bird dog as his eyes swept from photo to photo, then began again for a more leisurely look.

"Well cared for," Mercurio said. "The photographer should be fired."

Hunter waited.

So did Lina. She didn't need Hunter's neutral expression to know that he wanted her quiet right now.

"Anything else?" Hunter asked when Mercurio remained silent.

"What is their provenance?" Mercurio countered.

"Zero."

The other man didn't look surprised.

"You missing any pieces from your digs?" Hunter asked.

"None that I know of. Certainly no artifacts of this quality. My digs share a similar style—especially with that scepter, but I've found nothing like that mask. Is it real or of modern manufacture?"

"I don't know," Lina said. "I've never studied the artifact itself, only the photos."

"And you think I have?" Mercurio asked, looking at her. "You flatter me, *querida*. I have found some hints of Kawa'il, some sigils on goods. But I can't prove they weren't imported from Yucatan. In fact, anything regarding Kawa'il can't be proved beyond academic doubt as indigenous to my Belize digs."

"Then why is Philip . . ." Her voice dried up.

"So paranoid about my digs?" Mercurio's smile was different from his earlier ones. Harder.

"Yes," Lina said.

"Because he is not quite sane. Digs of this quality and apparent age"—Mercurio gestured to the photos—"have only been discovered on Reyes Balam land. I don't know what your father has found since I left. Certainly he never found artifacts of this magnificence when I was with him, *querida*."

"If you wanted to buy them, who would you go to?" Hunter asked, his eyes the color of winter ice. He was really tired of hearing the other man call Lina "darling."

"To you, of course," Mercurio said. "You're the man with the photos."

"These photos are as close as I can come to the real thing," Hunter said. "Who would you try next?"

"Cecilia Reyes Balam," Mercurio said.

"Not Simon Crutchfeldt?" Lina asked. "Or Philip?"

"If Crutchfeldt owned these, he wouldn't keep them long enough for word to get out," Mercurio said. "He is a businessman as much as he is a collector. Only a collector would be fool enough to keep artifacts such as those. As for Philip, if he had them, I would be the last to know. He wouldn't spit on my grave. Vindictive bastard." Then, quickly, "My apologies, Lina."

"Not necessary." Her voice, like her face, revealed no emotion.

"That takes care of the obvious suspects," Hunter said. "Anyone else?"

"Carlos, of course," Mercurio said. "But, assuming those artifacts are as good as they look, he wouldn't sell them."

"He'd give them to the museum," Lina said.

Carlos laughed softly. "Such beautiful innocence, *querida*. It is one of your greatest lures."

"I don't find it alluring to be called naive," she said evenly. "Are you saying Carlos would sell those artifacts on the black market?"

"No. I'm saying that the only way Carlos would let go of those artifacts is if he had better pieces in his collection."

"We have nothing to equal them in the museum," Lina said.

Mercurio's smile was both gentle and amused. "You must be the only person in Mexico who doesn't know that Carlos has a personal collection, and I'm not referring to your Houston museum."

"So he might know about these arti-facts?" Hunter asked quickly.

The quick flare of temper in Lina's eyes had warned him that she was reaching her limit on being patronized by Mercurio ak Chan de la Poole. That was fine with Hunter, but they had more questions to be an-swered before he let her shred the hand-some Mexican.

"Carlos?" Mercurio shrugged. "He is a man who keeps his own counsel. Lina's *abuelita* might know. She and Carlos are close."

"Why?" Hunter asked. "She's two gen-erations older than he is."

"He is the only reasonably direct male descendant of the Reyes Balam line," Mer-curio said. "He is the focus of the back-ward villagers who see him as a conduit to the old gods."

"He's CEO of a cement company," Lina said. "Not real godlike."

"To you and me, no. He is just one more spoiled son of an old family. The villagers are more foolish. They look for anything to make their dirt-scratching lives more im-portant."

"Take a good look at those photos," she said impatiently.

Mercurio's disdainful attitude toward poor Maya villagers was one of the major reasons she hadn't let their relationship go beyond a few dates with him. Despite his handsome face, fit body, and love of field archaeology, Lina couldn't see him as a potential mate.

Too bad Mercurio didn't feel the same way.

"What do you see?" Lina pressed. "What do you think the function of the artifacts was?"

"Is that cloth really a god bundle?" Mercurio countered.

"I don't know," Lina said.

He looked at Hunter.

"Same here," Hunter said. "That's why we knocked on your door."

"If I assume that the artifacts are as represented in the pictures," Mercurio began.

"This isn't a peer review," Lina said. "You're not being recorded or judged or asked to buy or sell. Spare me all the academic qualifiers."

"So direct," Mercurio said. "So American."

*About time you noticed,* Hunter thought sardonically.

"I'm not the starry-eyed teenager you knew on the digs," she said. "I'm way past that."

"You were beautiful, a bird just learning to fly." His voice was like a stroke, his eyes hot with memories.

"That was years ago," she said. "The pictures are now."

Hunter measured Mercurio like an undertaker sizing up future business.

Lina's dark eyes watched the other man, hoping he would accept that she had long outgrown her crush on her father's handsome assistant.

"People are dead because of those artifacts," Hunter said. "We don't want any more deaths on our hands."

But his tone said he wouldn't mind some of Mercurio's blood on his knuckles.

Mercurio studied the photographs again, his mouth flat rather than seductive. "Were they found together?"

"At the Texas-Mexico border," Hunter said. "Where they'd been before that is unknown."

"I can't tell you anything Lina can't." Mercurio shrugged. "They came from Reyes Balam land."

She started to protest.

Hunter cut across her. "What is their function?"

"Religious," Mercurio said. "Specifically, sacrificial. The quality of the knife, the scepter, the mask, the Chacmool, the incense burner—it all speaks of priest-kings communicating with gods. If there ever was a cult of Kawa'il, these goods belonged to its high priest."

"Why couldn't they have come from Belize?" Lina asked.

"I have several digs in Belize, most of them close to historic villages, places where traders came from the Yucatan peninsula to conduct business. Two of my digs are deeper in the jungle. Some of the sites have wall paintings. There is even one— just one—with the sigil of Kawa'il."

Lina's breath came in and stayed.

"The sigil is on the order of Mexico City graffiti," Mercurio said, shrugging. "It is a crude statement that someone was there at some time with some paint. I've never found artifacts of high quality produced on any post–Terminal Classic site in Belize.

Everything I've found is crude, made in the shadow of Yucatec memories by untrained people who barely survived the onslaught of the Spanish. The people who lived there were Maya, yes, but they had no greatness left in them. Like the villages today. Their gods are gone, and it shows in the poor rubble of their lives."

"Yet you have that scrap of paper," Hunter said. "Paper is the product of a high civilization."

"Or the remnant of what once was," Mercurio said. "If the scrap is from Belize, it was carried there." He looked up from the photos, took Lina's chin lightly in his hand, and turned her to face him.

Hunter eased forward, ready to deck the touchy-feely archaeologist.

"If I'd found artifacts as good as those in your photos," Mercurio said, "I'd have quit my post and started my own foundation. Money to sponsor my digs would have flooded in. *Madre de Dios, National Geographic* would have me on speed dial! Do you understand what I'm saying yet? If real, that mask alone is better than anything the Aztecs made, and they're considered the pinnacle. *Who has those artifacts?*"

"If we knew, we wouldn't be here," she said, stepping away from his grasp. "Thank you for your time." She turned to Hunter. "We'd better go. My family will be impatient to meet you."

Mercurio finally seemed to get the message. The look he gave Hunter was as hard as a blade.

"Thanks for showing us around, Dr. de la Poole," Hunter said, hand extended.

Mercurio grasped it angrily. "Of course."

This time Hunter didn't hold back his grip.

# CHAPTER SIXTEEN

OUTSIDE, THE SUN WAS A MEMORY AND DARKness real. Lina and Hunter walked down the pathway, casting strange shadows from the knee-level lighting. No voices came to their ears. Nothing moved farther back in the landscaping.

"Old boyfriend?" Hunter asked blandly.

"Don't start." Lina all but snarled into the night. "Sometimes I wonder what goes through Mercurio's head."

"I don't. He wanted you sweaty and horizontal."

She grimaced. "In his dreams. By the

time he noticed me sexually, I had outgrown my crush on him."

"Bad timing."

"In hindsight, it was brilliant."

Hunter's arm slid around her shoulders. "Yeah."

She turned toward him and started to say something.

His mouth came down and suddenly Hunter was all Lina knew, all she *could* know. There was no darkness, no stone path, no wild jungle breathing fragrance over the land. There was only Hunter's heat, his taste of coffee and lightning, need coiling in her until she couldn't breathe.

"I want you naked," he said against her mouth.

"And horizontal?" she teased. But it sounded more like a suggestion.

"Any way I can get you, including straight up."

"Like an ice-cream cone?"

"You change your mind about being shy?" he asked.

"I've been thinking about it. A lot."

He shuddered when Lina's tongue caressed up his neck and along his jawline, pausing over the dent in his chin. He lifted her until her legs were wrapped around his hips and his cock rubbed against her hot, moist center.

"Yeah, just like an ice-cream cone," he said roughly. "I wanted to lick you all over last night, but I was afraid you'd bolt."

"That was last night."

"And now?"

"You make me adventurous."

A door slammed somewhere behind them. Reluctantly Hunter allowed Lina to slide down his body until she was standing so close to him he could feel her hard nipples against his chest. He breathed out roughly.

"Car," he said.

For a moment all Lina could think about was getting closer to him. Naked close. Then reality came like a cold rain.

"I'll drive," she said huskily. "The last part of the road is confusing if you don't know your way, especially in the dark." She shivered despite the warmth of the night and the heat of the man so close to her. "What you do to me should be illegal."

"Not yet. We'll get to that part later tonight."

"My family is old-fashioned."

"So am I." He smiled, a flash of white in the darkness. "I've always wanted to climb up a trellis to a woman's second-floor bedroom."

"Naked?"

"Only after I get inside."

Lina laughed. She wanted to kiss Hunter again, but didn't trust herself. So she turned to the Bronco waiting out front. By the time she got in and fastened her seat belt, she could almost take a full breath again.

Almost.

If she didn't look at Hunter's lap.

She turned the key and drove onto the highway. Within minutes, the colorful lights of Pueblo Tulum had been replaced by the occasional eerie flash of animal eyes reflected in the Bronco's headlights along the roadside. Shrines loomed and vanished like random ghosts congealing from the shadows of the jungle.

Eventually Lina turned off the highway onto a series of roads that became more and more narrow until they unraveled into tangle of dirt tracks and semipaved lanes.

"You were right," Hunter said. "I'd be lost

by now. GPS only shows where you are, not where you want to be. The maps I have of this area don't show nearly this many trails."

"That's because we're on Reyes Balam lands. The main access to the estate is kept in reasonable shape, but the rainy season hasn't officially ended. Only the worst washouts will have been repaired, and nothing will be scraped and oiled until things dry out more."

"Looks fairly dry to me."

"Yes," Lina said without looking away from the road. "The rainy season was stingy this time. But it's not too late for some real drenching storms. For the sake of the villagers, I hope rain comes."

"No irrigation?"

"Only where the ancient stone ditches have been patched. And even then, the ditches lose more water than they carry."

Hunter waited until Lina had negotiated a rough segment of washed-out road before he said, "Mercurio thinks one or more of your family is involved in the illegal artifact trade."

There was a long silence while the thinning jungle rippled by in the headlights.

More and more limestone outcroppings poked through, like fangs fighting the plants that struggled to rule.

"So do a lot of people," she said finally. "Nobody has had any luck proving it. And plenty have tried. Being local aristocrats isn't the same as being bulletproof. Without Carlos's success in the cement business and our mahogany farms, the family would be land-poor and getting poorer. Celia contributes as well."

"What about the villages on your estate?"

"They're black holes for money. We pay for their religious celebrations, doctor their sick, bury their dead, give money for marriages and births, and send their children to schools. In return, they work on the estate lands, keep us in fresh food and game, and pay to rent croplands."

"Sounds downright feudal," Hunter said.

"It works for them. They can leave whenever they want. The ambitious or restless do. Many of them come back. Cities are cruel to the poor."

"So is the countryside."

Lina swerved to avoid a downed tree. The tires crunched over small branches.

The smell of crushed foliage flowed like oil through the open windows.

"So you've never known any of your people to dig illegally in the ruins?" Hunter asked.

"There are always rumors," she said slowly, "but once Carlos took over the family mahogany and cement businesses, the rumors dried up. The source of our money was obvious even to people who disliked us."

"Sounds like Carlos rules with bare knuckles."

Lina's mouth flattened. "Sometimes it's that or go under. Or have our lands pockmarked with illegal digs, new and old."

"Leave enough bodies and word gets out that the reward isn't worth the risk," Hunter agreed. "It's a management technique that never ages."

"Bodies?" She laughed. "Nothing that dramatic. Money works quite well. Carlos keeps the villages happy. They keep him happy. It's what the Reyes Balam family has always done."

"Yet Rodrigo, who knows more about this part of the Yucatan than the devil himself, believes there are tomb robbers on

Reyes Balam land. Mercurio would have said the same, but he was too busy trying to charm your shorts off."

"And you?" Lina asked tightly. "Do you believe my family is little better than the narco cartels? Money first and everything else second?"

"I believe you're honest." Hunter's fingers skimmed down her cheek. "I believe the jungle hides as many secrets as hell does, and damn near as many bodies. Until we know some of those secrets, we're running naked through places where angels in armor would tiptoe."

Lina chewed delicately on her lower lip. "I know my family—especially my parents—aren't angels, armored or otherwise. That's not the same as believing they've lied to me all my life."

Hunter picked over all the possible responses, trying to find one that wouldn't push Lina away from him.

"Whoever has those missing artifacts is corrupt to the bone," he said finally, remembering the basement abattoir, "and more dangerous than a bag full of grenades with loose pins. I don't want you hurt, sweetheart."

"It wasn't exactly safe in Houston."

"No. And we can't assume it's safe here."

"So . . . you *do* believe my family is dirty."

"Dirty as in narco dirty? No. Rodrigo didn't say anything about drugs or El Maya," Hunter said. "He just told me I should get the hell out of the Yucatan. He didn't hint at any danger to you."

"But you're still here."

Hunter didn't say anything. He didn't have to. His presence was the only statement that mattered.

THE ENTRANCE TO THE REYES BALAM ESTATE was guarded by nothing but jungle. The grounds were only partially illuminated, just enough to tell Hunter that the landscaping was expansive and not heavily pruned. Smaller homes—probably separate quarters for guests—orbited the big house like cottages around a high-end hotel. The architecture was a mix of Spanish and Maya, modern and ancient. Construction seemed to follow the fortunes of the Reyes Balam family. Older buildings had been renewed and new ones had been built when the family had money.

"Carlos obviously has done well," Hunter said.

"Once he was through his rebellious years, he has worked tirelessly for the family. Unlike my grandfather, who nearly ruined the family by picking the wrong fight, Carlos has avoided politics."

"Avoided the limelight, yes," Hunter said. "No one with real money avoids politics, especially in Mexico."

What Hunter didn't have to say was that Carlos was listed among the top tier of wealthy businessmen in Mexico. If people bought cement or mahogany, chances were good that they bought from some arm of Reyes Balam enterprises.

Lina turned off the headlights. The jungle flowed closer, part of the darkness. The stars were lost to the high overcast. Somewhere the moon glowed, but not here, not now.

She drew in a deep breath and let it out slowly. "I love the smell here. Green, living, laced with a hint of flowers and heat."

"Home," Hunter said.

Her answer was a soft laugh. "I never thought of it like that, but you're right. The early memories are the deepest. The sweet mysteries of the jungle, the music of children laughing, women calling to one another at the market, the smell of pork and chiles and unsweetened chocolate. The shocking coolness of jumping into a cenote on a hot day. Playing hide-and-seek among the ruins while the faces of gods watched. The music of life that is the jungle at night. It seems so long ago for me and yet close enough to touch."

"A lot different from Houston."

"Houston has its own beauty," Lina said absently, listening to the jungle. "The rush and tumble of human life, the feeling of being within a giant's heartbeat, shops offering goods from all over the world, the rhythms of different languages."

"And the artifacts that tie past and present together," Hunter said.

"That most of all. The people who lived in the Yucatan before the Spanish have always fascinated me. The resort cities . . . not so much. They don't seem quite real, like they landed from outer space."

The ticks and pops of the cooling engine blended with the random animal noises of the jungle that surrounded the compound.

Though neither Lina nor Hunter said anything, they weren't eager to leave the intimacy of the vehicle and the conversation that had nothing to do with blood and fear.

"I've never been able to decide which I like better," Hunter said, "exploring the marshes of my childhood or the jungles of my adulthood."

"What about cities?"

"A great place to get supplies, clean clothes, some shows, good food, and see friends. Overall, I prefer greenery to cement. But I'll take a big city over a small town any day. My uncles are the opposite. They hate cities and love Brownsville."

"I'm torn between my love of being on a dig and the richness of knowledge that comes with a city," Lina admitted. "I finally realized that I need both."

"Me, too." Hunter linked his fingers with hers, savoring the smooth warmth of her hand in his.

She leaned close enough to smooth his hair back from his face with her free hand. He turned slightly and kissed her palm.

"I suppose we have to go in," she said.

"Probably. Someone is sure to have noticed us by now. Is your neck itching?"

Her smile was bright in the darkness. "I'm used to being watched by family when I'm here. I am the only Reyes Balam of my generation."

"No wonder you live in Houston. Nobody there is nagging you to be barefoot and pregnant."

"And married," she said. "That's very important to my family."

"What about you?"

"If it happens, wonderful. But there's no nail-biting frenzy to get it done. I don't want the kind of marriage my parents have."

More lights came on at the front of the big house. A second row of knee-high lights came on along the main walkway to the house.

"I think that's our cue," Hunter said.

She sighed. "Good-bye, privacy. Don't get me wrong. I love my family, but they can be overwhelming."

"I've never met a family that wasn't."

Neither moved to get out of the Bronco. Hunter studied as much of the estate as he could see.

Lina studied him.

Despite architectural differences, the various buildings managed to blend to-

gether into a pleasing whole. Crushed limestone paths connected outlying buildings to
the main house. Gardens thrived with native and imported plants. The blended perfumes of flowers were a silent welcome
and an invitation to stay and enjoy. Foun-
tains splashed invisibly, joining all sounds
into a gentle music. Native palms and imported bougainvillea interrupted the stucco
and tile of the buildings. Sweeping balco-
nies anchored cascades of flowering vines.

"This is what Crutchfeldt was trying for
with his monstrosity," Hunter said in a low
voice. "But nothing beats old money and
roots that have grown through the centuries." His eyes adjusted to the darkness,
revealing more and more detail. He let out
a soft whistle. "I knew the Reyes Balam
name went back a long way," he said,
speaking as much to himself as to her, "but
it's beginning to sink in that you were born
on an estate the size of Rhode Island. Must
have been interesting."

Lina saw enjoyment rather than envy in
his expression. So different from Mercurio.
Hunter appreciated the age of the combined Reyes Balam family lines, but he felt
no need to been seen as an aristocrat in

the eyes of his fellow man. Nor did he feel somehow inferior for being "common."

She leaned closer, brushing her cheek against his arm for an instant. She had been looking for a man like him for a long time—confident rather than arrogant.

"I like the main kitchen and Abuelita's family table," Lina said. "The rest of it is simply there. When I was a child, most of the house was off-limits. After I was four, I rarely spent more than a few days at a time in the house. The rest of the time I was shuttled between digs and galleries until I told my mother that I was old enough to live on my own, with my own rules."

"I'd like to have heard that conversation," Hunter said with a slight smile.

All Lina said was "I think of the estate as belonging to others, not to me. Which is accurate. I may be the only pure Reyes Balam descendant, but I'm female. The lands and estate aren't mine and never will be. If I happen to produce a son, everything will pass to him. If I have daughters, it will be held in trust until their first son inherits."

"Your family didn't follow the Spanish custom of dividing land among sons and money among daughters?"

"I guess the Maya model held, though most grandsons of Maya rulers inherited nothing but death. Usurpers took the previous king's name or began their own dynasty, celebrated their own name." She looked at the flowers and the jungle surrounding everything. "I never really thought about all of this. All I cared about was being allowed to dig in the family ruins."

"So who owns it all now?" Hunter asked.

"Abuelita's name is on the deed. She came into it by inheritance. Funny thing is, she lived out in a village called Ixúmel most of her life."

"Is there a lot of the Balam family left?" Hunter asked.

"Not many. The mainline Balams are all but gone. The 'cousins' want nothing to do with Tulum. Even Carlos lives in Houston and only visits here."

"Interesting. Aside from the weird shrines and some scary dude called El Maya," Hunter said, "I like Tulum. But then I've always liked the Yucatan."

"Well, for Mexicans, being from Tulum is like being from . . ."

"Brownsville?" Hunter asked, smiling. "Barely a step above Hicksville?"

"Pretty much."

A lone figure came out of the front door of the main house, backlit by a hallway of brilliant chandeliers. The porch lights flooded on, revealing Celia Reyes Balam.

As always, Lina was struck by what a beautiful woman her mother was. She looked every bit the aristocrat that her birthright pronounced her. Tonight she was wearing exquisitely fitted black slacks and black heels with more height than leather. An emerald-green silk scarf embroidered in gold thread with Maya glyphs lay softly about her shoulders, partially covering a black silk blouse that had been created to highlight her assets in a sleek and stylish manner. A large, emerald-embedded gold cross hung between her breasts. The gold chain holding the cross was twenty-two carats, gleaming like a well-loved dream.

Even in her five-inch heels, Celia was inches shorter than her daughter.

*That's how she gets away with it,* Lina realized all over again. *Someone that tiny and voluptuous is always underestimated. Men never get past that "Pocket Venus" thing.*

Celia paused at the top of the many

steps leading up to the entrance. Mounds and waterfalls of flowers framed her.

"Your mother," Hunter said, though he couldn't see her face clearly.

"How did you know?"

"You have her elegance and curves."

Lina made a startled sound. She'd never considered herself as lushly built as her mother. To know that Hunter thought of her that way sent heat rippling through her.

Celia waved casually, then started to walk down the stairs one swaying step at a time. Even in the low lighting, the sensuality of her walk was striking.

"I don't move like she does," Lina said.

"No, you're sexier. Those long legs add an extra punch that high heels can't match."

"Stop it before I crawl right into your arms."

"That's supposed to discourage me?" Hunter laughed softly.

Then he bit down on her hand with a tender intensity that took her breath. She forced herself to remember that her mother was approaching.

The wind blew warm into the car, like a huge animal breathing.

"Hunter," Lina said huskily.

"Yeah, I know. That's your mother coming toward us like a thunderstorm. Time to see how bad it's going to be."

Hunter got out and walked quickly around the Bronco. He gave Lina an unnecessary hand out of the car and shut the door behind her like a good courtier. She smiled slightly and held on to his hand, telling him without words that she wasn't going to pretend he was just a business associate.

"You sure?" Hunter asked in a low voice.

"Yes." Her voice whispered against his ear as she went up on tiptoe. "Celia only respects strength."

"Which is your bedroom?"

"In the back, on the second floor. Southeast corner room." She smiled suddenly. "Wrought-iron trellis up to the balcony. Watch the bougainvillea. It has thorns."

"I'd expect nothing less leading to the bed of a princess," Hunter said. He gave her neck a quick, biting kiss.

Celia hurried forward.

Hunter and Lina walked more slowly. He had time to size up the woman who looked more like Lina's older sister than her mother.

The files Hunter had read told him that

Celia had had her first and only child after a difficult birth at age seventeen. Yet she looked barely a handful of years older than her daughter, a testament to good genes and better plastic surgeons.

"Lina," Celia said, stretching up to embrace her daughter. "It's about time!" The words were in Spanish.

Although Lina leaned down into the hug and her mother stood on precariously high heels, Lina was still taller than Celia.

**Those long legs add an extra punch that high heels can't match.**

The memory of Hunter's words made Lina feel much more feminine than her travel-wrinkled clothes.

"I told you I'd be here for Abuelita's birthday and the holidays," Lina said in English.

Celia's mouth shaped into a delicious pout and she said in Spanish, "It's fortunate that Abuelita insisted on an intimate family celebration this year. You know I depend on you for family arrangements."

"Really? I've never noticed," Lina said in English.

Hunter told himself he hadn't heard Celia emphasize "family" twice, but he knew he had.

So had Lina.

"Cecilia, this is Hunter Johnston," she continued in English, deliberately standing very close to him. "Think of him as a very, very good friend. I do. Hunter, meet Cecilia Reyes Balam, my mother."

Hunter's poker face held, but it was a near thing. Lina's emphasis on the second "very" had been a declaration of intimacy. When it came to throwing down gauntlets, she'd been taught by experts.

He smiled at Lina, letting every bit of the heat and possessiveness he felt shine through.

Celia would have to have been blindfolded to miss it. The flat line of her mouth said that she didn't like what she saw.

"Señora Reyes Balam," Hunter said deeply in Spanish, his voice caressing the words like a native speaker. "It is my pleasure and honor to meet you. I now understand the source of Lina's beauty."

Then he waited for Celia's next move.

With the smoothness of a businesswoman and the elegance of a queen, Celia held out her hand. Hunter took it in both of his, letting her measure the difference between his big, work-hardened fingers and her own fragility.

"Mr. Hunter." Celia nodded, switching to English. "How . . . unexpected."

"A thousand apologies," Hunter said in Spanish. "Lina and I just decided it was time for me to meet her family."

Lina had a good poker face, too. She'd been wearing it since she'd bent down to greet her mother. Deliberately, Lina rubbed her cheek against Hunter's arm in a lover's caress.

Celia watched with eyes that missed nothing. She didn't like what she was seeing, but she was too shrewd to leap into uncharted territory.

"But of course," Celia murmured. "Lina's little friends are always eager to meet her family."

Translation: *Men saw Lina as a way to marry well.*

"She is her mother's daughter," Hunter said. "I imagine that your marriage to Dr. Philip Taylor was quite a surprise to your family." Then he smiled.

It wasn't his warm and fuzzy smile. It was a statement that if Celia wanted open warfare, he'd deliver it. Philip might have come from an old Boston family, but they were hardly aristocrats. Yet Celia had married him despite his lack of great money and noble pedigree.

Celia blinked and reassessed Hunter. He might be a fortune hunter, but he wasn't weak or stupid. Which was truly unfortunate. Celia's grandmother had made no secret of her desire for Lina to marry a Mexican man of good family.

Lina spoke casually, as though she was unaware of the dangerous tides shifting beneath the conversation. "I thought it would be a lovely birthday present for Abuelita. I know she worries that I don't like men."

Hunter almost choked. He gave Lina a fast sideways look. She responded with a smile that announced just how much she liked a particular man: Hunter Johnston.

Lina was enjoying this entirely too much, but he couldn't bring himself to spoil her fun. He had a feeling that she was well and truly fed up with being shoved at men and reminded it was her duty to have children.

"You look exhausted, dearest," Celia said, tugging Lina toward the house. "Mr.

Johnston will bring your luggage while you greet—"

"Hunter isn't my lackey," Lina cut in. "Is the second-floor guest room across from me prepared?"

"No. All the rooms in the house are assigned."

*That many guests for Abuelita's intimate family party?* Lina thought sarcastically. But all she said was "Then one of the casitas will do."

Celia stopped. "Abuelita and Carlos won't tolerate you sleeping in the same room as your . . . guest."

"We'll each take a casita," Lina said, shrugging like it made no particular difference to her.

"You will take your regular room. Mr. Johnston will be in the casita next to Philip."

"I thought you just said that all the rooms in the house were assigned to guests," Lina said.

"Carlos didn't assign your room to anyone else. The men living in the house are guards, not guests."

"Guards?" Lina asked sharply.

"Of course. Guards have lived in the house for years. You just haven't noticed because you're never here for more than a few hours before you take off for one of Philip's grubby little digs."

"Carlos must be as paranoid as Philip," Lina said.

Celia shrugged. "The world has changed. Especially now. Every crazy in the world has come to the Yucatan to celebrate the destruction of the old and the coming of the new." She looked at Hunter. "I do hope you aren't one of those deluded souls?"

Hunter smiled.

Lina winced.

"No, ma'am," he drawled in English. "Your beautiful daughter is all the lure this boy needs to come to the Yucatan. But Tulum sure did look crowded."

"Idiots," Celia said. "Chasing legends like village children after butterflies." She turned toward one of the paths leading into the shadows. "Come, Mr. Johnston. You can settle in Casita Cenote while I take Lina to her room. After you have time to refresh yourself, dial three on the phone. Someone will come and bring you to the house."

Lina didn't object to the separate quarters. Casita Cenote was old, but better than the stable, which she'd bet was her mother's first choice for Hunter. "I'll show him the casita. I'm sure you're busy juggling Abuelita's celebration and a house full of guards."

For a moment Hunter thought Lina's mother would object to letting them out of her sight. Then Celia gave him directions to the casita and turned to her daughter.

"Come with me," Celia said. "We have much to talk about and very little time together."

Lina looked at Hunter, who smiled with a warmth that made her flush.

"No problem, sweetheart," he said. "I'm good at finding my way around."

# CHAPTER SEVENTEEN

CELIA LOOKED UP AT THE YOUNG WOMAN WHO was such a complicated mix of many cultures—Lina had the stunning facial structure of a female who could trace her royal Balam ancestors back six centuries, the height of her noble Spanish ancestors, and the tongue of an independent American woman.

All of it, thrown away.

"A gringo?" Celia demanded. "Is that how you repay your family? It is your duty to carry on the family line."

"Me?" Lina said, shocked. "What about Cousin Carlos?"

"Fifteen years of marriage, remarriage, far too many mistresses—no children. As Americans put it so crudely, *mi primo* is shooting blanks. That leaves you."

Lina didn't know whether to laugh or wail.

The tight line of her mother's jaw told Lina neither would get the job done. Same for the dutiful daughter routine. She was tired, tense, and repelled by being treated like a walking womb.

"The Reyes Balam family has married out of Mexico as often as it has married in," Lina said.

"Aristocrats," Celia said in a clipped voice.

"Really? Last time I checked, Philip was the son of two university professors. A gringo with no rich inheritance coming. You married him and you were only half my age at the time. The world kept turning. Your parents survived having an ordinary gringo in the family just fine."

"You will not speak to me with such disrespect!"

"Lies are disrespectful. I'm speaking the truth."

"Are you pregnant?" Celia demanded.

Lina stared at her mother. "No." *Not yet, anyway.*

"Then you have no excuse for embarrassing the family like this," Celia said.

It took Lina about three seconds to understand what she'd always suspected was the truth of her parents' marriage.

"I'm surprised your mother didn't just send you to a convent to have me instead of marrying you off to Philip," Lina said softly.

"Nobody knew Carlos was sterile," Celia said with faint bitterness. "I was young and foolish. I wanted out of Tulum, out of the jungle, into a bigger world. I saw Philip as my entrée into that world. For all that he was thirteen years older, he was . . . naive. When I became pregnant, he offered marriage. We eloped."

"And then you discovered that all Philip wanted in life was to dig in the jungles around Tulum," Lina said, understanding more of her parents and their choices. "He wanted a world whose center was Reyes Balam lands. Maybe he wasn't as naive as you thought."

Celia's nails flashed like blood as she

waved her hand, dismissing the past. "I won't let you repeat my mistake."

"It's my life, not yours."

"Carlos is unhappy with you. He could make your life difficult."

"In other words, do as he wishes or find myself out of a job."

Celia bit her lower lip unhappily. "Please, Lina. Now is not a good time to push Carlos. Abuelita is becoming . . . difficult at times."

"Difficult? How?"

"She is old, very old."

"Are you saying that my great-grandmother is senile?" Lina asked.

"I—no, of course not. She is simply Abuelita."

But Celia didn't look Lina in the eye when she said it.

"Does she need specialized care?" Lina asked softly.

"Don't even think it. Carlos won't hear of it and Abuelita . . . no, the best thing is to simply . . ."

"Pretend that everything is fine?" Lina said.

Celia smiled despite the unease in her

dark eyes. "Yes, that's exactly right. I knew you would understand, dearest. We don't contradict Abuelita. Carlos simply agrees and sees that things are as comfortable as possible for her."

"Which makes things comfortable for you."

"But of course. Abuelita will not live forever. It is little enough to do to make her last time pleasant."

Lina felt the heat of tears stinging her eyes. Abuelita could be headstrong and demanding, but she was one of the few constants in the shifting landscape of Lina's life.

As though sensing weakness, Celia bored in. "Mr. Johnston can't comprehend your position in Mexico, your family obligations. Enjoy him—he certainly looks like he is built to be enjoyed—but don't fool yourself into believing it is something it can't be."

For a moment Lina was too shocked to speak.

"Ah, little one, you look like you swallowed a live mouse," Celia said, laughing without malice. "We are women, yes? Sex is something we use. We don't let it use us. So go, sneak out to the casita in the night and roll around in the darkness with your gringo lover. But be in your own bed before dawn, ready to pay Abuelita and Carlos the respect they are due, and to be the Reyes Balam woman you were meant to be."

"Or at least pretend to be that woman?"

Celia smiled and hugged her daughter. "I knew you would understand. Once Abuelita is dead, things will change. Carlos is a man of the world."

When her mother released her, Lina said, "As long as you understand that Hunter will be treated as a guest while he is here. If you insult him, we will leave. Please tell your cousin."

"Abuelita won't—"

"Abuelita has the excuse of age," Lina cut in. "You don't. Carlos doesn't. Philip is rude to everybody, so he'll just be treating Hunter like one of the family."

There was a long silence while Celia digested the change in her daughter. She had always wondered what it would take for Lina to dig in and demand respect as an adult.

Now Celia knew. She couldn't say she

was relishing it. It had been much easier when Lina had been eager to please.

"How long will you be staying?" Celia asked finally.

"How long can everyone be civil to Hunter?" Lina asked in return.

Her mother nodded tightly. "Abuelita will expect to see you, and your *guest*."

"As soon as Hunter and I have had a chance to bathe and change our clothes, we'll be eager to see her. Or would she rather have us as we are now?"

Celia looked at her daughter's rumpled travel wear. "Abuelita is resting. Meet us for canapés in the library at eight."

HUNTER OPENED THE DOOR AT LINA'S LIGHT knock. Obviously she kept clothes at the estate, because she sure wasn't dressed tonight out of a cut-rate chain store. She wore a simple teal silk dress that probably cost its weight in diamonds, and strappy heels to match. A heavy gold bracelet was clasped around one wrist. Matching earrings swayed gently. He couldn't read the glyphs in the dim light of the porch.

She looked uncertainly at his black, artificially faded jeans, bare feet, and bare chest. "Didn't the maid give you my message?"

Hunter barely heard the question. The soft silk dress flowed over her like a lover's mouth, hinting at the full nipples on her breasts, clinging to the lush curves of her hips and thighs. He wanted to go down on his knees and worship every female inch of her.

"Hunter?"

"Excuse me while I reel in my tongue," he said, his voice deep.

Lina felt heat rise in her cheeks. "I should have warned you. On the estate, I'm expected to dress for dinner."

"I'm not complaining. You look damned edible. Will I get parent points subtracted if I leave drool marks on your dress?"

She laughed, stepped into the casita, and closed the door behind her. Seconds later, she was wrapped in Hunter's arms.

"Just don't bite me anywhere it shows," she said.

His glance went to her breasts and the sweet place between her thighs. "I can work with that."

She felt ravished, and she loved every hot instant of it. Anyone who saw Hunter's eyes now would never describe them as cold.

"Later," she said, her voice breathless. "Celia kept me from coming to get you until the last minute."

"I figured. She doesn't want you to have time even for a quickie," he said.

"In some ways, she is old-fashioned," Lina said against the warmth of Hunter's skin. Chest hair tickled softly, making her smile.

"So am I," he said.

"Really?"

"Yeah. For me, quickies just don't get the job done. Unless I'm going to be locked in the casita tonight. Then I'll take whatever I can get now, however I can get it."

"I know where the keys are kept," she whispered teasingly against his chin. "I'll set you free."

Hunter bit her neck very gently, very thoroughly. When he lifted his head, the only mark he left was her quickened breathing and heightened color.

"I'll count on it," he said. "Now turn on the TV or something while I get dressed."

Reluctantly, she went to the remote on

the small coffee table. In the quiet, the bar refrigerator in the tiny kitchen hummed, shuddered, and went still. Sounds of the jungle seeped through the thick limestone walls of the casita. The door to Hunter's bedroom closed.

Sighing, she flicked on the TV remote.

Every news channel she hit had something on the Maya baktun. It was being treated like the New Year's Eve countdown in Times Square. Clocks ticked away the hours and seconds until midnight, December 21. Subtly amused reporters stood in front of shrines and iconic ruins, interviewing crystal huggers and wannabe priest-kings. Some of the spectators wore costumes right out of popular-culture books and videos purporting to be about the Maya, except the feathers were from chickens rather than quetzal birds. Everyone shuddered deliciously at the false excitement of the end of the world that nobody sane really believed would come. Each person interviewed was more ridiculously earnest than the last.

"Just one big party," Hunter said from behind her. "Step right up and take your cup of Kool-Aid."

Lina grimaced. "The blood at those shrines was real."

"Blood is always real."

"Have you heard anything more from Jase?"

Hunter wasn't surprised that she associated blood with Jase. "Cell connection here sucks. The call was dropped halfway through Ali's assurances that Jase was feeling good enough to pat her butt and other interesting bits."

Smiling, Lina shook her head. "It's amazing that they only have two kids and one cooking."

"It's early yet. Give them a few more years. Jase always wanted a houseful of children."

"What about you?" Lina asked, then bit her lip at the sadness that etched around Hunter's eyes. "Sorry. I wasn't thinking."

"No problem. Will I pass dinner inspection?" he asked.

She looked from his clean, if well-used, dark jungle boots to the jeans and the square-bottomed dark shirt he wore open at the throat. "You sure pass my inspection."

"Parents are harder."

"Don't worry. Carlos will probably go with the conservative businessman look or Maya gentry, depending on his mood. Abuelita usually makes do with canapés and goes off to be by herself. Mother will be dressed like a dictator's wife, and Philip will show up in whatever he's wearing when he remembers dinner. If he remembers. It wouldn't be the first time he worked through meals."

As Lina spoke, she looked through the casita window. Less than a hundred yards away, a larger casita glowed quietly in the darkness brought by foliage and night.

"Is that where Philip lives?" Hunter asked.

She nodded.

"Your mother, too?"

"No. She and Carlos each have a wing of the main house. Abuelita, too. The guards stay there as well."

As Hunter straightened a pant leg, he quietly checked the knife in his boot. After a short argument with himself about paranoia, he had cursed the lack of a safe in the casita and secured the gun at his back.

"Anyone mention the reason for all the guards?" he asked.

"You heard Celia. They've been here for years. But I think all this Maya New Year stuff has them on edge. Strangers in Tulum, those wretched shrines." Lina moved uneasily. "There's something out there. I can feel it."

"Like Houston?" he asked sharply.

She frowned. "No. I think I'm just creeped out by those shrines."

"So am I."

Her eyes widened. "You don't show it."

"Contrary to Y-gene myths, I'm not fond of blood and guts," he said dryly. "Speaking of which, just how civilized am I supposed to be?"

"You mean, what kind of crap are you expected to take?"

"Yeah."

"Abuelita is very old. From what my mother hinted, she may be getting senile, so I can't vouch for her manners. Philip has no manners to speak of. If Celia and Carlos are openly rude, we walk out."

Hunter whistled softly. "You're pissed off."

"I'm an adult. If I have to be polite, I require the same from others."

"How did your mother take it?"

"Like a business deal she didn't like but couldn't change," Lina said. She glanced at the thin gold watch her mother had given her last Christmas. "We'd better get going."

As Lina turned her head, her heavy gold earrings caught the light.

"Those are Kawa'il glyphs," Hunter said.

"The jewelry was Abuelita's gift to me last Christmas. I suspect it was her way of saying that she accepted my bent for archaeology. And probably a little slice at me for being so much Philip's daughter."

"That's a really expensive insult," Hunter said.

"I choose to focus on the acceptance. Insults, civilized and otherwise, are a part of Reyes Balam life."

"I can't wait for dinner."

"Oh, it's not as bad as I sound. I'm just still angry at Celia's rudeness to you."

"She's not the first," Hunter said, latching the door behind them.

Despite Lina's joking words about keys—and the guards—there were no exterior locks, only an interior bolt. Maybe that was why all the guards were armed. Or maybe that shadow walking on a limestone perimeter pathway was a gardener with a really odd-shaped hoe.

A banana clip was hard to disguise.

Lina followed Hunter's glance. "He's just one of the compound's night guards."

The tone of her voice told him that the sight was as ordinary to her as the crushed limestone walkways stitching the Reyes Balam compound together.

*Banana clips,* Hunter thought to himself. *The new must-have accessory for the narcos and the rich who hide from them.*

The guard must have found Lina and Hunter equally ordinary. He didn't glance their way.

*All the banana clips in the world won't help unless he's a lot more alert than he looks,* Hunter thought.

He knew firsthand just how boring the job of being a night guard could be.

Until it wasn't.

Lina ignored the grand front entrance and went through the kitchen entrance instead. The scents of peppers both hot and mild permeated the air, along with roasted pork and corn, coffee, and the dark breath of unsweetened chocolate. Other spices clung to the room, telling Hunter that while dinner might be socially uncomfortable with the Reyes Balam family, it wouldn't be boring to the palate.

A tiny woman was sitting at a small, very solid mahogany table, sipping from a demitasse. The china was antique, both proud and subtly faded, as though it had come to the Yucatan via Spain centuries ago. The contents of the demitasse were all New World—thick, unsweetened chocolate laced with very hot peppers.

*The drink of the gods,* Hunter thought. *In the old days, I'll bet a woman wouldn't have been allowed to get any closer to it than preparing it for a man.*

"Abuelita," Lina said, hurrying across the tile floor. "I thought you would be in the library."

Abuelita held out a hand. She was thin as only the very old can be. Her ligaments and tendons had been forged in a jungle village, where women ground corn daily between heavy stones and carried water to the fields.

"Rosalina," she said in a voice like wind through reeds. "Finally you are here."

"I couldn't miss your birthday." Gracefully Lina kneeled to be closer to eye level with the old woman. "How many is it now?"

"I am as old as the Long Count," Abuelita said, her laugh a whisper. "I will see the final Turning of the Wheel and the changing of the gods. It is enough."

Lina bent and gave Abuelita a gentle hug, putting smooth skin against the weathered teak of the other woman. Abuelita's hair was white, like her clothes, which had a simple country style that was belied by the intricate white embroidery that glowed against the pale cotton. It was the sheer absence of the vivid colors that most native Maya wore that made Abuelita almost regal, her clothes and hair a white flame burning against rich skin and eyes blacker than any night.

Looking at those eyes, Hunter understood that Abuelita was indeed different. She lived in the jaguar's world, where human concerns were like the buzzing of flies. Once she would have been called a wise woman, a *bruja,* a priestess. Now she was labeled senile.

"Abuelita, permit me to introduce Señor Hunter Johnston," Lina said, speaking in

Spanish. "Hunter, this is Señora Kuh Chel Balam."

"I'm honored, Lady Chel," Hunter said, tilting his head in acknowledgment of her age and regal presence.

Abuelita's eyes sharpened at the formal title "lady," which was a more exact translation from the Mayan than "señora." She gestured for Hunter to come closer. When he did, she stared at him with an intensity that would be called rude in other circumstances. But this was Kuh—Owl of Omen—watching him.

Lina's subtly pleading glance at Hunter asked him to make allowances for Abuelita's age. His fingers brushed Lina's briefly, silently reassuring her that he wasn't offended.

"You were born in the wrong time, warrior," Owl of Omen said in a liquid Yucatec dialect. "The Turning Wheel will crush you."

Hunter looked to Lina for a translation. The slight motion of her head was negative. Whatever the old woman had said, he would have to wait until he and Lina were alone for a translation.

Then Owl of Omen blinked and Abuelita was back. She took a final sip of her fiery chocolate. The fingers that set the demi-tasse in its delicate saucer had the visible tremor of age.

"Rosalina, it is time for us to go to the library," Abuelita said in Spanish, holding out her left hand.

A gold band set with small rubies gleamed on her ring finger. The ring, like the china, had been passed down through the generations. The thick white embroidery on her clothes was as Maya as her heritage, but the glyphs were impossible for Hunter to make out for lack of contrast.

As Lina came to her feet, she looked at Hunter with sad eyes and said, "Follow us."

It was a plea, not a demand.

"Of course," he said quietly.

He watched while Lina helped Abuelita to her feet—not that she really needed it. For all her appearance of frailty, she was as tough and almost as supple as the flat leather sandals she wore. Lina's help was a gesture of respect, not a necessity.

When Abuelita was standing, the top of her head barely came up to the bottom of Hunter's rib cage. Yet she had a presence that had nothing to do with height. It was in her eyes, her bearing. She might have been born in a jungle hut, but she was born of a royal line.

Silently Hunter followed great-grandmother and great-granddaughter out of the kitchen and into the main part of the house. The furniture was antique, weighty, with richly woven brocade upholstery. Heavy, gilt-framed paintings of European ancestors were scattered throughout. The Balam side of the family was barely represented—a vase on a side table, the figurine of a Maya noble in a corner display, an ancient ceramic flute in a mahogany niche. If a rug interrupted the handmade tiles of the floor, it was ancient, Persian. Three suits of armor in varying styles—all of them dented in battle—stood at attention in the wide hallway, gleaming beneath crystal chandeliers.

The Spanish had married into royal Maya lines, but almost all of the furnishings had come on ships. The household was like Mexico itself, an uneven and sometimes uneasy blend of Old World and New.

Two heavily carved mahogany doors led to the wing where the library was located, the part of the house where Carlos lived. Although the glyphs on the wood were ancient, the doors looked newer than the rest of the house. Hunter wondered if Abuelita had commissioned the doors from native carvers.

Lina knocked lightly before she pushed open the library doors. Immediately she was swept up in Celia's conversation, giving Hunter an opportunity to study the room and its occupants.

The room claimed him. The overwhelming impression was blue on blue, the world viewed in every shade and tint and tone of blue—turquoise, royal, midnight, teal, cobalt, peacock, sapphire, lapis—the whole creating a sense of *blue* that had no name. Only gradually did he realize that the radiance of blues covered just two of the four walls. The furnishings were modern, with leather-upholstered chairs and low bookshelves of wood stained black as sharkskin. The occasional rugs looked modern, though they held Maya glyphs in shades that echoed the tiled walls. The unique fragrance of burning copal hung in the air.

Celia was dressed richly, with exquisite attention to detail—crimson silk dress, makeup flawless, nails and lipstick to match, hair expensively casual around her face, stiletto heels over four inches high—but she wore it all naturally, without thought, like her skin. Her jewelry was more aristocratic than nouveau riche. Around her throat was a heavy antique necklace of gold and emeralds in a baroque design, with bracelet, brooch, and earrings to match. They glowed against the rich color of her skin.

*If they ever get down in the pocketbook,* Hunter thought, *they could always hock the family jewels.*

*Or the artifacts,* he realized, his attention drawn by their quiet, ancient presence. *My God, this room could be in a museum. A world-class one.*

Masks, figurines, Chacmool figures in jade, blocks cut from limestone stelae thick with glyphs, knives, scepters, vases, faces, jewelry, and other Maya artifacts lined glass shelves and filled glass cases that covered two walls of the room. The lighting was subdued, almost reverent, as though not wanting to awaken the very gods that were being illuminated.

Silently Hunter whistled. As a whole, the room was a staggering display of wealth and position, the abode of a modern king or CEO.

He looked at Lina.

She was looking at the people, not the decor. Obviously she took everything for granted with the ease of a woman who had grown up in halls filled with armor, a mother who wore antique jewelry from the Spanish court, and a library that held brilliant fragments of a culture whose books had been burned.

A man—Carlos, from his richly colored skin and dark eyes—rose from a leather chair behind a mahogany desk that was square and solid enough to hold up the weight of the world. The wood was a red so pure and deep that it glowed. He wore very dark blue slacks and a loose, short-sleeved shirt of the same color. The embroidery on the shirt was silver blue. The Maya glyphs flowing down the center of the shirt and around the hem made a stark contrast with his clothes.

Hunter doubted he could translate the glyphs even if he stood within touching distance. He made a mental note to ask Lina about them later.

The man greeted Abuelita with a gentle

brush of lips over her cheek and a white smile. Then he turned to Lina. He was the same height as she was, which made him tall for the average Maya male. Carlos's hair and skin were darker than Lina's and Cecilia's, his features more blunt. He weighed probably twice as much as Lina did. Some of his heft came from food and beer. Most of it was simply genes; he was broad-boned and sturdy. His hair was black, straight, almost as long as Lina's, but held in place by a silver ring studded with blue stones. It was a style few men outside the entertainment business could pull off. On Carlos, it looked as natural as his full lips and broad cheeks.

It reminded Hunter of a parking garage where bullets sang of death.

But then, a lot of men he had seen since landing in the Yucatan reminded him of things he'd rather forget. It also made the street name "El Maya" next to useless for tracking down identity.

"*Mi prima,*" Carlos murmured to Lina. "I am glad to see that you don't ignore Abuelita as you do me."

Lina smiled. If Hunter hadn't known her better, he would have thought it was warm.

"As you know," she said lightly, "my job at the museum is very demanding. It seems like my last class was only yesterday."

"Family is always first," Carlos said.

"Of course," she said, but her eyes said she was biting her tongue.

Hunter stirred.

Carlos's head snapped to the side as though he hadn't noticed the other man until now. He looked at Lina. "Who is this?"

*Like Celia didn't tell him two minutes after I arrived,* Hunter thought sardonically.

But he was familiar with the kinks and knots of family life, so he simply waited like a good guest while Lina introduced him to Carlos. Instead of the head-of-the-family grilling Hunter had half expected, Carlos shook hands and turned his attention back to Lina.

*Message received,* Hunter thought. *I don't exist.*

Two maids ghosted into the room and put plates of seafood canapés on a heavy coffee table that already held a ragged stone face. Celia complained to Carlos that Philip wasn't here, yet she knew he was on the estate. She also said she preferred the previous chef, who had been trained in Europe.

Carlos shrugged and turned to Lina. "Come, *mi prima,* you must see my latest artifacts."

The blue-tiled wall leading to the artifacts glittered like it was underwater.

Hunter offered to get canapés and drinks for Celia and Abuelita. Celia declined. Abuelita didn't seem to hear him. He excused himself and went to investigate the food.

It was going to be a long night.

# CHAPTER EIGHTEEN

THE DISTINCT CRUNCH OF CRUSHED LIMESTONE meeting hard-soled combat boots came like bizarre jungle calls from around the perimeter of the compound. Hunter waited until the guard closest to him continued on his predictable rounds.

*If I was handling security,* Hunter thought, *there would be a lot of job openings. These clowns should be dancing with elephants in a circus.*

On the off chance that the guards might be backed up by other, more subtle men, Hunter waited in the shadow of a group of sabal palms whose trunks were buried in flowering vines and gardenias allowed to go feral.

**I'm going to smell like a vase of flowers when I get out of here. Plus fresh blood from the damned insects eating me alive. Good thing all my shots are current.**

There were diseases out in the jungle that were a lot more dangerous than the armed men making their mechanical rounds of the Reyes Balam compound.

Hunter waited, a semiwilling sacrifice to the insect gods.

No hidden guards moved. No sharp odor of cigarettes or matches hung in the darkness beyond the lighted paths. Toward the big house, two young women called from the huge kitchen, teasing the men who would rather be romping in bed than stomping around in the dark with guns.

When the guards had completed two rounds, Hunter picked his moment and ghosted through the landscaping, ignoring the noisy pathways. There were only a few flickering lights on the second floor at the southeast corner of the house—candles beckoning him. The rest of the floor was dark.

He wondered if the rooms were truly given over to guards, or if Cecilia had used that as an excuse not to let him sleep under the same roof as Lina, princess of the Reyes Balam line.

The muted, liquid illumination of the candles through screened windows drew Hunter as surely as his hunger for Lina. The landscaping lights around the house provided more ambience than security. It was way too easy for him to drift among the shadows that dipped and danced with every mood of the wind. The ancient bougainvillea was more ladder than barrier. The thorns drew blood he barely noticed. The sturdy wrought-iron balcony was an invitation he took with both hands. He went over the railing like a jungle cat, more imagined than seen in the shadows.

The French doors leading inside weren't locked. Hunter dropped to the balcony floor, eased open the doors, and listened.

Nothing but his heartbeat.

Silently he went low through the doors, closing them as he slid behind one of the heavy draperies that had been gathered at either side of the door. The sitting area was empty of all but half-consumed candles, the TV silent. A partially open door waited to the side. He stood near the door, listening, watching, wanting.

The scent of cinnamon and woman curled from the bed to him in a silent caress. The alluring line of shoulder and waist and thigh called to him. The pale, fragile silk of her nightgown revealed and concealed with every shifting breath she took. The dark shadows of her nipples, the shadow between her thighs, her slightly parted lips slid like a knife into his heart. For an instant he couldn't move, couldn't breathe, could only feel the ache of certainty sweeping over him.

She was everything he'd ever wanted, ever dreamed, ever hungered for in the loneliness that was his life.

Abruptly Hunter decided they could talk about artifacts and death later. At this moment other things were more important.

Lina's bed was draped in a fragile fall of mosquito netting. A single candle flickered at her bedside, beyond the reach of the netting. Slowly Hunter licked the finger and thumb of his right hand, pinched the wick, and let the room slide into a radiant kind of darkness. Exterior lights glowed beyond the screened windows, turning them into luminous silver.

With quick motions he stripped off his boots and clothes, making sure his weapons and condoms were within reach. He pushed through the gauze, feeling it slide like breath over his naked body. He put one hand over Lina's mouth as he let the mattress dip beneath his weight.

The electric change in Lina's body told Hunter that she was awake.

"Easy, sweetheart," he murmured against her ear.

He felt her smile beneath his hand, but it was the hot lick of her tongue over his skin as she breathed his name that told Hunter she knew exactly who was in her bed.

"Go back to sleep," he said softly. "Don't mind me."

His erection prodded her hip in bold contradiction.

She would have laughed out loud if his hand hadn't covered her mouth. As it was, she bit the base of his thumb slowly, deliciously, then sucked one finger into her mouth for a hotter caress, the kind of tasting she wanted to do all over him.

"Is anyone else on this floor?" he asked.

Lina savored the unique flavor of his skin—jungle and salt, a metallic hint of blood and dusty thorns—before she reluctantly gave up teasing his finger to answer.

"Only the night guards, and they're out making rounds," she said softly.

"I noticed. Bunch of clubfooted clowns."

"Their guns are clean and loaded. Carlos checked them before they began their shift."

"Your *primo* struck me as a demanding sort of employer," Hunter said, but his lips and teeth tracing her flaring cheekbone said that there were other demands a man could make.

Hungry ones.

"He is. That's why he's successful. Celia checked their clothes and fingernails. She won't abide dirty guards inside the house."

"Did Abuelita check their ammo?"

Lina's soft laugh was a rush of warmth over his lips. "She's asleep in her suite off the kitchen." Lina's lips went from the corner of his mouth to the hinge of his jaw. "The suite used to belong to the housekeeper, but when she quit last year, Abuelita took over the job. She even oversees the making of the candles she so loves." Teeth nipped his ear. "The house has never been so spotless or held so many candles. No one dares displease her."

"Her husband must have had huevos." Hunter's mouth nibbled Lina's lips in sweet retaliation.

"I don't remember him. He drank himself to death long before I was born."

"Huh. Can't say I blame him."

Teeth nipped, then sucked on the pulse in Hunter's neck. "Abuelita's soft underneath her armor," Lina said.

Hunter doubted it, but he didn't doubt Lina's affection for the old woman. "Did the family give you more grief after I left?" he asked.

Which had been as soon after dinner as was civilly possible.

"They understood you were tired," Lina breathed against his hair.

"More like they were glad to be rid of me."

She would have argued, but suddenly didn't have the breath. Hunter's warm mouth had found the valley between her breasts at the same moment as his hands had slid around their soft weight. The edge of his teeth on one nipple was sweet lightning ripping a sound of surprise from her.

"Okay?" he whispered, waiting.

In answer she shifted her thighs open. The scent of cinnamon and arousal lifted to him.

"God," he groaned. "You work on keeping quiet."

"What are you going to do?"

"I've always wanted to ravish a princess."

Her breath broke as he sucked on one breast, then the other. Her fingers tightened in his hair and she fought to be silent while his mouth worshipped her. Minutes slid by in a breathless silence that ended when small whimpers broke from her. His mouth alternately tormented and delighted her breasts, sending sharp streaks of lightning from her nipples to her womb.

When she was twisting slowly beneath his mouth and hands, her nipples stiff and quivering, glistening from his tongue, he lifted his head to admire the beauty his slow caresses had created. He kissed one nipple, then the other.

Her eyes opened dark with need, watching him.

"Hunter?" she whispered.

"Shh. Ravisher at work here."

Her smile became a hiss of indrawn breath when his mouth skimmed down her body, his hands slid beneath her hips to hold and mold her buttocks, and his teeth left a stinging caress on one hip bone and then the other. With a dark, fluid motion he shifted over her, pressing her legs farther apart to make room for his shoulders.

The scent and heat of her filled him like a drug.

He made a rough sound against her thighs as his fingers shifted to her nipples, squeezing and plucking in caresses that would have been painful just moments before. But not now. Now she was lifting into his hands, her body focused on the luxuriant whips of sensation uncoiling through her, arcing her.

Then he bent his head and took her in a way he'd taken no other woman, wanting to drown in her.

She would have cried out if she could, but he'd stolen her body. She lived only where he touched her, and he touched her everywhere. Without knowing it, she drew her knees up and gave herself to whatever he wanted, because with him she wanted everything. Ecstasy shivered through her, brilliant pulses that exploded like fireworks behind her eyelids, blinding her.

He lifted his head long enough to see her lost in the pleasure he had given her. Then he bent his head and drove her up again, less gently, fingers and teeth and tongue caressing and demanding until she came in a wild, writhing rush that destroyed her.

When she could open her eyes again, he was there, holding her, sealing her soft cries with his mouth. The taste of him, of her, of passion tangled with their tongues. With a long sigh, she separated their mouths and nuzzled the hands that held her face so tenderly.

"Gardenias," she murmured. "Why do you smell like gardenias? Did you steal Celia's perfume to fool the guards?"

Hunter smiled despite the driving hunger that made every muscle of his body hard.

"I waited in the bushes," he said, tracing her mouth with his fingertip. "Watching the guards."

She blinked slowly, a thick sweep of

eyelashes. "That explains it. Were the bougainvillea thorns bad?"

"Wicked. Make it up to me."

His blunt erection nuzzled at the lips of her sheath.

"Come here," she whispered. "Deep, Hunter. I want you deep."

"Then hold your knees high."

She would have been embarrassed, but she was too caught in their mutual sensuality to care about anything but pleasing him. She opened herself as much as she could, then watched him sink into her, inch by thick inch. Seeing the joining set fire to her all over again. She had never known a lover like Hunter, a man willing and able to enjoy every aspect of making love, not just his own release.

His pleasure in her was as surprising as it was arousing. She breathed his name as he filled her until she overflowed. Her hidden muscles flexed, held, caressed, until his control gave way to powerful, twisting thrusts. He rode her with a strength and power that made the world go black and red and wild until he shuddered above her, unable to hold back anymore.

Then they lay tangled, sated, their sweat mingling, breaths ragged, bodies joined.

WHEN LINA AWOKE AT DAWN, SHE WAS ALONE but for the sunlight turning the mosquito netting to ripples of liquid gold.

She wanted Hunter. Wanted him close to her, holding her, laughing while she kissed each tiny wound inflicted on him by insects and thorns. Then not laughing when she kissed the flesh that had given them both so much pleasure. There had been no more condoms, but she hadn't cared. She just wanted to worship his body as he had worshipped hers.

And she had.

Smiling, stretching, feeling each sensual ache from Hunter's tender, demanding lovemaking, Lina pushed through the mosquito netting. She showered and dressed in clothing suitable for jungle hiking, then took her backpack downstairs and tucked into the canvas enough food and water to last until evening. She filled a canteen with strong, rich coffee, left a note for her mother, and slipped out the back door before the maids arrived to

begin grinding corn for Abuelita's breakfast tortillas.

As always, there were guards along the
perimeter of the compound. Lina barely
registered their presence. She was too impatient to see Hunter.

The door to Casita Cenote opened before she could knock. Hunter's eyes blazed
a silver blue that took her breath. He was
dressed, as impatient as she was.

As hungry.

"I'd kiss you," he said in a deep voice,
"but then I'd lose my head and go right to
the top of your family's shit list."

The way Lina's eyelids half lowered as
she licked her lips told him that she'd awakened with the same thing on her mind.

"You're killing me," he said, touching her
damp lips with a fingertip.

She smiled, touched the tip of her tongue
to his skin, then stepped away. "We've got
to leave before Celia or Abuelita thinks of
a way to keep us apart."

Hunter peeled the backpack off Lina,
lengthened the straps to fit him, and said,
"At your service, beautiful."

She hesitated, smiled. "I never felt beautiful before you."

"Have I mentioned that you're killing me?"

"Maybe I like the way you 'die.'"

The crunch of boots on crushed limestone was all that stopped Hunter from dragging Lina inside and bolting the door.

"Start moving," he said huskily.

She turned and took a path leading away from the guard, walking quickly. He followed a little more slowly, just far enough back to appreciate the natural motion of her hips.

"You have a seriously fine ass," Hunter said.

Lina gave him a you-have-got-to-be-kidding look over her shoulder.

He grinned.

"What am I going to do with you?" she asked, laughing.

"You did real good last night . . . and then some. Now change the subject or I'll be walking bent over."

Her dark eyebrows rose. "So it's all my fault?"

"Every little bit."

"There was nothing little about last night. Bitty either. You may be used to your whacking great equipment, but I'm walking funny today."

Hunter laughed even as red burned along his cheekbones.

Smiling, she resumed her "funny" walk to the parking area of the compound. He took a long breath and followed her, wishing every step of the way that he had the right to drag her back to his bed for another up-close-and-personal loving from said equipment.

The Bronco was waiting where they had left it, limestone dust dimming its deep green paint. She held out her hand for the keys he had reclaimed yesterday. He dropped them in her palm. They were still warm from his pocket. She started to say something about how hot he was, then told herself to stop teasing the jaguar.

**But it's such fun.**

Beneath the scraped-back hair and jungle wear, Lina felt more female than she ever had in her life.

"Where are we going?" Hunter asked as she unlocked the Bronco.

"First, the Cenote de Balam, or Jaguar Cenote, as Philip calls it," she said. "Then to a very special place I've never taken anyone."

"Breakfast along the way?" Hunter asked hopefully.

"In my backpack. The canteen clipped to the bottom is coffee. I ate while I was throwing stuff together."

"Beautiful, sexy, intelligent, and understanding," Hunter said, smiling wolfishly as he released and opened the canteen.

"I'll remind you of that when I irritate you."

Hunter was too busy swigging coffee to answer. But he winked.

"There's a good limestone-paved walkway to the cenote from the compound," Lina said, "but I don't want to meet anyone. The villagers and workers use that path."

He grunted something agreeable around a mouthful of pork, chiles, and hard-boiled eggs wrapped in yesterday's corn tortillas. Four more fat bundles just like it waited for him in the backpack. He was hungry enough to eat every one.

"What about your cousin's artifacts?" Hunter asked between bites.

"Gorgeous. Echoes of Kawa'il. Nothing close to what we're looking for."

"Did he say anything useful?"

"Not to me."

On either side of the long estate drive-way, elegantly spaced and manicured gardens flowed by. Before Hunter finished his second tortilla, she turned the Bronco onto what looked like a maintenance road. Moments later they were deep in the jungle. Untamed, unmanaged, raw with life. The jungle had a different kind of allure than the estate, the beauty of single moments framed in every shade of green—a bird flashing through a shaft of sunlight, a butterfly resting with blue incandescence on a white flower, the sudden rush and screech of howler monkeys passing overhead.

The sun filtered through the intertwined growth of the canopy, enclosing the Bronco in a living green world. As the trees grew bigger, the spaces between them increased, though the sunlight didn't. Despite the overwhelming shade, the inside of the vehicle got hot, then hotter.

Hunter barely noticed. He expected heat in the Yucatan, even in December. It was the cool days that surprised people. But here, as in Texas, winter was being real slow about chasing summer from the land.

"Does the estate get its water from the cenote?" he asked as he swallowed the last bite of breakfast. "Or from cisterns during the wet?"

"Cisterns. Nearly all of Quintana Roo sits on a limestone shelf. Water flows through it, rather than being held back or pushed to the surface by denser, less water-soluble rock. During the wet season, rain fills the underground cisterns we've built. In the old days, the dry season was difficult, especially after the Maya fell and the ancient cisterns and canals fell apart."

"So you don't use the cenote at all?"

She shook her head. "Not anymore. We just drill down into the limestone 'sponge' to reach freshwater stored in stone from rainfall. You don't drill too far, though. Close to the sea, freshwater floats on top of salt-water. It's easy to punch right through to undrinkable stuff."

"And if you don't have a well?" Hunter asked. He enjoyed watching the relaxation and anticipation that spread through Lina with every minute away from the estate.

"Then you go to the nearest cenote, dip out water, and carry it back up the path. You'll see signs of the old trail worn into solid limestone around Cenote de Balam. The trail is older than local memories, far older than Bishop Landa and his soldiers." She downshifted deftly and whipped around a washout. "The actual word isn't 'cenote.' It's *dznot*. The Spanish mangled the Mayan word."

"Pretty much what they did to the natives."

"Oh, the natives were good at going to hell all by themselves. But yes, there wasn't a whole lot of cross-cultural understanding, then or now."

Laughing at the dry understatement, Hunter handed her a bottle of water.

She braced the wheel with her knees and one hand and drank. A thin line of water dribbled down her chin and dampened the khaki blouse above one breast, slowly revealing the dark shadow of a nipple.

Hunter forced himself to think of someone who might be following them. A fast check of the side mirrors revealed that they were the only limestone dust cloud on the road. Not that he could see all that far with the jungle crouched around like a huge green cat.

"Without the cenotes," Lina said, handing back the water, "the very ancient Maya would have died out long before the Spanish arrived. That and the fact that freshwater floats on top of salt."

"Fire, water, earth, and air," Hunter said. "All the rest is decoration. No matter where you are in the world, that doesn't change."

"The lowlands of the Yucatan peninsula could use more of the decoration called fertilizer," she said wryly. "In the ceiba and copal jungle, the ground beneath our wheels is thin, crumbly, and poor. Survival is hard. Take the strangler fig tree. It lives by being supported by a host tree, using the host as a ladder to climb up to light. Eventually the fig vines harden, extend roots, and strangle the host. Despite its lush look, the jungle plants survive more by force of will than the generosity of nature."

"Like the people. Still here. Still surviving, come hell, high water, and the Spanish. But then, we're all survivors descended from survivors. The rest of them are buried in the dust of time."

"Sometimes," she said, "the weight of all that history is . . . crushing. And sometimes it's so exciting to be a part of it that I want to dance."

His fingertips trailed gently down her cheek. "I'll dance with you."

Dark eyes flashed gold when she looked at him and smiled. Then the rough road claimed her attention again. The dual tire tracks zigzagged around clumps of rock as the jungle slowly melted away into a different, sparser growth.

"We're almost there," Lina said. "I'll park off in the scrub."

"No problem with the locals and a rental car?"

"Not if it's seen at the Reyes Balam estate first," she said.

Hunter nodded. "You've got more guards than the ones in the compound."

"We take care of the villages. They watch out for us."

They got out of the Bronco, and she reached into the back and took out a wide leather belt. A machete dangled from a clip on one side of the belt.

"I'm stronger than you are," he pointed out mildly.

"The path shouldn't be too bad. It's only been about eighteen months since I've used this route. But if I get tired, the big knife is all yours."

"Knife?" He looked at the forearm-long blade that had been invented by natives for the sole purpose of whacking through jungles. "More like a sword."

He followed her as she set out for a section of scrubby jungle—or jungly scrub—that looked no different from any other piece of the landscape. Trees struggled on the harsh land, lifting vine-burdened arms to the relentless sun. Bushes fought for their place in the light.

Lina slid sideways between several closely spaced, barely ten-foot-tall trees. Vines dangled only to be cut away by efficient strokes of the machete. She moved down the path like she wielded the machete, with an unconscious ease that came only from long experience. No hurry, no hesitation, just steady walking and random swings of the machete at whatever blocked the trail.

Hunter settled back to enjoy the walk. There weren't as many bloodsucking clouds of insects as he'd expected. The rainy season had been light enough to deny mosquitoes the stagnant puddles they used to breed, and then breed again, repeating the cycle of life and death until the standing water dried up. The wind helped keep the insects down, too. At least when it blew enough to push insects under cover.

The path had only a thin layer of dirt, with limestone knobs shoving through like blunt teeth. Tree roots humped up. They were smaller and thinner than those deeper in the jungle, but enough to trip unwary feet. Plant growth waxed and waned according to a complex balance of light, water, and slope of the land. Birds and monkeys called in the distance, but a moving pool of silence spread around Lina and Hunter.

When predators walked, the jungle held its breath.

After ten minutes the amount of light gradually increased. Somewhere ahead there was a hole in the canopy.

Lina went still.

Instantly Hunter faded into the foliage close to her.

Muted voices came on the wind. The words Hunter could make out were in the local dialect. He watched Lina.

After a few moments the voices faded and she moved forward again, then stopped, framed by trees far taller than she was. She clipped the machete in place at her hip and motioned Hunter forward. When she felt him behind her, she took a half step left, letting him see ahead.

As Hunter squeezed next to her, he saw the breathtaking drop into the limestone cenote less than a yard beyond their feet. Trees crowded right up to the edge of the cliff and beyond, roots clinging to limestone ledges no bigger than his hand. Vines trailed from trees and rock alike, yet after the thousand shades of green that was the thickest jungle, the overall impression of the cenote was of muted pale cliffs and water that blazed blue under an empty sky. Where shadows fell, the water darkened to a murky shade of green.

Across the cenote, where the cliff was lower and less steep, a pale thread zigzagged down to the water. He estimated that the far side was about two hundred feet away, with a cliff perhaps twenty-five feet high. Where he and Lina stood, the cliff was at least ten feet higher, probably more. Without a point of reference, it was hard to tell. The mouth of the cenote was a rough circle left when the roof of an ancient limestone cavern had collapsed.

Freshwater lay at the bottom of the limestone cliffs.

"Jase would be strapping on dive tanks,"
Hunter said in a low voice. "You ever dive
the cenote?"

"Not with equipment. The water is deep,
but even deeper at this side than the other.
We used to jump in over there," She
pointed to a place where the jungle at the
top of the cliff had been cleared and covered with crushed limestone, creating a
flat area. The cliff below was steep, almost
overhanging the water. "Hundreds of years
ago there was at least one altar there, but
it didn't survive the Catholic mandate. Generations of Maya have gradually restored
the limestone causeway from the village to
the cenote, though after we put wells in the
villages, people no longer had to risk their
lives just to get a drink."

The red and yellow of heaped flowers
announced the presence of a different,
modern shrine near the edge of the limestone platform.

"Is that usually there?" Hunter asked.

She shrugged. "It varies, but it has become bigger, more permanent, than I remember as a child. It looks like it has

doubled or tripled in size since the last time I really noticed it."

Hunter weighed the presence of the shrine and decided that it could wait to be investigated. It looked like just one more really big pile of flowers nearly engulfing a long-armed cross. From the thin veil of insects that seethed over the place, it was a good bet that there was food and/or blood among the bright petals.

"What's over there?" Hunter pointed to a gap in the cliff-side foliage that lay to the right of the shrine, just beyond the head of the ghostlike trail descending the cliff.

"The path from the estate. We have technicians who check the wells and the level of the cisterns so we know if water has to be rationed or pumped up from the cenote."

"That happen often?"

"Only a few times. Abuelita doesn't like pumping from the cenote. Once she made everyone haul water in buckets. Said it was better that way. In fact"—Lina put her hand on Hunter's shoulder and leaned out, trying to see better—"I'll bet that the pump doesn't even work anymore. The pipe down the rim into the water is gone."

Hunter absorbed the ancient cenote and modern shrine, the ghost path and cloudless sky. "Could be a long summer."

"My mother's mother had more underground cisterns built after the last drought. If we had to, we could irrigate enough of the estate crops to keep the villagers and ourselves alive. I barely remember my grandmother, but she was very determined that the estate be self-reliant."

"Governments come and go. The need for food and water doesn't."

"We have other cenotes on Reyes Balam lands, but none of the size and accessibility of this one. Some are so steep that even a jaguar would get a workout on the way to water. Others are little more than ponds with muddy bottoms. A few archaeological divers mucked about in them, but didn't find much."

"Any divers in this one?"

"Philip dived it after he and Celia were married. He found the usual knives, faces, pots, figurines, jewelry—all of it broken during the act of sacrificing to the gods. What is given to the gods isn't taken back."

"People, too?" Hunter asked.

"Apparently. This cenote was an important center for the lowland Maya, especially after the Spanish came. Philip dredged the cenote for a sample of what was on the bottom. He recorded the length and type of bones, the variety of artifacts, and then threw the bones back."

"Surprised he didn't study them."

"Some of the villagers were angry at Philip's 'violation' of the cenote, so he returned the bones, concentrated on ruins, and everyone settled down."

The sound of more voices came on the wind.

"Busy place," Hunter murmured.

"The wheel of time turns tonight. The Long Count ends and the Fourteenth Baktun begins. It will be a lot more quiet after that. Until then"—she shrugged—"we'll leave the cenote to the villagers. It costs us nothing and pleases them."

"And they'll be in church on Sundays and holy days."

"Their lives, their choices."

"A very modern point of view," Hunter said quietly as he eased back undercover. "Neither the Maya nor the Spanish were so broad-minded. For a lot of cultures, religion is a blood sport."

Lina followed Hunter's move to leave. As she started to go back, her body stroked over his. Even if the trail hadn't forced them close, she still would have touched him. She'd wanted him since her first breath this morning. Face-to-face with him, she paused, absorbed in how the silver in his eyes reflected the green shadows of the enclosing plants.

The voices from the other side of the cenote became louder, then faded, absorbed by the jungle.

"We haven't really been alone since we left the estate," Hunter said quietly in English. "That's why we're not finding out just how hard a limestone mattress is."

She hesitated, not even a breath away from him, and switched to English. "We're being followed?"

"Does your neck itch?"

"No more than usual in the jungle," she said wryly. "Getting used to the insects takes me a week or two."

He nodded. "But you know that we're being watched. Not by the same people, but we're never alone for more than a few minutes at a time."

She shrugged. "There are three villages

within several kilometers. Cenote de Balam is sacred, and this is a big holy day for the Maya. I'd be surprised if there weren't people gathering around the area. Plus, I'm a Reyes Balam with a strange male at my side. Naturally they would look out for me."

For a long moment Hunter weighed what Lina had said. Then he nodded. "So much for my fantasies of jungle sex."

Lina smiled. "C'mon. Maybe we'll get lucky in the ruins."

"You're laughing at me."

"I've never had so much fun in my life," she admitted.

"Will you enjoy it as much when you fig-ure out it's not a game?" he asked softly.

Before she could find an answer, Hunter was moving down the trail, away from the cenote.

And Lina.

## CHAPTER NINETEEN

HUNTER STOOD AT THE EDGE OF THE SMALL clearing where Lina had parked the Bronco. The vehicle looked undisturbed, yet they had rarely been without the presence of voices on the wind.

"Wait," Hunter said as Lina headed for the Bronco.

He circled the vehicle, saw nothing suspicious, and waved her over. After they got in, he watched Lina back the Bronco until she found a place to turn. She hadn't said a word since the cenote.

"You drive very well," he said.

"I thought you were mad at me."

"I'm mad at the situation, not you."

She got the vehicle straightened out and gave him a long look.

He smiled gently.

After a moment she put the Bronco in gear and headed back toward the main road.

"I've been driving estate roads since I was old enough to see over the dashboard," she said. "Philip liked having someone to run errands for him on the digs. That way he didn't have to leave a site for months at a time."

"The villagers don't drive?"

"Once a dig is set up, Philip doesn't allow any vehicle but his own in the area."

Hunter smiled thinly. "That puts the brakes on the size and quantity of what people can steal."

"We have very little theft here."

Crutchfeldt's words about grave robbers at work on Reyes Balam lands echoed in Hunter's mind, but he didn't say anything. Whoever or whatever El Maya was, he terrified people to the point that outside artifact poachers apparently didn't set foot on Reyes Balam lands—or if they did, they died.

"Loyalty is good," Hunter said, "but not all humans are."

"If theft occurs, it's punished the Maya way."

"Which is?"

"If the thief is from outside the estate lands," Lina said reluctantly, "the villagers beat him. Savagely. If the thief is from one of our villages, he gets the beating after his right hand is chopped off with a machete."

"That would limit the thieves," Hunter said mildly. *No scary El Maya mastermind necessary. Just a kind of pragmatism the civilized world shuns. Life lived very close to the bone.*

"It's the dark side of a quiet village," Lina said. "I understand why the customs exist, but I don't like all of them, any more than I like their preferential treatment of men over women. I don't like the second-class citizenship of most Maya in Mexico either. Things are changing, but slowly. It's education that works in the long run."

"Choices," Hunter said.

She nodded, then concentrated on a difficult stretch of the miserable "road." He settled back and kept note of the state of the track, the compass in the dashboard, and any landmarks the jungle permitted. He could mentally retrace every bit of their way, starting at the compound and working outward. It was a skill that had become habit in his childhood, where river marshes and brush formed an enticing maze for a curious boy.

Lina turned onto the main estate road, followed it for a time, then turned off onto a side road that slowly unraveled into a limestone track barely worn through the relentless vegetation. The track dodged around bigger and bigger trees until only trunks and vines and the most shade-hardy shrubs existed at ground level. The effect was almost parklike, but experience told Hunter that walking wouldn't be easy.

With automatic motions, Lina turned the Bronco and backed down the roughest trail until she finally came to a stop.

"We're here," she said, turning off the engine.

He looked around and saw nothing much different than he had been seeing. "If you say so."

"The foot trail is off to the left."

She reached for the backpack, only to have him snag it first.

"It's less than a kilometer," she said.

"What is?"

"A surprise."

Hunter compared where they were to the map he had built in his mind of the Reyes Balam estate. Right now they were perhaps two kilometers as the crow—or macaw—flies from the compound itself, and about a quarter of that to the Jaguar Cenote.

Eagerly Lina got out and headed for the trail that experience rather than her eyes told her was waiting. Hunter shut the Bronco door quietly behind him and walked into another aspect of the jungle world.

Copal and ceiba trees dominated the jungle, tall and mighty, their branches lifting to an unseen sky and their roots gripping the earth like a thousand snakes. For a moment Hunter saw the world as the Maya had. A huge ceiba tree was the only thing stitching the world together, the World Tree rooted in hell and holding heaven in its arms.

If the tree released its grip, reality would fly away.

The hair on the back of his arms and neck stood up. The last time he'd sensed anything like this, he had been far out from civilization, alone in the desert, at the edge of lost, in the presence of something that was far bigger than he was, something utterly indifferent to all things human.

The raucous call of a macaw grounded him again. Up above his head, a toucan snapped its bill. The thick, heavy bill looked like a fighting claw without a crab. The green on green of the jungle seethed with hidden life. Even when the jungle looked quiet, it was alive, moving, breathing, as restless in its own way as the sea.

And as relentless.

"Hunter?" Lina called softly.

He turned and walked toward her. She watched him, enjoying the lithe efficiency of his movements. He was the only man she'd ever known who was as comfortable in the wilds of the inhuman jungle as he was in the human jungle of a big city. She could picture him on a dig with an ease that was frightening.

**I've always wanted a man who could handle both city and jungle. Question is, can I handle him?**

She didn't know. Part of her—the part that thought of her parents' marriage—was wary of finding out. The rest of her hummed with anticipation.

"Are we there?" he said.

Lina realized she'd been standing and staring at Hunter. She shook herself.

"Until we reach the path, try not to leave any sign that we were here," she said.

He gave her a questioning look.

"I . . ." she began, then stopped, wondering how to explain. "Where we're going is very special. Villagers know about it, of course, but rarely visit."

"Taboo?" he asked.

"Not exactly. Their lives and ceremonies center around the Jaguar Cenote, the Cenote de Balam, so there's no reason to hike deep into the jungle. Village life doesn't leave a lot of time or energy for sightseeing."

"No tours?" he asked dryly.

"None, thank you very much. We don't want this place trampled or loved to death. Leave that for the better-known sites, with their groomed grounds and guards and partially excavated ruins."

"I'll be more careful with the jungle than it will be with me," Hunter promised.

Lina smiled. "The jungle thanks you."

She turned and pushed gently through a barrier of young trees, vines, and shrubs struggling against one another in the small opening left when a copal monarch had fallen.

Watching, listening, Hunter followed, feeling like a water bug in a marsh. Everything was much bigger than he was, older, tougher. The vegetation's struggle for light—for life itself—was timeless, all the more primal for its silence.

"Why didn't the Maya worship the strangler fig tree?" Hunter asked. "It can kill the biggest of trees."

"Many of the ceiba trees have just four main branches, like the four cardinal points. The roots are thick and obvious, their shoulders visible at the base of the trunk." Carefully she picked a way through the thicket of shrubs and vines. "The ceiba trunk goes up and up and up, like a pillar separating the overworld from the underworld. No other tree is quite like it."

Only after Lina and Hunter had passed through the tangle of plants did she unclip her machete. She checked her wrist compass, adjusted course, and set off. He followed her over rocky ground, around godlike ceiba trees growing taller and taller despite the weak soil feeding them. Some of them had grown together until their trunks were intertwined in unnatural embrace. The ground around them was sterile, sucked dry by the needs of the mighty trees.

The trail Lina followed was more unreal than real, better suited to four feet or wings. Claw marks reached above Hunter's head on one of the copal trunks. Resin bled out, hardening in the air, ready to be used for the sacred, scented fire of Maya ceremonies.

"Jaguar," Lina said, gesturing to the claw marks. "Though I don't think we've had anyone on the estate grounds killed by one since I was a little girl."

"You better be kidding."

She smiled and then spoke with the softness the jungle seemed to demand. "I am. Mostly. Our entire holdings are protected land for jaguars. No hunting allowed. No scientific study either. Abuelita firmly believes the cats should be left alone as long as they leave the villagers alone."

"What happens if a cat starts snacking on the locals?" Hunter asked.

"Then the family or the villagers take

care of it. That's as it must be. If the cats didn't respect and avoid people, there soon would be no jaguars at all."

The path became more obvious, although far from a well-beaten trail. Their feet made little noise and less impression on the jungle debris covering the ground. Only the occasional stain showed where boots had left marks on limestone rubble. The strident bird and monkey calls became part of the background, like an erratic heartbeat, noticeable only in its absence.

A striped iguana watched them, clinging to the side of a rock as big as the Bronco. There was a rough face carved on the stone, barely visible through an overgrowth of lichen and moss. Hunter couldn't tell whether the face was a finished work or started and then abandoned because of one crisis or another.

Lina never paused. Nor did she find any need for her machete. Finally she clipped it back in place, deciding that Philip must have been on the path recently.

**He promised not to dig here without telling me. It was the price of me leaving him alone for the last four summers.**

But she knew that sometimes Philip's

promises were forgotten before the echo of the words had died. He wasn't treacherous, simply self-absorbed. Something else would claim his attention and mere words exchanged between people would fade to nothing at all.

The canopy above them rustled and a flock of macaws burst through, leaving in their wake a random rain of droppings and half-eaten fruit. Red and blue streaked by, like tropical fish fleeing danger through a green sea.

Gradually Hunter noticed a random scattering of modern debris mostly hidden among the vines and moss—cigarette butts, scraps of greasy paper, broken glass winking from beneath green leaves, petals where no flowers were blooming nearby. Some of the petals were fresh.

Lina paused, listening.

Faint voices came from ahead.

Hunter's hand touched the small of her back. His lips brushed over her ear.

"More villagers?" he asked very softly.

"Sounds like." Her voice wasn't as soft as his. She was curious rather than wary. "Probably they're including some of the old places in tonight's celebration. It's a very big moment for the Maya."

Hunter was remembering Crutchfeldt's words about grave robbers and a man whose name it was death to speak. All things considered, assuming El Maya was a legend wasn't smart.

"We'll come back tomorrow," Hunter said.

She waited, listening. "They're gone now."

"The back of my neck itches," he said.

"Use more insect repellent."

"Lina—"

She held up her hand, stopping his words.

Nothing came through the jungle but silence.

She waited for a long ten count, then another. When the small and large sounds of the jungle slowly returned, she looked at him.

"They're gone," she said.

"So are we," he said, turning back toward the Bronco.

"I'm on Reyes Balam land. The locals know me. As long as you stay with me, they won't bother either of us. In fact, they probably left rather than disturb me."

Hunter stood and smelled the air, listened, and waited.

"Smoke of some kind," he said finally.

"The jungle is too wet to burn," she said impatiently.

"Cigarettes aren't."

"I've seen the litter. We'll pick it up on the way out. If it's messy again in a week, Abuelita or Carlos will send someone to clean up. The locals can treat their villages like garbage dumps, but not the rest of the Reyes Balam lands, especially around ruins."

With that, Lina headed up the trail once more, her stride purposeful. Hunter knew he had the choice of dragging her screaming back to the Bronco—dumb idea, considering the protective natives—or following her.

Muttering curses that could shrivel leaves, he walked quickly after her.

"It's just over the next rise," she said without turning around.

Hunter eyed lichen-covered rubble that was more green than gray. Emerald spikes of aloe plants dotted the ridge like a low fence. Where the limestone pushed through the thin soil in great lumps, shrubbery flourished in the sun beyond the overwhelming reach of ceiba and copal trees.

Lina pushed through the undergrowth, gathering new welts to match her old. Behind her, Hunter did the same. Neither of them commented on the small wounds. Both understood that the jungle was its own master and exacted its due from soft-skinned trespassers.

In tandem, Lina and Hunter climbed down to a low outcrop of limestone that overlooked a small clearing ringed with more of the misshapen ceiba trees. The roots were unusually gnarled and twisted, more like strangler figs than ceiba. Even for vegetation powerful enough to hold overworld and underworld together, life right here was a raw struggle.

At the center of a clearing Hunter saw a mound that had once been far taller than he was. Now it was about his height. The rubble surrounding it was at least twenty yards across. All of it had been consumed by the jungle, though the biggest lime-stone blocks were still fighting for their place in the sun.

Hunter took a slow, deep breath. Perhaps smoke from clove cigarettes, perhaps a dead campfire, perhaps his instincts working in overdrive. Whatever had happened here recently wasn't happening at this moment. He no longer felt watched with predatory interest.

And he still didn't like the fact that he had felt that way.

"Any back roads from here to Tulum?" he asked.

"None that don't pass over estate lands. As a cat sanctuary, we're off-limits to tourists and hikers. Besides, there's not much here to see. No beaches. No mountains or canyons worth mentioning. No striking ruins. No village fairs. Bird-watching is average, at best. Cenote de Balam is barely known beyond the boundary of the estate itself."

Hunter nodded slowly. "What you're saying is that the area is pretty much a blank spot on the map."

"A lot of the Yucatan is like that. Without rivers to provide food, freshwater, and relatively easy access, or any wealth to be mined once you manage to get deep into the jungle, this area has been left alone. Around Tulum there is the biggest underwater cave complex in the world, all gnawed out of limestone one drop at a time. But none of the underground passages connects with our cenotes."

"Somebody liked it a long time ago," he said, looking at the rubble mound.

"Even before the Maya came, there were people here. Some of the oldest human skeletons in the New World have been found deep in the flooded caves of Tulum. They come from a time when an ice age locked up so much water the sea level was much lower than now."

"What about this site right here? Has this been dug?"

"No. There were—and are—more promising sites. But this one is my favorite. There's something about the isolation, the feeling of time made tangible." She half smiled. "I've never been able to explain it. This site simply draws me."

He studied the overgrown remnants of what had once been a substantial structure. Very faint paths webbed around the mound, leading to the far side.

"So, what is this place?" Hunter asked as he looked for any sign of an entryway.

"It's a tomb. We think."

"'We'?" Hunter asked. "Philip comes here?"

"Not since we measured it. Ten years ago I found this site and some others by using remote sensing techniques. Spectral analysis of satellite images of the jungle pointed me in the right direction. Even overgrown sites reflect light differently from undisturbed jungle. Philip listed them in order from most promising to least and went to work."

"With your help?"

Her mouth tightened. "When I insisted. And I insisted that I be here for any excavation at this site. So"—she shrugged—"he put it at the bottom of the list."

"And you're still waiting."

"Most of the time, I don't mind. Part of me likes knowing the mound is here, untouched."

A breeze came, swirled. It sounded like snakes crawling around them, a dry scrape of scales. The haze in the sky was still thin, barren of rain.

"What do you think the rubble once was?" Hunter asked.

"Philip says it was like the rest of the

Reyes Balam sites, only much smaller, a sixteenth-century pimple on the bitter end of the Maya road."

"After the Spanish?" Hunter asked, measuring the rubble and the jungle with the eyes of a predator rather than a tourist or an archaeologist.

"We're not entirely sure, but yes. Most of our Reyes Balam sites were created by people fleeing population centers after the fall of the Maya civilization, which preceded the Spanish. Some of the sites we've found were active several generations before 1550, but after that, the sites grew quickly in size and number."

"Vanquished kings looking for new thrones."

Lina smiled. "I doubt that our Maya ancestor was a king. More like a favored son who saw the Spanish handwriting on the wall and put his *X* on the winning side. But the Balam genealogy insists he was a king. We have a family crest in Madrid to support that claim."

Hunter shook his head. "And you just want to be plain old Lina Taylor, Ph.D. Must really make your family crazy."

"They return the favor."

The breeze lifted again, almost secretive in its hushed presence.

With pale eyes Hunter searched the jungle. If there were any more mounds, he couldn't see them beneath the thick growth.

"Mind if I walk around the edges?" he asked.

"Go ahead. If there was anything of obvious archaeological significance, Philip would have been here, rather than scrambling around in Belize."

"Philip sounds like the type who couldn't overlook any chance, however slim or distant, to get one up on a rival."

"You haven't even met him, yet you already know him."

"You're a good teacher." Hunter jumped lightly down from the outcropping, then turned and held his arms up for Lina.

She could have jumped down just fine without him, and both of them knew it. So she smiled and let him lift her. Before he put her down, he gave her the kind of kiss that made the world spin around her.

"Your father may act like an ass," Hunter breathed against her lips, "but he contributed sperm toward one extraordinary offspring."

Lina blinked against a sudden sting at the back of her eyes. "Thank you."

"I didn't do a thing. You did."

Before she could say anything, he lowered his head just enough to sink into her mouth. She flowed against him like warmth from a fire, sinking into him in turn. Finally, slowly, he raised his head.

"Either we stop now or we go for ticket sales and a limestone mattress," he said hoarsely.

"Ticket sales?"

"The locals lurking out in the jungle."

"Oh." She sighed. "I'm willing to try the limestone mattress, but not the tickets."

"You sure?"

"Yes."

"Figured." He blew out a hard breath and reminded himself of all the reasons it would be really stupid to let down his guard long enough to do what his body was demanding. "C'mon, let's take a walk around the ruins."

She led him to a reasonably clear thread of path and set out toward the mound.

"Who do you think is buried here?" Hunter asked.

"Somebody more important than the

folks who built the tomb," she said dryly. "But on the scale of Maya monuments, this is really small change. It's isolated, unconnected to any other sites."

"Could have been a secret place."

She gave him a startled look over her shoulder. "That's what I think. Or rather, what I feel. This is an unusual site."

"Why don't you explore it?"

"Philip has first rights on all the ruins on Reyes Balam land. It was part of the prenuptial agreement he signed. In return, he gave up any legal claim to Celia's name or inheritance."

"He gets first dig rights and walks away from the sure thing—money."

Lina laughed oddly. "Celia married to get out of the Yucatan. Philip married to get exclusive digging rights in the Yucatan. The old Chinese curse—may your fondest wish come true."

Hunter whistled softly. "Life's a tricky bitch."

"Oh yeah. Even back then, Philip was drawn to hints of Kawa'il. He met Celia on a university-sponsored dig on Reyes Balam lands. When I read *Moby-Dick* on the way to my undergrad degree, I thought of

Kawa'il. It's Philip's white whale, his obsession. The more it eludes him, the greater his need to pursue."

"I saw the movie. Didn't end well."

The feeling of being watched returned. It wasn't simply the sensation of being in a jungle that felt alive and *other*.

"Are you sure we're alone out here?" Hunter asked, switching to English.

"As long as we aren't testing mattresses, we're okay," Lina said in the same language. "The local Maya knew about this place long before anyone cared. It wasn't disturbed then. It won't be looted and sold on the black market now."

Something rustled out at the edge of the clearing, twigs whipping against what sounded like flesh. The wind blew hot, feeling too dry for the jungle.

Hunter followed Lina around to the back of the mound and nearly ran into her when she stopped dead in the path.

"What—" he began.

She pointed, her finger trembling. Her voice made clear it was rage, not fear, coursing through her. "Some of the rubble has been moved."

Whoever had done it had been careful

to disturb as little of the overgrowth as possible. It took Hunter a moment to see what Lina saw.

"I can't believe looters are here," she said hoarsely.

Hunter had drawn his gun from beneath the backpack. He held the weapon along his leg, not wanting to spook Lina unless he had to.

"Neatest looters I ever saw," he said.

She closed her eyes and tried to manage the rage that had flooded her at the thought of her secret place being pillaged. After a moment she opened her eyes and saw what Hunter had.

A casual visitor wouldn't have noticed the subtle movement of rubble and overgrowth. There were none of the potholes and garbage and careless piles of dirt that were signatures of an illegal dig.

The breeze shifted shadows and sunlight. Something gleaming in the disturbed area caught Hunter's eye.

Metal, not glass.

He followed a very faint trail winding amid overgrown blocks of rubble. Within four steps he saw the gleam of fresh brass. He bent and picked it up with his left hand.

It was slightly cooler than his skin, no warmer or colder than the ground itself. On the back of the cartridge, the head stamp read $7.62 \times 39$. He rolled it in his fingers and passed the open end under his nose, smelling for gunpowder but getting only the faintest trace. Probably his imagination.

"How long since the last rain?" Hunter asked Lina as she hurried to him.

"I don't know," she said. "It can rain every day, but the weather's been weird here just like it has up in Houston."

He wrapped his fingers around the spent cartridge. "This smells dead. It could have been fired days or weeks ago. Brass is still shiny."

She looked at the gun in his right hand.

"Wrong caliber," he said, smiling faintly.

What he didn't say was that he would bet good money that the spent brass had come from an AK-47.

"But—" she began.

"Quiet," he breathed. He pressed her behind him into a shallow alcove in the mound of rubble. "Someone is out there."

# CHAPTER TWENTY

LINA'S PULSE HAMMERED AGAINST HER WRISTS. She had trouble keeping still while being held off balance with one side of her head pressed to the stone and the rest of her pressed against Hunter.

He stood quietly, his pale eyes raking shadows for a target.

Changing direction and strengthening, the wind kicked up, no longer dry. It was like jaguar breath, hot and moist. Bits of man-made and natural litter danced along the ground, covering any sounds that might have come from farther away, beyond the edge of the clearing.

Hunter waited, knowing there weren't enough shots in the magazine to manage a standoff. Rodrigo's illegal gun would put out a lot of stopping power, but not at a great range, certainly not enough to be much good against the thick cover of the encroaching jungle. Concealed by wind and vegetation, a dozen men could be closing in.

But the shadow that had alerted him was no longer there.

The exhalation of wind faded.

"Stay here," Hunter said.

He eased away from her, then made a sharp motion that no watcher could have missed.

Nobody cared enough to shoot.

Deliberately Hunter shrugged out of the backpack and swung it out into the open. Nobody shot at the sudden target.

He retreated to cover, shoved the gun into the back of his pants, put the backpack on, and returned to Lina.

"Nada," he said.

She nodded without looking at him. Her fingertips were digging along a faint, straight line among the stones. Now that she had called his attention to it, he could see that other fingers had been there before hers, rubbing against lichen and moss, and keeping bigger jungle plants at bay.

Hunter's curiosity fired. "Is it a door?"

"Looks like."

She worked her fingers along the tiny seam where the limestone blocks came apart. These huge pieces of stone were squared off, unlike the more uneven, harshly weathered blocks that had fallen from higher. It looked like a wall mostly concealed by rubble.

"Is it stuck?" he asked quietly.

"Probably hasn't been opened in centuries. We should get an engineering study to make sure that—"

With only the faintest grating noise, the stone moved.

Lina made a shocked sound and peered into the darkness. She could see just enough to tell that the door had moved aside into a prepared niche in the wall.

"It worked," she said, astonished.

"Too well."

"What do you—oh. It's been maintained. How odd. Philip never mentioned anything. But then, he wouldn't," she added with faint bitterness.

Hunter checked over his shoulder. Nothing but jungle, no sound except the faint rub of leaf against leaf as the wind slowly twisted. Whoever or whatever was out there wasn't interested in confrontation.

"What is this place?" he asked.

"I don't know," Lina replied. "It doesn't feel like any tomb I've ever been in. Something is . . . odd."

He nodded. His eyes never stopped probing the surrounding jungle.

"Look," Lina said, her voice urgent.

Hunter spun back to Lina's position and glanced inside. She stood half in light, the rest of her consumed by shadows. A few feet farther into the mound was what looked like a wall, yet a faint light came from one side. It took only a few steps before a blunt, short hallway, perhaps three feet by five feet, maybe more, opened at an angle deeper in the rubble.

Pale candles that smelled faintly of flowers burned in the darkness along one wall.

"Someone lit these," she said, going through the opening into the ruin.

He stepped inside after her, pulling the gun once more. When he moved to the right, the door slid back into place behind him.

"What the hell?" he muttered.

"I think whoever was here is gone," Lina said. "The candle-lined passage is empty and the flames are still. The opening of the door didn't really affect them. Nobody has hurried by lately, disturbing the flames."

"Stay put. I have to check something." He set the gun in an empty waist-level niche and took a penlight from his pocket, the same burglar's tool he'd found in his uncle's house in Padre. The thin beam revealed a finger-smoothed line around the rim of the door, just like on the outside. He pushed, prodded, cursed, stepped to the right—and the door opened. He stepped back across the entrance to the left and it closed again.

"Must be some kind of counterweight system," Hunter said, retrieving the gun and putting it at the small of his back.

"As long as we can open it, I don't care if it's PFM."

"PFM?"

"Pure flaming magic," she said, feeling her heartbeat settle.

He laughed softly. "As good an explanation as any."

"It's cooler in here than I expected," Lina said.

Hunter took a breath. "And dry. More PFM?"

"Works for me right now."

"Want more light?" Hunter asked.

Her teeth flashed against her skin as she smiled. "Not yet. I like seeing it as the Maya did."

"Sorry I left my copal torch at home," he said dryly, switching off his penlight. "I only have the twenty-first-century kind."

Smiling, she started to walk toward the end of the short, candlelit hall.

Hunter's hand clamped around her wrist, stopping her barely a step inside the blunt passage. Startled, she looked at his face. In the knee-high candlelight he looked hard, almost demonic. She froze, listening as he was listening.

Nothing. Not even the faintest rustle of a lizard.

Gently he released her. Then he switched on his penlight again.

"I don't—" she began.

"Let me look at the floor before you go exploring."

The beam was thin as a laser, a cold slash of blue white. Unlike the floor, the walls and ceiling were finished in limestone stucco. The uncovered stone on the floor had been worn away by the passage of feet, leaving a dull streak against the surface. The streak led to the far wall, and what looked to be a dead end.

"Dirty feet," Hunter said. "Or sandals. If it's safe for them, it's safe for us." He clicked off the beam. "Go ahead."

"Pit traps only happen in movies," she muttered.

"I saw that one, too," he said. "Ended well."

Candlelight bent and straightened as they walked down the hall. At the back, there was another hall branching off at a right angle. On the far side there were stone steps leading down to a place where no candles glowed.

Lina counted six steps before she lost them to the darkness. What she could see was polished limestone, dimmed at the center by the passage of many feet.

The air was definitely cool, dry. A slight draft flowed out from the dark opening at the bottom of the steps.

"Okay, I'll think about going modern." She reached for the flap of the backpack Hunter wore and fished blindly around for one of the heavy flashlights she'd packed.

But when she retrieved it, she hesitated.

His small beam switched on again. The thin light burned blue across the darkness.

"Is that some kind of censer at the back?" he asked.

She moved to stand beside him on the narrow landing at the top of the steps. At the far side of the large room there was a stone carved like a grimacing face. Air seemed to breathe out from the mouth and eyes and cutout sigils in the cheeks and forehead.

"More like a grate, I think," she said. "The air coming out is fresh, dry, quite cool. Eerie."

She felt Hunter beside her, close and warm, definitely real.

"The grate could lead to an underground opening into a cave system," Hunter said.

"The would explain the temperature, but the dryness?"

"Damned odd," he agreed. He moved his hand to the left, revealing another bit of the room. What had looked like a dim shadow flared into startling life. "But so is a shrine with only red petals. No whole flowers that I can see."

"At least the flies don't like it."

"Bodes well for the local wildlife," he agreed.

Candles of varied thicknesses, height, and color were scattered throughout in the room. Thin wisps of smoke still curled from hastily snuffed wicks.

"This is the smoke you smelled," she said suddenly. "The candles were put out when we got near. But where is all the smoke going? We should be choking."

There was no answer but the sigh of air through the room. Though the grate was at the back, the whole room seemed clear.

"Whoever was here, it wasn't looters," Hunter said. "They would use better light and not worry about fresh flower petals."

"Not looters," Lina breathed, shivering lightly. She moved his hand, guiding the beam of light while she spoke. "Look at the big candles at the four corners of the room, look at their colors. Sak, the north, is white; Kan, to the east, is yellow for the sunrise; Boox, to the west, is black for sunset; and Chak, to the south near the shrine, is red for blood. This is a sacred place."

"Or it's narcos stashing stuff here and trying to freak out any locals," Hunter said, but he didn't really believe it.

"There's nobody out here to frighten. No water but rainfall. Very little game to eat. No fruit trees to draw even monkeys. If narcos set this up, they're only scaring themselves. Besides," she said, releasing his hand, "can't you *feel* it? This is a place of power, of worship."

Hunter felt it. He just wasn't happy talking about it.

Looking for a vent or some way for the smoke to escape, he moved the beam of his light overhead. Lines of blue raced over the ceiling and down the wall, everywhere blue, gleaming and silent, calling across the centuries. Gradually he realized that there was red and white and black, even jade green gleaming in polychrome pictures; but the impact came from the many shades of blue, the voice of a god pouring from images of feathered deities and serpents.

There was not an inch of walls or ceiling left bare.

Lina let out a sound that could have been awe or disbelief or both mingling as the serpents did, indistinguishable.

"Late Post-Classic Mayan glyphs," she said faintly. "Very refined glyphs, very precise. As elegant in their own way as the Lindisfarne manuscript. The culmination of millennia of culture striving to describe the unknowable."

Slowly Hunter played the thin light beam over the walls around the entrance where they stood.

"That's not a mass of snakes as I first thought," Lina said. "It's a single gigantic serpent, made up of countless others."

"I can't see where one ends and the other begins," he said.

"You're not meant to."

A sea of scales and massive wings covered in rainbow feathers arched over the entrance to the room. Each movement of the flashlight revealed more details, more complexity, more colors that seemed to change as they watched.

"This is impossible," she said in a whisper.

"The clean air?" he said, still clearly caught by that unexplained reality.

"No. The range and subtlety of color is fantastic. Look at these rich greens. You expect to see blues endure, but none of these colors has degraded at all."

The coils of the serpent were all around them, above them. Some of the scales were rippling masked faces; some human, some demonic, and some animal, each of them idealized, all of them a great artist's representation of Maya fears and hopes.

"The depth . . ." Lina said. "There's a strange kind of dimensionality to everything, a depth that most Maya art shuns. This isn't intentionally flat or linear. It . . . breathes."

Hunter could only stare. Every time his flashlight moved even slightly, he would swear that the coils of the snake twitched. Like all great art, the serpent had a life independent of its maker. It simply *was*.

Another light clicked on. He started, then realized Lina had turned on her flashlight while he stared in awe at the slowly writhing snake. Her light was broader, warmer, more gold than blue. Closer to candlelight, but without its grace. The broad beam moved with deliberation over the walls and ceiling, up and down and then up again, a serpentine motion that was hypnotizing.

He moved his flashlight enough to see her face without distracting her. The gold buried in her dark eyes flashed and sparked, a mystery he would never solve, even more compelling to him than the images covering the walls.

The beam continued its circuit of walls and ceiling, then began all over again. Silent tears gleamed on Lina's face as the beauty and meaning of what she was seeing began to sink in.

"And to think Philip wrote this place off as a pimple on the history of the Maya," she said after a long silence. "This is one of the biggest complete wall paintings I've seen in the Maya style. The technique is incredibly refined. It must have taken years to execute."

Hunter could only watch the serpent watching him.

"You know what this is?" she asked finally, her voice husky with excitement.

"A snake. A really, really big one."

"It's Kukulcán in his serpent aspect. It has to be."

"So you've seen something like this before?" Hunter asked, unable to take his eyes off the endless, seething sea of scales and feathers.

"No, not this big, not this detailed," she said. "Even the paintings in the Petén don't compare to this. Petén's art is shallow and flat. But this . . . Bonampak might compare, maybe, but I don't believe it. I can't believe this."

"Is there any way to date the room?" Hunter asked. "I mean the painting, not the site itself."

"We can try to find soot for carbon dating, maybe even take some paint samples." Yet even as she spoke, she was shaking her head. "I couldn't bear to chip off a single piece of this. You could reach out and touch Kukulcán, feel the wind off its wings, breathe the sacred presence."

"That's the breeze through the hallway," Hunter said.

She gave him a glance from gold-shot dark eyes. "You hope it is." But she smiled, understanding a modern man's unease with ancient things that had no good explanation. "I'd guess that this temple is between four and five centuries old. I'd have to do some soil analysis and compare construction styles and techniques. Someone— generations of someones—have kept this in beautiful shape."

"PFM," he said absently.

Hunter was compelled by what his penlight revealed. The snake figure ended or changed before repeating itself. It was hard to tell. The whole painting flowed, seethed at the edges where darkness was.

The broader beam of Lina's light joined his, and he saw the serpent's jaws were gaping, revealing rows of teeth and a very wide red human tongue. There was an eerie, almost human aspect to the face, but it wasn't benign or inviting. The artist had captured the raw, primal majesty of a god that was worthy of awe and reverence. Its eyes were open, glowing gold with ruby irises. When the angle of the light changed, the pupils seemed to flicker between the vertical slit of a reptile and the rounder aspect of the human.

In candlelight, the effect would be terrifying.

The mouth was big enough for a large man to be swallowed inside. Hunter wondered if the man would emerge again, filled with godlike knowledge, or simply disappear to be digested by darkness. His skin rippled in primal response, making body hair stand on end.

He had no desire to be the priest-king swallowed by this god.

Hunter's pencil beam moved on to another part of the wall. A figure leaped out of time. He was a tall, muscular, idealized man wearing a mask.

"Lina," he said, "I need some more light over here."

With a reluctance that said more than words, Lina's light moved slowly to join his.

The figure was wearing a mask made of obsidian, gleaming and black as midnight water. The mask had aspects of bird and bat, beast and human.

Her breath came in, stopped. "That's a painting of the missing mask. It shows how it was meant to be used, in whose honor, in which ceremony."

Hunter stared at a representation of the

mask that had been stolen from the shipment seized by ICE.

The figure wearing the mask had a single hand outstretched to the mouth of the
serpent, fingers wide in courageous expectation. The other figures around him
were very small, barely ankle-high, signifying their relative unimportance.

"This was a priest-king," Lina whispered.

"The marking on his chest." Hunter's
voice was like hers, hushed.

"Blood. See the torn edges of the skin
around the nipples? The blood dripping
from beneath the loincloth? He cut himself
beyond the point of pain to reach a different kind of consciousness."

Hunter winced. "Glad I was raised in a
church where all we did was peel off a little
cash for the Communion plate. Damn, it
takes huevos or insanity to slice into your
own dick."

"Look at the pattern of the fallen blood,"
Lina said. "There, between his feet."

Uneasily Hunter looked. Blood that had
dripped and streamed red became transformed into a blue glyph on the floor.
"Kawa'il. Again."

"That's who the offering is for, but who

is the man performing the ceremony?" she asked. "I don't see any sigils or historical glyphs indicating house and lineage and battles."

"Is that unusual?"

"Very. There should be exploits, explanations, genealogies." She swept the beam around but found only a sea of colored scales, the serpent in its thousand aspects, watching her.

"Over there," Hunter said. "The priest or king or whatever is reaching for something."

Slowly she turned her flashlight to find the figure of the priest-king and then followed his arm out to the hand, fingers gently splayed.

**There.**

She and Hunter both saw something in the space between the serpent and the man's outstretched hand.

"It looks like a small niche cut into the wall," Lina said.

Hunter followed her, keeping close.

Flames or beams of radiance were painted around the niche, but they glowed a faint blue instead of red or orange or gold.

"Lightning," she said. "Another manifestation of Kawa'il."

Hunter played the thin beam over the niche. "Wonder what was in here. It can't have been much more than fifteen inches long and maybe ten high, ten deep. Too small for a decent shrine."

She thought of the missing artifacts. "The obsidian mask wouldn't fit there, not with its ceremonial feathers and fastenings. The opening's not long enough for a scepter. A censer, maybe."

He went closer, ran a finger lightly over the ceiling of the niche. "No soot. No matter how magic the ventilation, burning enough copal leaves a residue."

"Okay, the niche didn't hold a small censer. The god bundle would fit, but not its sacred box. A ceremonial knife isn't compatible with the narrative."

"What narrative?"

"The room is a story of the opening of a conduit between gods and man," she said. "The giving or taking of knowledge."

"Knowledge? You mean like a book? A codex?"

"Impossible," she said instantly.

"So is this room."

Shaking her head, Lina held up her hand. "Let me think."

Silently Hunter studied the glowing scales and eerie eyes of the massive serpent. No matter how often he told himself otherwise, the damned thing was alive. Not bad, not good, just unnervingly *real*.

"Remember the wood piece in the museum?" Lina asked abruptly.

Hunter thought back to the time before Jase had been shot. It seemed like a year rather than only days.

"The plaque was a new piece that we had on loan," she said. "It depicted a Kukulcán figure and another masked figure like this one, reaching to one another. There was something between them, but whatever it was had been broken off."

"Empty, like the niche."

"I studied the wood. I made sketches and took photos. The sketches are back in Houston. The photos are on my phone. Maybe they can give us an idea of what was in the niche—if the narratives are the same."

"Won't know until we compare them," Hunter said. "Is your phone in the backpack?"

"No. It doesn't work here, so I left it at home. I was expecting a little walk around my favorite ruins, not this. I don't even have my camera." The last was said in something close to a wail.

His penlight clicked off and one of his arms went around her shoulders. "Easy, sweetheart. This has been here for centuries. It will be here when we get back with cameras and measuring tools and the whole dig thing."

Her head thumped against his shoulder. "All I was thinking about was getting you alone. I'm an idiot!"

His other arm came around her and he held her close. "I like the way you're thinking. And don't call my favorite woman an idiot. You're insulting my taste."

She banged her forehead against his chest. "You're softer than a wall. Barely."

"Go lower. Things get harder."

He heard muffled laughter against his chest. Then, more clearly, she said, "I like you, Hunter Johnston. A lot. Only you could make me feel good about being so stupid as to leave the most basic work tools behind."

"Thank you. I think."

Her arms went around him as she stood on tiptoe and brushed her lips over his. The touch lingered, deepened, became a sensual mating of tongues. After a long time Lina lifted her head and sighed.

"But I have my sketchbook in the backpack, and you to hold the flashlight," she said.

Hunter sensed some long hours ahead. The look on her face kept him from protesting.

"Good thing you packed lots of food and water," he said, sighing.

"UH, SWEETHEART, UNLESS YOU BROUGHT MORE batteries, it's time to go," Hunter said.

Lina looked up, startled. "What time is it?"

"Time to go."

Stretching her cramped fingers, she stood. And groaned. "Sorry. I forgot everything but sketching."

"I noticed," he said, smiling.

She blinked and looked around, reluctant to leave even though her flashlight was dead and his was losing intensity.

"You owe me a big favor for standing here like a floor lamp all this time," he said.

"Repayment will likely involve costumes and sexual excess."

She looked intrigued, then interested. Very interested.

He groaned. "I should have thought about that hours ago. C'mon. I don't want to mess up the religious juju happening here."

She nipped at his chin. "Unlike other cultures, the Maya have almost no artistic tradition of depicting the act of reproduction. Likely, sex wasn't that important to them as a culture."

"Huh. No wonder their civilization fell."

Lina laughed. "You are such a man."

He smiled slowly. "That's because you're such a woman."

With a shake of her head, she followed the light beam back to the entrance of the tomb. Most of the candles had burned out, but a few were still waiting for the faithful man or men who had kept the temple clean. Despite the subtle draft from the back of the hall, the remaining flames burned bright and straight, bending only when she passed them.

It took Hunter a few tries, but the stone slab door opened onto the jungle. He let his eyes adjust to daylight before he drew Lina out of the tomb and into the cover of jumbled limestone blocks.

There was no unexpected shadow lurking, no sense of being watched.

"How's your neck?" he asked.

"Good."

"Let's go."

They covered the distance back to the Bronco quickly. Again, the vehicle was untouched.

"I know a lot of places that would pay big money to have this neighborhood watch system," Hunter said.

Lina smiled. "Want to drive?"

"How'd you guess?"

"The way your foot kept looking for the brake the whole time I was at the wheel."

"Did I say anything?"

"No. You earned major points for it, too. Almost as many as you earned last night."

He gave her a long, sideways look. "Yeah?"

"Oh yeah." She tossed him the keys.

"That's supposed to help me concentrate on driving?"

"Concentration equals more points."

"Huh. Definitely costumes are on the

schedule. Along with a few other things the Hindu culture was clever enough to illuminate in the Kama Sutra."

Lina bit back a laugh and climbed into the Bronco. She didn't have to give any directions as Hunter negotiated the confusing tracks that ultimately would lead to a better road. She relaxed into the seat, realizing that he was as good at backcountry driving as she had guessed.

"Sometimes I worry that you're too perfect," she said.

"What?" he asked, thinking he'd heard wrong.

She started to explain, then made a choked sound as he turned a blind corner and slammed on the brakes.

An old truck was approaching about fifty feet away. When the other driver saw the Bronco, he yanked the wheel and parked across the track, blocking it.

# CHAPTER TWENTY-ONE

"THAT'S PHILIP," LINA SAID. "BUT WHAT'S HE doing here?"

"Stopping us," Hunter said.

He eyed the growth on either side of the truck. Too thick and sturdy to muscle through. No other routes in sight, not even the faintest trace of a footpath.

"Wonder what kind of mood he's in," she muttered.

"What?"

"Philip can go from jovial to surly in a heartbeat." She reached for the door handle. "Better get it over with. Waiting won't improve whatever mood he's in."

She opened the door and got out with all the eagerness of someone heading for a root canal without anesthesia.

Hunter was one second behind her, then he was beside her. His glance swept the jungle before focusing on the man waiting in the truck. He was thick through the shoulders and tall enough that his head was close to the Rover's roof.

"Who the hell is this?" Philip demanded through the open window. "What's he doing on my land?"

"His land?" Hunter murmured. *Who made him king of the Yucatan?*

Lina gripped Hunter's hand and shook her head. "Let me handle him. You'll just make him more upset. And don't take it personally. He's rude to everyone."

"So I've heard."

She made the introductions through the open window. Other than a flat look from gray eyes, Philip ignored Hunter.

"You aren't supposed to be out here," Philip said to Lina. "Go back to the house right now."

She blinked. "I was just—"

"I told you there was nothing out here

worth looking at," Philip said over her. "You have no business here."

"But—"

"You heard me!" Philip shouted.

Hunter decided that he and Philip were never going to be buddies, so there was no point in playing nice. Begin as you mean to continue and all that.

"Lina is the Reyes Balam heir," Hunter said calmly. "She's also fully adult. She comes and goes as she pleases."

She looked at him. "It's okay."

"Actually, it isn't," Hunter said.

Philip began yelling, telling Hunter to get the hell off his land before he shot him, then repeating it again and again with emphasis, as if he shouted loud enough, long enough, Hunter would get it.

"Philip," Lina said, her voice sharp. "Hunter is my guest. Because of him, we made an astonishing discovery. Site number nine isn't a tomb, it's a temple. It's beautifully decorated with polychrome art of a fineness that has to be seen to be believed. I don't expect you to be grateful, but you can at least be—"

"You went inside?" Philip demanded.

"Yes, we—"

"You had no right. I have first excavation—"

"We didn't excavate anything," Hunter cut in. "And we're not the only people who know about it. The passages and main room were clean. Candles were lit. There's a shrine with fresh petals inside."

Philip's weathered skin flushed red, making his eyes appear almost white. "That's *my* temple. Every scale on Kukulcán is *mine.*"

At that instant Lina realized that not only did Philip already know about the temple, he had studied it.

"You promised you wouldn't explore it without me," she said.

"Don't be childish," Philip said, dismissing her with a look. "We'll discuss your behavior at the house. And don't think I won't check your car for stolen artifacts."

With that, Philip threw the Rover in reverse and began the tedious process of turning the vehicle on the narrow track.

Hunter and Lina went back to the Bronco.

"So that's Philip," Hunter said as they both got in.

Flags of anger burned high on her cheekbones. "He's in rare form."

"That's really special. Are we going back to talk with him?"

"Maybe he'll have cooled off by the time we get there."

*Or maybe I'll shove him in a cold shower,* Hunter thought. But he didn't say it aloud.

"I suppose I should apologize for not letting you handle it," he said. His tone said he wasn't going to. "Gotta say, you deserve better than him."

"If life was fair, we wouldn't invent so many religions."

He gave her a sideways look and a gentle stroke along her tense jawline. "I'll remember that."

They drove in silence for a time. Then she smacked her palm against the dashboard.

"I can't believe he dug without me," she said. "Oh, wait. I can believe. It just makes me want to take a shovel to that limestone block he calls his head. And now I sound like Celia."

"You sound like a woman who has been treated like a six-year-old."

"I should be used to it by now. But . . ."

"But?" Hunter asked when she remained silent.

"It seems that every time I come back he's worse. Well, not worse, just more like himself than I remember."

"That would be worse."

"Yeah."

More silence and rough road.

"I keep hoping he'll change," Lina said finally.

Hunter didn't say anything.

"Bad to worse is a change, right?" she asked.

"Not one I'd be happy about."

He maneuvered around a washout just before the main road. Philip's vehicle was nowhere in sight. Air flowed through the open windows, rich with the living breath of the jungle.

"Tomorrow morning we're gone," Lina said. "I'd leave now, but I promised Abuelita I'd be here for her birthday celebration. Unlike some people, I keep my promises."

"It's one of the things I really like about you."

She looked at him. "Same goes. I'm sorry you had to see him like that."

Hunter shrugged. "It's not your fault. If anything, it's mine."

"What do you mean?"

"You told me to let you handle him. I just really didn't like how he was handling *you*."

"I used to get mad about it," she said. "Then I figured it was a waste of energy. Today . . . he was way out of line."

"He ever hit you?" Hunter asked casually.

She looked startled. "Of course not."

"No 'of course' about it, sweetheart. It's a slippery slope from verbal abuse to physical. He wouldn't be the first man—or woman—to slide down."

"He's just blustery and rude."

Silently, Hunter thought someone should have taught Philip manners a long time ago. Or at least fear. But kids were stuck with the parents they had, and loved them despite everything.

"I'll try to behave better than he does," Hunter said. "What time are we leaving tomorrow?"

"Early," she said flatly.

"I'm going to be in your room again tonight."

Despite her anger and frustration with

her father, she gave Hunter a slow smile. "I'm counting on it."

What Hunter didn't say was that he'd be there even if he was sleeping on the floor. He didn't trust Philip. Her father wasn't lock-him-up crazy, but he wasn't a poster boy for rationality, either.

Silently they drove to the compound, parked, and walked down a crushed limestone path to Philip's casita. The morning haze hadn't thickened into afternoon rain, though thunder rumbled far away. The Casita Cenote guesthouse where Hunter was supposed to be sleeping was barely a pale shadow beyond the fairly mannerly tangle of greenery.

Philip's residence was a single-story, whitewashed L, with weathered storm shutters and a faded red-tile roof. Despite its occupant, Hunter liked the place a lot better than the mansion where Old World splendor reigned.

At least, he liked it until they knocked on the door and Philip opened it, looking like a wild man. Immediately he started cursing Lina for stealing his life's work, his only entrée back into the closed world of scholars, and the most valuable Maya artifact ever found.

After about thirty seconds of abuse, Hunter shoved Philip back into the entrance far enough for all of them to come in. Then Hunter shut the door and waited for the old man to run out of breath. From the look of his face—sweaty and pale—it wouldn't be long. When Lina started to walk closer to her father, Hunter held her back.

"Let him run down," he said.

And he revised his opinion of Philip from eccentric to borderline nuts.

"Anything he's saying make sense to you?" Hunter asked Lina when Philip paused for a breath.

"He thinks we stole an artifact from him."

"I got that. But what?"

Lina bit her lip and shook her head. "That's where it falls apart. He says we stole the Kawa'il codex."

Philip erupted again at her words and grabbed her shoulders, shaking her hard. "You traitorous bitch, you think I don't see through your lying—"

The flat of Hunter's palm landed on Philip's cheek. The blow wasn't hard, but it was shocking. With another swift movement Hunter knocked Philip's hands away from Lina. Then he got right into her father's face.

"Settle down before I put you down," Hunter said flatly.

Philip stared at him. "You—you—"

"You hearing me?" Hunter asked.

For a moment Philip's eyes went vacant. Then he nodded and sat heavily on an old couch.

"It's gone," Philip said hoarsely. "Everything is gone."

"What's gone?" Hunter asked.

"Ask her. She—"

"—was with me every moment she wasn't with her family," Hunter cut in.

Philip looked at him, baffled, almost childlike. "But it's gone."

"We got that," Hunter said calmly. "When did you miss it?"

"As soon I knew you had been to the temple, I came back here to check it."

"What—" began Lina.

Hunter's hand closed over her arm.

She looked at her father and understood he was only relating to Hunter right now. She bit her lip and looked away, tears stinging at the back of her eyes. Nothing new, really. Philip had ignored her all of her life.

"You came back here, checked, and it was gone," Hunter said.

Philip nodded.

"Show us where you kept it," Hunter said. His voice was like his eyes, patient. Relentless.

Her father tried to get up, wobbled, and started to go down. Hunter put him back on his feet with an easy strength Lina found as startling as the slap had been. The contrast between Hunter and her father rocked her. Even after she had begun to understand her father's emotional limitations, she still had thought of him as physically strong, indomitable, ageless.

He wasn't.

With Hunter's encouragement, Philip pulled himself together enough to lead the way back to his study. Hunter noticed the heavy lock on the study door and knew without asking that no one went in without Philip being present. Certainly not the maids. The place was dusty, messy, piled with papers and artifacts in haphazard heaps.

Lina's breath came in hard and stayed. The artifacts so carelessly stacked everywhere were extraordinary. The jade jaguar pendant she had found and he had kept was on a bookshelf, on top of a tilting pile of scholarly archaeology bulletins. Automatically she looked at every artifact in sight, searching.

Hunter watched her.

After a moment she shook her head. "Not at first glance. Excellent, wonderful, fascinating—but not what we're looking for."

Hunter nodded and centered his attention on Philip, who was still fumbling with the dial of an old-fashioned safe. Vault, really. It was at least seven feet high and five wide. Unlike the rest of the room, the lock looked well cared for, oiled, clean. Bookcases flanked the vault door on either side from floor to ceiling.

Just when Hunter thought he'd have to try his hand at drilling out the safe's locking mechanism, Philip managed to get the combination right. When the door swung open, Hunter was glad that he hadn't had to wear out steel drill bits and himself on the safe. It was at least four inches thick, way beyond what would be necessary to protect against burglary or fire.

Cool, dry air wafted out of the safe, reminding Hunter of the temple.

"No burning candles," Lina said, telling him that she was thinking the same thing he was.

Not surprisingly, Philip ignored his daughter. Whatever emotion had driven his outburst had been spent. Now he was a leaky balloon, deflating a breath at a time.

She gave him a worried glance but made no move to intervene as he pointed a shaky finger at a small, climate-controlled glass museum box at the back of the vault.

"There. It was there. Now it's gone," Philip said.

Hunter walked forward to look at the box. He could have checked for fingerprints, but he didn't have the right equipment—or temperament—right now.

A glance had told Lina that more than an empty climate-controlled box filled the vault. The walls were a mosaic of shelves and niches and cases. Boxes had been stacked waist-high, leaving very little floor space to move around. She realized that, unbelievably, the reason the jade pendant and other superb artifacts had been left in the study was that Philip had run out of room in the vault.

She turned and went to her father, who was leaning against the vault door. His hand hung limply on the handle. His expression was glazed.

"What was in the box?" Lina asked bluntly.

He shook his head as if her words were cold water instead of breath. "I . . ." His voice died. He swallowed. "A codex. Kawa'il's, I believe."

"How long have you had it?"

He looked confused, irritated. "Years, but what does it matter now? It's gone!"

"Years," she said, her expression a fluid mix of disbelief, anger, and disappointment. "You hid it for years."

"I had to study it," Philip said. "Without me, it's just drawings on paper. I found it! Once I've finished translating it, I'll publish and take my place with the foremost names in archaeology. But it's hard, so hard . . ."

"What is?" Hunter asked.

"Translation, of course," Philip snapped. "The glyphs are very intricate, very idiosyncratic, hard to understand. Almost cryptic."

"You never were very good at translation," Lina said, her voice neutral. "Yet you never asked me to help. Even Mercurio noticed it."

"You were on *her* side," Philip said. "She's the one who ruined me with her greed for artifacts and money. Trust you? You must think I'm as stupid as Mercurio did."

"What are you talking about?" Lina asked.

"You. Your mother."

"Philip, I was eight years old when you and Celia separated. What on earth makes you believe I was on anyone's side?"

"You're a woman. Selfish. Like her. Just when you were finally old enough to become useful to me, you were mooning after Mercurio. Nobody cares what I want. But I outsmarted all of you." Philip grinned without humor, more of a grimace. "I found the codex."

"A work whose meaning you could barely

decipher, much less truly appreciate," Lina said. "So you hid it for years and picked away at something that was as far beyond your reach as the back side of the moon."

"I made progress," Philip said defensively. "Glyphs aren't as impossible as people like you make them out to be. They just require more intelligence than most people have. Especially these glyphs. History as allegory, just like the *Popol Vuh,* worse than the *Chilam Balam.* All but useless to a real archaeologist."

Hunter looked at Lina.

"I understand," she said to Philip. "This codex wasn't a linear compilation of names and events. The glyphs required nuanced interpretation rather than measurement in situ. Shades of possibility and meaning, like poetry."

"Rubbish, not science," Philip agreed. "But there were solid facts. The Spaniards had already arrived. They were called ghost men, greedy and grasping, forever hungry. And the creator or creators of the codex scorned the phonetic alphabet the Spaniards introduced. This codex is true to the Maya."

"So you have a translation?" she asked.

"It's in my book," Philip said.

Lina glanced around the study. "Which one?"

"The one I'm writing."

"I remember when you started it almost ten years ago," she said, her mouth tightening. "The first thing you took for your 'scholarly study' was the jade pendant that is presently gathering dust in your study. Where is your manuscript?"

"In my head. You think I'd trust it on paper or in a computer where anyone could steal it?"

"In your head," she repeated. "What about your notes?"

"You must think I'm as stupid as you are." He tapped his head. "It's in here, all of it."

She slumped back against Hunter's chest and asked, "Is it ever going to come out?"

"Not until I have enough proof that no one can question it, or me," Philip snapped. "I'll never be made to look the fool again."

"Really?" Lina gestured to the empty box in the open vault. "Looks like someone fooled you but good."

The reminder bled the heat of indignation

out of Philip, leaving him hollow and pale again.

"Who else knew about the codex?" Hunter asked.

"No one."

"Pull your head out of your butt," Hunter said impatiently. "Someone else had to know. The jungle only *looks* empty. Who helped you get into the temple? Who watched you leave with a codex? Who knew you brought the codex here? Where did you get the climate-controlled box? Who helped you learn about the glyphs that baffled you? Somebody else knew. Somebody talked. Somebody always does."

"They wouldn't have betrayed me," Philip said, shaking his head. "I have too much information."

"Who?" Hunter asked.

Philip just shook his head.

Hunter abandoned the direct approach. He'd circle back to it in a few minutes, then go in and around and back again and again and again, until Philip forgot where he had been, where he had drawn lines, what he had said, and what he didn't want to say.

"Was the vault open when you came in today?" Hunter asked.

"No."

"Who else knows the combination?"

Philip's eyes widened. "No one. Do you think I'm crazy?"

Hunter doubted the other man truly wanted the answer to that question.

"If no one knew the combination," Hunter said, "how did the codex go missing?"

The older man blinked, confused. "Lina must have—"

"Try again," Hunter cut in. "That dog don't hunt."

Philip floundered, then said, "Celia."

"How?" Lina straightened. "You said no one else knew the combination."

"I don't know." Philip said sullenly. "I don't trust females and I never have. You're taking her side. You always have."

Hunter wondered if that pout had got Philip far with his parents, peers, or estranged wife. It sure looked ridiculous on a grown man.

From the expression on Lina's face, it wasn't working on her either.

"Where do you write down combinations,

passwords, that sort of thing?" Hunter asked.

"Why would I tell you?" Philip asked, but his eyes flicked toward his desk.

Lina headed for it.

"What are you doing?" Philip demanded.

She didn't bother to answer.

"When was the last time you saw the codex?" Hunter asked.

A blink, a frown, a confused shake of Philip's head.

"Yesterday?" Hunter asked.

Silence.

"Look at me," Hunter snarled.

Philip stiffened and started to argue. A glance at Hunter's eyes changed the older man's mind. Whatever Philip saw made him even more wan.

"When was the last time you saw the codex?" Hunter repeated, his voice much softer than his eyes.

"I . . . what day is today?"

"The twenty-first of December, 2012," Lina said without looking up from her search through the desk's belly drawer. "Abuelita's birthday."

"I know the year," Philip said, contempt dripping.

"Good for you," Hunter said. "The codex. When did you last see it?"

The older man frowned, trying to remember. "Three weeks ago. Maybe four."

"Wow," Lina said as she ran her fingers over the underside of the drawer. "You sure were working day and night on that translation."

"You will show respect to—" Philip began.

"Why?" Hunter asked. "You sure as hell don't respect her."

"I'm her father!"

"Yeah. I have a hard time believing it. Makes me understand the whole idea of changelings and babies mixed at birth."

"Fuck you!"

"Not even if you had tits," Hunter said.

"Found it," Lina said before the conversation could degenerate any further.

"Okay, so anyone with a brain and twenty-twenty vision could have found the combination," Hunter said.

"My study is always locked."

"Not a problem," Hunter said. "I could get in without leaving a mark. Big locks don't make a big difference."

"You're in this with her!"

Hunter told himself to be patient, he was dealing with a man under a lot of stress, a man who apparently hadn't been too stable to begin with. He wondered if giving Philip another smack would settle his thoughts into more rational lines.

**Doubt it.**

**But, damn, it's tempting.**

Reluctantly, Hunter let go of the idea. "Lina, when was the last time you were here?"

"End of July. Then I had to go back to Houston and prepare for my classes."

"It was you," Philip said almost desperately. "No one else could have understood the glyphs. You always thought you were better than—"

"If you accuse Lina again," Hunter said, "I'll turn you over my knee and spank your bony butt until you cry like your not-so-inner child. You hearing me?"

Philip's mouth flattened, but he nodded, which proved what Hunter had begun to suspect. Philip wasn't truly crazy. He just needed someone to remind him of his manners frequently—someone stronger than he was.

Hunter didn't like the older man any

better for the realization that Lina's father was a bully with a side order of irrationality.

"When was the last time Celia was here?" Hunter asked.

Philip shrugged.

Lina walked over to stand at Hunter's side. "She came in October. Abuelita was ill."

Philip made a rude sound. "That crazy old bitch will live forever."

Lina shook her head and wondered if her father had always been this self-absorbed or if being unable to translate the glyphs from the codex had rubbed him raw. *Or maybe he was just imagining the codex all along, a way to get back the academic respect he'd lost.*

She didn't know she had spoken the last thought aloud until Hunter caught Philip's hand just before it landed on her face.

"You're trying my patience," Hunter said to Philip. "Now either fight me or put your hands in your pockets and grow up."

Philip glared at the younger man. When it came to strength, whether of will or body, there was simply no contest. He didn't like it, but he took it. He lowered his hands and shoved them in his pockets.

"It is good that you did not strike her," said a voice from the doorway. "That would have displeased me."

"Carlos?" Lina said.

He tilted his head in a gesture of respect. "It is time, *mi prima.*"

"What—"

"You have many questions," Carlos said over her voice. "I will give you the answers."

## CHAPTER TWENTY-TWO

"WHAT'S GOING ON?" LINA DEMANDED THE IN-
stant the casita door shut behind them.

"Abuelita and Celia are waiting in my
study," Carlos said. "We will talk there."

"But—" Lina began.

Carlos made a sharp motion with his
head. "Patience, *mi prima*."

It wasn't a request.

Irritated, silent, Lina followed Carlos
along the path of crushed limestone that
led to the main house. The feel of Hunter's
hand resting at the small of her back was
an anchor in the storm of questions and
emotions seething inside her. She didn't

even notice the estate guards standing discreetly aside for them.

Hunter did. Back at the casita, the six full-blooded Maya who had arrived with Carlos had neatly separated Philip from Lina and Hunter. Then the guards had shut the door in front of Philip's face. Two of the men had stayed behind to make sure it stayed shut.

*Maybe they didn't like the way Philip acted,* Hunter thought. *Or maybe Carlos ordered them to beat the hell out of him once Lina was gone.*

The men looked more than tough enough to do the job. In fact, several were bruised and scraped like they had been in a fight recently.

Even though none of the men with Carlos had made a move against him or Lina, Hunter's instincts were up and prowling the dark edges of his mind, howling that something was very wrong. Maybe it was the fact that two of the men had slowed until they were walking behind him.

Hunter really didn't like having strange men at his back.

*And maybe it's just that creepy guayabera Carlos is wearing,* Hunter told himself.

The loose white shirt was heavily embroidered with what had at first looked like blue flowers, as many shades of blue as on his study walls. Only they weren't flowers. They were skulls set among ragged petals.

**Or is that lightning around the skulls?**

There was no answer to Hunter's silent question. Like smoke, the designs changed with every movement Carlos made, frustrating any attempt to decipher them.

"Cool shirt," Hunter said.

Carlos ignored him.

Lina looked more closely. She was accustomed to seeing the pattern within Maya embroidery. Her full mouth flattened.

*Must be skulls,* Hunter decided.

Skulls or flowers, he was glad to feel the weight of a gun at the small of his back. His neck was itching like it was hosting a chigger reunion.

Wind flexed, bending the jungle beneath it. The thinly overcast sky hadn't changed as the afternoon slid toward evening. The air smelled of lightning, a dry storm. Carlos's shirt rippled and shifted, reminding Hunter of the drawings in the temple, where blue lightning glowed.

One of the stocky, long-haired men who had come with Carlos opened the front door of the main estate for him. Carlos swept in, trailed by Lina and Hunter, whose silver-blue eyes never rested, checking possible exits and keeping track of the full-blooded Maya around them who wore guayaberas and jeans instead of uniforms but acted more like guards than the men outside clomping around the perimeter of the family compound.

Another thick-boned, dark-skinned man waited beside the open study door. He was wearing the jeans, boots, and loose pale shirt that Carlos's other men did. Hunter told himself not to get paranoid about it. A lot of the men in the Caribbean, Mexico, and Central America wore loose shirts and jeans.

He glanced at Lina, but if she noticed all the men, it didn't bother her. He wished it didn't bother him. But it did. He'd rather have had an AK-47 stashed under his shirt than a pistol.

Abuelita and Celia were waiting inside the study, sitting side by side on one of the couches, silent. A pitcher of water, ice, and lime slices waited within reach on the coffee table. Near the pitcher, fresh fruit and sparkling glasses were lined up like offerings at the feet of a life-size limestone face.

Celia was turned out like a city woman going to a fancy dinner, except for the temper that narrowed her eyes and added years to her looks. She looked even less happy to be there than Hunter was.

Abuelita's skin gleamed like polished wood, tight across her skull, hands interlaced like tree roots on her lap. Her face was a ghost of Lina's, plucked out of time past. The bones were the same, but the years had been pulled across them differently, skin weathered yet still alive, as enduring as the ceiba tree itself. She wore a long ivory dress with pale embroidery that shimmered mysteriously. A shawl lay loosely around her shoulders. The saffron fabric was as radiant as the sun would be tomorrow.

Two men stood in front of Carlos's desk. Their cinnamon-brown faces were impassive, their hair long, their hands broad and strong, their bodies thick and patient. The blood of the Maya ran rich in their veins.

Outside the open window, trees swayed in a wind that was too hot for the season.

Despite the wind, the room's air smelled of copal smoke and something else, something Hunter couldn't identify.

Abuelita's eyes tracked from Celia to Lina. The old woman's irises were like obsidian caught in the folds of her eyelids. With a gesture, Abuelita told Lina to come closer.

Lina smiled and took her great-grandmother's hands in her own. The old woman's skin was as warm as a lizard in the sun.

"You are looking well," Lina said, swallowing her irritation at Carlos. Despite her complaints about Lina's unmarried state, the older woman had always treated her like a princess, someone to be hugged and petted and fed special tidbits. "Your dress is very beautiful."

Abuelita squeezed Lina's hands and released them. "It is good you are here."

Flanked by two men, Carlos went to stand in front of his desk. At his signal one of the men began serving iced water with slices of lime. As the man moved, Hunter noticed that he was dressed like the others, walked like he had a sore gut, and in addition to a bruise or two, he wore what looked like a bulky bandage around his ribs under the loose shirt. All of the men had hair as thick and black as night, worn pushed back over their shoulders like a mane.

Hunter assumed they were armed because it would be stupid to think otherwise.

The man offered Carlos the first glass of water, Abuelita the second. When he held a glass out to Lina, she shook her head. Much to Hunter's disappointment, no one else was offered a drink. Broken crystal had intensely sharp edges.

"Who are these men?" Lina asked Carlos, her voice caught between impatience and unease.

"They are my people. The one with the bandaged hand is called Blood Lily," he said in the local Mayan dialect. "No Tomorrows is in the hallway. Two Shark and Water Bat brought you here."

If the others had names, Carlos didn't mention them.

Hunter didn't understand the words, for they were as Yucatec as the men. Lina translated for him, and added that she would continue to do so unless people spoke Spanish or English.

Carlos shrugged.

Celia moved restlessly, like someone who was about to stand. A sharp gesture from Carlos kept her seated. The lines on her face tightened, telling anyone who cared that she was barely tolerating her cousin's demands.

Hunter looked behind Carlos, where the server had previously blocked the view. The dense mahogany desk was clean but for a handful of artifacts. A scepter with obsidian teeth. A censer with openmouthed skulls decorating it and faint tendrils of copal smoke oozing out like sly tongues. A Chacmool of green stone, probably jade.

A mask of seamless obsidian.

Understanding crawled over Hunter like insects, but it was too late. He was way outnumbered. All he could do was wait for a chance. Or make a chance, if it came to it.

And pray that Lina didn't notice the artifacts behind Carlos's body.

"Speak to Carlos only when you are spoken to," Abuelita said to Lina. "Listen before you judge."

"What—" Lina began.

**"No. Listen."**

Lina stared at Abuelita, for the first time wondering if her mother had been right, if her great-grandmother was senile. Abuelita ignored Lina, watching Carlos, her old eyes filled with the love of a woman looking at her god.

Uneasiness condensed into ice, making Lina shiver.

Wind blew through the open window, but there was no moisture with it, no living scent of jungle and flowers. There was only a hint of ozone, distant lightning giving a burned edge to the air.

Carlos breathed deeply, smiled. "Kawa'il is sharpening his blades."

Without looking, he reached behind him and picked up a leather-wrapped bundle. Holding it like a fragile gift, he walked to Lina. As he placed the leather in her hands, his expression was both possessive and loving.

The fact that Lina backed up until she was almost on top of Hunter told him that she was no happier with the situation than he was. He wished he could do something about it, but he hadn't seen an opening.

Yet.

"Finally you are here with me," Carlos said to Lina, coming closer despite her retreat. "After so many ignored invitations and other, firmer overtures."

Drawn by the unexpected gleam of obsidian on the desk, Lina looked past Carlos. Then she went pale, shaking her head as though refusing to accept what she didn't want to know.

But she did know it, and nothing would ever be the same.

"The parking garage," she said to Carlos, her voice too tight. Like her hands, her body, her throat. "Those were your men." She looked at the silent Maya men around the room. "These men."

Hunter knew that she had figured out how deeply they were in trouble. *Don't lose it, sweetheart. You need every nerve you have.*

**We both do.**

Yet the desire to clamp his hands around Carlos's throat and squeeze almost overwhelmed Hunter's control. Motionless, he fought himself. Lina needed him more than he needed to punish Carlos for Jase's near death.

"Yes, they were in the parking garage," Carlos said calmly. "If they had hurt you, they wouldn't be here. They would be in Xibalba, waiting for the wheel to turn."

"Why?" she demanded. "Why hurt Jase? He bled so—" Her voice broke. The package Carlos had placed in her hands started to slip away. Automatically her fingers clenched, holding on to the supple leather.

"You can blame your own stubbornness for that," her cousin said. "You refused to honor the obligations of your own blood."

"What are you talking about? You could have just called me. You didn't have to shoot someone!"

Hunter's hand touched Lina's back soothingly, telling her that she wasn't alone, he was with her, watching for the instant he could grab her and run beyond the reach of her cousin.

"I tried." Carlos sighed. "I used honey upon honey, artifact upon artifact, lure upon lure, but still you did not come to me. My men would have driven you to a waiting plane. You would have been home within hours. You would have learned from me, prepared for this as I have for years.

But no, you ignored me. Now there is no more time."

Lina stared at Carlos. His eyes were as dark as Abuelita's, deeper than night. And like the night, without limits.

He touched the loosely wrapped package in her hands. "Open it. Learn. Understand."

Grateful to have an excuse to look away from her cousin's eyes, she lifted a flap of leather and carefully unrolled it. On the inside was suede, black as the space between the stars. When she unwrapped the soft, resilient leather, she was holding a long, wedge-shaped piece of mahogany. Two of its edges were lighter in color, a pale cinnamon red instead of the dark garnet gleam of the finished wood.

On the side she couldn't see, her fingertips traced zigzag lines carved deeply into the wood. As she turned it over, she knew she held the piece of wood that had been missing from the fascinating artifact sent to her by Mexico City's Museum of Anthropology.

Lina was holding the fragment of wood that had been floating between the gods and men. The markings that had been removed from the whole were a representation of a codex, accordion folded in the Maya style, partially open to hint at the revelations inside.

"This is the crucial part of the instruction glyphs on the box holding Kawa'il's god bundle," Carlos said, his voice vibrant with memory and awe. "Before I could prevent it, Philip discovered the box in the temple. He needed money, I needed something to appease the federal government."

She waited, full lips flattened, not wanting to hear any more and not able to stop listening.

"I kept the contents and sent the rest to the government for study. I didn't think you would be able to resist it when I prevailed upon the museum director to send it to you. Surely you would see its message, surely you would know that it had come from Tulum. You would be drawn here, to Kawa'il's wisdom. But you had lived too long among the ghosts. You no longer recognized Kawa'il even when you held his covenant in your hands."

"You broke the wood," Lina said, hardly able to believe it. "Deliberately. Broke it."

"Of course. It was a lure, nothing more. Beyond that key message, the box wasn't significant. The god bundle inside had already been removed to be kept safe in Kawa'il's own temple."

"Site nine," she murmured, seeing again the rainbow glyphs, the serpent without beginning or end. Carlos had merged Kawa'il and Kukulcán in his mind, or perhaps the builders of the temple had.

Carlos nodded and watched her with veiled eagerness, as though expecting something more.

"Everything that you did for the Museum of the Maya and the museums in Mexico, all the explorations on Reyes Balam land that you paid for," she said, "none of it was for the love of knowledge and history. It was all for you."

"For me?" Carlos shook his head. "No, I am nothing. Kawa'il is all. I planted seeds and watered them with money. Today, before midnight, Kawa'il will come for the harvest. And you, my cousin, you are the key to all."

Lina stared at her him. "You're—"

"Let him explain," Hunter cut in softly,

not wanting her to tell Carlos how crazy he was.

There hadn't been any bloodletting yet. Hunter really wanted to keep it that way.

Lina started to protest Hunter's soft order, but didn't. The fear she had been trying to ignore had slid clammy fingers over her flesh. She finally understood just how fragile the skin of normality was right now.

If it split, there would be violence.

Almost desperately she looked at Celia. Her mother was staring at Carlos, her expression confused, almost stunned. It was obvious that she knew less than Lina did about what was happening.

"I thought your reluctance to come to me," Carlos said, "to learn, meant Kawa'il was angry with me because I didn't have the proper tools to communicate with him through ceremony and ritual. But when I tried to send the sacred artifacts to myself in Houston, they were seized at the border. Soon after, the place of worship that I had built for Kawa'il was desecrated by ignorant American police."

Lina wanted to scream at Carlos to shut

up, that she didn't want to know just how crazy he was.

Hunter touched her back lightly, reminding her that Carlos's words weren't the only reality in the room.

"I took my most holy objects and went to a new place, a place already dedicated to death," Carlos said. "There I sought Kawa'il in blood and smoke, but the tools I used to cut, to bleed, to worship, were inferior. Yet by Kawa'il's grace it was enough. His sacred objects came back to me. They were beautiful, powerful. I gave glad sacrifice to my generous god and came home to Quintana Roo."

*That's one way of looking at it,* Hunter thought sardonically. *My view of reality is different. Snakeman twists LeRoy to steal the artifacts from ICE's evidence warehouse, good old LeRoy loses his heart to Kawa'il, and Carlos beats feet back to Mexico. Nothing holy about it.*

"But still you didn't come to me," Carlos said to Lina. "Still Kawa'il tested me."

Air moved like a dry river through the open window. Without looking away from her, Carlos coughed and held out one hand. Water Bat gave him a glass of cold water with translucent green lime slices floating beneath ice. The wind swelled again, bringing the smell of lightning and the malaise of a storm that would not break.

"You're thirsty," Hunter said very softly in English to Lina. "Hold out your hand for a drink."

Before he finished, she was asking for water. Apparently the same thought had occurred to her—a broken glass could be a weapon.

Two Shark brought Lina a glass of liquid. He and Water Bat withdrew, watching everyone in the room equally.

Despite the dryness in her throat, Lina's stomach knotted at the thought of swallowing anything, even water. She sipped anyway. The liquid coolness and the fragrant kiss of lime made her feel better. When she took another small drink, Carlos began talking again.

"When my men failed to bring you to Quintana Roo, I knew that somehow I had continued to displease Kawa'il." Carlos swallowed water, sucked on a stray piece of ice, and watched Lina with leashed anticipation, waiting for her to understand.

She fought for control by counting the

tiny beads of condensation that formed on the outside of her crystal glass. The taste of lime went metallic in her mouth.

"I came here, to Tulum, to Kawa'il's land, his people," Carlos said when Lina stayed silent. "I studied the twenty panels of Kawa'il's instructions."

"The codex," Lina said despite herself. "*You* have it."

Carlos kept talking. "I realized I must have misinterpreted one of the panels. I sacrificed my blood until I knew the ecstasy within the soul of agony. Each time I used the sacred stingray spine, pulled the knotted twine, breathed the sacred copal smoke, I came closer to knowing Kawa'il. With his wisdom, his guidance, I learned until the god found me worthy." Ice crunched between strong teeth. "Kawa'il brought you to me. Who am I to refuse the gift of Death himself?"

For Lina, reality narrowed to the jagged chunk of limestone sitting on the coffee table. The stone's edges looked chewed, signature of having been chain-sawed off its anchor wall in some unknown ruin. The stone face with its empty eyes stared at the world serenely, eyes relaxed and easy, mouth open, with just the hint of a broad tongue touching the lower lip.

No one had taken a piece of the fruit heaped like flowers around the limestone face that ruled the coffee table.

She watched the stone, half expecting it to comment on what was happening in the room. That would be no less crazy than Carlos, calmly waiting, standing on a small rug that looked like a pool of turquoise water lapping around his feet.

Bare. His feet were bare. Strong. Clean. His toenails gleamed from a recent pedicure.

Lina swallowed laughter she was afraid to release. She knew there would be no end to it until she was as mad as her cousin.

The warmth of Hunter's hand moved slowly on Lina's back, pulling her away from her cousin, anchoring her in something that wasn't crazy, wasn't murderous.

Death or love. The choice was simple, terrifying, because she knew her life and her love were in the bloody hands of a madman.

"Rosalina," Carlos said, his voice almost hissing, echoing the sacred snake with the human tongue. "Our people have been hiding for five hundred years. Abuelita and our ancestors are descendants of priests and kings. Instead of waging a losing war against the Europeans, or signing over their souls to the invaders, our people took their knowledge and disappeared into the jungle. We survived. And we waited."

Without moving anything but his eyes, Hunter watched the men in the room.

They watched him in return, dark eyes alive with the patience of a jaguar.

*Not good,* Hunter thought. He had hoped the English ramblings of their boss would bore them, make them careless.

It hadn't.

"The hidden people kept the covenants with the gods," Carlos said, his voice resonant with time and certainty. "During the years, priests of Kawa'il filtered out of the jungle. They helped villages, showed the people how to bend the required worship of the European Christ so they could escape the Spaniards and still appear to have bowed to them."

"The Vatican allowed it," Lina said, feeling like a sapling engulfed in a deep wind, fighting to hold the very earth she was rooted to.

"The pope believed his god would overcome ours in time," Carlos said, satisfaction in his voice. "Foolish. While we kissed the European beads in churches built on the ruins of our temples, we planted our crosses of corn and blood and kept the true gods alive."

Her throat too dry to speak, Lina just shook her head.

"The truth of the world was written down," Carlos said, his eyes burning. "The Codex of Kawa'il is not only a celebration of the real gods. It instructs us in the proper ceremonies to keep them alive, to keep the bargain that the gods made with their new creation so many thousands of years ago."

Lina looked at her mother. Celia was shaking her head in silent denial while tears ran down her cheeks, leaving dark trails of mascara.

"The Chel family was first and highest among the hidden priests," Carlos said. "Like the Balam side of my family, Chel blood is older than Palenque, as old as the first breath. We have not only the blood of priests and kings, but of the gods themselves infusing our lines with greatness.

The gods will reward those of their children who have honored them."

"Carlitos," Celia said, her voice breaking.

He ignored her, focusing only on Lina. "Imagine the gods' gratitude when the Great Wheel turns, the Long Count ends, and we present them with a sacrifice that honors both them and the Balam line."

His eyes gleamed but Lina could only see black emptiness beneath their glow. Like obsidian. All that kept her from freezing into stone was the warmth of Hunter's hand.

**Am I as warm to him? Am I his anchor in Carlos's mad storm?**

Hunter's hand caressed, reassuring both of them that there was a reality beyond madness. A reality he held on to as surely as she did. A reality they held between them.

Carlos reached beneath his shirt to a sheath of leather bleached white as bone. He drew out an ancient knife.

Obsidian.

Lina's breath froze.

"How can you not believe?" Carlos asked Lina. "Could mere man make such as this? Never. It was the hands of our ancestors, the very gods, Kawa'il himself, that shaped this blade."

Hunter didn't need Lina's sharply indrawn breath to recognize the knife as the one in the photos. The blade shimmered and seethed with an extraordinary light, as though life had somehow been trapped within.

Delicately, Carlos's long fingers traced the lines of the knife. "Look at the proof of Kawa'il. The blade is smooth and even, flawless in comparison to other obsidian blades. Its like has never been seen before or since. Kawa'il's sigil wasn't carved into the blade, it was breathed there by gods, again and again, until the stone itself accepted the mark. To hold this blade is to hold black lightning, the power of Kawa'il and Kukulcán, living as one. This is the key to the end of our corrupt age." Carlos pinned Lina with his obsidian gaze. "And you, Rosalina, you are the lock to be opened."

A terrible understanding ripped through Celia. She came to her feet so violently that she nearly upset the coffee table. The limestone head shivered, swayed, then settled among the tumbled fruit.

"Take me!" she cried. "My blood is as royal as Lina's."

With surprising strength, Abuelita yanked Celia back to the couch.

"Quiet, my granddaughter. Neither of us is worthy of being made holy."

"My blood is—" Celia began.

"We are sterile," Abuelita said, her voice dry, terrifyingly rational. "You by choice. I by age. Carlos by the will of Kawa'il. Of what worth is our blood to the gods? Only Rosalina carries the seed of future Balams. Her death is the end of the Balam line. What greater gift could possibly be given to the gods? What time could be more sacred than the end of the Long Count? Rosalina will be made holy and the gods will favor the Maya once again. Carlos will lead our people out of slavery. He will lead our world, as it should be led, in the ways of the old gods."

"How sweet for you," Lina said to Carlos, not bothering to hide her anger any longer. "You, the only survivor, Kawa'il's favorite, king of the new age. No doubt you'll be made fertile in the bargain and given twenty fertile virgins to screw."

Carlos shook his head at her lack of understanding. "I will merely unlock the doorway to the gods. Kawa'il will be first to come through. He will sacrifice the four sacred Bacabs to Kukulcán and the sky will fall. Then the world will end. If it pleases Kawa'il and Kukulcán, I will live. If not, another Long Count of slavery to a foreign god will begin for our people, until another is born who is worthy of the attention of the gods."

Beyond the windows, incandescent white light seared across the sky, revealing the ghostly shapes of jaguar-spotted clouds. Something rumbled in the distance, too hollow to be thunder, too empty to be anything else.

"But you don't really expect the gods to be displeased," Lina challenged. "Do you?"

"Like everyone else," Carlos said, "I await the judgment of the gods."

But his eyes said he knew what that judgment would be.

Lina bit her tongue against a scream, tasted her own blood in her mouth, swallowed it. But she couldn't swallow the rest.

"You really are insane," she said.

Hunter gathered himself for the explosion.

It didn't come. Other people's reality simply didn't touch Carlos.

"Every day you believe in things that you can't see, can't touch, can't explain," Carlos said, trying to make Lina understand. "The power behind an electrical switch. The fragmented heart of atoms. The music your tiny machines steal from the air. The movement inside your television. You don't understand these things, can't create them yourself, yet you accept them. Kawa'il is simply a different kind of acceptance, a different kind of power."

He sounded so calm, so reasonable, that Lina shivered. "You believe you're the chosen one. The one who will save the world."

"I have no intention of saving this world," Carlos said. "It will be cast off like a snake's skin. And what will be left will be shining and new, ruled over by a wise king and Kawa'il's sacred warriors. After more than five hundred years of sleep, our people will awake. I just wish that you could see it, Rosalina."

There was something terrifying behind his eyes, a jaguar weeping for the cornered prey.

And hungering.

Thumping and scuffling came from the hallway, along with grunts of effort. Two long-haired, unsmiling Maya pushed Philip fully into the room. His hands and mouth were efficiently bound with duct tape.

Carlos laughed, a sound like faraway thunder. "The idiot arrives, the soulless one who can't understand the words of the gods, much less the beating heart of a living people. The codex was never yours, fool. Be grateful that Kawa'il wants only pure blood today."

"Then let Hunter go," Lina said immediately. "He has nothing to do with this."

At a single gesture from Carlos, Philip was thrown facedown on the couch, all but burying Celia. Abuelita made an expression of distaste and stood up so that she wouldn't touch Philip.

"Don't worry," Carlos said tenderly to Lina, his fingertips rough against her cheek. "You aren't the first I have suckled. It will be swift and certain. You are the last and most perfect. Only you will be kissed by the sacred knife of Kawa'il."

Lina smashed the glass into her cousin's face. Icy water flew. Blood appeared from a long cut on Carlos's cheek.

Hunter spun and took out the nearest man with a backhand that sent him tumbling into another man. "Run, Lina!"

One high, one low, two other guards jumped Hunter. Lina turned to help him, the broken glass held in her fist. Carlos struck from behind, sending the wicked crystal spinning away. A gun flashed in a guard's meaty fist and the barrel slammed into Hunter's head. He fell forward in a boneless sprawl.

Lina screamed until a guard took her from Carlos and silenced her with a broad hand across her mouth. Celia wept. Abuelita smiled.

Outside, lightning raged over the horizon and the dry wind whipped. The burned smell in the air increased.

Carlos felt the familiar heat and texture of the liquid running down his cheek and smiled with white teeth whose gums were rimmed with blood. "Kawa'il is pleased."

# CHAPTER TWENTY-THREE

WHEN WATER BAT PARKED CARLOS'S LAND Rover near the Temple Four site, Carlos seemed to come out of the trance he had been in. Lina had been watching her cousin warily, waiting for him to break out in tongues or froth at the mouth, or both. He had done neither, simply sat silently, swaying with the rough road, his black eyes searching the dark, dry night.

Lightning arced and branched and sheeted in awesome display around the Rover, followed by the hollow applause of thunder. Yet no rain came down to bless the thirsty land.

Two Shark opened Lina's door and pulled her out. As he bent down, his knife flashed in the gleam of the headlights. The duct tape hobbling her ankles came apart. She held her wrists out in front of her, expecting to be freed. She wasn't.

The headlights went dark.

With a grunt Two Shark sheathed his knife. Water Bat and the other men who had come with Carlos had already vanished, nothing but shadows among the handful of torches suddenly flaring in the jungle.

Carlos appeared at her side. The mark she had left across his cheek looked black in the weak light. He'd done nothing to clean his face.

"Follow me," Carlos said.

"My hands—" she began.

"If you fall, Two Shark will carry you."

The thought of Two Shark touching her made Lina shudder. She turned away from the silent guard and followed Carlos. She had been dreading taking the path in the dark with her hands bound, but more torches were lit as soon as his guards told people that Carlos was on the way.

Within minutes they had arrived at temple grounds that were alive with the movement of flames. They danced to the music of the wind that was whispering and calling through the night, bending trees as easily as it did fire. Another line of torches went beyond the temple, in the direction of Cenote de Balam. Mixed with copal smoke from the torches, Lina smelled bruised leaves and sap from recently chopped branches.

*They've cut a new trail to the cenote since Hunter and I left,* she thought. *There was no sign of it earlier.*

For every torch there was a Maya standing solid as stone, reflected fire licking over each face. She didn't see warmth, or welcome, or even curiosity. She saw only the expectation of a jaguar that had finally seen its prey.

But not in Carlos. His eyes were alive with something else, more fierce and less human than his followers. His expression could have been a god's confidence or a devil's satisfaction, or both together, burning like flames in the wind. His fingers touched the wound on his face. Like the night, it was dry, waiting.

As he walked into the temple, Lina slowed

and tried to slide away among the shadows and wind, into the bottomless darkness of the jungle. Two men appeared to block her, a wall of flesh short enough for her to see over but too strong for her to break through. Each man grabbed her by an arm. Without a word, they pulled her in the direction of the temple, making it clear that she could go with them willingly or she could be dragged like a donkey.

Lina looked longingly at the scarred steel machetes each man wore. They were stained and scented with the blood of the plants they recently had hacked through. Her palm itched for the feel of a machete handle.

*Not yet,* she told herself fiercely, fighting the fear that made her want to panic. *Wait for them to get careless. They aren't warriors or guards. They're simple farmers. They expect nothing but obedience from a woman.*

**Wait.**

**Just wait.**

**And don't think about Hunter.**

But he was there, always, part of her heartbeat, part of her fear, part of her hope.

Promising herself a panic attack when

she could afford one, Lina walked at the same speed as the men beside her, wanting to appear willing or cowed, anything so that they wouldn't watch her so closely. The men walked slowly, more slowly than Carlos, who soon disappeared into the open mouth of the temple.

By the time Lina reached the short hallway inside the temple, Carlos was out of sight. The candles that lined the narrow passage were the color of fresh, pale cream, and smelled like vanilla and cinnamon. The thought of Abuelita making each one of them with loving hands for this night sickened Lina.

She could understand the madness of her cousin wanting to be priest-king; she couldn't understand the madness of her great-grandmother wanting to worship him.

The inner temple room was both cool and ablaze with clumps of blue candles, every shade of blue from light to dark.

Carlos was naked.

It was the last thing Lina had expected. It was too much. Throat straining around screams she refused to voice, she closed her eyes and tried not to break down completely. As she fought for self-control, she heard rustling sounds, footsteps leaving, returning, echoing her wild heartbeat.

*You can't get away if your eyes are closed,* she told herself. *Stop acting like a child. You've seen a naked man before.*

An image of Hunter suddenly consumed her mind—male, hard, reaching for her as she reached for him and they joined bodies in a lush tangle of pleasure. Hot. Alive. Everything she had ever wanted.

**I love you, Hunter. I never let myself know, never told you how I felt. I was afraid it was too soon.**

**But it was too late, and that was something else I didn't know.**

Lina set her teeth and opened her eyes. Somehow she would free herself, find Hunter, and tell him.

Then the memory of him falling bonelessly to the floor flashed through her mind like icy lightning.

**No!**

**He's alive. I'd know if he were dead. Wouldn't I?**

*Don't think about it,* she told herself fiercely. *Think about getting away from*

*Carlos. It's the only thing you can do right now that matters.*

Hunter ran like blood through Lina's body, her bones, strengthening her. She forced herself into the moment, the crazed modern man in the ancient temple, and her own eyes alert for any opportunity to escape.

Carlos was now wrapped in a long loincloth of fine, midnight-blue cotton. On his head he wore the cured skin and skull of a jaguar. The cat's eyes were gleaming obsidian, eerily alive. The rest of the jaguar's spotted skin swirled down Carlos's back, the back paws nudging against his legs, the front paws clasped around his shoulders in a horrifying embrace. Beneath the long, curving claws, two necklaces held a jade pectoral representing an open-mouthed jaguar surrounded by lightning.

The jade was spectacular, fully twice the size of the one Lina had found. One of the heavy necklaces was made of carved, thumb-size obsidian beads. The other was of jade. Both felt as ancient as the temple to her.

One of the men stepped forward, using

his fingers to paint Carlos in all the colors of ritual—black, red, yellow, white. When he was finished, another man stepped forward with a headdress of feathers that rippled like blue-green lightning. Their jobs complete, both men left the room. Carlos opened the small bag he had been given. His movement and the candlelight made the feathers of his headdress, the paintings overhead, and the jaguar skin writhe with terrifying life.

Stubbornly Lina refused the awful allure of the scales and the endless serpents, the supple cat skin mocking life.

"Who do you think you're fooling?" she asked Carlos in English, afraid if she spoke the native Mayan dialect she would be sucked deeper into the nightmare. "You hear the echoes in your own head, not the voices of the gods."

Carlos ignored her. Slowly Two Shark approached him. Like everyone in the room except Lina, he had switched to ancient Maya dress—loincloth and bare feet, paint and decorations topped by feathers. Their drapes were of cotton rather than jaguar fur, their costumes less noble than their leader's. As the men moved, jade and obsidian objects sewed onto their clothes caught light. The cloth Two Shark wore was the color of Kan, the east, the yellow blaze of sunrise. He held a small, carved box in his hands.

Water Bat was dressed as Chak, the red of the south, the color of fresh blood. His burden was the sacred jade Chacmool that had been among the stolen artifacts that had brought Hunter to Lina. Silently Water Bat kneeled in front of Carlos.

No Tomorrows wore the black of sunset, Boox. Another man wore white, Sak, the north.

*The four pillars, the Bacabs,* Lina realized, *separating heaven and hell.*

In the ancient belief, when the Bacabs fell, Xibalba would rise to the gods and everything in between would be cleansed, destroyed, a storm of change that would make room for the next creation, the next age.

The Age of Kings, which Carlos believed he would lead.

Grimly Lina looked around the temple. Its shadows were empty, no man-size limestone altar lurking nearby.

**He won't be killing anyone here. So**

**why are they posed like costumed actors waiting for the director to appear?**

As though Carlos had heard her silent question, he spoke to her in soft English. For all his men responded, it might as well have been the wind rustling.

"I regret that I didn't have time to make you understand," he said. "But know this, it is not only your blood, your pain, that Kawa'il needs today. I will bleed, too, an act of reverence to strengthen me for what comes."

"Really? Last time I checked, you weren't the one dying."

"Silence, or I will tie knotted twine in a loop through your tongue and yank on it each time you speak."

Put that way, silence had definite appeal. She shut up.

Carlos went back to preparing himself to turn the key that would open the lock on the Age of Kings. As he did, he continued to instruct her in English.

"The twine I hold in my right hand is from a wild cotton tree growing near my natal village, gathered as our people have for over six thousand years. I wound the twine myself and knotted it twenty times, following the instructions in the Codex of Kawa'il. On one end of the twine is the barb from a stingray I hunted and killed myself with a stone knife."

Lina found herself unable to look away from the ancient ritual Carlos was reenacting. The stingray barb was almost as long as his hand and nearly as thick as his little finger. At either side of it were curved spines that had only one purpose—to dig into flesh and not let go.

Carlos set the box on the floor, moved his loincloth aside with his left hand, and pinched a deep fold of foreskin between his thumb and forefinger. He plunged the barb through the hypersensitive skin, stopping only at the first knot.

Lina didn't know whether he gasped or she did. She did know that it couldn't have been the first time Carlos had performed this agonizing rite. His hands were too steady, too sure. Blood welled and began to drip down his penis. Bile crawled up her throat. She swallowed hard. Twice.

"With each knot pulled through, I draw closer to Kawa'il," Carlos said. "When the whole cord is dipped in my life, Kawa'il speaks to me."

*Twenty knots embedded beneath and then pulled through his foreskin,* Lina thought, feeling a bit dizzy. *That would bring enough pain to hear voices in your head and make you believe in an alternate reality rooted in blood, flowering in agony.*

Carlos tugged the twine and more blood flowed as the first knot pulled through the slit in his skin. The cord turned crimson in the candlelight. Blood trickled into the jade Chacmool held by the kneeling Bacab.

Lina forced herself to breathe. From the corner of her eyes, she watched the men dressed as the Bacabs. Three of them were absorbed in the ritual.

No Tomorrows watched only her.

The metallic scent of fresh blood curled through the small room like copal smoke.

Knots kept crawling into the slit and emerging drenched in red.

"Earth lies flat on a field of four colors, black and white and red and yellow. Each of the field's corners is held up by a man who is becoming a tree, roots plunging down, drinking earth's blood, flowering in the heavens . . . the four pillars of creation . . . hot wind blowing . . . stars glowing . . . Xibalba in black pulses reaching for the stars . . . my breath is his breath, hot, hotter, too hot . . . agony . . . Kawa'il . . . is all . . ."

Carlos's words wound through the room with the smoke, and the smoke became a serpent whose blood rippled in feathers the color of rainbows, jaws opening and opening more, until the room was swallowed and the last knot was red and Carlos was ecstatic, held within the pulsing center of agony.

For a long time there was silence but for Carlos's ragged breathing. Then, at a nod from him, Chak stood and placed the blood offering in front of the pile of red petals at the south corner of the room.

"Now," Carlos said, his voice transformed by pain and something else, something others called madness and he called transcendent communication. "I am cleansed, renewed, blessed. Kawa'il has spoken. I am ready for the most beautiful of sacrifices." His voice boomed. "Come. The end of the world awaits us at the Cenote de Balam."

PAIN SPIKING OUT FROM BEHIND HUNTER'S LEFT ear drove him from the black embrace of unconsciousness.

**Lina.**
**Danger.**

Hunter tried to sit up. Pain stabbed and he discovered that his hands were taped behind his back, his ankles were taped together, and his feet were bare.

**Boots.**
**Knife.**

He rubbed his face against the floor to clear blood from his right eye. The pain was breathtaking. He forced himself to breathe anyway. Then he listened.

From beyond a closed door came the voices of two men. They were on guard and they were bored. One of them talked about robbing and raping Cecilia. The other told him that El Maya would have his balls and the balls of every one of his male relatives. Better that they just wait and do what they had been told to do. Soon the wheel would turn, El Maya would come back to the house, and his men would be rewarded for their service.

Hunter smiled unpleasantly. *Doubt that they know their boss expects the world and everything in it—except himself—to be destroyed. Or if they know, they don't worship at that altar.*

The subject of conversation in the hallway changed to which of the housemaids had the best ass.

Carefully Hunter looked around as much as he could. Shadows. Rug. Wooden floor. Vine-choked windows outlined by landscaping lights. He was on the second floor and it was night. The weight of the gun at the small of his back was gone. He was tied, defenseless.

**Lina.**

**What is Carlos doing?**

Hunter pushed away his fear for Lina. He couldn't help her until he helped himself. From the corner of his eye he saw his boots about four feet away.

**Did they find the knife?**

Ignoring the pulsing pain in his head, he inched closer to his boots. He saw the shadow of the black-leather-wrapped knife and grinned despite the surly throb of his skull. He managed to swing his feet over the boots and drag them closer to his bound wrists. Slowly he struggled to get the knife out and position it so that he could saw away at the duct tape coating his wrists. By the time his wrists were free, his shoulders were burning, he was sweating, and the clock counting down in his head was screaming at him.

**Hurry.**

**Lina.**

**Hurry!**

He pushed aside the pain streaking through his head and attacked the tape binding his ankles. Moments later the silver material gave way. He shoved his feet into his boots and stood.

The dark lure of unconsciousness spiraled around him. He breathed through his clenched teeth until the dizziness passed.

Outside in the hallway, the guards were talking about the Mexican lottery. Both wanted to win it. Neither really expected to. One kicked idly at the wall as he talked. The hollow thud of his boot told Hunter that this was likely one of the banana-clip-carrying elephants brought in from stomping the perimeter to more stationary duty.

**Hope the clumsy bastards still have their weapons. I'll need them.**

Untrained people who carried weapons had a touching certainty of their personal invincibility. Hunter had learned long ago that a trained body was a weapon that couldn't be taken away or used against him.

Sheathing the knife because it would only get in the way, he eased carefully toward the door. Like all of the doors he had seen so far on the estate, it locked only from the inside, which explained the guards outside.

Listening to the voices, placing the position of each man in his mind, Hunter flung open the door. He took out the guard on the left with a backhanded fist to the throat. The second guard barely had time to put his idly kicking foot on the ground before Hunter's boot sank into his gut. A second kick knocked the man out.

Someone jumped Hunter from behind. At first he thought he'd missed his mark on the first guard. Then he realized that there had been a third man who had been doing his job rather than jawing with his buddies. Hunter slammed an elbow backward. The third man grunted and let go just enough for Hunter to turn and face him. The guard's chin was tucked to protect his neck.

But the rest of him was up for grabs.

Fingers hooked, Hunter's left hand went for the man's eyes and his right for the man's crotch. The guard saved his balls but couldn't evade the fingers digging into his right eye socket. Desperately he threw his head back and grabbed Hunter's left wrist. With his other hand, the guard pulled a knife and stabbed. As the blade cut through cloth and skin on the inside of Hunter's leg, Hunter's right fist smashed into the man's now-unprotected neck.

Retching, coughing, fighting to drag breath through a ruined windpipe, the guard joined his groaning buddies on the floor. A few swift kicks put them out of their vocal misery. Gutter fighting at its dirty and brutal worst, but it got the job done in reasonable silence.

Hunter felt blood running down his leg. He widened the slash in his pants, saw that the blood wasn't pulsing and the wound wasn't to the bone, and set about disarming the guards. AK-47s weren't his weapon of choice, but they had a way of evening odds in a crowd. He checked one weapon quickly, found it good to go, and slung it across his back. He tucked an extra banana clip in his belt. He left the rest of the weapons behind. The guards wouldn't be using them any time soon, if ever.

Lightning sheeted through the night,

overwhelming the darkness. Thunder rumbled, but no rain hit the windows.

Hunter used the prolonged thunder to cover his footsteps. He didn't find any other guards on the second floor, or the first. In the kitchen Abuelita sat at her table sipping pepper-laced cocoa from china as fragile as a breath. Philip and Celia were duct-taped to separate table legs. Even if they had worked together, they wouldn't have been able to jerk the solid mahogany table anywhere useful.

But they weren't working together.

Philip was ranting about treachery and his career and the codex. Tears and mascara ran down Celia's cheeks. She was screaming at him to shut up, his daughter was in danger.

"I never wanted a damned brat!" Philip yelled back.

"Then you should have kept your cock in your pants! I was an innocent!"

"You were the biggest whore since Lilith!"

Obviously it wasn't the first time they'd had this discussion. They flung insults and accusations with the ease and timing of actors in the fourth year of a Broadway play.

"Where is Carlos?" Hunter demanded, cutting across the old argument.

"I don't know," Celia said. "His men kept Philip and me out of the way until Carlos had gone." Then she wailed, "He took Lina with him!"

Hunter had already figured that out.

Sheet lightning blazed through the night. The blackness that followed was absolute, all electricity gone. The house creaked and groaned and trembled under a blast of wind and thunder.

A wooden match flared, followed by the biting smell of sulfur. Abuelita lit the first of four candles that were set at cardinal points around her table.

"It is too late for words." Abuelita said in Spanish. Her voice was as dry and thin as the flame touching each candlewick in turn. "The gods are with Carlos. He will be reborn as the ruler of the Age of Kings."

Philip turned his invective on Abuelita.

She blew out the match and drank her cocoa as though she was alone. Her eyes gleamed with reflected fire.

Hunter would get the truth from Abuelita somehow, but he would try sweet reason first.

"Lina told me your name means Wise Owl," Hunter said.

Abuelita's black eyes focused on him. She nodded.

"You know where Carlos has taken Lina," Hunter said.

"It cannot be stopped."

"Then there is no harm in telling me, is there?"

She laughed.

He stared. With her dark, glittering eyes lit from beneath by candles, she didn't quite look human.

"Carlos lived among you ghost men," Abuelita said, "but only enough to earn the wealth to buy the old secrets that had been stolen from his people. He listened to me. I told him who he was and who he could become. After the wheel turns, a new generation of kings will come from his loins."

"He's sterile!" Celia screamed.

"The wheel has not yet turned," Abuelita said calmly. "Carlos is in the temple now, consecrating himself so that he will be favored to make Lina holy."

Lightning flashed again, this time so close that the feeling of electricity playing through the air made Hunter's skin ripple.

"Where's a flashlight?" Hunter asked Celia.

"In a bracket by the back door."

He bent, slashed the knife blade through Celia's wrist restraints, and handed her the weapon.

"You can free Philip or cut his throat, your choice," Hunter said, not caring which she decided on.

Celia closed her trembling hands over the handle of the knife.

Hunter ran to the back door, grabbed the bulky, waterproof flashlight, and headed for the Bronco. Lightning blasted across the sky. For an instant everything looked frozen. Then thunder rode on the back of a wind that felt desert-dry. Blinded, half deaf, Hunter put the AK-47 in the passenger seat and climbed into the Bronco by touch more than sight. He fumbled several times before he jammed the key in place.

The Bronco started, died, started again. Hunter hit the lights and accelerator at the same instant. Wheels churned through crushed limestone, sending white gravel spitting out from beneath the tires. Following the map in his mind, he raced down the main estate road, then made a series of turns that ended in a small track. The Bronco lurched, bounced, banged, and scraped, but held to the track.

Hunter's leg burned and his head was on fire. He set his teeth and took the punishment, wishing only that he could be faster. He didn't know what personal witching hour Carlos had chosen, but Hunter didn't want to be late for the ceremony. Not with Lina the central attraction. He kept hearing Abuelita's words ringing in his head, louder than pain, more urgent.

**Carlos is in the temple now, consecrating himself so that he will be favored to make Lina holy.**

**Make holy.**

**Sacrifice.**

The knowledge was like fingers beneath Hunter's ribs, in his guts, digging, twisting. He drove faster than even a fool would think safe, but it still seemed like a month before he saw a Land Rover and several trucks blocking the narrow track.

The vehicles were empty. Just beyond them was the trail to site nine, the Temple of Kawa'il. He killed the lights, half expecting shots to explode around him. Opening the door, he went out low.

No shouts. No shots. Nothing but trees thrashing beneath the wind like drunken dancers.

**Guess everyone is in the temple, getting ready for the main event.**

The blood sticking Hunter's pants to his thigh pulled free in a slash of pain. Blood ran down his leg to his boot.

*It's a long way from my heart,* Hunter told himself.

He turned on the bulky flashlight, slid the AK-47 over his shoulder again, and headed for the concealed trail to the temple. Except it wasn't concealed anymore. Sap bled and recently cut branches gleamed like bones in the flashlight. The pain banging in his head was his heartbeat, routine, barely noticed. It wasn't the first crack on his skull he'd taken. He knew he had at least a mild concussion, but he saw mostly one of everything, so he wasn't worried.

His head was a long way from his heart, too.

In every pause of the wind Hunter expected to hear voices—shouts or incantations or screams—anything but the silence that filled the usually noisy jungle.

*This has to be the right place,* he told himself. *Those vehicles didn't just fall out of the sky.*

Before the jungle gave way to the small clearing, he turned off the light. He knew he should wait for his eyes to adjust, but there wasn't time. He slipped the AK-47 off his shoulder, readied it, held the darkened flashlight along the barrel, and continued down the path.

He smelled the torches before he saw them. They burned on either side of the temple doorway. He froze, listening, listening.

Not one human sound.

The image of Lina lying bloody on the temple floor was a knife in Hunter's guts. He shoved the thought away. It couldn't help him, but it could bring him to his knees.

A shadow in the darkness, he hurried over the open ground. Every uneven step made the pain in his head flash lightning. If anyone noticed his approach, no one cared. That should have been good news.

It wasn't.

With growing fear, he went into the temple entrance. Candle flames bent as he rushed by. There was no sound but his footsteps, nothing but the mixed scents of vanilla and cinnamon and blood. He hoped it was just the blood from his leg he was smelling. Candles burned in the temple room.

He was alone.

Wildly Hunter raked the room with his flashlight. No sign of Lina. No sign of Carlos. No sign that anyone had ever been there.

Then he found the Chacmool in front of the petals. Blood, yes, but not enough for a severed artery, a beating heart ripped from a chest. Next to the Chacmool was a bloody stingray spine and an even bloodier piece of knotted twine. Hunter remembered Abuelita's words.

**Carlos is in the temple now, consecrating himself so that he will be favored to make Lina holy.**

Hunter hoped Carlos's hand had slipped and he'd cut off his own dick.

"Okay, he's consecrated now, but he doesn't finish the ceremony here," Hunter said, talking aloud because he was tired of hearing nothing but candle flames. "He must have another holy place."

An image of Cenote de Balam shimmered in Hunter's mind, the huge mound of flowers, the natives weaving through the jungle like snakes, watching Lina.

Watching their beautiful sacrifice.

**But the vehicles are still here. There must be a trail.**

Hunter walked back out into the jungle quickly, limping now, not caring. The clock in his head beat harder and faster than any pain.

Recklessly he swept the flashlight around the clearing, looking for any sign of where everyone had gone. The new cuts in the surrounding jungle leaped out. Someone had hacked an opening.

A trail.

Ignoring the blood seeping down his leg, he ran.

**Lina will be at the cenote.**

**Alive.**

**She has to be.**

# CHAPTER TWENTY-FOUR

DRESSED ONLY IN A WRAPPED SKIRT OF RED cotton held in place by an obsidian pin, Lina should have felt exposed, even humiliated as she followed Carlos across the freshly swept limestone pavers leading to the cenote. She was too busy calculating her best chance for an escape to worry about being half nude. In any case, breasts weren't a Maya fetish; they were simply a means of feeding babies.

As she walked between lines of men to the waiting altar, none of them leered at her. If anything, there was respect in their attitude. She was their gateway to the creation of the next Maya world. Her head was high and her hair was unbound, lifting and falling in the unpredictable wind.

She wished her hair was shorter than her little finger. Hair was too easy to grab, to use as a binding, to imprison her as surely as the lines of short, muscular men standing close to her.

She had to escape.

Somehow.

**I waited all my life for Hunter. I'll be damned if I lose my future to my nut-case cousin and his equally crazy followers.**

Without moving her head, Lina looked for a chance to run. No matter how many slow steps she took, escape seemed farther away.

As she walked out of the jungle toward the cenote, a feeling of dreamlike unreality condensed around her, a combination of torchlight, ancient costumes, the dry wind making the jungle bow, and lightning clawing the night with thin, incandescent fingers. There was a surreal beauty to seeing Cenote de Balam as it had been dreamed by her ancestors, the edge thick with worshippers, the water a portal to another world, silently waiting for the beginning of a new age.

Her naked feet barely noticed the flat, cleanly swept limestone pavers that led to the edge of the cenote. When the wind paused, there was no sound. The silence was as dreamlike as the cenote, darkly shimmering, waiting. Then the wind blew again. The cenote became a vast open mouth breathing in and in and in, drawing reality with it. When the cenote finally exhaled, all would be a dream.

A nightmare.

The four Bacabs walked to a mound near the edge of the cenote. They surrounded it, then bent and lifted as one. What had looked like a pile of flowers when Lina had seen it from the other side of the cenote turned out to be a cape made of vines and flower petals.

From the edge of the crowd, conch horns blew, sounding a long, low note. The four Bacabs moved like dancers to the brink of the cenote and flung the petal-thick cape into the waiting water.

The cenote sucked the offering down.

The conch horns went silent.

Where the cape had been, a long, waist-high Chacmool altar made of deeply carved limestone blocks stood gleaming in the torchlight. Sturdy legs carved to resemble serpents supported the altar. Torchlight made the painted legs twist and writhe like snakes. Copal smoke lifted on the returning wind, seeping from a huge censer that stood at each end of the Chacmool.

Both censers had the same design as the one Lina had seen in Hunter's photos. She had never seen the altar before, which likely meant that it had been concealed in the jungle and brought piece by piece to the cenote for this ceremony.

**I'd feel flattered by all the preparations, but it's nothing personal. Just blood.**

**Mine.**

The four Bacabs, dressed in white and black and yellow and red, took their places at cardinal points around the reclining Chacmool. The stone face looked alive in the torchlight, with the faintest smile of satisfaction or amusement. Most of all, the face looked expectant.

Carlos turned toward her. The long, exquisite feathers in his headdress quivered delicately with each breath of wind, yet they had been strong enough not to break during the walk from the temple to the cenote.

Still looking at Lina, Carlos held his left hand out from his side. Immediately a bone scepter with obsidian blades set like rows of black teeth was brought to him, resting on a piece of jaguar skin. His hand clenched around the scepter until his flesh ran with blood.

The expression on his face didn't change.

"It took me many years to understand the sacrifices Kawa'il required to make me worthy," Carlos said. "The disappointments, the blood, even my manhood. But agony . . . *that* I learned to accept most of all. It is Kawa'il's gift."

Lina watched in a combination of fascination and horror as Carlos lifted the rod high, so that everyone could see the glistening of fresh blood running down his arm. A sigh of agreement, almost release, went through the gathered crowd.

Slowly, fist clenching to increase the blood flow, Carlos turned in a circle, showing everyone his willingness to give his own blood. Lina expected him to pull off his loincloth and reveal his bloody penis, too, but apparently that wasn't part of the ceremony.

She let out a breath of thanks for small favors. She had seen more than enough of her cousin's body in the temple. His eyes were still wild with pain, his body still riding the high of agony.

Carlos completed his circle and placed the sacred scepter back on the skin.

"You may choose to put yourself upon the altar," he said to Lina in English, "or my men will carry you respectfully and bind you in place."

*Don't want to bruise the sacrifice,* she thought with bleak humor.

But the sacrifice sure wanted to bruise them.

"I choose not to be bound," she said through her teeth. *Can't run if I'm tied to the damn altar.*

Carlos closed his eyes and tilted his head toward her in something very close to reverence. "You please Kawa'il greatly. You are worthy in every way."

Fire swept over Lina, a kind of anger she had never felt before. *Thanks so much for complimenting me on being scared stupid. I can't wait for the moment when I kick your useless balls into the new age.*

"To the altar," Carlos said in English to Lina. "Go alone, that all may know your willingness. Lie down on your back, with your arms above your head and your feet touching Chacmool's thighs."

Lina didn't argue. The sooner she got Carlos close to the altar, the sooner she would have him within striking distance of her feet.

**I will escape.**
**I have to.**

She took a step toward the grinning stone and climbed unaided into the Chacmool's deadly embrace.

Carlos sank to his knees. A group of men closed around him, hiding him. When they stepped back and he stood again, he was wearing the obsidian mask.

It transformed him into something terrifying.

From beneath his elaborately embroidered wrappings, Carlos withdrew what looked like a box. Lina realized she was looking at the Codex of Kawa'il. Blood from his cut hand seeped into the cover of the codex, adding to other dark stains. Carefully, reverently, he unfolded a panel and began to read.

"The four Bacabs shall don the faces of the gods and their clothes so that the Four Corners shall hold for the sacred night."

*"And the blood of the offering blood shall be primeval,"* chanted the Bacabs.

"The sacred copal smoke shall lift and the sacred light of Venus shall inhale it into the darkness."

**"And the offering shall be a personage."**

"The sky shall be manifest in incandescence and the earth shall tremble with the grinding of the Great Wheel's final turn."

**"And the offering shall be precious."**

"He who tends the *ah mun,* the green shoot of maize with its roots in the underworld and frail tassels reaching to the heavens—"

**"And the offering shall be prepared."**

"He who planted the kernel—"

**"And the offering shall be pliant."**

"He who kept the covenant—"

**"And the offering shall be at peace."**

"He who received the sacred truths of the gods—"

**"And the offering shall be perfect."**

"He shall wield the sacred black knife."

**"And the offering shall be made holy."**

"The Chacmool shall feed Ah Puk, who shall be sated. Xibalba shall become one with the middle world," Carlos said, his voice carrying across the expectant silence. "Kukulcán shall allow the skies to fall. Once destroyed, all will be remade in perfection."

Everything was silent, even the wind.

"I know who my master is and what is required," Carlos said. "His promise will be kept."

When Carlos held the codex high in his right hand, the worshippers made a hissing sound, like an ancient serpent waking.

Lina shivered and wished Carlos stood a few yards closer to her, within reach of her unbound feet. She watched two men dressed in trailing loincloths and finery in the ancient style approach him with their heads bowed. They brought something wrapped in jaguar skin with them.

"You may reveal it," Carlos said to the men in Mayan.

With trembling hands, one of the men unwrapped the cloth, revealing a roughly heart-shaped bundle of cloth.

The cenote seemed to inhale air, then exhale wind with a low, hollow sound. Torches shivered.

The crowd waited raptly.

Carlos reached out with his bloody left hand. As he grasped the cloth, he was utterly tender, as though holding the beating heart of a hummingbird in his grasp. When he held his hand up high, revealing the bundle, all but the most richly dressed worshippers made a moaning sound and went to their knees.

"This," Carlos said in Yucatec, his voice carrying across the faithful, "this is the promise given form. This is the essence of Kawa'il, waiting to be joined with the first priest-king of the Age of Kings."

The worshippers moaned in awe.

Lina saw a piece of the cotton bundle lift on the air, then dissolve and fly away. She wanted to cry out at the exposure of the ancient cloth to blood and wind, yet she didn't make a sound. She knew she had very little time left. She had to hold herself in silent readiness for the single instant of her revenge.

"This has endured," Carlos said, looking into Lina's eyes, "waiting for my hand while the wheel counted down the time of man. It has already begun. The lightning is Kawa'il's ax blade chopping at the Bacabs, gnawing away their strength, readying everything. I am key. You are lock. Together we will open time."

A low, monotone exhalation rose from the crowd, like the shifting of a vast stone door deep beneath their feet.

WHEN HUNTER SAW THE TORCHLIGHT AHEAD, he turned off his flashlight and slowed from a painful run to a more cautious walk. His breathing was rapid, hard. He readied the AK-47 for firing and eased forward, letting his eyes adjust and his breathing slow. From what he had seen this morning, the cenote had a cleared area large enough to hold more than a hundred people. The new trail he had followed entered the cenote clearing at a right angle midway between the path he had taken this morning and the broad limestone-lined walkway leading to the Reyes Balam compound.

A low, sustained sound, rhythmic, like the panting of a great beast, spread through the jungle around the cenote. Ceramic flutes began to play from somewhere close, but out of sight. The notes seemed to lift from the cenote itself, echoing and reinforcing the sound of the crowd.

The hair on Hunter's neck and arms raised in primal response.

He slid from shadow to shadow until his next steps would push him into the kneeling, chanting Maya gathered in the clearing. What he saw over their heads made his heart jerk.

Lina.

She was alive, half naked, wrists bound, lying on the altar. Nothing tied her feet or her body to the stone. Shaped like a Chacmool, the altar had been placed about two yards back from the edge of Cenote de Balam. With each breath she took, the sound the flutes made edged higher, then higher. The wind flexed hard, all but tearing fire from the torches. The drone of massed voices chanting flowed over the cenote, filling it with expectation.

Lina's body looked taut, not slack with drugs. No blood showed anywhere on her. If Hunter started firing, he hoped that she would be able to flee, or at least take cover behind the altar.

The flutes sang higher with every

moment the living sacrifice lay waiting. The Chacmool's face looked taunting, teeth parted to receive all the sacred fluid it could drink, telling everyone in vast silence that humans were only temporary vessels for blood, and the Chacmool itself was blood's ultimate destination. The shivering torchlight gave eerie life to the serpents supporting the altar's legs, snakes winding about one another, twining, devouring, with neither beginning nor end.

The keening wail of the flutes lifted to the night, notes climbing until they were just short of a shriek.

Hunter sighted the AK-47. The weapon hadn't been designed for accuracy. It had been created to lay down a storm of lead, not to pick off targets one at a time.

**No good shot. Too many Maya near Lina. Too much stone to ricochet against. I have as much chance of hurting her as freeing her.**

**Which one is Carlos? Not one of the Bacabs. Maybe one of the two dressed in glittering chunks of obsidian and feathers.**

**Wait, the one in the jaguar skin with**

**the black mask. Obsidian. Yes. That has to be Carlos.**

Hunter sited down his weapon's barrel and his finger slowly tightened.

Without warning the crowd stood, blocking Hunter's shot.

**Shit.**

Spraying lead might wound Lina, might push Carlos into killing her right now, and would certainly level the crowd until he ran out of bullets. As a last resort, he'd do it.

But not yet.

Cursing silently, steadily, Hunter worked through the jungle at the edge of the clearing, finding a place where the land rose enough to give him a good angle on Carlos. The chanting of the worshippers and shrilling of the flutes rose relentlessly.

Lina lay on her back between the Chacmool's mocking face and its upraised knees. Slowly she lifted her bound wrists above her head. Her body was taut, vibrating with life.

Carlos walked forward until he stood at the edge of the Chacmool. He thrust his hands up to the darkness and wind. One hand held the codex. The other held the god bundle. An obsidian knife gleamed from a jaguar-skin belt circling his waist. Torchlight slid across the obsidian mask like oily water. It was impossible to read any expression behind the mask. Blood dripped from his lacerated left hand, smeared over his skin and the god bundle that he held.

Lightning made the mask he wore glow like black water lit from within. It was mesmerizing, terrifying, reaching deep into the primal core that most humans denied even existed.

Lightning turned the darkness brilliant, then plunged everything into a night that seemed twice as deep.

More flutes cried above the droning of the crowd. The sound of the ceramic instruments was close to a scream and still climbing, climbing, climbing toward an unbearable climax, a sound more goading than melodic, driving the crowd to the edge of madness and ecstasy.

The flutes poured out a shattering, terrifying shriek, then fell silent.

"I hold your most sacred objects," Carlos cried to the sky, to Kawa'il. *"Give me the sign."*

"That's my codex, you son of a bitch!" Philip's bellow ripped through the night.

Everyone flinched and turned toward the sound.

Lina brought back her knees and then lashed out with all her strength. Her heels sank into her would-be executioner's crotch. She rolled off the Chacmool on the side closest to the cenote. Running hard past a stunned Bacab, she hurtled off the rim of the cenote and into the dark water below.

The night exploded.

With the strength of madness, Philip shoved and kicked through the crowd, rapidly reaching Carlos. Hunter pointed his rifle up and fired a short burst, magnifying the confusion into chaos. Using the gun butt when he had to and his feet the rest of the time, he circled around the edge of the crowd, heading for the Chacmool, the place he had last seen Lina before worshippers blocked her from his sight.

Carlos screamed "Noooooo!" as he went down under Philip's attack.

The worshippers shifted, howled, and surged toward the Chacmool, where Philip clawed at the codex Carlos still held. Machetes flashed like teeth as the human wave rolled over the two grappling men. Torches went out when the wave swept to the brink of the cenote, paused . . . then withdrew, retreated, dissolving into the darkness and jungle with eerie speed and silence.

The few torches still burning showed nothing. No Bacabs, no Philip, no Carlos, no artifacts. Hunter was alone but for the empty altar and the limestone pavers leading up to the rim of the cenote. Even the wind was still.

"Lina!" he shouted.

Nothing answered his cry.

Assault rifle in one hand, flashlight in the other, he ran to the cenote's brink and shined the light over the black surface of the water. The first thing he saw was two bloody bodies tangled in a shroud of flowers and vines, Philip and Carlos slowly sinking into the dark water.

"Lina!" Hunter called again.

Again silence answered.

He swept the arc of the light back and forth over the dark water. Pieces of the Bacabs' clothes floated, red and yellow, white and black. He saw dark hair, bound wrists, and the graceful line of a woman's shoulders. She was struggling against something that was trying to pull her below the water.

He set down the rifle, backed up enough for some running steps, and leaped forward into the cenote. The flashlight was nearly torn from his hand by the force of the water as he plunged deep, but he hung on to it. He opened his eyes, followed bubbles of air to the surface, and probed the darkness with the flashlight, looking for Lina.

He heard her before he saw her, a coughing, strangled sound that was his name. He jackknifed enough to pull his boot knife, put it between his teeth, and then kicked out toward Lina, who was fighting to stay above water with her hands tied and her feet tangled in scarlet cloth. The first thing he touched was her long hair. He used it to hold her head above water.

"Roll onto your back," he said. "Lie still while I cut your hands free."

Lina gulped air, coughed, and trusted him despite the water trying to suck her deep and drown her. Awkwardly she rolled over.

"I've got you," Hunter said.

She drew a ragged breath, coughed, and tried to explain. "Had to—be quiet—until I—was sure—" She kept coughing.

"It's okay now. Everyone's gone." *Or dead.*

When Lina managed to breathe without her body jerking into coughs, Hunter sliced through the cords tying her wrists. She floated much more easily then, helping him as he carefully cut and pulled away the cloth tangling her legs.

"Any injuries?" he asked when he finished.

"No. You?"

Hunter's head throbbed in helpful reminder. So did the knife cut on his thigh. "Nothing major."

"I was afraid I'd never be able to tell you."

"What?"

"I love you."

His smile was a pale flash illuminated by the bobbing flashlight. "That makes the night worth it. I love you, too." He pulled her close enough for a quick, hot kiss. "Come on, sweetheart. Let's go home."

Together they swam toward the trail up to the rim of Jaguar Cenote.

# CHAPTER TWENTY-FIVE

Two weeks later

HUNTER SAT IN THE ONLY OVERSTUFFED CHAIR in the living room of his apartment. It was almost midnight, he and Lina had barely arrived back in Houston, and Jase had showed up as soon as he saw the light in Hunter's apartment go on. Jase had an icy six-pack of cerveza under one arm and Ali under the other. Lina had taken one look at Jase's unusual pallor and dragged him to the couch.

Jase stretched out with his head on Ali's lap. Lina had liked Jase's wife on sight; she had the most beautiful smile Lina had ever seen. The other woman's loosely curled black hair was as shiny as her eyes, and her skin was a rich color that most Anglos broiled on the beach or sprayed out of a bottle to achieve.

"I can't believe Jase dragged you out of bed to come over here," Lina said to Ali, handing her a glass of ice water.

Ali flushed. "Um, we weren't asleep. My sister has the kids. It's our anniversary."

Despite the cocky smile Jase gave his wife, he was still recovering from his wounds. He was pale and drawn. And fighting it.

"You knew I was going to grill you like a steak as soon as I got the chance," Jase said to Hunter. "One lousy phone call to tell me you were both safe doesn't get it done, old man."

"We were busy," Lina said.

"I get that," Jase said. "You're not busy now."

"Some people actually like to sleep, boy wonder," Hunter said mildly.

"Talk," Jase said.

Hunter pulled Lina into his lap, settled in, and talked, beginning with Crutchfeldt and going on to Rodrigo, Mercurio, the Reyes Balam estate, and the Temple of

Kawa'il. Ali looked both fascinated and re-pelled by Lina's family, then horrified at what Carlos had done.

"He was El Maya?" Ali asked.

"Yeah," Hunter said, breathing in Lina's presence. "Leader of Los de Xibalba. A killer who even the narcos stepped aside for."

"You must have been terrified," Ali said to Lina.

"You can't imagine," Lina said, shivering, "and you don't want to."

"How could you be so brave?"

"Brave? I was shaking."

"But you did what had to be done," Ali said quietly. "That's brave."

"Hey, don't forget Hunter," Jase said. "He was good, really good."

"Of course," Ali said. "He has been trained, been in battles. He's a cop."

"Ex-cop," Hunter reminded Ali.

She sniffed. "Like your job is any safer now."

Amused, Lina bit her lip against a smile and realized that Ali must have been Hunter's friend for almost as long as Jase had.

"Put it on pause," Jase said, interrupting

them. "The baby kicked. Damn! I know it's a girl now."

Ali just shook her head and ran her fingers through Jase's hair. "It's too soon."

"It's a girl," Jase repeated, smiling a very satisfied kind of smile. "About time, too."

Ali stroked his cheek and said to Hunter, "Go on."

"Not much more to tell," Hunter said, smiling when Jase's hand settled on Ali's rounded stomach. "We walked out of the cenote, and walked back to the main house. Didn't see anyone on the way."

"When we got there," Lina said, "Abuelita was dead. Heart attack, stroke, old age. Nobody official cared. Celia—my mother—was frantic. She had stayed with Abuelita until the end."

"So the local authorities really bought your no-frills version of what happened?" Jase asked, looking at Hunter again.

"Two men settled old grudges with machetes at the edge of the cenote during the end of the Maya year. Both were injured. Both fell in. Both drowned. Too bad, how sad, count your money, and on to the next job."

"Did they recover the bodies?" Jase asked.

"Celia told the authorities to leave Philip and Carlos in peace in the cenote," Lina said. "After a suitable amount of money changed hands, the authorities did. Abuelita had a private burial in the family cemetery. Celia assumed the reins of the Reyes Balam businesses and disappeared into her work."

"Nothing floated up in the cenote?" Jase asked, cop to the core.

Lina winced.

Hunter took it in stride. "Nope. The disappointed worshippers cut everyone so thoroughly they sank like limestone blocks and stayed at the bottom."

Remembering a rain of bodies as she struggled to stay afloat, Lina closed her eyes. That time seemed unreal, like a nightmare.

And yet it was as real as her own heartbeat.

"None of the artifacts were found?" Jase asked.

Lina opened her eyes. "Nothing. By sunrise, even the altar had vanished."

"So the cause of all the fuss got swept into the cenote with the two wack jobs," Jase said.

"Jase," Ali chided.

"What? They were crazy and now they're dead as Geronimo. Tiptoeing around it won't change it."

"I'm sorry," Ali said to Lina. "He's hopeless."

Lina smiled sadly. "He's also right. Carlos and Philip weren't sane. And they're dead."

Sometimes she wept over the loss of the man she would never please. Sometimes the child in her refused to believe he was dead. And Abuelita, the woman whose smile and affectionate pats were like bright embroidery stitching through her childhood . . .

**Maybe it was a nightmare after all.**

Yet Lina knew it wasn't.

Gently Hunter stroked her hair. He could feel the wave of sadness in the tension of her body. The waves would come further and further apart, but they would never go away entirely.

"Some of the villagers live in the same

Maya fantasyland that Carlos and Abuelita did," Hunter said.

Lina sighed. "They believe there will be a new Maya world someday."

"They'll have a long wait," Jase said.

"They're patient," Lina said. "Frighteningly so."

"Or nuts."

Hunter shook his head. "They're just different, Jase. It's a whole other world back in the jungles of the Yucatan."

Lina ran her fingers through Hunter's hair. He kissed her palm and pulled her even closer, breathing in the scents of cinnamon and heat and woman.

"Are you done with the cross-examination?" Ali asked, caressing her husband's cheek.

"For now. I'm a cop, after all. I always have more questions."

"Make a list. We're going home," Ali said firmly. "You've been up too much."

Despite his drawn face, Jase grinned and said, "You never complained before."

Ali punched his good shoulder lightly, got to her feet, and turned to help him stand.

"I've been out of the hospital for a week," he grumbled. "I'm not an invalid."

"The doctors really wanted to keep you."

"Shows you what they know." Jase stood carefully. "You're the best medicine for me."

Ali stood on tiptoe and whispered something in Jase's ear. His smile made him look years younger. His hand stroked her rear. She swatted at him and blushed.

"Why don't we go to bed so these nice people can go home?" Hunter asked Lina dryly.

With a smile and a wave, Jase and Ali headed for the apartment door. The door shut behind them.

"They're good people," Lina said, snuggling closer to Hunter.

He rumbled agreement as his hand went to the first button of her blouse. Her breath broke. The second button gave way. She started to turn toward him, but he held her in place.

"Let me just touch you," he said. "I still see you laid out on that damned leering altar."

"And I still see you falling unconscious to the floor at my cousin's feet."

"Not my best moment."

The catch of her bra came undone. His fingers savored the warm, soft flesh they had revealed.

"My beautiful Amazon," Hunter breathed, stroking her.

Her breath came out on a sigh. "That's Brazil, not the Yucatan."

He laughed softly and licked her neck where it curved into her shoulder. "Now, tell me what's been going on behind those gorgeous eyes of yours."

"Hmmm?"

"I can feel you thinking."

"That's not my brain you're feeling," she said as he teased one nipple.

"I know. What I don't know is what you're thinking."

She smoothed her cheek against his chest. "I love you."

He pinched her nipple delicately. "And I love you, but I can't read your mind. You've been chewing on something ever since we crawled out of that damned cenote. It's not grief or fear, yet half the time your mind is somewhere else. Is it the lost artifacts?"

She arched into his touch. "You're a mind reader."

"Tell me anyway."

"I just *feel* that the artifacts didn't end up in the cenote. And I'm worried that's crazy, like Philip."

He lifted one breast and bit her neck gently. "You don't feel crazy to me. You feel all woman."

"Hunter . . ."

"Don't worry, sweetheart. You won't be going off any deep end without me right there with you."

"But . . ."

Both of his hands slid beneath her breasts, supporting and caressing them at the same time.

"I mean it," he said. "You're stuck with me. What do you think—feel—happened to the artifacts?"

At the moment all Lina thought or felt was Hunter's hands, his breath, his body hot and hard wherever she touched him. She held her hands against his, stilling him, while she caught her breath and un-scrambled her brains.

"You said that the villagers just broke over Philip and Carlos like a tidal wave, and when everyone retreated, there was nothing left but the altar."

"Mmmm," Hunter said, tasting her neck.

"I think in all the confusion, some of the worshippers took the codex, the god bundle, the mask, all of it, and disappeared back into the jungle. I think they put the sacred artifacts in a very safe place and went back to their usual lives. They'll stay like that, apparently normal, working and waiting until their belief burns out or the Maya renaissance comes."

Hunter's body went still, then one hand slipped away from her. He found new flesh to touch, to caress. Her breath came in with a small whimper of pleasure and need.

"You want to find the artifacts," he said.

"Yes."

"Will it be safe?"

"The villagers could have killed me at any time while we climbed out of the cenote and walked back to the compound," she said simply. "We were watched every step of the way."

"I know." The memory still could make his skin crawl.

"Philip was right about the cult of Kawa'il. It existed. It exists now. *There is a sixth codex.* I can't just walk away from that."

"I didn't think you would." Hunter's voice was neutral.

"After we're married—"

He turned her swiftly and kissed her like a man desperate for warmth.

"What?" she asked when she could talk again. "You asked me to marry you when we were climbing out of the cenote and I said yes."

"All I heard was a cussword when you stubbed your toe."

"Which time?"

He smiled.

"Just for the record," she said, "yes"—she kissed his chin—"and yes"—she nipped the corner of his mouth—"and yes"—she licked his lips—"and—"

Whatever she was going to say was lost in a long, sensual tangle of tongues and breath and need.

Finally he lifted his mouth just enough to say, "Good and good and good and good."

"Can you spend part of your time on the Reyes Balam lands with me? Celia agreed to fund the digs and pay me more than enough for—"

He shut her up by kissing her again. "I already talked to my uncles. I can work from the estate or from the moon, so long as they don't lose their Mexico expert. And they expect to meet you real soon."

Squirming until she could reach his shirt and begin unbuttoning it, Lina murmured in his ear, "Are you actually volunteering to be my bodyguard and site artist?"

"I'll guard every sweet inch of your body."

She smiled. "How about the artist part?"

"Can I draw you naked?"

"Only if mosquito netting is involved."

He laughed softly. "I can work with that."

# Author's note

THE WRITTEN, PHONETIC VERSION OF THE MAYAN language is a work in progress. Scholars disagree about when or whether to use apostrophes to indicate a vocal hitch in a word. *C* and *K* are often used interchangeably. Names are spelled one way by one expert source and a different way by the next. About all I could find consistent agreement on was that "Maya" refers to the people, their customs, their artifacts, everything but their language. That is called "Mayan."

I also was confronted with many choices as to accent marks. If a word is commonly understood and printed in the United

States without any accents—for example, Mexico, Cancun, the Yucatan—I didn't use accents, even though they *are* used in Mexico.

Some Maya scholars agree there is a God K. Some don't.

Kawa'il, his cult, and his artifacts are my own invention.